MORE THAN FRIENDS

"I am not a beast, madame. You are safe with me. All you must say is a simple yes or no to my friendship. That is all it takes." Alexandre reached out and touched her cheek, cupping her jaw in the palm of his hand. The gesture was feather-light, the most tender caress Olivia had ever received. His hand slipped to the back of her neck, drawing her closer as he bent down. And then his mouth sank upon hers, warm and unbelievably gentle.

She had thought he would be the type of man to grab her and plunge his tongue into her mouth. But Alexandre's kiss was far from invasive. In fact, he didn't press her to open to him, yet she did so—willingly, shamelessly, and eagerly—wanting more of him than she cared to admit. She longed to close her eyes and wrap her arms around him, to sink against his solid body and let the kiss go on forever. Instead she pulled back, too flustered and confused to know what she did want.

"The answer is no, Alexandre."

Books by Patricia Simpson

Lord of Forever
The Lost Goddess
The Night Orchid
Raven in Amber
The Legacy
Whisper of Midnight

By Debbie Macomber, Linda Lael Miller,
and Patricia Simpson

Purrfect Love

Published by
HarperPaperbacks

Harper
Monogram

LORD OF
FOREVER

Patricia Simpson

HarperPaperbacks
A Division of HarperCollinsPublishers

HarperPaperbacks   *A Division of* HarperCollins*Publishers*
10 East 53rd Street, New York, N.Y. 10022

Cover illustration by Jeff Barson

First printing: September 1995

Printed in the United States of America

HarperPaperbacks, HarperMonogram, and colophon are trademarks of HarperCollins*Publishers*

❖ 10 9 8 7 6 5 4 3 2 1

To Carolyn Marino
Thank you for your insight and vision
these past four years.

&

To T.M.I.L.
Some flowers were meant to bloom forever—
Like the rose in my garden.
Everlasting.

LORD OF FOREVER

Prologue

October—Present Day

    "This is it, du Berry. Either I regain my mortality or I die."* Alexandre Chaubere raised a golden goblet full of amber liquid to his lips as thunder crashed outside his Charleston, South Carolina mansion.

"Alexandre, *non!*" Gilbert du Berry lunged forward to snatch the goblet away, but Alexandre nimbly stepped out of range. Gilbert sighed in exasperation and crossed his arms, splaying his manicured fingers over the satin sleeves of his cerulean blue frock coat. "Don't be foolish!"

"I don't intend to be," Alexandre replied, relaxing somewhat, sure he could thwart any further attempts made by du Berry to grab the elixir. Gusts of wind rattled in the palmetto trees outside and the lights flickered in the laboratory, glinting white and silver on his friend's elegant evening attire. Alexandre had called du Berry away from a Halloween party, Gilbert's favorite holiday because it allowed him to indulge in his penchant for historical clothing. He was sure that du Berry would be upset. But there would be other masquerade parties, and literally countless Halloweens for him to celebrate, so he shouldn't protest too much. A more important ceremony was slated for this special evening of magic—that of returning Alexandre's future to the hands of Fate where his life belonged.

"Alexandre!" Du Berry's impassioned voice pulled him from his thoughts. "Put down the goblet, I beg of you!"

Alexandre lowered the glass slightly, but only to speak. "I want you to be my witness, du Berry," he explained. "And to record the details of the experiment as it progresses. In that notebook, there." He nodded toward a journal on the counter.

Du Berry glanced impatiently at the black notebook, its pages marked by Alexandre's crabbed writing, and then back to his friend, his eyes full of anger and disbelief.

"Is it that you expect me to document the final minutes of your life, as if you were some laboratory animal? Forget the science, *mon ami*! This is your life with which you are toying!"

"Toying hardly describes what I do here tonight."

"Either way, it means death for you, if not tonight, then later when you might regret all that you are doing now!"

"And is death such a bad thing?" Alexandre cocked a black brow.

"Death, death, death!" Du Berry threw up his hands and paced the floor in great dramatic strides while behind him lightning flashed through the slits of the closed shutters. "We are rich, we have no cares, we can go anywhere we desire, Alexandre—"

"And we cut off friendships before anyone sees that we never grow old, and deny ourselves the recognition of our work so as not to draw attention to ourselves. I'm tired of it, du Berry! Never for a moment can we drop our guard, when even such a little thing as an outdated driver's license could betray us for what we are. It gets harder every day to invent a new persona, with computers and databases keeping track of every move we make."

"Details, Alexandre, these things are only troublesome details."

"No, it's the way of life that troubles me—the deceit, the constant vigilance, the loneliness—"

"Loneliness? Our lives can be one big festive party, Alexandre, full of music, full of art, full of fascinating people! How can you say you are lonely when there is always so much pleasure to pursue?"

Alexandre wondered if in the three hundred years Gilbert du Berry had spent on Earth, he had ever taken a moment to examine his life. It was quite possible du Berry had skipped such internal inquiry, for he had always preferred the chatter of salons and soirees over serious conversation and had always sought out gentle pleasures over the blood-racing adventures Alexandre pursued. Perhaps du Berry was too dissimilar in spirit to ever view life from the same perspective as Alexandre.

Alexandre had to smile. How he and du Berry had ever remained friends was one of the great mysteries of life, but companions they had been for what seemed like forever and quite possibly would be for an eternity.

"Why are you smiling like that Alexandre?" Du Berry came to a halt in the middle of the room. "I thought you were tortured and lonely, ready for death. And now this smiling. *Mon Dieu*! Have you gone completely mad?"

"Maybe I have."

"I am losing my patience, *mon ami*. You call me away from a most engaging party and make me come across town in a veritable hurricane, so that I can watch you die and take notes? I will not be party to the taking of your life, Alexandre, I simply will not."

"Perhaps it will be the resumption of my normal life, my friend. Consider that." He swirled the potion in the glass. "If my experiment proves successful, I will finally have the life I prefer—one that eventually ends." He glanced at du Berry, tall and imperially slim, dressed in the satin and lace fashion of two centuries past, an era both of them were particularly fond of, but for different reasons. Du Berry had adored the clothes and the art of the late 1700s, while Alexandre had enjoyed an extremely lucrative career as a privateer, capturing enemy ships for the French Republic. He had established his vast fortune from his daring adventures along the southeast American seaboard, and had made quite a name for himself. He'd even picked up a few titles of nobility along the way. But those days were long past, and chasing down happiness from such adventures was growing more elusive by the year. Like a man in his twilight years, he'd let the house fall into disrepair and the garden go wild, and sequestered himself from the rest of society behind a tangle of brambles and shrubbery, abandoning his soul as he abandoned his gardens.

The time had come for him to "disappear" and reinvent an identity, but he wasn't willing to go through the process again. Through the last three hundred years, he and du Berry had helped each other perform the necessary task of "modernizing" their personages. One would travel for several years to return with a new name, different mode of dress, changed accounts, and a renovated personal history, ready to form fresh acquaintances unrelated to the old life. While one was "modernizing" the other would manage the other's affairs and property. Alexandre was tired of all that. Dead tired. He smiled ruefully at his own pun, for he could never be *dead* anything. He could suffer any wound and survive. His physical body hardly registered the effects of any outside force, and he rarely had to attend to corporeal maintenance, such as eating and sleeping. Through the ingestion of a secret elixir long ago, his body had become a master of regeneration. So had du Berry's.

Three hundred years earlier, while living in Paris, Alexandre had developed a potion made from the extract of an exotic plant. He had experimented upon himself, believing the achievement of immortality would be the greatest triumph for an alchemist, and for many years he basked in the glory of his new-found invincibility. His casual friend, Gilbert du Berry, learning of the elixir and unconcerned with anything but the near future, had broken into Alexandre's Parisian laboratory, helped himself to Alexandre's potion and had never suffered a moment of regret. But over the years Alexandre had come to despise his everlasting life, and had worked ceaselessly to find an antidote. He was fairly certain the secret to mortality was to be found in the glass he held in his hand.

Alexandre shook off the memories and stepped closer to du Berry.

"After I take this draught, I may be in great pain. But whatever happens, observe it and write it down."

"Alexandre, think twice! It could kill you!"

"I am well aware of that, du Berry." Alexandre glanced at the ornate goblet in his hand and sighed. "If it kills me, then I shall be better off."

"Better off? You will be dead, *mon ami*! Dead as a doorjamb!"

"Dead as a door*nail*, du Berry."

"Idioms!" He shrugged elegantly. "The English language—so complicated, so disorganized! I will never grasp it, should I live to be a thousand years old."

Alexandre shook his head at his friend's massacre of the local language. He wasn't certain if du Berry lacked the ability to learn a foreign language, or used his disdain for all things British—even after three hundred years—as an excuse not to perfect his English. "Perhaps you are more suited than I to the life we have been cursed with."

"Cursed with? To me, it is a gift, *mon ami*! Cannot you see that?"

"It is all in the eye of the beholder, du Berry." He pushed back the long dark locks that had fallen along his temple. "I have often thought that our age difference might have something to do with our varying opinion on the matter." He glanced at du Berry, taking in the fine clothes and the powdered wig, which artfully concealed du Berry's receding hairline, and the expertly applied cosmetics that heightened the faded features of a man past his prime. "You entered this new life of ours as a man of sixty-four years—nearly at death's door."

"Death's door? Pah!" Du Berry waved him off with a flick of his hand.

"Regardless, you were and are not plagued by the appetites of a younger man."

"I believe you slander my virility, Alexandre!"

"Virility?" Alexandre smiled bitterly. "You and I both know the price we have paid for extending our natural lives."

"*C'est vrai*. And we Frenchmen are supposed to be romantic and hot-blooded, *non*?" What a cruel jest—" His voice trailed off in wistfulness. For a moment even the eternally gay du Berry appeared remorseful. He gazed at Alexandre, his dark eyes full of compassion. "And you, *mon ami*, you entered this life as a young man of thirty-one, with plenty of hot blood in your veins, *non*?"

"Yes."

"A taste for *les mademoiselles* and nothing to be done about it."

"*Exactement*." Alexandre knew well the frustration of feeling everything a man could feel for a woman without the physical ability to act upon it. The hibernating systems of his body included his reproductive organs. No matter how much he desired to make love to a woman, his cock remained maddeningly unresponsive. That, in itself, was enough to drive him toward death. He sighed. "And I can no longer bear it."

"Alexandre, you are in a morose mood, and quite unlike yourself, I must say. Tomorrow you will recover your senses, I am sure of it. Come back to the party with me. Laugh, dance, and flirt with the ladies as you used to do. Just do not do this thing tonight."

"This is no mood, du Berry. I have made my decision."

With a quick movement of his arm, Alexandre raised the goblet to his lips and in one fateful gulp, swallowed the amber liquid. The potion burned his gums and throat and spread like fire in his stomach. He dropped the goblet and hunched over in pain, and through a shimmering haze, glimpsed du Berry scrambling toward him.

Dropping to his knees, he clutched his abdomen in pain. Was the potion dissolving his stomach? He was vaguely aware of the thunderstorm outside and the wind and rain lashing the shuttered windows behind him. It was a fitting night to die—dark and stormy and intense— nature's echoing cry to the rage and frustration he had lived with for the last fifty years, the frustration that had forced him to this end.

"Alexandre!" du Berry shrieked, leaning over him, "Alexandre, say something!"

Then, nearly as quickly as the pain had come upon him, it ceased. The burning sensation let up, and the waves of agonizing spasms dissipated.

"Alexandre, what's happening? *Dit à moi!*"

Alexandre pushed the damp hair off his forehead and slowly got to his feet. He took a penknife from his trouser pocket and lightly pulled the blade across his finger. The knife cut into his flesh, showing a faint trace of red but no blood pooling in the wound, and an instant later the slit healed into a faint straight line.

"Shit," he said.

Du Berry stepped closer, staring intently at Alexandre's hand. "Sheet?"

"Nothing happened." Alexandre sighed heavily. "It didn't work."

1

Charleston, February

"Do you have that ad with you?" Sherry asked, pulling a chair off the table and setting it on the plank floor of Harry's Jazz Club, a popular spot for residents and tourists in the heart of the historic district of Charleston.

"Yes." Olivia Travanelle did the same with the chairs at a neighboring table. Ostensibly, someone had swept the floor the previous evening, but she could see cigarette butts and swizzle sticks near many of the table legs and along the front of the bar. "Why do you want to see it?"

"'Cause I want to check out the address." Sherry sidled closer, chewing her gum and absently scratching the back of her head, where her dyed red hair was pulled back in a careless knot. At twenty-five, she was three years younger than Olivia, but looked much older due to her hard-drinking, emotionally-draining life with a succession of rough boyfriends. She had told Olivia about them, even though the two women had known each other less than a week. In the five short days since Olivia had come to town and landed the part-time job at the bar, she had heard Sherry's problems in great detail, and realized how much deeper her own problems would be had she taken similar directions. Long ago, however, she had learned not to depend upon men to take care of her or trust anything they said. Such knowledge had served her well. Though she had sometimes been called a loner, she didn't mind the label, for she had kept her life free of trouble.

Olivia put her hand in the pocket of her jeans skirt and pulled out the classified advertisement she had cut from the morning paper. She gave it to Sherry and anxiously watched her read it.

Help Wanted: Landscape work on
historic Charleston estate. Inquire
at 17 Myrtle Street after 7 P.M.

"Shew," Sherry drawled, tapping the newspaper with her painted nail. "I thought I reckonized that address."

"And?"

"Seventeen Myrtle Street. That's the Chaubere House." She handed the slip of newsprint back to Olivia.

"So?" Olivia folded the clipping and returned it to her skirt pocket. "Should I know about the Chaubere House?"

Sherry rolled her eyes. "You've been here five days and nobody's mentioned it?"

"No." Olivia pulled down another chair. "What's wrong with the place?"

"It's the creepiest place in Charleston, that's what it is. Even tour groups avoid it. Everyone avoids it."

"Why?"

"People think it's haunted. It's all run down and over-grown. And hardly nobody ever sees the guy that lives there."

"Who does live there?"

"A man named Alexandre Chaubere." Sherry looked over her shoulder as if afraid of being overheard. "People claim he comes here to listen to the jazz if we've booked a good band, but I've never seen him."

It was Olivia's turn to roll her eyes. "Really, Sherry. You make him sound like some sort of monster."

"He's weird, that's what I've heard. And his place is a dump."

"Maybe that's why he's advertising for a landscaper."

"Why now? Why would he want to do anything to his property, after all the years it's been rotting away?"

"I don't know why and I don't care." Olivia brushed back a wisp of her red hair and straightened. "I need the job."

"You do landscaping?"

"Yes. My major in college is landscape architecture."

"Oh, yeah. I forgot." Sherry walked to the bar and poured them each a soda. "Here," she held out the cola and then leaned a bracelet-ringed forearm on the counter. "You're awful ambitious, aren't you?"

"I have some dreams, that's all. And I've got to make enough money for college this fall. The only way I can see to do it is take on two jobs."

"What about your boy?"

"I'll find someone to look after Richie when he isn't in school."

"That should be easy. He seems like a nice kid. Mrs. Denning thinks he's the best."

Mrs. Denning was the older woman across the hall from Sherry's apartment, who kept her ear on Richie dur-ing the evenings when Olivia was at work. Olivia had found a gold mine in the old woman, as well as in Sherry. Both of them had generous hearts. However misdirected Sherry seemed regarding her relationships with men and the world in general, she was kind and giving. She not only had befriended Olivia, she had also offered her a place to live until Olivia found a suitable apartment. Olivia liked Sherry and appreciated her help, but she couldn't wait to get her ten-year-old son Richie out of her cramped and littered one-bedroom place. The less Richie was exposed to the unrefined men that Sherry entertained, the better.

"Thanks." Olivia sipped her drink. "I hope he hasn't been any trouble."

"Oh, heck no!" Sherry laughed. "I've just never seen a kid read that much."

"Well, that's all he can do right now, what with his models and posters packed away. When we find a place to live, he'll make some friends and everything will fall into place, I'm sure." She glanced at her drink and heard the echo of her words, wondering if Sherry noticed the hollow ring to them. Richie had never made many friends and she often wondered if she had raised him to be too sensitive, too much a loner like herself. She tried not to worry about it, but the older he got, the more concerned she became. "In the meantime, I've got to find a way to apply for this job."

"What's the problem?"

"The ad says to show up after seven p.m."

"Seven P.M. at night?"

Olivia glanced up at Sherry's redundant question, and would have smiled, but for the dark expression on her coworker's face. She nodded.

"That does it!" Sherry slammed her glass on the countertop. "You're not going to the Chaubere House and that's final!"

"But I need the extra work—"

"*That* work you need like a hole in the head." She swept the air with her hand. "Why do you think he wants people coming so late in the day?"

"Maybe he sleeps during the day."

"Maybe the guy wants to lure people to his place so he can kill them after dark!"

"Have you ever heard of people being murdered there?"

"Well, no, but someone's gotta be first."

Olivia finished her soda and slid her glass across the scarred bar pocked with cigaret burns. "Maybe he works during the day, Sherry. Maybe he doesn't want his dinner hour disturbed. There could be a lot of reasons other than homicide why the man wants to interview people in the evening. And I really, really need the work." She frowned. "The problem is, that's when I have to work here, and he doesn't have a phone number listed."

"Well, hell." Sherry pursed her lips. "If you're so dog-gone determined to answer that ad, I suppose I could cover for you—if you aren't too long."

"You could?"

"The place won't be hopping for a few hours, not until the band starts. You could go right now if you hurry."

"What about Mr. Thomas?"

"If he comes by, which he usually don't until ten, I'll think of some explanation—Richie got hurt or something."

"Oh, Sherry!" Olivia hugged her. "You're a godsend. Thanks!"

Sherry pushed her away, embarrassed by the display of affection. "Just don't go staying too long. And call me if that Chaubere character gives you any trouble. We'll send Ed over there to lean on him."

Olivia tried to picture Ed, the bouncer, coming to her rescue, with his beer belly and his tattooed arms.

Somehow he didn't seem like hero material. But heroic or not, she thought he'd likely give it a try if she were in trouble. Olivia untied her apron and stashed it behind the bar, thinking how lucky she was to have met such nice people.

Though her coworkers were good people, she wasn't crazy about slaving away nights in a bar. She didn't smoke and rarely drank, and she disliked the way her clothes reeked of both cigarettes and beer when her shift was over. But she clung to the thought that this job was temporary and would provide an end to a string of low-paying jobs. Once she finished her college education, she would never step foot in a bar again, at least not as an employee.

"You be careful!" Sherry called as Olivia headed for the door.

"Thanks, I will." But she stopped on the threshold and turned back in chagrin when she realized she hadn't the faintest idea where she was going. "Sherry?"

"Yeah?"

"Draw me a map?"

"Shew, girl!" Sherry shook her head and chuckled as she shuffled a slow southern path across the room.

By the time Olivia reached the intersection of Tradd and Myrtle Streets, the streetlights had blinked on, throwing pools of light on the cobblestone roads. At first she had felt safe walking in the dusk, for there were many couples strolling around the historic district, and tour groups trailing into the gardens and drawing rooms of nearby mansions. She could hear them talking and an occasional soft laugh would drift through the evening toward her, which lent a festive air to the surrounds. But as she approached The Battery and waterfront, she soon found Myrtle Street narrowing to a single lane with a sidewalk that was heaved and cracked by ancient trees whose leaves swept her hair as she hurried past. She didn't see another living soul, and the farther she walked, the more nervous she became. She wasn't the type of person who normally let herself get worked up over unfounded hearsay, and she wasn't afraid to walk alone at night. In fact, it wasn't even all that dark out yet. But there was something about the shadowed silent houses, hundreds of years old, that made her skin crawl.

Sherry's voice echoed in her thoughts. *"It's the creepiest place in Charleston, that's what it is. Tour groups avoid it. Everyone avoids it."*

Her steps slowed. Suddenly the messy familiarity of Sherry's run-down apartment in a more modern section of town seemed much more appealing than she had first thought. Adding to her disquiet, a stiff breeze from Charleston Bay came up, whipping through her hair and the branches above, which produced shifting patterns on the street. Up ahead she heard the creak of an iron gate mournfully swinging on its hinges.

"Get a grip," she muttered to herself. Her imagination was running away with her usual good sense.

Then she saw the house, a large two-story mansion of brick, closed shutters, and a double set of regal columns hidden behind a jungle of live oaks and red bud trees. High above the trembling canopy of the oaks, she could just make out the sharp white pediment of the second story, where a round window stared in silent resignation at the Cooper River. Slowly, she walked by a high iron fence, shrouded in vines. The gate she heard creaking was in the center of the fence and was spanned by arched grillwork ending in iron spikes. Ivy tendrils and forbidding briars climbed up the iron bars and twisted around the gas lamps on either side of the gate, blocking the view beyond. Neither lamp was lit, and no light filtered through the shutters of the house—hardly a welcoming sight.

Still, she had come this far and wasn't about to turn back until she made sure this was the Chaubere House. Where was the address? Had the numbers faded over the years? Was there no historical plaque like the ones she had seen fastened to the walls of the other historic homes? Perhaps because tour groups avoided the Chaubere House, the city fathers saw no reason to provide the name or history of the place. She'd have to get a closer look.

Carefully, Olivia pulled aside a briar and stepped through the gate. She sucked at the scratch from a thorn as she inspected the shrouded yard on either side of her, where mounds of what appeared to be azalea bushes battled for precious space with oleander shrubs. Far in the distance, at the end of a gravel walk, rose the house, its twin staircases curving upward on either side of the porch, leading to the main level, which was elevated half a story from the ground.

With careful steps she ascended the stairs. Once on the porch, she discovered the dull metal numbers of the address to the left of the door: 17. So this *was* the Chaubere House. But was anyone home? She raised the tarnished brass knocker and let it fall. The sound seemed inordinately loud, even with the wind rustling in the trees.

When no one responded to her knock, she tried again and waited impatiently for the door to open. She glanced to the side. If the yard was any indication of the condition of the mansion's interior, she wasn't sure if it would be safe to enter the house, regardless of the mental condition of the owner.

After waiting a few minutes in the heavy silence, she retraced her path down the wide stairs to the walk below. Just as she took a step toward the gate, she was startled by a loud clanking noise at the back of the house. Her heart roared in her ears. What was coming over her? She had never been this skittish in her entire life! She fought down her initial alarm and marshalled her thoughts. Could Mr. Chaubere be working in the backyard, unable to hear visitors at his front door? If that was the case, she couldn't pass up the chance to talk with him. Though her heart still raced, Olivia turned toward the back of the mansion and picked her way down a leaf-strewn walk, barely more than two feet wide. It curved around the side of the house.

"Hello?" she called. "Anyone home?"

No more noises issued from the back of the house. She walked along the side of the brick home, past six white-trimmed windows and a metal vent pipe that angled toward the roof. To her right she could just make out the faint track of a gravel driveway and some outbuildings, but most of the details were obstructed by unpruned and unrestrained vegetation. At the back corner of the house, she was surprised to come upon a rather vast rear garden and a labyrinth of walkways. Not far from the stairs, at the center of the house, was a small garden which boasted a life-sized statue of a female nude. Though graceful and tastefully posed, the statue dominated the yard and captured one's attention, drawing the eye away from the trees and flowers. The statue would have been better placed in a quiet garden, where one came upon it unexpectedly. There the viewer could experience pleasure and surprise at the lovely sculpture, instead of being hit over the head with it in full view, where the delicacy of the form was lost to its stark availability. Besides, from a purely female standpoint, she found herself wanting to throw a protective wrap around the Venus. The nymph deserved the dappled shadows of wisteria or philodendron, where her lines would be modestly shielded from the ogling stare of sun and moon.

Olivia drew her gaze from the marble woman and looked at the house. The property sloped down at the back of the mansion, which allowed the masonry walls of the first level to show their full height. The first level was comprised of great stone arches filled with more of the forbidding iron grillwork, but Olivia was heartened to see light glowing in the two arched openings near the high back stair. She ventured closer, crushing the newspaper ad in her fist.

"Hello?" she called again.

"Please enter your encryption password," a loud mechanical voice instructed, startling her. She had heard such a sound on computers at school, but was still startled at hearing it issue from the lower depths of an old southern mansion. Another clank rang out, louder this time, and she heard a deep male voice swear in French. "*Sacre bleu!*"

Full of misgivings, but still determined to talk with Alexandre Chaubere, she pressed on to the back stairs and behind them found a set of narrow stone steps leading to the cellar. A gust of cool dank air swept across her face and arms. Once again she had a feeling of apprehension and wondered if she should turn tail and run. But running wasn't her usual way of doing things.

Slowly Olivia descended, one hand on the cool rough stones of the stairwell.

"Mr. Chaubere?" she called, hoping she wouldn't alarm him by coming upon him unaware. A door on the right showed a rectangle of light. She poked her head around the opening.

Before her was a huge room full of computers and lab equipment. Nearly every shelf, table, and countertop was covered with either stacks of paper and books or bottles of chemicals. Wooden crates littered the floor and were stacked against the walls. Row upon row of glassware glittered in the light from the fixtures high above—glassware of all shapes and sizes, from delicate flasks to giant five-gallon chemical bottles. In the center of the room was a long counter covered with scientific equipment—Bunsen

burners, scales, distillation coils, a sink, and more glassware. Beyond the counter she could see the shape of
someone with dark hair and a white shirt moving on the
other side of the room, his body distorted by viewing him
through a huge bottle of pale green liquid. One minute he
was a slender, wraithlike figure, the next a hulking shape
with monstrous shoulders. She suddenly wondered if Mr.
Chaubere was malformed and that was why he didn't venture out among people.

"Mr. Chaubere?" Olivia's voice cracked. Annoyed by
her own temerity, she cleared her throat and tried again.
"Excuse me, Mr. Chaubere?"

The shape turned. She could see the pale oval of a face
through the glass, the long, shoulder-length hair, and the
generous lines of a white shirt. For a long moment the
man regarded her, as if trying to figure out why she was in
his laboratory.

"What are you doing here?" he asked in a gruff voice.
"This is private property."

He had a strange accent, a mixture of the slow relaxed
enunciation of the south urged along by the fluid lilt
peculiar to the French language.

"I've come about the ad."

"The ad?"

"Yes, the one for the landscaper."

"Ah." He stepped toward her, his shape shifting once
more through the veil of glassware as he strode along the
counter that separated them, and came around the end,
into plain view.

Olivia stared at him, thunderstruck.

Alexandre Chaubere wasn't a wraith or a monster, but a
tall handsome man with wide shoulders and very lean
hips. In fact, he was the most exquisitely formed man she
had ever seen. His dark brown hair shone with glints of
gold and magenta as it fell in slight waves to his shoulders

from a widow's peak at the top of a wide and intelligent brow. His nose was prominent and determined, his lower lip a slash of vermillion above a distinctly square jawline. His physical beauty was in a class far beyond the norm and belonged in the garden next to the statue she'd seen earlier. But his human warmth easily surpassed the cool perfection of the sculpted marble. He literally glowed with a vibrant life force, from the deep golden tones of his skin to the intense and almost black fire in his eyes. He reminded her of one of the iris flowers she had cultivated years ago—not as frilly and showy as the others, but so deeply crimson, so wonderfully velvet-like inside, that it seemed more beautiful than all the others combined.

"I didn't mean to disturb you, sir," she stuttered. "But the ad said come at seven o'clock, and so I did."

"And so you did." He gazed at her, a smile lifting the corner of his wide and very masculine mouth. He didn't seem compelled to continue the conversation.

"Are you Alexandre Chaubere?" she asked.

"I am. And you?"

"Olivia Travanelle." She had taken an old family name after her divorce to distance herself in both the emotional and informational arena from her ex-husband.

"A French name."

"My grandmother was French."

"Ah." He tilted his head a fraction and his gaze wandered over her hair and face, and down her arm to her left hand and the golden wedding band she wore to keep men at a distance.

"And as to gardening, madame?"

"I know plenty. I've studied landscape architecture for three years and have—"

"Modern methods."

"Of course. Science has made many strides in the past few years in regard to—"

"Poisons. Chemicals."

"Well, some—"

"Modern ways are not necessarily superior, madame."
He looked away, almost as if dismissing her.

Olivia stared at him. What a strange man. He hadn't
even shaken her hand, and the interview had been short
and rapid-fire. She gazed at the line of his jaw where it
angled up to his ear, and knew by the sharp set of that jaw
he would be a stubborn man, probably as stubborn as she.

He reached down and picked up a crate, obviously
wanting to resume his evening activities. She watched the
movement while anger spiralled inside her.

Did Chaubere think the brief interview was enough to
make a judgment about her? He had hardly scratched the
surface, and was quite mistaken if he thought she used
harsh chemicals in her gardens. Of all the horticulturists
she had come in contact with through the years, she was
the least likely to resort to harmful sprays and harsh pow-
ders. And she wasn't about to leave without informing
Mr. Chaubere that he had jumped to the wrong conclusions about her.

When he turned to go back behind the counter, she
stepped in his path. "Mr. Chaubere, you haven't even
given me a chance to apprise you of my qualifications."

"I have seen enough."

"What is that supposed to mean?"

"Madame, you toy with me." He gave her such a dismis-
sive look that she almost reached up to slap him. He
seemed to read her mind and his eyes glinted in smoldering awareness. He didn't, however, move out of her way,
and he slowly lowered the crate to rest against his right leg.

"Look at you, madame. It is obvious that you do not
possess the physical attributes necessary for the task."

She felt color rising in her cheeks. "What physical
attributes, exactly?"

"Women of your diminutive size and delicacy are born for drawing rooms and galleries, not for mucking about in my reflecting pond."

"They are, are they?" Olivia sucked in a deep breath, trying to control her escalating rage. "And just what century were *you* born in, mister? Women can do anything they put their minds to!"

"Really?" He raised a brow. "Can they piss standing up?"

"If they found it necessary," she replied, knowing he was trying to shock her into abandoning the argument. "I, however, was thinking of more lofty achievements."

"Such as?"

"Knowing the proper placement for that statue out there. A sad waste of a piece of fine sculpture, if you ask me."

"And if I were asking, madame." He placed a hand on his hip in a nonchalant gesture which only made her angrier. "What would you tell me about that statue?"

"I would say it lacks proper presentation, which is a major flaw in the design of your garden."

She thought she saw a muscle twitch at the corner of his mouth, but went on with her analysis. "I must say, I'm surprised, for I recognize Dezallier's hand in the design of your garden, however overgrown it may be. And I marvel that his plans could have called for a statue to be placed in such a poor location."

"For your information, madame, the location was of my own choosing."

"Then you must have had your reasons?"

"Yes. The female figure holds some appeal to me. I like to look at it."

"And do you even notice it anymore, when it's in plain sight all the time?"

He paused. She couldn't tell if he was amused or incensed. Then quite suddenly, he threw back his head and broke into laughter, the rich deep sound echoing off the curved stone ceiling. Olivia blushed furiously. Did he find her that amusing, her words that preposterous?

She turned on her heel and stomped to the door. She'd had quite enough of strange Alexandre Chaubere. He could keep his gardens and his creepy house. She didn't want to work for such an insufferable man, no matter how much money was involved. She knew she possessed the talent and determination to transform his yard into a southern paradise, but he wouldn't even consider her solely on the basis of her gender, which made her all the more angry.

"You're right, madame," he called after her with a chuckle hanging in his words. "You're absolutely right!"

Olivia stormed up the stairs and past the diamond-shaped garden. She glared up at the statue's eternally calm face. "Poor creature!" she muttered under her breath, feeling sorry for any female subjected to Alexandre Chaubere's narrow views. She hurried around the side of the mansion, banged the iron gate after her, and strode down the sidewalk. For the first time in her life she felt out of control. No matter how she tried to push back her anger, the more upset she felt. How could she let a man do this to her?

She rushed back to the club, stubbing her toes on the cracked sidewalks and swearing under her breath.

2

"*Wow!*" *Sherry said* with a wide smile as she came up alongside Olivia later that evening. They waited for the bartender to mix their customers' orders. "Some night, ain't it?"

"I'll say."

"Must be the band. Lenny Hanfield and the Ambassadors. They always pack in a crowd."

"Are they local?"

"Naw. They're from Atlanta. And I could just die for that bass player."

Olivia glanced at the man playing bass, his eyes shrouded by sunglasses and his figure concealed by an oversized black suit. How could Sherry see enough of the man to find him attractive?

"Ain't he just prime?" Sherry continued. "Look at those hands. You know what they say about the size of a man's hands."

She wiggled her eyebrows while Olivia shook her head and glanced at her watch. It was nearly one o'clock, almost time for the bar to close. She was tired and out of sorts after her unsuccessful interview with Alexandre Chaubere earlier in the evening. How was she ever going to make enough money for college? Until she found a second job, she didn't want to look for an apartment for fear it would be too far from everything. And any day now she should enroll Richie in school, but couldn't until she knew for sure which neighborhood they would be residing in.

"By the way," Sherry leaned closer. "Did you notice the guy in the corner?"

"What guy?"

"The one with the dark hair over there. Drinking cognac. Check him out."

While Sherry took off with her round of drinks, Olivia looked around the bar until she spotted a man sitting near the band with a brandy snifter in his hand. Most of his body was lost to the darkness of that particular corner, but when he leaned forward, a light from above outlined his face and left hand. The man's sharp profile looked familiar.

Olivia delivered her beers and cocktails and returned to the bar for more when Sherry came up beside her again and barked her orders to the bartender.

"That has to be Alexandre Chaubere." Sherry pushed her empty tray onto the bar.

Olivia regarded the man more carefully. The hair was right, but a lot of men wore their hair that length these days, and the tall spare body shape was similar. He wore a dark shirt and black jeans. As she stared at him, he seemed to sense it and turned her way. Immediately, she averted her gaze and reached for her tray. "It could be Chaubere."

"I thought so, after hearing you describe him. Though I can't see him so good in the shadows."

"Didn't you say he comes here for the music some-times?"

"Yeah. The man hardly drinks, though. Hope he leaves a decent tip to make up for it." She winked and swept away to dole out the drinks perched precariously on her tray.

Olivia picked up her own tray and jostled her way through the crowd. Her tables were on the opposite side of the room and the joint was too busy for her to spend any more time gawking at a stranger in the corner. One of her customers was clearly drunk and seemed determined to make conversation and pull her onto his lap, keeping her distracted and wary for the rest of the evening.

After the bar closed, Olivia and Sherry walked down the stairs to the street together. As soon as they gained the sidewalk, a large overweight man on a Harley revved up his machine to catch their attention. Sherry laughed and slung her purse strap over her shoulder. "It's Larry," she exclaimed. "See you later, Liv!"

"Bye." Olivia waved and tried not to imagine the type of night Sherry had in store with her tattooed and bearded companion. She watched Sherry jump on the back of the cycle and stretch her arms around Larry's ample stomach. Then she walked another block and turned the corner, heading for the apartment a half-mile away.

"Hey, sugar pie!" a voice called behind her.

She glanced over her shoulder and in dismay saw her inebriated customer. He was a tall man, and though he couldn't have been much older than she was, he had a beer belly just beginning to creep over his belt and dirty blond hair already thinning on top. Not wanting to engage him in the slightest conversation, she didn't answer him and quickened her pace.

"Hey, what's the rush, babe?" His words were slurred.

Olivia heard the sound of his unsteady footsteps behind her. A sheen of sweat broke out on her skin as she veered in the opposite direction of the apartment. Maybe she could duck into a courtyard garden of one of the houses, hide until he gave up, and then run home. She kept walking as fast as she could without breaking into a trot.

Before she knew it, she found herself on Myrtle Street, in complete darkness.

"Damn!" she swore under her breath. Wildly she glanced around. Just as before, no lights were on in any of the surrounding houses, and she had nowhere to turn if the drunk behind her got nasty.

"Wait up, sugar!" the man cried.

Appearances be damned. There was no one to see, no one to hear. She dashed up the cobblestone street, trying not to twist her ankles. The drunk ran after her, and by the time she had gone two blocks, she could hear his strident breathing close behind her.

A few seconds later, he grabbed her left arm. Olivia's heart nearly pounded out of her chest as she was yanked backward against the man's paunchy torso.

"You sure ain't very friendly," he drawled. His breath reeked of beer. "What's the matter with you?"

Olivia struggled, but his grip was like iron.

"You're a damn Yankee, aren't you? Where you from?" She refused to answer him.

"You're cold as hell and that's a fact," he continued. "But I know just the thing to warm you up, you sexy little darlin'."

He clamped a hand over her breast and leaned down to nuzzle her neck, just as a car turned the corner, blinding them both with the glare of headlights.

Olivia squirmed in his arms, trying to break free, or at least alert the driver that she was in trouble. The car screeched to a halt, and to her relief a man jumped out of the driver's side.

"What's going on here, Jimmy Dan?" a deep voice boomed.

Olivia felt her assailant freeze.

"Please!" Olivia cried in desperation. "Help me!"

Jimmy Dan tried to pull her back into the shadows of the sidewalk, but she dragged her feet, hoping the driver of the car would see that she was being taken against her will.

"Mind your own business!" the drunk yelled. He clamped his hand over Olivia's mouth and dragged her to the side of the road. His hand was greasy, salty and rough, and she nearly gagged.

The driver of the car advanced, his long legs silhouetted by the headlights, his shoulders wide. The light behind of him plunged his features into darkness, but his voice held a familiar accent. "Let her go, Petersen," he said quietly.

"The hell I will."

"I said let her go."

"She's been teasing me all night," Jimmy Dan declared. "Wiggling her tight little ass, pushing her tits in my face. What do you expect?"

"I expect you will let her go."

Stiff with fright and outrage, Olivia stared at the driver of the car, praying he had the courage to stay and help her. She felt the drunk's grip tighten.

"Leave us alone," he said, growling. "This ain't your business."

"I'm making it my business." The driver advanced close enough for Olivia to make out his face, and she wasn't surprised to see it was Alexandre Chaubere.

Sensing the oncoming altercation, Jimmy Dan threw Olivia to the side. She careened for a moment, teetering on one foot and struggling to regain her balance, and then toppled into a holly bush. Each barbed leaf brutally scratched her hands and forearms as she fell through the glossy foliage. But she choked back her tears and scrambled to her feet, just in time to see the drunk take a wide swing at Chaubere.

Alexandre responded with a kick that hit the man in his midsection with a sickening thud. Then before Jimmy Dan could recover, Alexandre whirled around and kicked him again in the side. It was apparent that Chaubere was proficient in a form of martial arts. Karate? Olivia wasn't sure.

Jimmy Dan lunged for Alexandre in a blundering attempt to grab the man around his torso and drag him to the street, but Alexandre stepped aside and delivered a straight-armed blow to the man's solar plexus. The drunk collapsed to his knees, holding his chest and gasping for air. Alexandre stood above him, ready to continue the fight if the man got back to his feet.

"Had enough?" Alexandre inquired briskly.

"Go to hell, you bastard," the drunk replied in a muffled voice. He didn't look up.

Alexandre raised a brow and glanced at Olivia. "Are you all right, Madame Travanelle?"

She nodded, angling away from the drunk and toward the idling car so that Alexandre stood between her and the gasping man, who had retched upon the sidewalk.

Alexandre returned his attention to the drunk. "Get out of here. You're stinking up the neighborhood."

The drunk hunched over and wiped his hand across his mouth. Then he slowly got up, but Olivia could see a metallic glint in the hand he held behind him, out of sight of Alexandre. A knife!

"Watch out!" Olivia screamed.

Alexandre glanced at her in surprise, giving the drunk just enough time to lunge forward. He stuck his weapon into Alexandre's gut, and with a horrible wrenching motion, Jimmy Dan yanked the knife upward and pulled it out, while Alexandre fell back, both arms outstretched in disbelief at what had just transpired.

"You've killed him!" Olivia shrieked, running to Alexandre to try to catch him before he fell to the street, forgetting that she was too small to hold up such a large man. She grabbed Alexandre's arm, wondering how he could still stand after receiving such a serious injury.

The drunk gaped at Alexandre, as if he, too, was shocked at what he had done. Then, ashen-faced and shaking, he dashed away, making a coward's quick retreat.

"Mr. Chaubere!" Olivia struggled to hold him while he staggered backward. She glanced at his abdomen, at his ripped, bloody shirt, but couldn't see the wound in the darkness. He sank to his knees.

"I'll be—" he began but couldn't continue.

"Oh my God!" she cried, unable to keep him upright. He collapsed to a sitting position on the curb. "I'm going to call 911!"

"No!" He clutched her forearm. "Just give me a moment."

"You've been stabbed!"

"Merely scratched." His breathing was so uneven, she thought he was about to pass out. He was probably in shock and not even aware of the extent of his wound.

"He practically disemboweled you!" Olivia bent over to unbutton his shirt and assess the damage, but he stayed her hand with surprising strength.

"No!"

"But Mr. Chaubere!"

"I said I would be all right." He wiped the hair out of his eyes and looked up at her for the first time. "He just surprised me, that's all."

"But the blood!"

Alexandre glanced down at himself. "From the scratch." He passed his palm over his midriff to prove to her that he was not seriously injured. "See? It isn't as bad as you think."

She stood above him, incredulous. She had seen the knife plunge into Alexandre's body. She had seen the drunk yank the weapon upward, slicing through his flesh. How could he possibly say he had suffered only a scratch? Then to her astonishment, Alexandre rose slowly to his feet and took a deep breath, as if he had just arisen from bed.

"There you see? Nothing to worry about. Just a ripped shirt."

"But I saw the knife go—"

"You were mistaken. It is dark, hard to see."

"But—"

Maybe her eyes *had* played tricks on her, for after all he *was* standing there in front of her, as good as new. In amazement she stared at him. The breeze lifted tendrils of his hair, infusing his hair with the same strange vibrancy emanating from the rest of his body. He seemed taller than before, but perhaps her mind was playing tricks on her, inducing her to view him in a heroic light. But attributing hero status to this man was a mistake she wouldn't make, especially after his treatment of her earlier in the evening.

"At least you are unharmed," he observed.

"Merely scratched." She used his own words to make light of her injuries.

He glanced at her sharply and she knew her dark humor hadn't been lost on him. "Let me have a look." Without asking permission, he lifted her right hand and turned it, palm up. She didn't often let men touch her so casually, but given the circumstance, she resisted her natural inclination to pull away.

"How did you get these?" he asked, staring at the crimson scratches.

"From falling in that holly bush."

He shot a glare at the offending shrub and then inspected her bare arms, frowning in concern. "You suffered quite a few scrapes by the looks of things."

"I'll be all right." She withdrew her hand from his warm grasp, anxious to break contact with him. His touch unnerved her and his nearness alarmed her, for an odd humming energy seemed to vibrate between their shoulders, drawing her into his personal space. She stepped back from Alexandre and smiled at him, knowing her smile was unsteady. "Thanks for coming to my rescue like that."

"I am glad to have been of service." He gave a slight, courtly bow, made more graceful by the sweep of his arm. She could almost imagine a floppy hat with an ostrich plume curling around the brim in his hand, brushing the surface of the cobblestones as he bowed. She blinked away the image and moved even farther from him, coming up against the curb with the heel of her flats. There she stopped, still in disbelief at what had transpired.

"Are you certain you are all right, Mr. Chaubere?"

"Quite certain."

"Well, thanks again. Goodnight." She turned to leave but he reached out and lightly grasped her elbow.

"Madame Travanelle. Surely you can't mean to continue your way unescorted."

"That was my plan."

"But what if Petersen accosts you again? What if someone else sees you walking alone?"

"I walk alone all the time."

"But as you see, it is not safe."

"That drunk was the exception, not the rule."

"Regardless," he countered, "allow me to drive you to your home."

Surprised by the offer, Olivia stepped up to the sidewalk to distance herself from him, forcing him to release her elbow. Though Alexandre Chaubere had rescued her from a sticky situation, she wasn't sure if she wanted to get in his car or allow him to find out where she lived.

She held up both hands, palms facing him. "Really, thanks, but it isn't necessary."

"Then I shall follow you, to make certain you get home safely. Otherwise I will worry the rest of the evening."

"You're going to follow me in your car?"

"Yes." He crossed his arms. His eyes held a sparkle of humor in them, which she could see, even in the darkness.

Olivia hated being the source of his amusement, as if he viewed her as an inept child. And she couldn't imagine the embarrassment of being followed by a car all the way home. Her anger from their previous encounter in his lab suddenly resurfaced.

"I am not your responsibility," she declared, crossing her own arms.

"Tonight you are."

"For your information, Mr. Chaubere, I have taken care of myself for twenty-eight years, thank you very much. And I haven't had any trouble."

"You don't consider Jimmy Dan Petersen trouble?" he retorted, nodding his head in the direction her assailant had taken.

"He was just drunk."

"He is drunk nearly every weekend, madame." He tossed his mane of luxurious dark hair. "And he will try anything to make a sexual conquest of you. I've heard him boast to his friends about his conquests many times."

Olivia tried to maintain unswerving eye contact with Alexandre, but his last statement flustered her so much she had to turn away. His frankness disarmed her.

"If you are interested," he continued behind her, "I have developed a chemical substance that would render him harmless, and give you enough time to get away should he assault you again."

"I don't like to hurt people."

"I'm afraid Petersen doesn't share your philosophy, madame. And besides, my spray will not really hurt him, it will just make him sneeze long enough for you to flee."

She glared over her shoulder at him. "Why go to all this trouble for me?"

He shrugged. "I like to see my inventions put to good use."

Olivia gazed at the tall lean man, confused by his unusual character—a mixture of the exasperating domineering male coupled with the mannerisms of a courtier. Usually she classified men in two general categories: the jock-type who got everything he wanted through guts, coercion, and plenty of dependence on the good-old-boy network, and the sensitive man, who was willing to let life buffet him around, too timid to make choices, let alone act upon them, and far too caught up in convention and correctness to entertain the slightest individual thought. Most men she had met fell into one or the other categories. Yet this man, Alexandre Chaubere, defied generalization because he was both kinds of men, yet at the same time neither of them. This rattled her cage as Sherry would say.

At her silence, Alexandre walked to his car and opened the passenger door near her. "Please, madame. It will make the night shorter for each of us if you will permit me to drive you home."

Olivia took a deep breath, wondering why she should trust this man, but sensing nevertheless that he wouldn't harm her, regardless of the physical strength he had displayed a few minutes ago. She surveyed his vehicle, a neat little black sports car, a model and vintage she didn't recognize from her son's many car posters. It was most likely foreign. Though older, the car had been kept in immaculate condition and its engine purred smoothly beside her.

She sighed, hoping she wasn't making the biggest mistake of her life, and answered tentatively, "Well, all right. Thanks."

He stood to the side as she sank into the dark seat of his car, and when she was safely settled, he gently closed the door. Somewhat taken by his good manners, she breathed in the pleasantly pungent smell of the leather upholstery as Alexandre walked around the front bumper and got in.

She had never been in a sports car before, and once the man beside her closed the door and filled up the space with his wide shoulders and long legs, she realized with a shock what a sequestered and intimate universe a car could be. He reached over in front of her, and she sat back to avoid being touched, taking notice of his fine wrist and long slender hand, both of which spoke of quiet intelligent strength, not the type of bone structure to be found on a brute. He pressed a button to open the glove compartment, revealing a CD player cleverly installed inside. He touched a couple of buttons on the CD player and then leaned back and shifted into first gear. The soft strains of a jazz piano piece drifted up to her and she felt herself relax enough to let her weight press against the back of the seat.

Alexandre pulled away from the curb. "Where to, Miss?" he said, mimicking the manner of a New York cabbie. He smiled at her.

She almost smiled back before she caught herself. Alexandre might be charming, but she wasn't about to let him think he was having any effect on her. "Anson and Elm," she replied.

Undaunted by her serious reply, he continued with his cabbie impersonation. "Scenic route, ma'am, or ya in a hurry?"

"Direct route," she said. Then deciding to show him that she wasn't a spiritless idiot, she added. "And I'm watching the meter, buddy."

He chuckled and shifted into second. His moves were deft and sure, and not once did his driving make her reach for the door handle or brace herself against the dash. She appreciated his calm driving, and didn't expect such behavior from a man who owned a sports car and fought drunks in the street.

For a few minutes they drove without speaking as mellow jazz filled the comfortable silence. Sitting there in the dark with the soft music playing, watching the blocks of beautiful old homes passing by, Olivia almost forgot that seven hours ago she had stormed out of this man's house, angrier than she had been in years. Lost in her thoughts, she was surprised when Alexandre announced they had arrived.

"Anson and Elm," he declared. "Which house, ma'am?"

"The yellow one on the right." She glanced at him, with the realization that she had enjoyed the drive with Alexandre Chaubere far too much for her own good.

He rolled to a stop behind a parked sedan. Olivia looked up to the second floor where Sherry's apartment was located and noticed all the lights were still on. Either Sherry had brought home her Harley man or Richie was still up. She would have been happier had the windows been dark.

As soon as the car came to a complete stop, Olivia opened her door.

"Thanks, Mr. Chaubere," she said. "For everything."

"My pleasure." He got out of his side as she jumped out of the car. She hoped he didn't expect to escort her to the door. She'd had enough of his unsettling effect on her for one night, enough of his gallantry and humor, and quite enough of his soft, relaxing jazz. The fact that his humor and charm nearly induced her to drop her guard made him dangerous and off limits.

Alexandre came around the front of the car. Olivia could still hear the seductive soft music drifting from inside. She paused at the gate and turned.

"Shall I see you to the door?" he asked, his voice a soft rumble in the darkness.

"That's okay. I'll manage." She dug her keys out of the side pocket of her purse. "Goodnight." She pushed through the gate.

"Madame Travanelle?"

She turned.

"I'd like to discuss some ideas with you in regard to my house."

"Oh?"

"But it's late. We will talk tomorrow."

His assumption that she would agree to more contact was slightly irritating. "And if I am too busy tomorrow?"

"Are you?" he countered, raising one of his black brows.

She wanted to make a sarcastic reply, that she had more important things to do than speak with him, like washing her hair or going to the library, but found herself going along with the idea. "What time did you—?"

"Nine o'clock?"

"Mr. Chaubere, I work nights. That time is not convenient for—

"Well, then, come earlier. Say five o'clock?"

"If I can." She didn't want to be too agreeable.

"I shall be in my laboratory in the back where you found me before."

"All right. Maybe."

"Until then." He nodded toward her and returned to his car.

Olivia walked up to the front door, opened it, and climbed the stairs while she thought of Alexandre's offer, wondering if it had to do with something other than the landscape job. She jingled the keys in her hand as she reached the landing and then walked up to the second floor, not certain if it would be wise to work for such a man. She couldn't figure him out.

Shaking her head at the strange day she'd had, she unlocked and opened the door and stepped into the apartment. Richie bounded across the floor toward her.

"Richie," she admonished, relieved to discover that Sherry hadn't returned with her biker friend. "Why are you still up?

He ignored the question. "Who was that guy?" he exclaimed.

"Mr. Chaubere. He gave me a ride home from the club."

"Whoa!" Richie ran back to the window and peered out. "He's got a cool car! A '73 Fiat Spider."

"That may be true, but you shouldn't judge people by the cars they drive." Usually cars didn't matter to her much, and she wasn't impressed by ostentatious possessions, but she knew she had enjoyed being in Alexandre Chaubere's car far more than she cared to admit. And *his* quiet little Spider had been nothing like the souped up Trans Am driven by her ex-husband. She came up behind Richie and put her hand on his shoulder. "Never mistake possessions for character, Richie."

"Yeah, but Mom—a '73 Spider! It's practically an antique!"

"Antique or not, it's time you were in bed." She set her purse on a newspaper-strewn table and guided him over to his sleeping bag near the TV. The bag was tattered and the stuffing compacted into uncomfortable lumps. Richie's T-shirt was torn at the neck and faded. She sighed. There was so much she wanted to give her son, so much he needed. And yet he never asked for material things. Perhaps he sensed she couldn't afford them and spared her pride by not making an issue of their limited finances. She thanked her lucky stars for such a son, and told herself that soon she would have the resources to provide a decent life for him.

Richie sat upon the threadbare bag and looked up. "Do you think I could see that car sometime, Mom?"

"I don't know." Olivia looked away. Did she want her son to meet Alexandre Chaubere? Probably not. Since her divorce she had never allowed herself the luxury of a male friend, simply because she didn't want her son to get attached to a man and view him as a father figure, only to have the relationship fail and break Richie's heart. That was why she wore a wedding ring on her finger. The gold band gave her an excuse to keep her life uncomplicated by keeping men at bay. "Mr. Chaubere's a private man, I'm told. He likes to keep to himself. He probably wouldn't want a boy hanging around his car."

Richie's shoulders drooped.

"But if I see him again, I'll ask him, OK?"

He beamed and wiggled into the sleeping bag. "Thanks, Mom!"

She bent down and ran her hand through his auburn hair and then kissed him lightly. "Goodnight."

"'Night."

Olivia raised up and surveyed the apartment. She'd tidy up Sherry's mess, take a shower and then crash. In the morning she'd locate a copy of her résumé for the meeting with Alexandre Chaubere and dig out her best silk blouse to wear to the interview. If all went well, she might possibly have another job by tomorrow night.

3

"*So you're actually packing* up the lab," du Berry commented to Alexandre, surveying the crates strewn along the floor. "I never thought I would see the day when you would give up your alchemy."

"They call it science now," Alexandre put in, squinting down at the floor as a recurring and annoying film passed over his eyes. After a moment his blurred vision cleared. "Research and development, to be exact."

"Whatever." Du Berry waved him off. "It is all grease to me."

"Greek," Alexandre corrected with a smile, allowing the amusement of his friend's slip to distract him from his troubling ocular incident. Gilbert was attired in more modern clothes this time, having exchanged his frock coat and breeches for an off-white linen suit and Italian woven-leather shoes. He had returned to Charleston at Alexandre's request and was staying in a nearby hotel on

Meeting Street until Alexandre left for South America. Alexandre had offered the usual carriage house apartment for his use, but the older man complained that he could not abide Chaubere's reclusive way of life any longer and his objection to parties. Du Berry put a hand in the pocket of his trousers. "So you are actually going to leave all of this in the behind?"

Alexandre decided not to correct yet another of du Berry's fractured idioms. "Yes. Stored in the attic under lock and key."

"But what is it that you will do in South America without your precious chemicals and equipment?"

"I really don't know." Alexandre glanced at his bottle-covered counter and sighed. "Perhaps take up ranching in Argentina. Develop a better breed of beef. I don't know yet."

He hoisted a heavy case containing his state of the art oscillator and carefully stowed it in a crate, added some generously wrapped manuals and accessories, and then scattered biodegradable packing material around the lot.

"So when is it that you depart for South America?" du Berry asked, holding out the lid of the crate. "And where exactly are you going?"

Alexandre took the lid and set it on the crate. "Initially, I am going to Rio de Janeiro, and once I get there I'll let my fancy dictate where to start a new life. As to when, as soon as my ship is ready. Frank said he'd have it seaworthy by mid-March."

"That gives you a month more, *mon ami*. Can you be finished with all your affairs by then?"

"I believe so." Alexandre knelt to scribble the contents of the crate on an adhesive label, which he peeled from its backing and affixed to the wood while Gilbert idly wandered through the lab.

"Will you not miss this house, miss Charleston?"

"Hardly. I have seen far too much of both over the last two hundred years."

Gilbert fell silent for a moment as he walked along the counter. "Ah, I see that you have not given up your alchemy entirely," he remarked, pointing to a microscope and a line of beakers on a table at the end of the room. "What is it that you are studying now?"

Alexandre glanced at the table. "I'm still working on the antidote."

"Ah! Do not say it!" Du Berry turned to him in shock. "You haven't been taking any more of the lily, have you?"

"Every week."

"*Tiens!* There is so much danger in this!" Du Berry shook his head. "It's been nearly four months since the first dose, Alexandre. And you have been taking it every week? It is foolishness to take too much! You know that better than anyone!"

Alexandre frowned at the reminder. He knew too well the fate of some of his fellow alchemists in their search for immortality so long ago. Once the properties of the lily had been discovered in an ancient manuscript and the secret leaked to his comrades, everyone scrambled to be the first to achieve immortality. But none of his peers had arrived at the proper proportions in their concoctions. Some of his fellows had gone mad, blind, or had become paralyzed. Some had rotted from the inside out. But the one side effect that frightened Alexandre the most was the way the lily could heighten and distort a man's natural tendencies. If he were an angry person, he might fly into uncontrollable rages, enough to kill. If he were a troubled man prone to depressions, he might spend decades dragged down by acute melancholy. Scores of dabbling alchemists had forfeited their sanity or their health in their quest for eternal life.

He and du Berry had been the lucky ones, achieving relatively benign immortality, because he'd been extremely careful in his calculations, detailed in his documentation, and painstaking in his preparation of the elixir. Yet each time he tested the newest version of the antidote, he tempted fate, for the effects of the lily could never be depended upon to remain constant. Whatever had befallen his compatriots in their search for eternal life might happen to him in his search for death. Each time he tested a new version of the antidote, he took a terrible gamble. Still, he believed it was better than remaining in his present condition.

"Alexandre, tell me you will stop this experimenting."

"I can't, du Berry. Don't you see?"

"But are you getting any results?"

"Slight ones. I think I am getting somewhere."

"How can you tell?"

"My blood cell count is changing. And—" he broke off, not anxious to discuss his health problems with anyone, not even du Berry.

"And?"

"I've been having spells."

"What kind of spells?"

"Blurred vision, body cramps, and some nausea."

"Give it up, Alexandre. It sounds as if you are becoming poisoned."

"But I'm getting closer. My red and white blood cell counts are constant, but counts of the third cell type are getting lower, day by day."

"I don't like it. If you kill yourself or go mad, I will not be able to bear it. You and I are the last ones, my friend. The last ones! And if something happens, what will I do without you?"

"Have parties in my house, I expect."

"This is not a joking matter!"

"I know." Alexandre stood up and drew an ancient timepiece from his pocket. It was solid silver and engraved with his initials on the cover, a gift from Napoléon Bonaparte for services rendered to the Republic. For two hundred years the pocket watch had served him faithfully, with only a few minor repairs here and there, all of which he had performed himself. Alexandre flipped open the cover and glanced at the time.

"Five o'clock," he announced. For a moment he listened intently, wondering if he would hear Olivia Travanelle's approach, and wondering further if she would come at all. Last night, she hadn't seemed overly anxious to meet with him and had made no commitment whatsoever to honor his request to visit.

"Is it that you are expecting someone?" du Berry inquired.

"Yes."

"*Ici*?" du Berry pointed toward the floor of the cellar. "At your house? How unlike you, Alexandre!"

"It's in regard to the advertisement I submitted for a landscaper. She will have to see the house eventually."

"Did you say *she*?"

"Yes, I said she." Alexandre glared at his friend, hoping to wipe the grin off du Berry's face.

"This grows *intéressant*. Tell me more. Is she young, old? Ugly, pretty?" He held out his hands in front of his chest in a gesture every man on earth could interpret, regardless of language differences. "Perhaps a nice set of knickers, eh?"

Alexandre ignored du Berry and pulled another crate to the counter in front of him as he thought of his own description of Olivia Travanelle. Yes, she was young, but there was something very old in her eyes, as if she had seen enough of the world to make her wise beyond her years. And yes, she was pretty but not beautiful, with her attractiveness based on natural wholesomeness, from her tangle of red hair to her lithe figure and sensible clothing. If he recalled correctly, she wore no makeup, yet her fair skin and startling blue eyes were vibrant enough not to need cosmetic enhancement. Though at first glance he had made the mistake of judging her small stature and fine-boned limbs as a sign of weakness and frailty, Alexandre was quite certain after having talked to the woman that she would prove as wiry and tenacious as a terrier. She was a person of no artifice, a true exception to the female race as far as he was concerned, and the possibility of the existence of such a woman intrigued him. Could Olivia Travanelle be as guileless and straightforward as she appeared? He'd like to find out.

"There is not much to tell, du Berry," he replied at last. "She is just a woman."

"Just a woman? Then why is it that you have been standing there in a dream world staring at that wooden box?"

"Have I?" Alexandre grinned in surprise and looked up, just in time to see the lady in question appear in the doorway, a purse in one hand, a portfolio in the other. He felt his grin fade to a slow smile at the sight of her wild curls and ivory skin in stark contrast to the austere stone wall behind her. She looked like a nymph from the garden.

"Sorry to interrupt," she said, motioning toward the side of the stone doorway, "but there's no bell."

"No matter." Alexandre brushed his palms on his trousers and strode toward her as Gilbert turned, hands on both hips. "You haven't interrupted anything important."

"Nothing important?" du Berry wailed dramatically. "*Alors*, you cut me to the quicksand, Alexandre!"

Alexandre turned back to the woman to find her trying to suppress a grin. He gestured toward du Berry. "Madame Travanelle, allow me to introduce my longtime friend, Gilbert du Berry." He made a point to pronounce his friend's first name the French way, *geel-bare*, so that Olivia wouldn't make the mistake of Anglicizing it, which would highly offend his cultured friend.

"Nice to meet you, Mr. du Berry." She transferred her purse to her shoulder and held out her hand, and seemed momentarily displeased when Gilbert raised her fingers to his lips.

"*Enchanté*, madame," he murmured, holding up her hand and preparing to do a *pas de deux* with her. "Alexandre did not do your beauty justice when he described you to me."

"Oh?" she replied cooly.

Alexandre caught Olivia's somewhat withering glance, as if she didn't care to be discussed. Didn't the woman recognize a compliment when she heard one? Or perhaps she didn't value praise coming from a man as artfully charming as du Berry. Or was it possible that compliments had no effect upon her? This was something new. He bit back a smile and watched her joust with his friend.

Olivia raised her chin. "And what did Mr. Chaubere have to say about me?"

"That you were just a woman."

"Somehow that doesn't surprise me." She wrested her hand from du Berry's light grip and clutched her purse and portfolio in a businesslike way. Alexandre had to admire a woman who could resist Gilbert's well-honed social patois.

"Hah!" du Berry laughed, gesturing toward her. "A woman who can see through Alexandre Chaubere's outward charm to the real man beneath! I am oppressed."

"Impressed, you mean," Alexandre put in.

Olivia ignored his interruption. "I don't believe Mr. Chaubere has tried very hard to obscure his true character," she replied archly, without glancing his way.

"Ah, but he has obscured yours and to great injustice. You are a picture, madame, a veritable portrait! A delightful confection of freshness and beauty whose equal I have not seen in decades!" Du Berry turned toward Alexandre.

"Cannot you visualize her, Alexandre, dressed *à la polon-aise*, just like a precious little country maid?"

Olivia's smile grew rigid and she glanced at Alexandre, her gaze burning and direct.

Alexandre cleared his throat. "The manner in which Madame Travanelle is dressed is perfectly acceptable, du Berry. And for the work she is to perform here, a shepherdess dress would hardly be appropriate."

"*C'est dommage!*" du Berry commented in mock sadness, pressing the sides of both index fingers to his lips.

"You mean to offer me the landscape job?" Olivia asked.

"Yes."

"Even though I am a mere woman?"

"Yes. I've reconsidered—"

"Is it not because you are desperate, *mon ami*?" du Berry put in, aggravatingly truthful when he wanted to be a tease, which was as often as possible. "Is it not because no one else in Charleston would agree to work here, since you are considered so—"

"Enough, Gilbert," Alexander warned, "before you offend Madame Travanelle altogether." He couldn't keep his annoyance from cutting a hard edge through his words. Du Berry made a face and stepped back a pace.

"Is that true?" Olivia inquired. "No one else applied for the job?"

"Yes." He had no recourse but to admit the truth. Damn du Berry and his loose tongue. Alexandre wanted to throttle him, for now he had no bargaining power, thanks to his chatty friend. "And I don't wish to wait any longer to start the project."

"You mean to say you are offering me the job out of sheer desperation?"

"Well—" Alexandre noticed her expression had become frosty and her blue eyes so piercingly sharp that he could feel her glare pricking his skin. "—not entirely, madame. Your knowledge of Dezallier impressed me. Not many people are acquainted with the work of an eighteenth-century landscape architect."

"If you had taken the time to interview me properly, sir, you would have discovered that I have many more qualifications than that."

"I admit that I—"

"But I can see you are no different than other arrogant, egocentric men. Why should I seek your employ when it means subjecting myself to deprecating remarks about my person? You have no business discussing my appearance. In fact, you should be sued for sexual harassment over remarks such as that."

Du Berry made another face, apparently taken aback and amused at the same time by Olivia's controlled but fiery temper. Alexandre stared at her, his expression frozen, without the slightest notion how to respond to her. No woman had ever accused him of sexual harassment. In fact, he had experienced quite the opposite. The more he tried to back away from women, the more they usually pursued him.

She threw back her small shoulders. "I, sir, am not desperate enough to work for a man like you! Good-day!" She turned on her heel and stormed out of the laboratory while du Berry let out a nervous titter.

"Thanks ever so much, Gill-Bert," Alexandre remarked acidly in his best British accent, willfully insulting du Berry as he brushed past him.

Du Berry smirked sheepishly and shrugged.

Angered and baffled by the last few minutes, Alexandre ran after Olivia, hoping to catch up with her before she made it to the street. He had no wish to become a spectacle for his neighbors if Madame Travanelle chose to continue her tirade. He found her standing on the walk at the side of the house. Her blouse had become snared by a briar and she was trying to disentangle herself with short angry movements.

"Madame," Alexandre called softly, "Wait."

She whirled to face him. "Why? So you can insult me some more? Haven't you and your friend had enough fun?"

"I apologize for du Berry," Alexandre replied. "That's just his way. He meant no harm."

"That's what they all say."

"Believe me, it's true. A kinder man you will never find than Gilbert. He just likes to tease sometimes."

Alexandre could tell by her movements that she was too upset to attend to the task with the proper concentration necessary to free herself. And the more she struggled, the more briars stuck to her blouse.

"Allow me," he said, venturing closer. He wasn't sure if she would strike him or let him help.

She heaved a big sigh. "Okay."

Olivia stood quite still as he carefully pulled the briars from the fabric of her sleeve and the back of her blouse. Standing so close to her made him realize how tiny she was, how slender and feminine. Next to her he felt like a big hulking male, when he knew very well that compared to most men—though he was tall—he was not massively built. Perhaps when the world was viewed from the vantage point of a petite woman such as Olivia, men *did* appear callous and overbearing, although he got the feeling his attitude and words had more to do with her reaction than his physical characteristics.

He worked at the briars, trying not to breathe in the perfume of her hair that wafted up to his sensitive nose. The everlasting lily heightened all of his senses, sometimes to a nearly unbearable level, and he found the touch and scent of Olivia Travanelle highly stimulating.

To his regret, he noticed a small tear near the hem of her garment. "I am afraid the thorns have ripped your shirt," he said. "We are both destined to suffer rents in our clothing, it seems."

She inspected the rip and frowned. "Great. My best silk blouse."

"I will be happy to replace it. Just name the price."

"Forget it. I ran into the briar. I should have seen it."

"But you were running because you were made to be angry. I am responsible for that, not you."

She studied him intently and he stared back, making sure not to let his gaze drop. If she got the slightest impression that he appreciated the slender lines of her feminine figure and the swell of her "knickers," she'd probably slap him and turn a deaf ear to the entreaties he planned to make.

"All right," she stated. "Forty dollars."

"Done." He reached into the back pocket of his pants and pulled out his wallet. She waited silently while he selected two twenties, slipped them out, and gave them to her.

"Thanks."

"If you can't find one for that price, I will make up the difference."

She narrowed her eyes, obviously not ready to believe him, but then put the money in the pocket of her dark blue slacks. When she turned to leave, he reached out for her. The touch of her warm flesh set up a humming vibration in his palm.

"Madame," he began, and then realized from her stiff posture that she didn't like being grabbed by the arm. He let his hand drop and was relieved when she didn't walk away.

"Yes?"

"I hope you will reconsider taking the job. I promise that neither du Berry nor myself will make disparaging remarks. And I assure you that I value your knowledge of gardening."

"Oh?"

"It's true that only you answered my advertisement, madame, but that is of no importance. I am confident of your ability to do the job successfully, however much Gilbert made you think otherwise. He was unaware of my reasons for wanting to hire you."

"He was also quite overbearing."

Alexandre bowed his head slightly in silent agreement. Then he went on. "If you don't accept the job, it will simply remain undone." He paused. "I plan to leave the country in a month or so, perhaps for a few years, perhaps forever. I want to sell the house, and get a decent price for it in the bargain. So you see, I *am* desperate."

She narrowed her beautifully clear blue eyes again. "How desperate?"

"Desperate enough to agree to any reasonable fee."

Olivia sniffed and glanced around the yard, slowly taking stock of her surrounds. Was she playing hard to get? He didn't care. He needed her services. "I don't know, Mr. Chaubere."

"What if I offered to pay you enough so that you didn't have to work at Harry's?"

"And what makes you think I don't want to work there?"

"Men like Jimmy Dan Petersen," he replied. "And the way you looked last night when you were waiting on people."

"You saw me?"

He nodded. "Serving beer in dim surroundings is not what you were meant for, madame. Anyone can see that."

She glanced at the ground and he couldn't read her expression. Had his remark offended her again? She was so unfathomable, unlike any woman he had ever come across, that he was quite at odds at how to handle her. He couldn't afford to offend her sensibilities; she'd walk out of his yard forever. So, in case he had offended her, he'd sweeten the deal just to be safe. He had one more card to play.

"What if I offered you free lodging?" he ventured.

Olivia's head whipped up. "In your house?"

"No, in my carriage house. I've got quite a nice little two bedroom apartment above the garage where du Berry used to stay when he came to town."

He could see the wheels turning in her head.

"I have a son," she put in. "He's ten."

"As long as he minds his own business," Alexandre shrugged. "It's all right with me." He glanced at the ring on her finger, curious why she hadn't mentioned her spouse in all this time. "And your husband?" he asked.

"My what?"

He nodded toward her hand. "Your husband. Will he be living on the premises, too?"

"Um, no."

Alexandre surveyed her carefully and watched her quickly recover her composure.

"He's, uh, he's out of the country right now. He's an engineer, you see. Builds bridges all over the world."

"I see." Alexandre sensed she wasn't telling the complete truth, but now was not the time to delve deeper. "Well, before you make a decision, would you like to see the apartment?"

"Yes." She raised her chin. "Not that I'm agreeing to anything."

"Oh, completely understood, madame."

He motioned her through a break in the oleanders and walked with her down the gravel drive to the carriage house.

The sun was setting as Olivia accompanied Alexandre across the yard. In the golden light, the carriage house appeared cozy and welcoming, unlike the mansion behind her. Though the brick walls were just as old, the trim around the doors and windows had been recently painted a bright white. On the bottom floor was a three-car garage and what appeared to be an office or workroom. Alexandre walked to the south end of the building and opened a door.

"After you," he said, motioning her through.

She stepped into a small foyer with a coat rack and mirror on one wall and stairs ascending to the second floor. She went up them, her hand on the sturdy banister, and noticed the building smelled of fresh paint and not the overwhelming mustiness she expected from a two-hundred-year-old structure. A Palladian window greeted her at the top of the stairs and to her right she saw a door.

"It's unlocked," Alexandre said behind her.

She opened the door and stepped into the most charming apartment she had ever seen. The walls were white, the floors were polished oak planks, and there were plenty of windows to make it bright and cheerful. Even though it was on the second floor, the ceilings were high, giving the rooms a spacious feel, far different than most of the places she had lived. Expensive but simple pieces of furniture in cherry and chintz graced the room.

"It's lovely," Olivia remarked. "Who did the decorating?"

"Du Berry, during his provincial stage, when he wanted everything to have the charm of a country garden." He shook his head. "Gilbert hasn't set foot in the country, here or on the Continent, I'm sure of it."

Olivia caught herself smiling again and enjoying Alexandre's company far too much to maintain proper professional distance. She made herself revert to a more sober attitude and wiped the smile off her face.

"The dining room is straight ahead," he indicated with a wave of his hand while he closed the door behind him with the other. "And the kitchen to the right of that."

Olivia had brought nothing with her but clothes, her most favorite plants and tools, and some small appliances packed in her old van, for she had left all her possessions, shabby as they were, in storage in Seattle. None of them would have been right for this apartment anyway. But that was not a problem; she wouldn't mind being surrounded by du Berry's notion of roughing it. The man obviously didn't know the meaning of the phrase, just as he seemed not to entirely grasp the English language. Though it was obvious he had little talent for language, his taste in decorating was impeccable. Everywhere she looked, she was pleased by the arrangement of furniture, the clusters of paintings, the muted blues and creams of the upholstery and drapes. To Olivia, the apartment seemed like a model home for a designer exhibition. She absolutely adored it.

Olivia breezed into the kitchen, conscious of Alexandre slowly ambling behind her, and was pleasantly surprised to find herself surrounded by fairly modern cupboards and appliances. A large window at the sink afforded a view of the rear gardens, an expanse of green trees, and a glimpse of one of Charleston's major waterways, the Ashley River, in the distance over the rooftops. Olivia paused at the sink, entranced.

"What is the matter?" Alexandre asked.

"Oh," she glanced at him, beaming, "it's just that every place I've ever lived has looked out upon an alley, or a parking lot, or another group of apartments. This is so different, so beautiful!"

"This?" He stepped up to the counter beside her. "Why it's just the city."

"But such a beautiful city, your Charleston!"

She glanced up at him to find him gazing at her with an odd crooked smile on his lips, and wondered why she had let herself be so effusive. It wasn't like her.

"I have been in Charleston so long, I'd forgotten to really look at it," he commented. "Rather like the misplaced statue in my rear garden." He stared at her, seemingly puzzled, and then returned his gaze to the scene outside the window. "It's refreshing to see things with the eyes of someone so young, Madame Travanelle."

She stood beside him, watching the sun melt behind the rooftops, and wondered at his odd remark about her age. He wasn't much older than she was, unless he hid his age extremely well. She'd guess he was in his early thirties, and he certainly wasn't older than forty. Gradually, however, she became aware of the intense energy buzzing between their shoulders again, and once more she broke away, alarmed by his effect on her.

"What about the bathroom?" she asked, wondering if he felt the odd energy field, or if it was just in her imagination.

"There are two. One across the hall." He led her out of the kitchen through a doorway at the end of the living room. "Here. And one in the master bedroom."

Master bedroom? Olivia tried to conceal her excitement. She had never enjoyed the luxury of having a private bath. She poked her head into the main bathroom, done in blue and white and then walked with Alexandre down the hall to the two bedrooms separated by a walk-in storage closet. Alexandre showed her the smaller bedroom first.

"Your son can stay here," he said. "What did you say his name was?"

"Richie." She slowly pivoted, admiring the spacious room and the window seat, certain Richie would think a room like this was the best thing that ever happened to him.

"Short for Richard?" he asked, pronouncing the name in the French manner, as *ree-shard*.

"Yes, but no one calls him by that name."

"Soon he will outgrow the nickname. And you must allow it."

She felt a twinge of resentment at his words. "Oh?"

"Women sometimes fail to recognize their sons are growing up, and they do them grave injustice not to notice such things."

"Maybe he won't like being called Richard either," she replied, neither agreeing nor disagreeing, and slightly perturbed by the way he assumed he could comment on her relationship with Richie. Without close family relations and no intimate friends, Olivia had never dealt with criticism or suggestions from outside sources regarding her son.

"Perhaps," he averred quietly.

"And the master bedroom?" she asked, her voice frosty, hoping he would take the hint that some subjects were off limits.

"Across the hall. This way."

She followed him to an even larger room, dominated by a large flounced bed with a canopy. One wall was comprised entirely of mirrors, behind which was more closet space than Olivia had ever had in an entire apartment. She wandered to the bath where she discovered a large soaking tub and shower, decorated in subdued tans. Her Boston fern, which she had nurtured for seven years, would look grand hanging from the skylight above the tub. Olivia drew her hand along the large cabinet of the sink and knew without a doubt that she wanted to live here. It would be like living in a luxury hotel, almost as if she were on vacation, an indulgence she had never been able to afford.

"It gets warm here in the spring, you know, especially by next month," Alexandre explained, walking to a set of French doors. He opened them and motioned her to join him. "There is a piazza on this side of the apartment that extends from here to the dining room."

Olivia walked out onto the narrow wisteria-hung piazza. A slight breeze rustled her blouse and hair with air cooled and sweetened by the greenery of the garden. "This is lovely, Mr. Chaubere."

"The breeze off the harbor will cool the rooms in the evening, but we here in Charleston spend a lot of our time on our piazzas."

"I've noticed that. People seem to languish in the evenings here."

"Sometimes it's too hot to do anything else." He returned to the bedroom. For a moment she breathed in the cool air, heavy with the smell of damp earth and growing things, a smell she loved better than anything else in the world. She felt at home here, as though her spirit recognized its rightful place in Charleston, a feeling that was as alien to her as the weird energy that buzzed between her and her possible employer.

Reluctantly she returned to the bed chamber where Alexandre waited.

"Well?" he asked, his dark eyes hooded and unreadable. "What do you think?"

"I like it. Shall I submit a bid to you in the next few days?"

"Instead of a bid, how about a budget of twenty-thousand dollars?"

She thought she'd choke. "Twenty thousand?"

"Yes, which would cover your own fee plus supplies and services you might have to subcontract."

"I would say that is generous, Mr. Chaubere."

"Then you accept?" He raised one of his black brows and the corner of his mouth.

She looked past his shoulder. "Twenty thousand in addition to free rent?"

"Yes."

Her heart pounded. She couldn't believe her luck. There had to be something wrong with this deal, because it seemed too good to be true. Yet no warning flags went up, the kind she usually heeded and was later grateful for.

No small voice whispered in the back of her mind, telling her to go elsewhere. She took a deep breath and made her decision.

"Mr. Chaubere?" She held out her hand. "You have yourself a landscaper."

"Excellent." They shook, and she wasn't surprised by Alexandre's strong, warm grip. "Can you start tomorrow?"

"Yes. After I get settled."

"I can't stress enough that I am in a hurry to get this job completed. Can you work six days a week?"

"Yes."

"I hope to have the major part of the job completed before the end of March. Do you think that would be possible?"

"Perhaps, but I'll have to inspect the grounds before I give an actual time estimate."

"Good. I shall leave the carriage house open for you in the morning, as I will not be available. If you have need of me, leave a note on the cellar door. I prefer not to be disturbed during my work hours. But I will respond to inquiries in the early evening."

"All right." Olivia wondered if Alexandre slept late, but he didn't seem like the type of man to linger in bed. Perhaps he just kept odd hours.

"As to the landscaping itself, I wish to see your plans within the next few days. And I want to make it clear that you should consult me before pulling up any plants. I have a few rare varieties growing on the grounds which mustn't be disturbed."

"All right."

"Good."

She followed him down the stairs and out to the driveway. He turned.

"My only request is that you and your son respect my privacy," Alexandre went on, his face more serious than she had ever seen it. "I do not countenance visitors and I don't want anyone wandering around my house or lab. I have extensive and very sensitive equipment which I am in the process of packing, and I don't want it disturbed in any way."

"Of course. I understand."

"Good. Then I shall see you tomorrow evening, madame."

"Good night." She set off down the driveway, but his voice stopped her.

"Be careful tonight after work," he called after her. "And don't walk home alone."

"I won't." She waved and continued toward the large gate at the end of the drive, wondering why Alexandre Chaubere thought he had the right to give her advice. Although, instead of making her angry, she was surprised to find his last words gave her a warm feeling inside, the kind evoked by knowing someone genuinely cared for her welfare, which hadn't occurred very often in her life. Olivia slipped through the tall wooden gate and admonished herself for succumbing to an emotional state she disdained so much in other women. It was perfectly obvious why Alexandre would worry about her welfare. It wasn't because he cared about *her*, but because he would lose his gardener if anything should happen to her.

Olivia shook her head at her own silliness and walked briskly home, anxious to break the news to Richie that they had a place to live by themselves. Granted, it would only be for a month or more, but such a place! And not to have to dole out rent money would help her financial situation considerably. On the way, she kept thinking about how wonderful it would be to live in the apartment. But best of all, she would bet her ex-husband, Boyd Williston III, would never be able to find them on Chaubere's seemingly abandoned estate.

Boyd Williston III. She hadn't thought about him for years. There had been a time, long ago, when she believed Boyd's handsome Nordic face would be emblazoned on her mind forever. She had been seventeen then, new to Seattle, full of innocence and convinced that love could conquer all, and that Boyd would be in her life forever. Life had taught her otherwise and she had learned the hard way that "true love" wasn't always true, and that people could say things they didn't really mean.

She had met Boyd in their junior year in high school, when her mother had moved to Seattle after the devastating break up with her father. From the moment Boyd Williston set eyes upon her, he was constantly at her side. She loved it, for Boyd was not only attractive, he was intelligent and active in all facets of school life. He was the captain of the football team, homecoming king, and president of the student body. To be known as his girlfriend vaulted her to instant popularity, and made what might have been a miserable two years as a new girl in a metropolitan high school into a whirlwind of dates, dances, and heavy petting sessions in the back of Boyd's Trans Am.

As the months went by, however, she found little satisfaction in his social circle, for she never felt entirely accepted by Boyd's affluent friends. Besides that, she found most of them to be overly materialistic and self-centered, both qualities for which she had little patience. All the girls talked about was clothes, boys, and the latest cosmetics, and all the boys did was tell off-color jokes and flirt with her, whenever Boyd was out of earshot. She would have been just as happy to make friends of her own choosing and concentrate on her own school career. There was plenty to do, for she was involved in a lot of activities herself—drama club, the school literary magazine, and choir. She also maintained a straight-A average, which she would not jeopardize by choosing Boyd over her homework, no matter how he pleaded some weeknights. Occasionally she would give in and agree to do homework together, but Boyd could never keep his hands off her, and a few times they nearly made love in the kitchen while her mother sewed upstairs.

One night in her senior year as they were parked in their favorite spot overlooking Lake Washington, she was overcome by the moonlight, the wonderful time they'd had at a Christmas party, and her burgeoning love for him. Without much thought to the future, she gave herself to Boyd. All the books she had read, all the movies she had watched, convinced her to expect ecstasy in Boyd's arms. She remembered how women cried out with passion when making love. But nothing of the sort happened with her and Boyd. Sure, the experience had been pleasurable—although cramped, sweating, even desperately clumsy at times—but not the glory she'd anticipated.

She said nothing, however, convinced that her ignorance was the source of the problem, for Boyd seemed to have enjoyed himself immensely.

Even though she felt a disappointing flatness in their first experience of lovemaking, she held Boyd close, happy to give him such pleasure, for she thought she was deeply in love with him. And she fully believed he was in love with her. After that first time, she didn't have any grounds for putting him off, and she couldn't deny she craved closeness with him just as much as he wanted her. They made love every chance they got, and though she never reached any particular height of ecstasy, she loved the feeling of being in his arms, of touching his trim athletic body, of kissing him for hours and hours. She was extremely careful though, and kept track of her cycle, having studied the rhythm method of birth control and considering it her only recourse. She would never have asked her mother for a doctor's appointment to get contraceptives, and Boyd didn't like using condoms.

With the advent of sex, their relationship intensified and deepened, and for many months she sailed through the days in a blissful state, thinking she had everything under control and sure that Boyd Williston III was everything she could possibly want. From some of the things he hinted at, she was fairly sure he was considering some kind of future with her. She spent hours writing her name combined with his. *Olivia Williston. Mrs. Boyd Williston. Ms. Olivia Williston.*

Then in the spring of her senior year, she missed a period. By April she suspected she was pregnant and finally was forced to go to a clinic where tests confirmed her worries. Scared, but dying to tell him, she broke the news to Boyd on his birthday.

At first he stared at her for a long, incredulous moment, and then he sank back in the booth at their favorite hamburger joint. A thin smile broke on his pale face, as if he'd eaten something questionable and didn't know whether to swallow or spit it out.

"Boyd?" she ventured, taken aback by his reaction. She had hoped for a joyful grin or a supportive hug, not this half-hearted smile.

"God, Olivia." He licked his lips and tried another smile, but it was more of a grimace. "What a surprise! I mean it's great and all, but—"

"I thought you'd be happy." Her voice trembled. "I know we didn't plan this, and I know it might make things complicated, but Boyd—think of it! There's a little baby growing inside me. Our baby!"

"Yeah." He glanced at her, but the table concealed her from the waist down. "It's hard to believe it's true, not being able to see anything yet." He laughed stiffly and shifted on the bench seat.

"We can manage though, can't we, Boyd? We love each other and that's all that matters."

"Yeah, we do." He leaned forward, his forearms on the table. "But damn, Olivia, this just isn't the time to be having babies."

"Why? I'll be out of school when it happens. I won't even be showing when we graduate."

"But I can't be a father yet. I'm too young!"

She curled her fingers around her crumpled napkin as worry twisted inside her. She lowered her voice. "You weren't too young to make love to me."

He looked down. "But I'm going to Stanford in the fall. I won't even be around when the baby is born."

"Why can't I go with you? We could be together and you could attend college, just like you planned."

He stared at her as if she had uttered the most preposterous statement in the world. "Go to Stanford with a wife and kid?"

"Why not?"

"Olivia, I'm going to live in a frat house, play football, and have some fun. College is supposed to be the best years of a guy's life. It just won't be the same if I have to come home at night and watch you change a kid's diapers."

Olivia was shocked. "What am I supposed to do then, Boyd? Stay here in Seattle? Let you have your fun while I wait for you to come back?"

"I don't know!" He balled up the paper covering of the straw. "Hell, Olivia! How am I supposed to know?" He tossed the ball of paper on the table. "I thought you were taking care of things."

"I was!"

"Well, what happened?"

"I'm not sure! I don't think I miscalculated."

"You must have messed up somehow. And now you think you're going to drag me right down with you?"

"Drag you down?" Olivia blurted, trying to keep her voice lowered so the other diners wouldn't hear. "There's a child growing inside of me, Boyd. We made this child together. We are both responsible for it."

"You said it was all right, that the coast was clear."

"Well, it wasn't. Something went wrong!"

"I'll say!" Boyd jumped to his feet.

"Where are you going?" she asked, struck by the fear that he might walk away and never come back. "Boyd?"

"I've got to get out of here."

Olivia slid out from behind the table. "Please don't go like this." She reached for his arm. "Boyd—"

"Thanks for the birthday surprise." He brushed off her hand and stepped away. "Thanks a lot!"

He strode to the door of the restaurant, leaving Olivia alone and shaken. She hadn't considered the possibility that Boyd might reject the idea of fatherhood. She had been so sure of his love for her.

Gradually she became aware of the curious faces turning to gawk at her as she stood in the aisle of the restaurant. Blushing and heartbroken, she grabbed the check and her purse and stumbled to the till near the front. She walked home in a miserable daze, wondering what she would do if Boyd abandoned her altogether. How would she manage? How would she ever admit she had gotten in the same predicament her mother had found herself in eighteen years ago, when she'd been forced to marry before completing high school? Olivia walked for hours but knew this was one situation she could not outdistance.

Three days later Boyd took her for a ride and told her he'd been utterly miserable since their fight. He'd thought things over. He wanted to work it out with her, wanted to marry her even, if that's what she wanted. They made love that night in his car, and a sweeter, more wonderful night she had never known. A few days later, Boyd announced that his parents wanted to meet her. She was invited to tea at the Williston house on Lake Washington. His parents had never expressed the slightest interest in getting to know her and she viewed this as a turning point in her and Boyd's relationship.

The day of the tea, Boyd arrived to pick her up, jaunty and smiling, but with a strange distant edge to his light mood.

"Will they like this outfit?" Olivia asked, slowly rotating to give Boyd a view of her new dress bought especially for the occasion.

"Sure." He smiled and drew her into his arms. "I'm crazy about you, you know," he murmured, swaying with her a little. She smelled the faint but unmistakable fragrance of marijuana on his clothes. Olivia pulled back. "Did you smoke some pot?"

"Sure. What of it?"

"Won't your parents notice?"

"Hell no. They don't notice anything. You'll see."

Her bliss disappeared altogether on the ride to Boyd's home. When had he started smoking pot? She knew Boyd well and could tell he had put on a jaunty air to cover up something that disturbed him. Was he nervous about her meeting his folks? Did he think she would embarrass him in some way? Though she didn't come from a wealthy family like Boyd, she was intelligent, hard-working, and talented and in no way felt less a person for her middle-class roots. But did Boyd share her view?

She glanced over at him as he drove along the highway, and her gaze slipped down his perfectly formed Nordic profile, his impeccable hair, cut to brush just the tips of his ears and blow-dried to sweep off his forehead. He sensed her regard and turned with a smile. Then he fumbled for her hand and held it on her thigh, while he gave it a light squeeze.

"Nervous?" he asked.

"A little."

He returned his attention to the road. They sped along the lake drive and soon turned into a long lane that led to a colonial style house set on a knoll near the water. From what Boyd had told her, the house was more a symbol of emotional frigidity than a home, and his parents as unassailable as the cool marble columns that flanked the front stairs. At least he admitted that money hadn't brought his family happiness. She was proud of the fact that with her help he had learned to judge people from the inside, and not by their possessions. But had his independent thinking allowed him to separate himself from his family? She wasn't sure. Boyd pulled around to the side of the huge house and parked. He turned to her.

"Let me handle them," he warned. "I know them."

She picked up her purse. "What do you mean, handle them?"

"I'll do the talking, all right?"

"I suppose." She opened her door and got out. Boyd led her to the front steps and with each stair she felt her anger rising, because she realized what Boyd had really said to her. He didn't want her to talk. He didn't think she was capable of holding her own.

When they walked into the main hall of the large house, Olivia glanced up at the sparkling chandelier and let her gaze travel down the gleaming oak banister of the graceful staircase on the other side of the room. Suddenly her new dress seemed inadequate, her shoes not quite right, and she became highly conscious of her frayed purse strap. She slipped the strap down and carried the purse in her hand, throwing her shoulders back and reminding herself that she was proud of who she was.

He showed her into a room comprised mainly of glass, which commanded a gorgeous view of the lake below. She stepped across the threshold and her feet sank into the deep pile of a light cream carpet. Every piece of furniture was upholstered in off-white with brass and glass accents, and the walls were painted the same light tone. The only color in the entire room was a restrained arrangement of pink roses on the coffee table. This was not a lived-in room, not a place to put up one's feet and relax. Olivia marveled that a room could remain so spotlessly sterile, and wondered what it would be like to live in such a place. She could feel her naturally reserved personality tightening even further. Then she noticed the older couple standing near a liquor cabinet.

"Ah, there you are, Boyd," his father greeted him. He strode forward, shorter and stouter than his son, but wearing an expertly tailored suit that camouflaged his portly form. He held out his hand and shook Boyd's while his gaze darted over Olivia. She thought it was odd that a father should shake his son's hand like that, as if they hadn't seen each other in weeks.

"And you must be Olivia," he said, smiling briskly.

Olivia noticed the smile hung around his lips, but failed to light up his pale blue eyes.

"This is my father, Boyd Williston, Sr.," Boyd said.

"Pleased to meet you, sir," she said. Regardless of the older man's coolness, Olivia held out her hand.

She could tell her action surprised him, but he quickly recovered and gave her hand a limp shake meant for women, the kind Olivia particularly disliked.

"My pleasure," he mumbled.

Olivia glanced over his shoulder at the slight woman hovering in the background, sizing her up, her lips a tight line in a pinched and unhappy face. She wore a gray wool dress with a navy and gray scarf artfully draped around her shoulders. One look at Boyd's mother and Olivia knew that in entering this sterile white room, she had just crossed over the Arctic Circle. She would find no ally in Mrs. Williston.

"Mother," Boyd said. "This is Olivia Martin."

"How do you do?" Mrs. Williston declared, her frosty voice making a statement out of the question.

"Nice to meet you, Mrs. Williston."

"Martin." She paused, as if searching her memory. "There's a Mrs. Martin who takes care of the houseplants of a friend of mine. Barbara Martin, I think her name is. Any relation?"

"Yes." Olivia tilted her chin a bit higher. Her mother ran a one-woman plant care business which catered to wealthy homeowners. Though the work was demanding and her clients were sometimes unpleasant taskmasters, her mother had always made a decent living for them. That her mother owned a business, set high standards for herself and met them, and provided for her without fail, was enough to win Olivia's respect, no matter what she did for a living. Barbara Martin was smart and hard-working, and could have been anything she wanted, but her lack of skills and education, having a child to raise, and her husband's alcoholism had kept her slaving away for wealthy women like Mrs. Williston, with no time or energy left to better herself. "Barbara Martin is my mother."

"She is?" Mrs. Williston spread a fine-boned hand over her expensive scarf while she shot a dark glance at her husband. "Why, isn't that a coincidence! It's quite a small world, isn't it, Miss Martin, where my son can date the daughter of my best friend's gardener."

Olivia raised her chin even higher. "She isn't exactly a gardener—"

"Whatever," Mrs. Williston waved her off. "Perhaps I should try to steal your mother away from Sylvia and get her to do my plants. The company that does it now has the laziest help. I can't tell you how hard it is to find decent help these days."

Olivia fought down a flush. Her mother wasn't a servant; she was a businesswoman. Yet, what good would it do to belabor the point with Mrs. Williston, who obviously didn't see a distinction. She wished Boyd would take her hand, touch her arm, or do something to shield her from his mother. But he stood to the side, seemingly unaware of the subtle digs his mother made at Olivia's social standing.

"And what about your father?" Mrs. Williston continued. "What does he do for a living?"

"My father?" Olivia swallowed, extremely uncomfortable about discussing her father. "He's a—he's a fisherman."

"Really? Does he own a boat?"

"No, he goes up to Alaska, places like that."

"How adventurous," Mrs. Williston put her hand to her mouth as if to suppress a yawn. Then she smiled again. "Tea will be served in a few minutes. Why don't you sit down and make yourself comfortable, Miss Martin."

Comfortable? Olivia glanced at the hard white couch. Who could make herself at home in this room? The decor reflected the personality of the mistress of the house, who was cold and inhospitable, at least to those of lower social standing. Olivia could find more comfort on a block of ice.

Olivia chose her seat carefully. She didn't want to sit on the couch in case Mrs. Williston needed to perch there to serve tea. And she didn't want to sit in the wing-back chair, because it seemed like a place more suitable to Mr. Williston. So she took the lighter, harder side chair and carefully sat down. Boyd moved to a position behind her, his hands on the back of the chair. She wasn't sure if he stood there in a gesture of support or to hide. Olivia tucked her purse near the leg of the chair with hope that its worn edges and strap would be hidden from view.

No one spoke a single word. Mrs. Williston fussed with the wrinkles of her dress and her diamond bracelet, and Mr. Williston, judging by the intensity of his gaze, stared at something important on the lake. Olivia shifted nervously in her chair, crossed her legs, then remembered it was more socially acceptable to cross them discreetly at the ankles. She put her ankles together, struggling to relax, while she endured the longest three minutes of her entire life.

A maid bustled in with the tea tray and broke the uncomfortable silence. Everyone watched Mrs. Williston pour tea as if it were the most fascinating activity imaginable. Olivia accepted her dainty cup and saucer and prayed she wouldn't betray her nervous state with a loud clatter of china. Forcing herself to settle down, she managed to maneuver the teacup to position, and waited for everyone to be served before she took a sip.

After another weighty silence while Mr. Williston added sugar and cream to his tea, and Mrs. Williston silently offered a plate of cookies which no one accepted, Mr. Williston sat back in his chair.

"Now then," he began, politely clearing his throat behind his napkin, "Boyd tells us you've got yourself in a difficult situation."

"Situation?" Olivia repeated, forgetting her promise to let Boyd do the talking. Boyd's right hand bumped her shoulder, warning her to be quiet, but she was too surprised to heed his signal. She had expected to talk about marriage, not her pregnancy, and felt betrayed by Boyd for having told his parents of her condition before they had a chance to meet her. They'd probably already formed an opinion of her without ever having talked to her.

"Really, Miss Martin," Mrs. Williston put in, "You must admit that your present condition will cause problems— for all of us, granted—but especially for you."

Olivia lowered her cup to protest, but Boyd interrupted her.

"She knows that, Mother. Olivia's not stupid."

"I'm sure she isn't, dear, but she might not realize what's at stake. Having a baby is a big responsibility, one that is overwhelming, even for the most prepared woman." She took a sip of tea and carefully returned the cup to its saucer. "It's difficult enough when the proper foundations are laid, such as being married and established, having a home, and earning enough income to provide for the child. You, Miss Martin, have none of these. We don't wish to see you suffer. We don't like to see anyone suffer needlessly." Mrs. Williston tilted her head and smiled, but her expression remained cool.

"And Boyd shouldn't be saddled with children at this point in his life," Mr. Williston continued. "He's got an education to pursue."

"We know this is a difficult time, Miss Martin, an extremely difficult time," Mrs. Williston placed her cup and saucer on the tea tray. "And to make it easier for you, we're not even going to raise the issue of paternity."

Olivia stared. "Paternity?" she gasped, realizing what Boyd's mother had just said. She jumped to her feet, aghast, and put her palm on her belly. "You think this baby might not be Boyd's?"

Both of his parents gazed up at her with dispassionate eyes, unaffected by her harsh question. Mrs. Williston dabbed a napkin to the corner of her mouth. "In some cases it's difficult to be sure of these things."

Olivia felt the tips of her ears blazing. "Mrs. Williston, I'll have you know that—"

"You must understand our concern for Boyd. Some girls use pregnancy as a weapon, you know. Of course, I'm sure you would never do such a thing, Miss Martin. You seem like a nice girl."

Olivia couldn't believe her ears. In their eyes, she was promiscuous and their son was her innocent victim. Rage and regret swept over her—rage that they could think she might have slept with someone other than Boyd, and regret that she had allowed herself to get in this predicament. They probably thought she had got pregnant on purpose to trap Boyd into marriage, when it was never her intention at all. Why wasn't Boyd sticking up for her?

She turned to him. "Boyd!" she implored.

Mr. Williston got to his feet. "Now, just calm down here, little lady. There's no need to get upset. We want to help you."

"In what way, exactly?" she stared at him, refusing to break eye contact. These people were masters at avoiding eye contact and she wasn't going to let Mr. Williston off the hook.

"Well," he began, running his hand over his hair, "we can have the problem taken care of."

"Problem?" Olivia retorted. "This isn't a problem to be taken care of. This is a human life we're talking about!"

"Of course, Miss Martin," Mrs. Williston calmly agreed, her tone never raising above a certain well-modulated level. "And we respect human life. Of course we do. But what kind of life will you be able to give this baby? And what kind of life will you have? You're little more than a girl yourself."

Olivia couldn't believe what they were saying to her. The Willistons wanted her to have an abortion. They wanted her to get rid of her baby. Never in her wildest dreams had she suspected her visit to the Williston home would come to this. She had expected to meet Boyd's parents, chat about college plans, and get to know the family. She had expected to be observed and judged—but not this.

"We are willing to see you through the unpleasantness," Mr. Williston said after a long pause, "for Boyd's sake. We know he doesn't want to see you suffer. We've got a great specialist lined up and a nice little recovery vacation planned for you and a friend of your own choosing. You can do it over Memorial Day weekend. All of this can be behind you in a matter of days."

"Days?" Olivia exclaimed. "You want me to get rid of my child and then expect me to go on *vacation*?" She felt her cheeks burning. "You think I'll forget about it in a matter of *days*?"

"I know you can't see it now." Mrs. Williston folded her hands in her lap. "But in the long run, it will be better for all concerned."

"Not for the baby!" Olivia countered, nearly shrieking. Was she the only one with feelings in the room? How could they talk so calmly about taking the life of a child? "Boyd?" Olivia whirled to face him. He had offered to marry her. Marriage would solve most of their problems as far as she was concerned. Why wasn't he bringing up the subject? "Haven't you told your folks about our plans?"

Mr. Williston's head came up. "What plans, Boyd?"

Olivia watched the color drain out of Boyd's face and knew he hadn't mentioned marriage, and was probably too afraid to do so, or had decided against it. His glance darted away from her and veered to the floor. At that moment her love for him shifted as she saw how he faced a difficult situation for the first time. It was easy to appear strong in his bulky football uniform and in front of the student body when all he had to do was follow rules and use his natural charm and athletic ability to succeed. Success had always come effortlessly for Boyd Williston III. But along the path of success, his character and values had never really been tested. Not until this moment. With that glance downward and his telling silence, Olivia realized he had just failed the exam.

"You weren't considering marriage, were you?" Mrs. Williston asked, her eyes wide.

Boyd shuffled his feet behind Olivia's chair. "Well, as a matter of fact, we—"

"Boyd, it would simply be out of the question. Both of you are far too young."

"But if I—"

"No, son," Mr. Williston shook his head. "It's a nice gesture, but we can't let you ruin your life."

"So marrying me would ruin his life?" Olivia questioned, turning to face his parents. "Is that what you think?"

"Of course not, dear," Mrs. Williston smiled. Olivia was sick to death of her phony expression. "We simply want to ensure Boyd has every advantage in life. Marrying young would limit so many of his options, don't you see?"

Olivia heard the sugar-coated words but knew what had been said to her. Mrs. Williston might just as well have slapped her. Olivia wasn't good enough for their son. That was it. She didn't have the bloodline, the background, or the assets to make a proper match for their precious son. No matter how intelligent she was or how hard she worked, she would never have the pedigree to become a member of the Williston family. Olivia had never been so insulted in her life, and she'd never been so desperately disappointed. She was on her own. She could see it as clearly as the spotless glass table near her leg. Olivia snatched her purse off the floor and straightened.

"Don't bother worrying about the quality of your grandchild's life," she remarked. "I'll handle it on my own." Before anyone could say anything more about her character and family, Olivia strode across the immaculate carpet to the high double doors at the end of the room.

"Olivia!" Boyd called after her. "Wait!"

She heard his footsteps behind her but ignored him. Boyd was the last person she wanted to see. She stormed out of the house, choking back the urge to cry, and had every intention of walking all the way home, even though it was miles away and would take her hours.

"Olivia!" Boyd ran down the steps behind her. He took her arm but she shook him off.

"Get away from me!" she blurted, hurrying down the walk.

"Olivia!" He ran around in front of her and took both her arms. "Give them time."

"Why? They won't give me the time of day!"

"I still want to marry you, Olivia. I will, as soon as they see it our way."

"They're never going to see it our way, not when you just stand there like a lump. How could you let them say those things to me—treat me like that!"

"Like what?"

Olivia stared up at him. His tone sounded so innocent.

"Like what, Olivia?"

"They treated me like dirt."

"That's because they don't know you."

"So that gives them the right to treat me like dirt?" she retorted, angry and hurt, and holding back tears which were dangerously close to the surface.

"I'll work it out, Olivia. Somehow, I promise. Just don't cry."

"I'm not crying." She raised her chin and blinked.

"Let me take you home. We can talk." He reached up and tilted her chin with the curve of his index finger. "Still love me?"

"Of course I do." She sighed. But even as she reassured him, she felt the hollow echo in her words and knew that her love for him was faltering, and would never be as strong or as pure as she thought it had been before. She glanced up into his face, into his blue eyes, recognizing the needy expression in them for the first time. Boyd needed her. He needed her love because he didn't get it from anyone else but her. Was that enough to hold them together?

Satisfied with her assurance of undying love, he dropped a light kiss on her mouth and then guided her to the car. He drove her home. She expected to talk with him about the travesty they had just experienced. But Boyd was silent and her energy seemed at an all time low. All she wanted to do was run into her house, crawl into bed, and cry. She didn't want to talk to anyone about anything. A heavy feeling of despair descended upon her, and she was certain her future had taken a sudden plunge into darkness—even if Boyd decided to defy his parents and marry her—because after today, she wasn't sure if she did want to marry him. And she would never know one way or another if she truly loved him, for now she would have to marry him for different reasons other than love. From here on out responsibility toward the child growing within her would color every decision she made. She could no longer let her heart lead her. From now on she would have to follow her head and learn to put the needs of someone else before her own. That afternoon she was acutely aware of stepping out of her adolescence, and she wondered if Boyd would ever do the same.

Olivia found herself standing at the foot of the stairs of Sherry's apartment. She hardly remembered the walk from Alexandre Chaubere's house to here, so deeply had she been engrossed in thoughts of the past. Now that she was older, she could look back on her relationship with Boyd and see the bald truth. All the time she had spent with him, she had interpreted his emotional hunger as love. How could she have been so blind? She shook her head. Their attempt at marriage had lasted only a few brief weeks until pressure from his family and her own disappointment in his weak character drove him away. He left her pregnant and desperate and never once looked back. In the time it had taken to raise her son, she had done a lot of growing up herself. She'd never be that naive again.

For ten years she had placed Richie's needs above her own. For ten years she had given all her energy and time into making a life for her child. It had been extremely difficult and lonely, too, without a single penny of help from the Willistons. Sometimes she was so tired she didn't think she could go on. But Richie gave her the strength to keep plugging away. From the moment she had heard his cry, she had dedicated her heart and soul to him. And little by little life was improving for them both.

Olivia placed her hand on the knob of the newel post of Sherry's apartment and looked up to the second floor where her son was probably eating dinner with their neighbor. *Her* son. The son Boyd was trying to track down now, ten years later. He'd sent a detective snooping around her workplace and apartment in Seattle, making inquiries about Richie. Why, after so many years of silence? She didn't have a clue. All she did know was that the scholarship for college in Charleston had come through just in time, conveniently getting her and Richie out of Seattle before Boyd could catch up with them. She wasn't about to let the Willistons barge into Richie's life. Not now. Not ever. They didn't deserve him.

She decided not to dwell on Boyd any longer and headed up the stairs. Richie would be excited to hear the plans she'd made to move to Alexandre Chaubere's carriage house tomorrow morning. She'd throw herself into her work and pray the Chaubere estate would hide her son from the Willistons.

5

"*Mom, here comes Mr. Chaubere,*" Richie said, turning around on the couch in the front room of the carriage house apartment.

Olivia knew the view from the couch by heart already—the long seventy-foot drive to the big gate, the strip of oleanders between the drive and the house, and the large overgrown garden between the house and street. Most of the homes in Charleston had been built close to the sidewalk, if not flush with the pavement. Alexandre Chaubere's home, set over a hundred feet from the street, was an exception, affording privacy and shrouded distance from passersby, which probably served to heighten the mysterious aura surrounding the man and his estate.

"He's walking this way!" Richie whipped back around and stared out the window again.

Olivia glanced up from her seat at the dining room table, where she was sketching preliminary plans for the rear garden. "I wonder what he wants?"

It was seven-thirty and nearly dark. By noon she and Richie had settled into the carriage house, with plenty of time to look over the grounds, take measurements of the property, buy some groceries, and then have a leisurely dinner together. She had tonight and tomorrow off at the club, and had given her notice the night before. Olivia promised to keep working until they found someone else and offered to pitch in whenever someone was sick or had to take time off unexpectedly. In a way she was sad to leave her new friends at Harry's, but she was glad not to be away from Richie during the evening.

Richie craned his head to get a better look. The tendons on his slender neck stuck out with the effort. Olivia leaned on the heel of her hand and surveyed her son's wiry body, wondering when the child would ever put on any weight. His bone structure was fine—he had nice little shoulders and long legs—but he was the thinnest kid. Sometimes he got teased for being a carrot-top, although his red hair was slowly darkening to auburn, and it wasn't as hard a cross to bear as it had been a few years ago. She recalled a few times he had come home crying, begging to stay home from school. But of course, she couldn't allow that, even if she didn't have to work. She wasn't about to let Richie be a baby. Olivia pushed the memory from her mind and noticed her son was now practically hanging off the back of the couch.

"Richie, it isn't nice to gawk out the window like that. What if he sees you?"

"He didn't. He's going into the garage."

"Well, I hope he didn't notice you spying on him." Olivia returned to her sketching, slightly disappointed to learn Alexandre wasn't coming up to see them. She had many items to discuss with him, including the possibility of hanging Richie's car posters on the walls of his bedroom. Apartment managers had always forbidden any kind of fastener that made a mark on the walls. As to that, she'd leave a note on Alexandre's door after he left and talk with him tomorrow. A few moments later she heard the muffled noise of a car ignition.

"Cool!" Richie exclaimed. "He's firing up the Spider." He scrambled to his feet and raced for the door.

"Where do you think you're going, young man?" Olivia demanded, stopping him in his tracks.

Richie wilted, one hand on the knob. He heaved a large dramatic sigh. "Mom—"

"Don't even think of going down those stairs. Mr. Chaubere expressly told me that he didn't want to be bothered."

"I won't bother him, Mom."

"You will if you run outside every time he gets his car out of the garage."

Olivia heard the car back up, stop and then roll down the driveway. Not until Alexandre was well out of range did she release Richie from her glare. He scowled and stormed down the hall.

"You never let me do anything!" he exclaimed.

Olivia heard him slam his door, and then looked down at her drawing and frowned. It was true. Richie didn't get to do much. She didn't have time to take him to organized sports, and she wouldn't let him go off on his own. They didn't have enough money for camp or specialized lessons. Usually Richie obeyed her rules and seemed content to putter around the house building models, reading, and riding his bike around the block. But it was true that he didn't get to do half the things other boys his age enjoyed.

She put her mechanical pencil on the table and walked down the hall after her son. At his closed door, she stopped, and turned her ear to the paneled wood.

"Richie, how about taking a walk with me?"

Nothing but silence issued from the other side of the door.

"Come on. We can go down to The Battery and check it out. There's lots of old cannons from the Civil War and before."

"You said you'd ask Mr. Chaubere if I could see his car."

"Yes. And I promise I will. First thing tomorrow, all right?"

"Why didn't you ask him today?"

"I didn't see him today. He's a busy man, Richie. But I promise I'll ask the first chance I get, all right?"

"Oh, okay." The door opened slowly. Richie came through it clutching his new Charlotte Hornets cap. He stopped in the hall, however, and peered up at his mother.

"But you have to ask him tomorrow, Mom," he said. "I've got to see that car."

"I know," she tousled his hair. "I know you do."

She watched him wait until he got outside to plop the cap on his head. Olivia smiled as she locked the door behind her. Richie might not have the financial advantages of his peers, but he was a good kid.

Later that evening when Richie was in bed, Olivia continued her sketches of the property. Around eleven, she heard Alexandre return and the sound of the garage door opening and closing. She wondered where he had gone, but it was really none of her business, so she dashed the thought and concentrated on her work. When she finished, she made a list of questions to ask Alexandre, and then wrote him a short note on a Post-It pad, suggesting a meeting as soon as possible. She rummaged around in one of the boxes she had decided to leave packed and found an old flashlight. The beam was weak but would have to do. Taking the note, Olivia slipped out of the carriage house, turned on the flashlight, and picked her way through the overgrown shrubbery to the walk on the side of the mansion, which she knew would take her to the cellar stairs.

The night was balmy, just cool enough to be comfortable in her shorts and tank top. Crickets sang in the jungle surrounding the house, and the crescent moon hung in the indigo southern sky like a graceful silver earring. Olivia breathed in deeply, enjoying the pungent smell and the peace and quiet of Alexandre's expansive property. In Seattle, she was accustomed to hearing traffic noises and sirens at night, and was surprised how her stress level fell in this tranquil place. Relaxed and happier than she had been for many years, Olivia strolled to the back of the house. She gave a quick derisive salute to the female statue and then turned toward the cellar stairs. Not a single light burned in the Chaubere house, not even in the laboratory.

Hoping Alexandre would see the note in the morning, she stuck the paper to the door of the laboratory at his eye level, which was nearly a foot higher than hers, and turned to go. At that moment her flashlight went out.

"Oh, great," she muttered. Her vision darkened momentarily as her eyes adjusted to the dim surrounds. She tried the stairs while bracing her hand on the stone wall for support, and climbed upward. She managed to stumble her way to the top and plunged into the deeper shadows of the grilled arcade, whose massive plastered columns supported the huge house above. Peering into the darkness, she tried to make out the shapes of the giant posts, praying she wouldn't run headfirst into one of them. Her peaceful stroll to Alexandre's house had suddenly turned into a disquieting expedition. The dark house had become a menace, both to her body and her mind, for the oppressively heavy ceiling of the arcade seemed to have shrunk to just above her head, and the trees beyond blotted out even the faint light of the moon.

With the failure of her flashlight, the entire mood had flip-flopped, leaving her apprehensive, claustrophobic, and—she hated to admit it—even a bit frightened. As Olivia minced across the stone floor of the arcade, she tripped over something—a wooden crate—and bumped her shin.

"Ow!" she cried and jumped at the sound of her own voice, which echoed in the blackness. She hopped on one leg while looking around her, not knowing what she expected to see, but hating being in the ancient house this time of night. The mansion seemed to have a life of its own, and she felt trapped in its jaws.

"Who's there?" a deep voice boomed from beyond the grillwork.

Olivia shrieked in fright and threw up her hands, even though the voice was familiar, for it belonged to the master of the house, and he didn't sound pleased to find someone near his laboratory.

A dark shape moved toward her. She backed up but slammed against one of the square columns of the arcade. The rough plaster scraped the tops of her shoulders. A cold sweat broke out beneath her shirt as she watched him approach.

"Madame?" he questioned harshly. He wore a white shirt. His shoulders loomed wide in the darkness. "What are you doing here?"

A million explanations for her presence near his cellar sprang to mind. *The note, her flashlight, the darkness, her son, the car, the night.* What could she say to explain herself? He probably thought she was snooping around, exactly what he had told her not to do. She thought back to the things Sherry had told her about Alexandre, that he was strange and kept to himself, that he just might be a murderer. What was he going to do to her? She hadn't felt this panic-stricken or tongue-tied in years.

"Madame!" he stepped closer.

She skittered around the edge of the column. "Keep away!" she warned.

"What's going on?" His tone was crisp and unfriendly. "What are you doing here?"

"I was—" She could hardly hear over her thumping heart. What a coward she was, to let the house and this man affect her so easily. She thought she had more backbone than that. Of course she had more backbone than that. She just wasn't seeing things for what they were. Olivia forced herself to return to rational thought. She was simply standing at the back of an old house, talking to an eccentric man. Nothing to get terrified about.

Olivia stood upright, away from the column. "I was—" She threw back her shoulders. "I was leaving a note for you and my flashlight went out."

"Are you hurt?"

"No. I just hit my shin on something."

"You should be careful. There are packing crates lying about."

"I couldn't see a thing!"

"I shall remedy matters. Wait here."

She saw his dim form pass by her and disappear down the stairs, heard his shoes ringing on the stone, the lock tumblers grating, and the old door creaking open. A few moments later, he returned, holding an old-fashioned lantern with glass sides. The flame flickering within emitted a surprising amount of light, and threw a warm glow over Alexandre's face and torso.

Olivia glanced up at him, relieved to see that he wasn't angry. His skin was appreciably more golden in the light of the lantern, and his expression relaxed. He wore a loose-fitting white shirt, with dropped shoulders and the sleeves rolled up on his sinewy forearms, and dark form-fitting pants tucked into tall black boots. She gaped at him, struck by the image, for though she forced herself to be pragmatic and practical for Richie, she had always been a romantic at heart and had loved swashbuckling stories as a child. This man could have stepped right off the set of a pirate movie.

A wry smile curved his lips as if he read her mind, aware she was admiring him, and his smile immediately popped her out of her fantasy. She didn't like any man, especially this one, second-guessing her or making assumptions.

"Thanks," she said, indicating the light with a sweep of her hand.

"Let's have a look at your leg." He lowered the lantern and leaned closer.

"It's just a scratch. Nothing serious."

He knelt on the stone floor. Before she realized what he was doing, he slipped his warm hand around her calf and slid it down to her ankle to raise her foot off the ground. The gesture was done with such gentle confidence that she didn't even think of protesting. She was glad she had shaved her legs that afternoon, so that her skin was silky soft to the touch. And yet, she shouldn't care what Alexandre thought of her skin. He was her employer. She was his landscape architect. Nothing more. Not now or in the future. Flushing at her own thoughts, she looked down, and noticed that his touch left her calf tingling like the aftermath of a shock.

"Looks like you've got a small bump here."

"I've had worse." She surveyed his lush sable locks, wondering what it would be like to reach down and stroke him and push her fingers through his long, shoulder-length hair. Shaking off such dangerous thoughts, she forced herself to a different topic. "Once I was building a rock retaining wall, and one of the stones rolled down the slope and hit my leg. The right one, see? There's a scar."

Alexandre released her left leg and moved the light close to her other leg for a better view. "I see."

"I had a bump the size of a golf ball on my shin."

He lightly stroked the scar with his index finger. "*C'est dommage, ma petite,*" he murmured.

She didn't know French, but she guessed the foreign words expressed his regret at seeing the scar. For a moment she gazed down at him, amazed that she could let him stroke her so easily, and that his touch would be so satisfying. Since Boyd, she hadn't let a man so much as hold her hand. She had kept her guard up, her wariness of men well-sharpened. And yet with this man, her guard continually slipped. She'd have to watch herself with him.

Then she noticed Alexandre staring at his hand, the same hand that had slipped down her leg. He turned it over, glanced at the back, and then studied his palm again. Olivia couldn't imagine what he found so puzzling about his hand and thought his behavior was unusual. Maybe it wasn't such a good idea to be alone in the dark with him like this. Olivia took a step back, enough to show him the conversation regarding the state of her physical welfare was over.

Effortlessly he rose to his feet. "And the content of your note, madame?"

"I've drawn up some preliminary sketches of some of my ideas and want to talk to you about them."

"Excellent. I will walk you back and have a look at them."

"Now?" she croaked, anxious to get away from him.

"Of course. The night is young, madame. Is it not?"

Olivia turned her wrist and glanced at her watch. "It's midnight."

"As I said. The night is young."

Regardless of the warmth in his voice, a cool shiver passed through her.

"Shall we?" he asked, motioning toward the walk, and holding the lantern aloft. The light streamed through the glass, illuminating the path.

"Well, all right. It shouldn't take long." She led the way, guided by the light he held. He walked close behind her, and she guessed he would have taken her elbow had she not made it clear earlier that she didn't like to be held in such a fashion by a stranger.

Their shoes crunched loudly on the gravel drive as they walked in silence to the carriage house. She opened the door and ascended the stairs, highly conscious of his tall form behind her. Olivia wasn't accustomed to taking men into her living quarters, and there was something distressingly unsettling about guiding this handsome but undeniably mysterious man into her world during the middle of the night. She had never been alone in a house with a man, had never made love with Boyd other than in a car. And though she hadn't the slightest intention of making love with Alexandre Chaubere, she found herself getting more and more apprehensive at the prospect of sharing her space with him.

She paused in the living room to put the flashlight on an end table near the couch so she would see it in the morning and remind herself to get new batteries. Alexandre looked around, still holding the lantern. "I expected to see boxes and trunks. You're all settled in."

"Yes. We only had what was in my van."

He nodded and walked toward the dining room, as if he owned the place. Well, he did actually, but she still thought he might have hung back, now that she had taken possession of the apartment. Perhaps Alexandre wasn't the type of man to hang back indecisively at anything. Or perhaps he thought he controlled all things in his domain, including the people. She felt another wave of unease. Perhaps it hadn't been prudent to allow him in the house.

"My sketches are on the table," she declared, hoping to get down to business.

"Let's take them out to the piazza," he suggested. "It's cooler out there."

"Okay. I'll get us something to drink."

He smiled his faint, enigmatic smile, opened the French doors and walked onto the balcony, his progress marked by the glow of the lantern. Olivia poured lemonade over ice, reflecting how strange it sounded to hear words like *us* and *let's* when it came to dealing with a man. She had been single so long, so fiercely independent, that her vocabulary had been restricted to the starkly separate *you* and *me* for years.

She carried the tall glasses out to the piazza, where Alexandre had arranged the lantern and sketches on a white wrought iron table. He stood nearby, studying one of her papers.

"I like this one," he commented. She walked over to him and stood near his shoulder so she could see which drawing he had selected. Holding the cold glasses in front of her, she peered across his forearm to the paper in his hand.

He had chosen the design with the "ruin", a plan she had developed to incorporate the statue with old stones to create a pleasant surprise for someone coming upon it unaware. The "ruin" would appear like part of an ancient temple half-swallowed by the garden and would make far better use of his beautiful statue. "Good," she replied. "I like that plan best myself."

"*Bien.*"

"You're aware that we'll have to move your statue."

"I expected as much, madame." He raised one of his expressive eyebrows and looked down at her with a wry expression of good humor and an obvious willingness to acknowledge her superior eye for design. Their eyes locked and held, and in that moment her wariness of him was drowned in a peculiar communion that flooded the space between them.

A shaft of pure unadulterated desire shot through her. She wanted to lean into his shoulder and experience the sensation of his height and strength, wanted to reach up and touch his square jaw just below his ear, and more than anything wanted to know how it would feel to have that sensual mouth of his pressed upon hers. She longed to close her eyes and bathe in the quiet confidence that streamed out of this man, and let it cleanse all the bitter restraint from her heart.

Something cold jerked Olivia to her senses. She found herself standing there still clutching the glasses, the icy lemonade burning her hands.

"Here you go," she blurted, thrusting a glass toward him.

Alexandre accepted the drink. "Thank you," he said, moving toward the table.

She hurriedly pulled out a chair and sat down before she could lapse into any more fantasies. Taking a long cold drink to douse the heat inside, she leaned over the drawings.

"Actually, the original design of the yard is very nice. I don't think many extensive changes are called for. Here," She pointed to a position on the drawing, "is where a ruin would be favorably placed, near the corner of the reflecting pool."

Alexandre nodded. His hand rested on the table beside her drawing and she was extremely conscious of the nearness of his wrist as they both hovered over the sketch in the lamplight. "I like the placement," he said.

"As for the ruin, I see a stone wall, old masonry blocks if I can get my hands on some, with ivy cascading over the top, creeping jasmine, some myrtle and the statue set there." She tapped the paper with her index finger. The light glinted off her wedding band and she was sorry she had used her left hand. "I'm hoping to find some old columns, too."

"My only concern is the existing flora in that location," Alexandre mused. "There are valuable plants there. In France we called them Everlasting Lilies, *Lis Perpetual*, and I don't want them disturbed."

"Everlasting Lilies?" Olivia repeated. "I've never heard of them."

"They are extremely rare. An ancient plant." He curled his hand around his glass, but didn't take a drink. "If you like, I'll show them to you tomorrow."

"All right. As to the bulk of the work, most of it is pruning, thinning, and getting rid of the weeds. Once that's completed, I'll make a list of plants we need to purchase."

"You have done well, madame. I am pleased."

"Good, because I have a favor to ask."

A shadow passed through his eyes. "Yes?"

"It's my son, Richie." She took a drink of lemonade. "He's crazy about cars. He's got a zillion posters, a hundred models, and knows every vehicle ever produced, domestic or foreign. He's dying to hang up his posters in his room and also to have a look at your Spider, Mr. Chaubere."

"My Spider?"

"Yes. He saw you drive up the other night when you took me home, and he's been badgering me ever since to ask you to let him see it."

Alexandre chuckled and drew his hand across his chin in the particularly masculine way men with beards stroke their faces. He sat back in his chair.

"I told him you were a private man, that you didn't like to be disturbed."

"Only during the day."

"And that you didn't want to be bothered by little boys."

"He's ten, didn't you say?"

Olivia nodded.

"If he is truly interested in looking at my car, I will show it to him."

"Oh, thank you, Mr. Chaubere. He'll be thrilled. He really will!"

"And I don't mind if you hang things in the carriage house."

She grinned. The balmy night became peaceful again, the twinkling city beautiful, and the garden below a haven of tranquility once more. Olivia sat back, fully content, even though she knew she had to get up early in the morning to enroll Richie in school.

Olivia tried to push thoughts of tomorrow away and enjoy the moment at hand. She was forever thinking of tomorrow—planning, scheduling, worrying—and just this once she wanted to relax.

"You are a stranger to Charleston," Alexandre said at last. "Where are you from?"

"Seattle."

"Ah, Washington. I have never been there."

"It's beautiful. Moody like Charleston, but with a chillier flavor. Charleston is sultry, like a beautiful woman aging gracefully. Seattle is crisp and busy. Much more masculine."

He shot a glance at her. "An odd comparison, madame. But I believe I know exactly what you mean."

"You should visit Seattle. It's been voted one of the most livable cities in America."

"Really?" He glanced at her again, this time more slowly, allowing his gaze to travel into her hair. "But I'm curious. What brought you here?"

Olivia turned her glass in her hand, unwilling to delve too deeply into her past or to divulge much of her life to this man. How and why she got pregnant at seventeen wasn't a tale to tell most people. "I came here to finish college. I won a scholarship."

"Oh?"

"Yes. A tuition grant from the Charleston Horticultural Society. I entered a contest and won."

"Hmm. So you will remain in Charleston until next year sometime?"

"I intend to."

"What will your husband do in the meanwhile?"

"My husband? Oh, he'll be out of the country for two years at least."

"How do you and Richie fare, living apart from him so much?"

"We fare all right," she answered, allowing a tinge of bitterness to creep into her voice. "In fact, we do just fine."

For a moment he studied her silently. Then he slowly got to his feet. "Well, I keep you up far too late," he declared. "I am accustomed to late hours. You are not."

"I didn't yawn, did I?" she countered with a smile.

"No, but your eyes tell me you have had enough."

Olivia felt a slight disappointment at his plan to depart. He had interpreted her bitter thoughts of Boyd as a reflection on his own company. She hadn't come across someone so attuned to the nuances of her mood before, and vowed to be more careful in the future.

She rose.

"I bid you good night, madame."

She walked him to the front door, where he turned. "Meet me at the statue at half-past six tomorrow evening and I will show you the lilies."

"All right."

"Ah, I'd almost forgotten about the car. Tell your son I'll be in the garage at six to show him the Spider. Have him come down then."

"Great. I appreciate this, Mr. Chaubere."

"You can come down, too, if you like."

"Maybe for a few minutes." Olivia opened the door. "But this car business is a male thing. I'd like to feign interest, but the fact is—"

"I assure you, madame, it won't be boring."

Olivia glanced up at him. Truer words were never spoken. Nothing about Alexandre Chaubere would ever bore her. She knew it more certainly than if the phrase were chiseled in the wall behind him.

"Okay. Six then." She watched him walk out to the landing. "Good night."

He gave her a fancy little salute with his hand to his forehead, and disappeared down the stairs.

Olivia closed the door and walked back to the piazza to retrieve her drawings and glasses. She tucked the papers under her arm and then picked up the glasses. One of the glasses was still full and she realized Alexandre hadn't even touched his lemonade. Perhaps he didn't like the beverage. She chided herself for not inquiring about his preference and vowed to remember to ask the next time, should he ever visit again. Olivia put away her drawing equipment and then walked toward her bedroom, stopping halfway across the living room floor. Something didn't feel quite right. The carriage house seemed empty without Alexandre's presence—too quiet, too ordinary. She hugged herself and closed her eyes. Alexandre was certainly no ordinary man. She found him fascinating and dangerous at the same time, and a bit of a mystery. What would Richie think of him?

6

The next morning she backed her van out of the stall on the ground floor of the carriage house, and drove Richie to Oakview Elementary, a mile north of the house. She filled out all the papers, was introduced to the principal, and had a brief tour of the building. Then they accompanied Richie to his new classroom and met his teacher. A large calendar in back of the teacher's desk was plastered with red and pink hearts with a big number 14 in the center of the display. Olivia had overlooked the fact that it was Valentine's Day. In all the upheaval and moving, her new job and new apartment, she had completely forgotten about the holiday. Richie had come to school without any cards to exchange. At this point, valentines would have no meaning since he didn't know any of the other children anyway, but she knew he would feel excluded at the end of the day. She felt a stab of guilt, even though Richie was the type of kid who would understand the circumstances.

Olivia's heart went out to Richie as she watched him walk to a desk at the back of the room, nervous and apprehensive but trying hard not to let it show. She knew what it was like to change schools, for she had done it frequently during her childhood when her father drifted from one job to another, city after city. She watched Richie as he sat down and stowed his pack under his chair. Then she said good-bye to the teacher and left, making a promise to herself to keep him in the same school, no matter how tight it made her schedule once she started college. Richie was at the point when he would begin to make lifelong friends. If she kept moving him around, he would never forge any close ties and end up a loner like she was. Solitude and loneliness was a legacy she refused to pass down to her son.

The rest of the morning she spent documenting all the plants in the garden and noting their exact placement on her drawing, which she had transferred to grid paper. During the heat of the day, she made calls to get estimates on the masonry job required to build the ruin, and to a local building supplier to see about purchasing blocks. More calls were made to a tree-topping service, and to the city waste company to make arrangements for a Dumpster in which she could deposit large quantities of yard debris. Then she drove to a hardware store and bought the tools she required for the job—shovels, rakes, hoe, fork, weed-wacker, wheelbarrow, and some new batteries, paying for the tools with her own money because she would use them for future jobs, not just for the Chaubere House. The rest of the smaller tools she'd need she had brought with her from Seattle—top of the line tools which she kept in immaculate condition.

Then, thinking of Richie coming home from his first day of school, most likely feeling alienated and excluded because of the Valentine's Day party, she decided to get him a present to raise his spirits. She found a hobby shop that sold models, and when she asked if the store carried any Fiats, the shopkeeper pursed his lips.

"Not much call for Fiats these days," he said, "But you know, I think I have one. It's kind of old, though. What make were you looking for?"

"A Spider."

"Ah, I believe that's what I have." He turned, reached down behind the counter to a shelf near the floor, and came up with a dusty box that had been reinforced on the ends with small pieces of yellowing cellophane tape. "I've had this around for years, ma'am, but it's a fine kit—metal, not plastic, you know."

Olivia picked up the carton. "Why, this looks just like the car I had in mind."

"It's a '73. Kind of old. There's a guy who drives one just like it around town, though. I see it every once in a while. Beautiful little car."

"It's perfect."

"I'll tell you what. I've had that model sitting around so long, I'll give you a deal on it. Fifteen dollars."

"Great." She reached in her purse and took out her wallet. "Can you also wrap it for me? It's a gift."

"Surely." The shopkeeper took her money and then hobbled into a back room. He emerged a few minutes later with a bright blue package topped by a blue and green bow.

"Thank you," she said happily, knowing Richie would be thrilled with the model.

"Come again."

She left the shop and stopped for a quick bite at Harry's where she caught up on the gossip with Sherry, who was amazed Olivia had survived unscathed an entire night on the Chaubere property. Then she drove home and unpacked the equipment, just in time to run down the block to meet Richie's bus.

Ordinarily she wouldn't have been able to meet his bus. She never before had the luxury of arranging her own work schedule, and had never been able to take late afternoons off. When Richie was younger, she had made arrangements with her day care person to see him safely home from school. As he grew older, he walked to the baby-sitter's house with a few other kids who spent the afternoons there, and always called her at work to tell her that he had arrived safely. Now, she was hoping he'd find a companion with whom to walk the few blocks home, although she wouldn't worry about him too much if he went unaccompanied, because the neighborhood seemed safe and quiet. For the first day at school, however, she wanted to watch for the bus and make sure he knew where to disembark.

The afternoon was humid, but not too hot. Olivia stood in the shade of a cypress and waited on the cracked sidewalk, going over the rest of the day in her head. If she worked in the yard until 5:30, she could dash back to the carriage house in time to clean up before they met Alexandre in the garage. Then they could have dinner afterward and she'd give Richie the model.

A few blocks away she heard the hiss of air brakes and knew the school bus was on its way. Olivia smiled softly, grateful to have a job at last that afforded her some independence. So far she enjoyed working for herself and was confident she could handle all the components of the project.

The long yellow school bus slowly rolled around the corner and lurched to a stop. Four boys and a girl emerged, most of them jumping from the last step, which was fairly high off the ground. The girl hurried around the front of the bus and crossed the street while the other kids filed out on the sidewalk. Olivia gave a small wave. Richie caught sight of her and slung his backpack over his shoulder while the other three boys jostled by him. He didn't take a step toward her, and he didn't smile as he usually did when she greeted him. Olivia stuffed her hand back in the pocket of her shorts and realized she had probably embarrassed her son by showing up at the bus stop.

One of the taller boys snatched Richie's baseball cap from the back. "Mama's boy!" he yelled, dashing off with his prize and leaving Richie's hair standing on end.

Richie whirled around, but the other three boys were already out of reach.

"Fraidy cat! Fraidy cat!" the tall one shouted again, "Nothing but a pussy!" They all snickered as they galloped away, their backpacks bouncing and their shoelaces slapping around their ankles.

Olivia watched her son's shoulders lower in defeat. Why did kids have to be so cruel to each other? As a child she had never teased anyone or derived any pleasure from seeing another human being suffer. What did boys like that get out of tormenting her son? And why was Richie always the one to get picked on—because he was skinny, because he had red hair, because he had no father? Why?

"Sorry, Richie," she commented, stepping toward him.

He turned, shaking his head and scowling. "Thanks a lot, Mom."

"I just wanted to make sure you got off the bus at the right place."

"Like I was in kindergarten or something?" he strode past her without glancing at her. "Thanks for nothing!"

"Richie!" Olivia sighed and watched him storm toward the Chaubere house. Was this the start of pre-adolescent problems? Would she be overprotective and smother him, just like Alexandre had said? How could she not want to look out for him? He was only ten years old, practically a baby. And he was all she had in the world.

She took out after him, her steps brisk, as she struggled with the predicament of raising a growing son and not knowing exactly what to do to help him face a man's world. At the corner of Alexandre's block, she passed by a gate where an elderly woman was snipping yellow roses.

"Yoo hoo, young lady!"

Olivia stopped and glanced back, surprised the woman had called out to her. The white-haired lady gestured to her to come closer, motioning her forward with a pair of scissors. Olivia retraced the few steps she had taken and stopped on the other side of the gate.

"Yes?" she asked, wondering what the woman wanted of her, and not anxious to chat with a neighbor when she felt compelled to go after Richie.

"I don't mean to be nosy, young lady," the woman began, holding a bouquet of long-stemmed roses in her hand and speaking through the bars of the gate, "but I couldn't help noticing you and your boy've moved onto the Chaubere property."

"Yes, we have." Olivia threw an impatient glance down the sidewalk after her son. "Into the carriage house."

The older woman opened her gate. "I'm sorry I haven't made a social call, but Mr. Chaubere frowns on that sort of thing. My name's Eugenia Foster."

"Nice to meet you. I'm Olivia Travanelle."

"Travanelle?" The woman surveyed her from her running shoes up to her hair. "You're the student who won the scholarship from the Horticultural Society, aren't you?"

"Yes."

"Well, y'all haven't been in Charleston very long, have you?"

"No, why?"

"Well, we all know better than to have anything to do with the Chaubere place."

Olivia centered her full attention upon Mrs. Foster. "It seems fine to me."

"There's something not right there, and I believe it's my civic duty to warn you about it."

"About what?"

"The man who lives there, Mr. Chaubere."

Olivia crossed her arms, anxious to nip malicious gossip in the bud but at the same time curious about factual information concerning her employer. "He seems like a nice enough man."

"Nice?" the older woman rolled her eyes. "Mr. Chaubere is the most antisocial man in town. Don't he seem awful strange to you?"

"Everyone has their quirks, Mrs. Foster."

"Quirks?" The older woman studied her closely. Then she stepped onto the sidewalk and glanced down the street toward the Chaubere house as if afraid of being overheard by the large round window of the portico. "Now I'm not the type to stick my nose into other people's business, Lord knows I'm not. But you look like a nice young lady, so I'm going to butt in this one time." She raised her gloved hand and wagged the scissors at Olivia. "I'm tellin' you, if you stay on at the Chaubere place you'll be gettin' into something that's better left alone."

"I can't imagine why."

"You can't? Well, I can surely tell you a few things about the place."

"Such as?"

"Lots of things." The woman looked at her flowers. "But I need to put these roses in water. Why don't you come on inside for a spell?"

"I really must be getting back, Mrs. Foster."

"It will just take a moment. And I have something I made for you and your boy, to welcome you to the neighborhood. My specialty—peach cake." She put her hand on the gate. "It won't take but a minute."

"Well—" Olivia didn't want to insult Mrs. Foster by refusing the invitation, and she was curious to learn more about Alexandre Chaubere. She decided to take a few precious moments and follow Mrs. Foster into the house. "All right. Just for a few minutes."

The woman smiled and passed through the gate. Then she led the way down the walk. "I'm Charleston blood, born and bred. Lived in this house all my life."

Olivia stared up at the yellow stucco walls of the double house, neatly trimmed in white and black, with a perfectly manicured patch of lawn and a brick walkway leading to a side door and alley garden. She couldn't imagine living in the same place her entire life. Mrs. Foster showed her into the main hall and let the screen door bang behind them while she hurried ahead. "I'll just set these beauties in a vase, and then we'll see if that cake is cool enough to box up. Come on upstairs."

Olivia followed her up a huge but slightly tilting staircase to the main floor above. The air inside the shadowy house was mellow with the fragrance of years upon years of home canning, bleached sheets, furniture polish, and mothballs. The place was spotless but nothing seemed to have been purchased since World War II. Even the photographs on the walls were black and whites, yellowed with age.

Eugenia took her to the kitchen. Olivia padded close behind, hoping she wouldn't be subjected to a complete tour of the house. Ordinarily she would be interested in seeing the old mansion, but today she was in a bit of a rush. In the kitchen Olivia watched Eugenia bustle around the yellow room, putting away her gloves and scissors. The kitchen smelled like cantaloupe and was lined with dated appliances and a black and white linoleum floor which probably hadn't been changed since the forties.

"I don't mean to be rude, Mrs. Foster," Olivia commented, "but I have to get back soon. My son just got home from school, and we had a bit of a misunderstanding. I need to talk to him."

"Of course. What's his name?"

"Richie."

"I've got a grandson just about his age. Is he nine?"

"No. Ten."

"Willie Lee—that's my grandson—practically lives over here. His mama just got remarried and her new husband don't have any kids. It's takin' some gettin' used to for him to have Willie Lee around. So the boy's usually here. Except for today. He's playin' at another boy's house." Eugenia arranged the flowers in a cut crystal vase.

"You have Richie come over and play anytime. You tell him he's more than welcome. We got a basketball hoop out back and a rope swing all the boys like."

"That's very nice of you, Mrs. Foster."

Eugenia laughed and waved her off as she picked up the vase. "It's not nice of me, it's an act of self-preservation, that's what it is!"

Olivia smiled. She liked Mrs. Foster and felt it would be safe if Richie spent time at her house.

"Would you like some iced tea?" the old woman asked as she set the vase on a doily in the middle of the kitchen table.

"No thanks. I really should be going soon."

"But I haven't told you about the Chaubere house." She washed her hands in the sink. "Do sit down for a minute and have a glass."

"Well, thanks." Olivia lowered herself to one of the ladder-back chairs with a woven rush seat while Eugenia reached into the refrigerator for a gallon jar covered with a tin foil cap.

Eugenia dropped ice in the tall glasses and poured from the gallon jar without spilling a drop. Then she returned the tea to the refrigerator and brought the glasses to the table along with two crocheted coasters.

"Thank you."

"You're welcome. You don't know how nice it is to have a decent neighbor to talk to, Olivia. Livin' on the corner like I do kind of limits the conversations over the fence, and havin' Alexandre Chaubere for a neighbor makes it even worse."

Olivia held her tea, anxious to get the conversation back on track. "So why is it dangerous to live at the Chaubere place?"

"Well, Olivia." Eugenia sipped her tea. "I've lived in this house all my life, and my daddy lived here before me, and his daddy before him. Charleston families are like that, you know. We tend to keep the property in the family. Why, this house has been in my family since the Late Unpleasantness."

"Late unpleasantness?" Olivia repeated, not following her.

"What you Yankees call the Civil War."

"I see." Olivia suppressed a smile.

"Anyway, my family lived here and the Chauberes lived there," she nodded to the side toward Alexandre's property, "since before anyone can recall any different."

"Is that odd?"

"It wouldn't be, except for the fact that the Chauberes never have any women at the house, no women and no children, not in my time and not in my daddy's time neither."

Olivia sipped her tea thoughtfully. "Maybe the Chaubere women don't like Charleston."

"Chaubere women? There's been no such thing. Folks rarely see anyone comin' or goin', no families bein' raised, no visitors, no nothin'. But there is always a handsome young Chaubere man keepin' house at the place. And if you ask me, they all look an awful lot alike. A strikin' resemblance." Mrs. Foster set down her glass. "Now I ask you, Olivia, just where do these young men come from?"

"I don't know. Maybe the family in France sends the young men to the United States to keep an eye on the property. Maybe the family doesn't want to live here."

"But this Alexandre—I've watched him over the years. In fact, when I was younger, I fancied myself in love with the man. He was a charmin' gentleman. Just charmin'."

He still is, Olivia thought to herself.

"I used to sneak onto his property and try to get a peek at him every once in a while, because he'd never accept invitations to the house. You know how young girls are— always attracted to the dark and mysterious types. Well, let me tell you, I was dyin' to get to know Alexandre Chaubere, even though people said he was odd, because he was the finest looking man in Charleston, no doubt about it. But he wasn't interested in me. He told me to get off his property and stay off. That was in 1940, and I haven't spoken to him since."

"Nineteen-forty?" Olivia did some quick math in her head. Alexandre Chaubere wasn't much older than herself. He couldn't have been alive in the 1940s. "You must be talking about a different man. The Alexandre Chaubere who lives there now is in his early thirties, I'd say."

"No, he's as old as I am. And a bachelor with no children, as far as anyone can figure."

"Perhaps the Chaubere you grew up with was replaced by a nephew or cousin. Really, Mrs. Foster, the man who lives there now is my age, not yours."

"See?" Mrs. Foster jumped to her feet. "That's what's so peculiar about the house. Nothin' changes over there. No one comes or goes, except Alexandre when he drives that little car away at night and his strange friend, that older man. Sometimes he gets deliveries, but that's about it. No one ever sees him shoppin' in the local stores. He rarely goes to any of the restaurants or cafes. He never sets any trash out for collection like the rest of us do. You just don't see the man much. It's unnatural, that's what it is. Unnatural."

"He says he doesn't like to be disturbed during the day, Mrs. Foster. Maybe he's a night person. Maybe he doesn't like crowds." She wondered why she took Alexandre's part, just as she had done with Sherry, and then decided she did it out of her habit of playing devil's advocate, more than out of loyalty to him.

"I have a friend who works at the post office," Mrs. Foster continued, "and she swears that Alexandre Chaubere never gets personal mail. Not a stick. And he don't have a phone. So how do you think he parlez-vous with this supposed French family of his?"

"I don't know," Olivia replied. "But he does have a phone in his carriage house."

"I bet you crullers to catfish he never uses it!"

"Maybe not." She stood up. "But he doesn't seem that odd, Mrs. Foster. He's been fairly nice to me."

"I wouldn't trust him, Olivia, no I wouldn't. How long are you stayin' there?"

"A month or two. Just until I finish the landscape job he's hired me to do."

"Landscape job?" Eugenia shook her head, "That's peculiar, him wantin' to do something about the place after all this time. Well, if he acts the slightest bit strange, you come runnin' over here, you understand?"

"Thanks, but I hardly think he'll—"

"Some give in to their dark sides more than others," Mrs. Foster put in, "wouldn't you say?"

"I suppose—"

"And that Alexandre Chaubere is a dark one."

Olivia stood up, uncomfortable with the turn in the conversation. She had never taken much interest in gossip and didn't like speculating about people behind their backs. "I have to be going, Mrs. Foster. Really. Thanks for the tea."

"I don't mean to frighten you, my dear. I just want you to be careful is all."

"I will."

"Let me get that cake for you." Eugenia carefully lowered the layer cake into a lidless cardboard box and covered the box with tin foil. "There you go!" she said, holding it out.

"Thank you so much," Olivia replied. "It looks wonderful." She walked toward the large staircase at the front of the house with Mrs. Foster following close behind. At the front door, Olivia paused to say good-bye, but the older woman spoke first, her elderly face etched with worry.

"Do you believe there are such things as vampires, Olivia?"

Olivia stared at her in surprise. "Pardon me?"

"Vampires. Do you think it's possible they might exist?"

"They're just fictional characters, Mrs. Foster."

"Sometimes I'm not so sure."

Olivia backed away from the ornate screen door. "You aren't suggesting Alexandre Chaubere is a vampire?"

"I'm not sayin' he is and I'm not sayin' he isn't. I'm just sayin' I can't explain what goes on over there. Lock your doors at night, young lady. Don't be alone with him after dark. And tell the same thing to that boy of yours."

"I'll be careful, Mrs. Foster," Olivia said, simply to appease the old woman, for she found the vampire notion ridiculous, "I promise."

"Anytime you want to have tea, just come on over, you hear?"

"Thanks."

Olivia waved and walked briskly toward the gate. She was amazed by Mrs. Foster's opinion of Alexandre. Sure, the man kept odd hours, and he possessed a peculiar sort of energy Olivia had never felt before from anyone. Yet she didn't sense danger from him. Was it because he had a psychological hold on her and used a form of supernatural mind control to put her under his spell? No. Ridiculous! Impossible! She was the last woman on earth to allow any kind of man to worm his way through her defenses. The notion that Alexandre might have blood-dripping fangs was simply preposterous.

Even so, Olivia could use an objective opinion on the matter. Richie hadn't met Alexandre yet. Her son was an honest and accurate judge of character. Maybe Richie could shed some light on the subject.

Olivia pushed through the heavy wooden gate, closed it behind her, and hurried up the Chaubere driveway. The more she tried to discount Mrs. Foster's fears, however, the more reasonable the old woman's conclusion seemed. She remembered well the phrase Alexandre had uttered the night before, when he had claimed they had plenty of time to look at her plans. *The night is young,* he had murmured. His words and tone had sent a shiver down her spine. Who and what exactly was he? And was she placing herself in danger by agreeing to walk with him in his garden at night? She'd soon find out. Olivia glanced at her watch. It was already three-twenty, little more than two hours until she would meet him near the garage.

7

Precisely at six o'clock, Olivia and Richie walked down the stairs of the carriage house to the ground floor below. Once he learned she had actually asked Mr. Chaubere about his car, Richie had forgiven his mother's appearance at the bus stop.

"Do you think he'll remember to come?" Richie asked anxiously.

"Yes. Mr. Chaubere doesn't strike me as the kind of man who forgets anything." She opened the door and motioned Richie through. Sure enough, she spotted the tall lean form of Alexandre Chaubere as he slipped through the branches of the oleander shrubs and walked across the driveway. He wore jeans and a forest green shirt with the sleeves folded up on his forearms. His long brown hair blew behind him as he came forward, accentuating the widow's peak on his tanned forehead.

A sharp thrill passed through Olivia at the sight of him,

and she wasn't sure how to interpret the reaction, because she wasn't certain if she was wary of Alexandre or wildly attracted to him.

"Ready to see the Spider, Richie?" he asked, without waiting for an introduction.

"Yeah!"

Alexandre smiled and in the dying light of day, his face glowed as if he possessed an inner light, and warm creases appeared at the corners of his eyes. This man could no more be a vampire than Santa Claus. He held out his hand. "I'm Alexandre Chaubere. How are you?"

"I'm fine, sir." Richie shook hands formally and Olivia was surprised to see how different the skin of their hands appeared when joined. Alexandre's was golden brown compared to the pink-tinged freckled hand of her son.

"Your mother tells me you're a car fanatic."

"Kind of. I like to build models and stuff."

"You do?" Alexandre smiled again, his attention completely centered on her son. She liked that. So often adults gave only cursory attention to children, believing kids couldn't tell the difference or didn't deserve their full regard. "I build models, too."

"What kind, Mr. Chaubere? Cars?"

"No. I fancy ships myself. Sailing vessels, mainly."

"You mean the kits with rigging and cloth sails and all that?"

"That's the kind. Although I don't work from kits, Richie. I cut everything myself. The kits can be too simplistic at times. And inaccurate, I've found."

"Wow!" Richie exclaimed. "That's cool!"

Alexandre smiled in amusement as he unlocked the garage door, stepped inside, and opened the bay. He poked his head out. "Stand aside and I'll back her out."

"Okay." Richie stepped onto the grass where Olivia stood with her hands in her pockets, content to quietly observe the proceedings. As Alexandre fired up the car, Richie glanced up at her. "He's neat, Mom."

She nodded and watched the Spider roll out to the driveway. Alexandre set the brake and got out, leaving the engine running.

"Want to look under the hood?" he asked.

"Sure!"

Deftly, Alexandre disengaged the latch near the grill and raised the hood, while Richie stood beside him, his thin boyish shape dwarfed by Alexandre's broad-shouldered adult figure.

"It's sure clean for a twenty-year-old car," Richie remarked.

"I take good care of what is mine." Alexandre sliced a glance at Olivia. She looked away, wondering what that glance had meant.

She heard them discussing the size of the engine and other specifications, but couldn't keep her mind on what they were talking about. All she could hear were Mrs. Foster's warnings about Alexandre Chaubere. Did she want her son to develop a friendship with a person of questionable character, for it was obvious from the way they were chattering that they shared deep and common interests.

"Would you mind if Richie took a turn at the wheel?" Alexandre inquired, carefully closing the hood.

"What?" Olivia couldn't believe her ears, nor could she believe the look of ecstatic incredulity on Richie's face.

"Do you mind if he drives the Spider?"

"Mr. Chaubere, he's only ten. He's never driven a car in his life."

"I could do it, Mom!" Richie dashed around the front of the car and skidded to a stop between Alexandre and her, his entire body stiff with anticipation. "Mom, I could!"

"We'll restrict ourselves to the driveway, madame."

"I don't know." Olivia stared at Alexandre and then at her son. Alexandre hadn't been kidding when he said this wouldn't be boring.

"Please, Mom? I'll do anything. Dishes for a week, anything!"

"Dishes for a week?" Alexandre raised a brow and gazed at her expectantly. "Hmmm."

She couldn't look at Alexandre's face anymore. He could charm her without saying a single word, just by cocking that one brow. Olivia forced her stare to drop to the Spider.

"Do you have insurance, Mr. Chaubere?"

"Of course."

"But what if Richie has an accident? How could you ever replace your car?"

"I'm not worried." Alexandre reached out and put his hand on Richie's right shoulder. "I can tell Richie's not the type to take chances."

Richie glanced at Alexandre standing behind him and beamed, and Olivia knew in that moment she had lost a small part of her son to this man. Her heart surged painfully in her chest, both from the realization that another person could win the affections of her son and that she had permitted this situation to develop with Alexandre of all people.

"Well, all right. But, Richie, you be careful. Do everything Mr. Chaubere says. You hear me?"

"Yes!" Richie turned to the black Fiat. "Oh, man!" he cried, happier than she had ever seen him.

"Go ahead, get in," Alexandre instructed. "But don't touch anything until I'm in, too."

Richie slipped into the leather seat and closed the door. Olivia crossed her arms as Alexandre walked around the Spider, gave her a thumbs-up sign, and then disappeared into the passenger seat. She could see the silhouette of his head and shoulders as he gave Richie instructions inside the car.

A minute or two went by. She could tell by the sounds of things that Richie was practicing shifting gears and checking out the brake and accelerator pedals. Then, with a crunch of gravel, the Spider slowly rolled forward. Olivia's heart rose into her throat, and she walked alongside the vehicle as her son drive it down the lane, carefully guiding the car so it remained exactly in the center of the road. She could have walked more quickly than he drove, but was glad for his prudence. At the end of the drive the Spider stopped. For a while she thought Alexandre was going to get out of the car and take over. But then the car moved in reverse, lurched, and died. Olivia shook her head, wondering why Alexandre would take such a chance to make her son happy. For all he knew, Richie might throw the car into the wrong gear and slam into the wooden gate across the drive.

Yet her fears went unfounded. The Spider started up again. This time Richie eased the car backward without killing the engine. With a few more lurches, he managed to maneuver the car around and drive back, coming to a respectably smooth stop in front of the garage. Olivia had to trot to catch up with them. Richie turned off the engine and put his hand on the door, but stopped while Alexandre said something to him. Olivia wondered what it was.

Then, his face glowing with pride and joy, Richie opened the door and jumped out. He barely looked at his mother, but instead turned and watched Alexandre rise up from the passenger's side.

"Thanks, Mr. Chaubere!" he exclaimed. "That was awesome!"

"You did well, son," he replied. "You're a natural."

Son. No one but Olivia ever called Richie son. She was surprised that Richie didn't call Alexandre on the premature familiarity, for Richie didn't countenance nongenuine remarks from people. Perhaps he perceived Alexandre as honest, or hadn't noticed the phrase in all the excitement.

"I've never seen anyone manage a clutch that well on their first try," Alexandre remarked.

"That's because I know how a clutch works, don't you think, Mr. Chaubere?"

"You're probably right."

Richie whipped around. "Did you see me back up, Mom?"

"Yes. That's pretty tricky for a new driver."

"I could drive the van for sure, Mom, since it's an automatic."

"I think you've had enough driving for one day, Richie. And I believe you have some homework waiting for you, right?"

"Aw, Mom!"

"I'll be up in a few minutes to fix dinner, and I want to see that you've made progress."

Alexandre slipped the car keys in the pocket of his jeans and said, "I've got to show your mother some plants I don't want moved. But when we're finished, you can take the car down to the gate for me, provided your school work for today is completed. Deal?"

"Deal, Mr. Chaubere! See you!" Richie dashed to the door of the carriage house, anxious to get to work.

Olivia stared at Alexandre. Just like that the man had gotten Richie to attack his homework, a major feat as far as she was concerned.

"You certainly have a way with children," she remarked.

"I've always thought it would be an interesting experience to have a son," Alexandre replied as he watched Richie disappear into the house.

"Interesting isn't the word I would choose," she chuckled. "Frustrating and difficult maybe."

"But rewarding, too, eh?"

"Many times." She glanced up at Alexandre, wondering why she had never run into a man like him before. She knew without a doubt that Alexandre wasn't saying things just to please her. She could tell he genuinely liked the boy.

He looked down at her. "Let me show you the lilies I told you about."

He set off for the wall of oleanders and she followed him, trying not to appreciate the sight of his lean male backside and line of his wide shoulders. She had never been attracted to men with long hair, but on Alexandre, long hair seemed appropriate, even romantic, and added to his otherworldly appearance which she found so appealing.

"I don't understand, Mr. Chaubere," she ventured as they walked. "If you're planning to sell the house, why are you concerned about the lilies?"

"Because they are extremely hard to cultivate. I've found they can't be grown indoors, otherwise I'd take a few with me. They're much too valuable to destroy."

"Valuable, in what way?"

"They have medicinal properties that are not yet fully explored."

They headed into the depths of the garden, circling around the end of the iris-encrusted reflecting pond, which contained more mud than water. By the time they reached the lilies, Olivia had to strain to see their color in the muted twilight.

"Here they are," Alexandre announced, drawing back the overhanging branches of a willow tree.

In order to see better, Olivia had to come up beside him and stand quite close to him. Had he positioned himself that way on purpose? She heard Mrs. Foster's words. *Lock your doors at night. Don't be alone with him after dark.* Was she a fool for trusting this man and allowing not only herself to get involved with him, but her son as well?

Yet what had he done to earn her distrust? Nothing. Cursing herself for believing malicious gossip, Olivia craned her neck and looked down at the low-lying shrub.

"These are lilies?" she inquired skeptically, never having seen a lily growing on such a tangle of foliage.

"Yes. An ancient strain, as I told you."

Olivia surveyed the dark crimson flowers, with fuchsia centers deep inside their bells, and reached out in fascination.

"Don't touch them!" he exclaimed.

She snatched back her hand. "Why?"

"They're poisonous. They might have an adverse reaction with your skin."

"How odd," she murmured.

"Odd?"

She could feel the puff of his breath on her neck. Goose pimples broke out on the surface of her skin and she moved aside a bit, wildly distracted by the closeness of his body.

"Yes," she stammered, trying to gain control of her pulse and her voice. "The flower looks dry, almost papery."

"But beautiful, no?"

"Exquisite." She glanced down at the plant. "They don't close at night?"

"No. They are nocturnal."

Olivia swallowed. The similarity between man and plant was not lost on her. She commanded her imagination to decrease a notch, and returned her attention to the clump of lilies.

"The foliage is green. Curious. I would think a night-blooming plant would be a saprophyte."

"What's a saprophyte?"

"A plant that feeds on decaying material. Like a mushroom."

"Something that doesn't depend on photosynthesis?"

"Yes."

"Perhaps because they bloom during the night and the day, they have properties of both kinds of plants." His deep voice, soft in the evening air, enveloped her in a velvety blanket, offsetting Mrs. Foster's remarks. The fact that he made no move to touch her, reassured her even further. If this man was a psychopath, surely he would not miss a chance like this to overpower her. Yet Alexandre kept his distance.

"Perhaps." She glanced over at him, and was sorry she did, for she found him studying her and not the flowers, disconcerting her again. "I would imagine the flowers preserve well, since they are so dry."

"Yes." Alexandre turned his attention to the plants at his feet. "The blooms last a very long time. This one is more than a century old."

"Pardon me?" she countered. "Did you say a *century*?"

"Yes. It has a long life span, like the Century Plant of the Southwestern deserts."

"How do you know this flower is a hundred years old? You haven't been around that long to keep track, have you?"

He blinked and looked away. "The Chauberes have observed this plant for years, madame. And I assure you, the observations are accurate."

Something in his tone, something in the way he failed to meet her stare, clued her to the possibility he was lying. He let the willow branch drop.

"Shall we be getting back?" he inquired.

"Yes, if that's all the lilies you have to show me."

"That's all of them."

He walked toward the reflecting pool and she stumbled

after him, her eyes not adjusting to the darkness as easily as his. At a time like this, she almost wished he *would* take her elbow, to keep her from tripping.

"I met your neighbor today," she said, to fill the silence.

"Oh?"

"Mrs. Foster. She seems nice."

"She's meddlesome."

"She thinks you're a hermit, that you aren't normal because you don't set out garbage like everyone else."

"Does she now?" His tone rang curt and crisp.

"Perhaps if you chatted with her once in a while, she wouldn't—"

"Madame," he turned abruptly, "If I chose to chat with her, which I don't, I would have done so long ago. But I see no reason to establish relations with a snoopy female."

"You don't care what your neighbors think of you?"

"No, I do not." He glared at her, his eyes blazing in the darkness. Then, quite suddenly his expression sagged and he staggered backward, clutching his chest.

"Mr. Chaubere!" Olivia cried, shocked by the sudden change in him. He seemed to be having a heart attack. She lunged forward. "What's wrong?" she cried.

His hand was like a claw on his shirt. "I—I—can't breathe!" he gasped.

She tore at the buttons of his shirt, but in seconds Alexandre had dropped to his knees.

"What's happening?" she shrieked, sinking down beside him.

"*Mon Dieu,*" he choked out.

"Lie down!" she ordered, guiding him back into a patch of dandelions. With hands that were surprisingly calm, she unfastened his shirt. "I'll be back in a moment," she said. "I'm going to call 911."

"No!" he wheezed. His eyes rolled back and he lay there panting.

"I think you're having a heart attack, Alexandre! I've got to get help!"

"No. No calls. I'll be—I'll be all right in a moment." He licked his lips and kept panting. His dark eyes were closed and his golden skin had faded to an ashen color that alarmed her.

"I'm going to call someone. Or take you to the hospital."

"No." His eyes fluttered open. "I'm feeling better already. Truly."

She knelt by his side. His breathing had become less harsh, but he still looked awful. He was sweating so profusely that tendrils of his dark hair stuck to his temples and cheekbones. His shirt lay open, revealing a muscular chest that rose and fell with each labored breath. Since Boyd, she had never been this close to a man's naked chest, and she had to look away.

"How are you doing now?" she asked.

"The pain is," he swallowed, "abating."

"Have you had your blood pressure checked lately?"

"No."

"Maybe you'd better."

"Yes, doctor." He gave her a slight smirk, his eyes still shut.

"I'm serious. This is nothing to joke about, Chaubere."

"You called me Alexandre a moment ago."

"Did I?"

"Continue to do so." He opened his eyes. "I like the sound of it when you say my given name."

She felt a hot blush creep up her neck, and decided to camouflage her disquiet with sarcasm. "Since you're back to giving orders, I take it you're feeling better."

"Yes." He continued to gaze at her. "Do you think you can help me get to the lab?"

"Of course. I'm small but I'm strong."

"I suspected as much." He held out his hand and she grasped it, rising to her feet and trying not to let the contact of his warm palm and fingers have any effect on her. She felt her hand tingling but passed it off, attributing the odd sensation to the slight contact she had made with the lilies. Tugging gently, she pulled Alexandre to his feet. He swayed for a moment, holding a hand to his forehead. Quickly she slipped her arm around him, under his shoulder and across his back, so that his torso was supported by her slight frame.

"Are you all right?" she asked, trying to see his face under the shadow of his hand.

"Give me a moment."

She stood there, trying to ignore the way he felt in her arms, trying not to feel the rippling muscles of his back or the heavy press of his weight against her. She steadied him with her other hand, bracing her palm against his bare chest. The sensation of touching his smooth firm chest jolted her like an electric shock. Boyd had been an athlete, but his body hadn't yet attained the powerful definition of this man's mature physique. Olivia was surprised to find she'd broken out in a sweat herself.

"Ready?" she inquired, anxious to get him to his lab and out of her awkward embrace.

"Yes." He took a tentative step.

They walked most of the way in silence, making slow progress through the tangled garden, for by now it was quite dark. Alexandre relied heavily on her for support, and seemed to have lost almost all of his strength. By the time they made it to the walk that went around the house, Olivia was exhausted.

"You want to go to the lab?" she asked, worried about Alexandre's weak condition.

"Yes."

"I think you ought to take it easy. Maybe retire for the evening."

"I promised Richie I'd let him drive the Spider."

"Forget that. I'll tell him what happened. He'll understand."

"But I left the car out."

"Give me the keys. I'll put it away for you."

"Thanks." He reached into his jeans and pulled out his keys. Then with a gesture born of his weak condition, he clumsily stuffed the keys in her pants pocket.

"So is it the lab or your bed?" she asked.

Alexandre paused and looked up at the front of the house. "Stairs," he commented, giving a shake of his head.

"Too tired?" she replied.

He nodded. "I can go down them, but not up."

"Okay. Let's go around back to the lab, then."

She struggled with him down the walk, past the statue, and around to the arcade and the laboratory stairs. She managed to guide him down the stone steps without too much trouble, and then stood aside as he opened the door to the lab. He flicked on the lights. Standing in the doorway, he ran a hand through his tousled hair. Olivia surveyed him closely.

"Are you going to be okay, Alexandre?"

He nodded. "I'm feeling better already."

"I hate to leave you like this. Do you want anything? A drink of water? Anything?"

"No. Thank you. I'll be fine in a few minutes. I've experienced this before."

"Is there some place you can lie down here?"

"There's a cot in the back."

"Do you want me to help you over there?"

"No." He sucked in a deep breath and ran his hand over his chest and down the muscles of his abdomen. "I'll be fine."

"Are you sure?"

"Yes." He glanced at her. "You *are* quite strong, Olivia Travanelle."

"I told you I was."

"And now I believe you." He reached down, and before she guessed his intent, Alexandre lifted her hand and kissed her fingertips. "Thank you, madame, for your care and your strength."

She felt another blush flood her cheeks and hoped the shadows hid her face. "You're welcome."

"I bid you good night."

"You'll be okay?"

"Don't worry." He smiled slightly, but she could see the strain in his eyes. He released her hand and slowly Olivia backed away.

"Good night," she said.

"Adieu."

Olivia tore her eyes away from his and hurried up the stairs. She'd worry about Alexandre the entire night. Why wouldn't he see a doctor? Why were men so bullheaded? Not until she saw him up and about the next day would she quit worrying about him. She returned to the carriage house and Richie, where they enjoyed Mrs. Foster's peach cake and Richie opened his present. Olivia watched joy blossom in Richie's face when he discovered the model was a Fiat Spider, but the small celebration was marred by Olivia's worry. From their table on the piazza, she kept glancing across the lawn to the dark Chaubere house beyond, wondering if Alexandre was dead or alive.

8

After Olivia disappeared, Alexandre closed the door and leaned heavily upon it, gathering his strength. He'd never felt so frightened in his life. During those few terrible minutes when he had collapsed upon the ground in the garden, he had been sure he was dying. His heart had raced and then pounded unevenly, galloping inside his chest until he thought it would burst out of him. What was coming over him? Had he drunk too much lily elixir? Or was the potion finally taking effect and killing him?

Alexandre pushed away from the door and stumbled across the room. A bout of light-headedness threw him off-balance. He careened toward the counter, slammed into it, and staggered to the table a few feet away. Half-blind and nauseous, he swayed and reached out for support, knocking a flask to the floor. It shattered, crashing through the silence of the night.

"Shit!" he swore, hoping Olivia wouldn't hear the noise and return. He didn't want her to see him like this, blinded and clumsy, nor did he want to have to explain his peculiar ailment to her. She'd demand to know what was wrong with him, or insist upon calling a doctor. The last thing he needed was some curious twentieth-century physician poking at him and discovering the odd state of his physical system.

Though he could barely see or walk, Alexandre forced himself to keep moving. He gained the table where his microscope and flasks of elixir sat. For the past three months, he had been taking blood samples every day, sometimes more than once a day, and analyzing them. He kept track of the results on a graph, charting the amount of normal cells in his blood compared to the number of abnormal cells—or what he had termed "immortal" platelets. The immortal platelets were a deeper red than the red blood cells, almost black, capable of carrying massive amounts of oxygen to the rest of the body, to which he attributed the highly efficient state of his being since he'd been an immortal. After a bout of dizziness or cramps, he had discovered a slight decrease in the immortal platelets, which he interpreted as a sign the lily potion was gradually having an effect on him.

The cardiac incident had been much more trauma than he had previously experienced, however, and he couldn't allow an attack of such magnitude to go undocumented, no matter how wretched he still felt. Alexandre found his razor-sharp scalpel, deftly slit the end of his finger and squeezed out a drop of blood upon a slide before his wound had time to heal. He spread the drop with a second glass slide and then waited until the sample air-dried. Then he dyed it with a quick stain and pushed the slide under his microscope.

For a few minutes he had to lean against the counter and close his eyes. Huge waves of nausea swept over him, as chills alternated with sweating. His knees shook, as did his hands, and he would have sat down except he didn't have the strength to stumble to the chair near the wall.

With this massive reaction, there was no doubt in Alexandre's mind that his body was changing. He might be on the way to recapturing his mortality. Soon he might be able to bleed, to eat, to drink, and to make love. Or he might be dying. He scowled at the thought. Three months ago, he'd spouted brave words about death to du Berry, but now, facing death—and most likely a painful one—he wasn't certain how he would handle it. He reassured himself with the thought that death was ultimately what he wanted. Then a vision of Olivia's worried face as she knelt beside him during his attack appeared in his thoughts, and he suddenly wasn't so sure of his course. Did he want his life to end at the same moment a fascinating woman had come into his world? It was just like Fate to deal him an untimely hand.

If the elixir was truly working, however, he had a concern far worse than death to worry about. Should the elixir transform him into a monster instead of a man, would he be a threat to Olivia and Rich? Would he be able to protect them from what he might become? Death or transformation. Whatever happened, he could do nothing to stop it. He had no choice, now that the potion had finally begun its dark work.

Panting and sick with apprehension, Alexandre pushed up from the counter and wiped his forehead with his sleeve. Slowly his vision cleared. He stepped up to the microscope, turned on its light, and bent over to begin screening. Just as he'd thought, his immortal platelet count was down from the check earlier that morning. Alexandre cleaned his equipment and then recorded the results on his graph. His hands still shook, but at least the nausea had subsided. After he finished, he dragged himself to the cot at the back of the lab and collapsed onto it. His head was splitting, he was exhausted, and all he could think about was sleep.

°   °   °

First thing Tuesday morning, before Richie got up for school, Olivia slipped out of the carriage house and hurried across the dew-covered lawn toward the Chaubere mansion. She sprinted down the walk and around to the back, half-expecting to find Alexandre's body sprawled upon the ground or collapsed on the stairs. All night she had tossed and turned, worrying about Alexandre and thinking she should go back and check on him.

The dank smell of the cellar wafted up around her as she descended the stairs to the chilly lab. Olivia rubbed the goose pimples on her arms and hurried down the steps. She turned the knob, but to her surprise, found the door locked. She knocked.

"Alexandre?" she called, wondering if he was in the lab or in the main house upstairs. "Mr. Chaubere, are you in there?"

Nothing but silence issued from the room behind the thick wooden door. The light had been turned off. She distinctly remembered Alexandre flipping it on the night before. If he had collapsed again, chances were the light would still be on and the door unlocked.

She waited a few moments and called his name again, chafing her bare arms all the while, and wondered what to do. Perhaps he had found the strength to drag himself to bed during the night. She hoped so. She'd have to trust that he was all right, for she certainly wasn't going to invade his privacy by searching for him in the rooms of the mansion. She didn't want to be accused of being a snoopy female.

With a sigh, she turned to go back to the carriage house. She wouldn't know how Alexandre fared until later in the day, not until he showed up for his car keys, which might not be until early evening if he observed his usual schedule. Olivia shook her head. It was going to be a long day.

Olivia spent the entire morning clearing the vines from the front fence and digging out the brambles. She stopped at noon for lunch. While grabbing a quick sandwich at the apartment, she was called and asked to work a shift at Harry's that evening, after a last minute cancellation by another waitress. Olivia told them she could manage, and decided to ask Mrs. Foster if she could baby-sit Richie. Just before Richie was due home from school, she took a quick shower and changed into a jeans skirt and white cotton blouse. Snatching up her pocket calendar, she hurried down the drive and set out for the end of the block, hoping that Mrs. Foster was home. She let herself into the Foster gate and rang the bell. To her relief, Mrs. Foster answered the door.

Fortunately, Mrs. Foster was happy to baby-sit Richie for the evening. They chatted until the boys got off the bus. Olivia intercepted Richie as he walked by the gate and introduced him to Mrs. Foster and Willie Lee. The boys decided to play computer games until dinnertime and Olivia left them, much relieved about Richie's welfare.

Olivia left the Foster house and stepped into the sunshine to head toward the Chaubere house, grateful that her affairs seemed to be settling nicely. When she walked onto the Chaubere property, however, a cloud drifted in front of the sun and cast a shadow over the house and yard. She glanced at the overgrown garden and the dark, lonely mansion. Was Alexandre lying in a room inside somewhere, dead? She pressed on, trying not to think about him. He was probably all right. She'd seen him in a lot worse shape, during the knife attack when she had been certain he had received a mortal wound. Yet he had reassured her that he would be fine, and he had recovered amazingly well. She should learn to trust in what he said. The man knew his body and his limitations better than anyone else. He was probably just fine.

Still she worried. Olivia didn't see Alexandre during the remainder of the time she toiled in the garden. At five-thirty she stopped to make dinner and get ready for Harry's. Richie breezed in a few minutes later, jabbering about all the computer software Willie Lee had, and anxious to get back to the Foster house with his Fiat model kit to show his new friend. She was thankful the boys seemed to have hit it off.

"You remember to take your homework over there, too," she reminded him. "And do it."

"I will." He dropped his backpack near the table. "What's for dinner?"

"Stir fry." She checked the rice and set it aside. "Wash your hands and set the table, will you?"

He did what she asked, but paused at the silverware drawer. "Mom?"

She kept stirring the chunks of chicken breast and ginger. "Yes?"

"How long are we going to stay here?"

His question surprised her. She turned, holding her spoon above the electric skillet. "You mean in Charleston?"

"No, I mean here."

"Two months at the most. Why?"

He shrugged. "It's nice here, living in a house like this."

"It is, isn't it?"

"I like Mr. Chaubere, too. And I like living where there aren't so many apartments all crowded together. Have you noticed how quiet it is?"

"I sure have. It's a nice change."

"Yeah." He set the silverware on either side of the plates. "Couldn't we ask Mr. Chaubere if we could stay here longer?"

"He's moving, Richie. He's going to sell this place."

"Maybe we could rent from the next owners."

"Maybe." She gave him a reassuring smile, even though she knew the chances were slim they could stay on after Alexandre's departure. For one thing, they could never afford the rent this apartment could likely bring the new owners.

Just as they sat down to dinner, someone knocked on the door.

"I'll get it!" Richie exclaimed, rushing toward the living room. Olivia turned in her chair and saw Alexandre's tall figure framed in the doorway. She felt a welcome sense of relief at the sight of him, for apparently he had recovered, since he was up walking around. The dying light of day behind him cast his body in silhouette while the shadows of the unlit living room veiled his expression, and for a moment he stood silently gazing across the room at her, more statue than man.

"Hi, Mr. Chaubere," Richie greeted, breaking the spell.

"Good evening." His voice was deep yet quiet, reaching across the room to her like a caress. "Ah, you're having dinner," he tilted his head and she caught the glint of his dark eyes, like obsidian in shadow. "I'll come back later."

"No, it's all right," Olivia said, getting to her feet. "Come on in. Would you care to join us?"

"We're having stir-fry," Richie put in eagerly.

Alexandre shut the door behind him. "Stir-fry?"

"You know, vegetables and chicken over rice. You like stir-fry?"

"I've never had it."

"You should try some. My mom's a good cook."

Olivia was surprised to hear such praise coming from her son. How could he say she was a good cook when her best recipe was a meal thrown together on the run between work and classes?

"Is she now?" Alexandre murmured, slowly walking across the carpet. Gradually he came into the light of the dining room. He wore a deep purple shirt, open at the throat, and black jeans. Though his clothing was simple, it fit both his body and his character well. Richie scooted ahead of him and raced into the kitchen while Olivia put her hand on the back of her chair.

"How are you feeling?" she asked.

He came to a stop before her. "Much better, thank you. I have come to pick up my keys."

"Oh, right. Let me get them."

"I don't wish to interrupt your meal." He motioned toward her chair. "Please sit down."

"It's no trouble," she protested.

"I insist."

"Only if you join us," she replied.

"I have dined already, madame. But I will sit down." He waited for her to resume her seat and pushed her chair into place just as Richie appeared with a full plate, a set of utensils, and a wide grin.

"Here, Mr. Chaubere. You gotta try some of this."

"I'm sorry, Rich, but I've already eaten."

"Just taste it then. You can sit right here." Richie placed the plate at the end of the table opposite his mother. Olivia looked up at Alexandre and raised her eyebrows, challenging him to combat Richie's eager enthusiasm.

"As you wish. Thank you." Alexandre moved to the end of the table and sat down. Olivia averted her gaze and focused on her meal. To have a man sitting down to dinner with them was such an unusual occurrence—a totally foreign experience actually—that she felt at a loss of how to act and what to do. Her father, an alcoholic for as long as she could remember, had rarely sat down to dinner with her mother and her, and Boyd had never eaten with her other than in a restaurant or in the car.

"Are you going out tonight, Mr. Chaubere?" Richie asked.

"Yes."

"Well can I—do you still need someone to drive the Spider down to the gate?"

"Of course."

Olivia shot a glance at her son and saw him grin from ear to ear, and then stuff his mouth with a huge forkful of rice. Alexandre, on the other hand, idly stirred his meal with his spoon. Perhaps the food didn't appeal to him. Perhaps he was accustomed to much finer cuisine. She wished Richie had never insisted he join them at the table.

"I see you've cleared the front fence," he began.

"Yes. You've got blackberries, Mr. Chaubere, everywhere."

"A hardy plant."

"Too hardy."

"Do you like blackberry pie, Mr. Chaubere?" Richie inquired.

"I don't recall ever having blackberry pie."

"Blackberry's my favorite. My mom can bake the best blackberry pie ever. "

"Can she now?" Alexandre smiled. He raised a small piece of chicken to his mouth.

She couldn't look at him any longer. By the sound of the amusement in his voice, he was probably smirking, well aware her ten-year-old son was trying to impress him with her culinary achievements. Olivia blushed, feeling more ill at ease than ever before in her life at Richie's fumbling attempt at matchmaking. She tried to finish her food, but the stir-fry sat in her stomach in a hard lump.

"Your stir-fry is excellent, madame," Alexandre remarked.

"Thanks." She noticed, however, that he had eaten very little of it.

"Why do you call my mother *madame*?" Richie asked.

"Because it's a title of respect for a married lady."

"But she really is—"

"Richie," Olivia broke in, jumping to her feet. "Please put the dishes in the dishwasher. We've got to go soon." She grabbed her plate and Alexandre's, and kept her expression hidden from him. Her marital status had never been a problem until this moment, when she was horrified that Richie might blurt out the truth. Then Alexandre would know she had lied to him. She kicked herself for not having advised her son about what she had told Alexandre—what she told all men, in fact, that she was married and unavailable.

Alexandre pushed back his chair and stood up.

"May I get you a cup of coffee?" she asked.

"Thank you, no. So you are going out tonight?"

"To Harry's. I have to work."

"Didn't you quit that job?"

"Yes, but I agreed to be available for the next two weeks. They called me."

"I see." He walked into the kitchen after her, carrying the milk glasses. "You are driving there, I trust?"

"Yes." She dumped the rice in a plastic container, marvelling that he still worried about her being assaulted by someone like Jimmy Dan Petersen.

"Rich," Alexandre said behind her. "Here. You did not finish your milk."

Olivia put the vegetables in the refrigerator, aware of the shortened name Alexandre called her son. The name sounded strange and Alexandre was a bit presumptuous to change it without asking, but she was grateful that he had noticed the unfinished milk. Richie had a bad habit of wasting his food.

She wiped off the counters as Alexandre retrieved the place mats from the table and Richie started the dishwasher. Olivia straightened from her task and for a moment she surveyed the odd scene before her, that of this dark quiet man joining them in their domestic tasks. A warm feeling poured over her. Was this what it was like to live in a household with a good man, a man who was a willing and participating member of the family unit instead of the force that pulled it apart?

"I have to freshen up before I go," she ventured, putting the dishcloth away.

"May Rich take the Spider out?"

She hesitated, wondering if she should trust her son alone with him. "Well, I guess so, after he brushes his teeth."

"I'll be right back, Mr. Chaubere," Richie exclaimed. "Don't go anywhere."

Alexandre leaned against the counter and chuckled, "I won't."

"Oh, your keys." Olivia breezed out of the kitchen to the small table by the door and retrieved them. She walked back to Alexandre who watched her approach with a slight smile on his lips.

"Thank you for putting the car away last night."

"You're welcome." She dropped the keys in his hand. "And I hope you see a doctor soon."

He nodded and for a moment they stood before each other simply surveying each other's face. Olivia had never been able to look a man in the eyes for so long a time and not feel embarrassed, yet Alexandre's calm silence encouraged her to continue to stare. His energy drew her toward him, and she felt acutely aware of the thrumming space between their torsos and hips, a magnetic-like compulsion that made her consider stepping into the space and against the front of his body. Olivia forced herself to ignore the sensation.

"I've got to get ready for work."

"I'll wait for Rich here, if you don't mind."

"Fine. Goodnight, Mr. Chaubere." She walked a few

paces away from him, relieved to break out of his power field.

"Perhaps I'll see you at Harry's," his voice said behind her.

She turned slightly. "There's just a local band playing. Nothing extraordinary."

"Do they have to be?"

"Someone told me Alexandre Chaubere only shows up for the best."

"Not just the band will be there tonight." His lips curved up in a slow smile.

His subtle compliment was not lost on Olivia and pleased her. He crossed his arms over his chest and smiled.

His intent gaze made her nervous. "Perhaps I'll see you then," she said in an airy tone that belied the flutter in her stomach. She turned on her heel just as Richie hurried past her.

"Be careful with Mr. Chaubere's car," she warned.

"I will!"

Olivia watched him dash down the stairs in front of Alexandre, and then she ambled into the living room to watch them from the couch. Richie drove the Spider to the front gate, hopped out, and spoke briefly to Alexandre as he came around the front of the car. Then Alexandre tousled Richie's hair—exactly the way she did it—and got in the driver's side. He had no right to touch her son like that, no right! Yet Richie hadn't backed away, and stood waving to Alexandre as he drove off. Olivia hugged her arms and gazed at the boy standing alone at the side of the gravel drive and at the car as it turned onto the street and disappeared. One day soon, Alexandre would repeat the scene she had just witnessed, never to return. How would they feel then?

Olivia waited at the couch until Richie ran up to the carriage house. Then she hurried to her room to change. She intended to wear her black jeans and white cotton shirt to the club. But when she glanced at her reflection in the mirrored wall of her bedroom, the outfit appeared too much like a uniform. She decided to change into a black scoop-necked body suit and a pair of dressier loose-fitting rayon pants in a black and lavender print. As she pulled on the pants, however, she stopped, one leg in and one leg out. Why was she doing this? To look more feminine and more attractive for Alexandre Chaubere, just in case he decided to show up at the club? Olivia shook her head at her own behavior. She had no reason to preen herself for anyone, and no business thinking of Alexandre as anything but her employer. It would be idiotic and a bit tawdry of her to start something with a man for whom she worked and on whose property she lived. What if something went wrong? Her job and excellent living quarters, not to mention her son's newfound sense of stability, would be put in jeopardy if she and Alexandre didn't work out.

She shouldn't even consider it. Hadn't she learned anything in the last ten years? Where was her head? Men took. Women gave. And suffered later. It was as simple as that.

Scowling, Olivia changed back into her jeans and shirt. Then she walked down the hall to the living room.

Rich burst through the door just as she grabbed her car keys.

"Get your things, Richie," she said. "We've got to go now or I'll be late."

"Okay." He slung his backpack over his shoulder.

"And before I forget, Richie," she continued, tucking her purse under her arm, "I need to mention something."

"What?"

"A few minutes ago you were about to tell Mr. Chaubere that I wasn't really married, weren't you?"

Richie shifted his weight. "But you're not, Mom."

"You know why I tell people that, Richie, and the same reason applies to Mr. Chaubere."

"But why? He's not going to bug you."

"Perhaps he isn't, but I still don't want you to tell him differently."

Olivia could see Richie's stubborn reaction in the way he glanced to the side and stuck out his lower lip.

"And there's no reason for you to be bragging about my cooking to Mr. Chaubere, either."

Richie squinted his right eye and glared at her. "Don't you like him, Mom? Don't you think he's a neat guy?"

"He's all right. But I work for him, Richie. It isn't a good idea to get too friendly with someone you work for. Do you understand?"

"Kind of. But I don't see why I can't tell him the truth."

"Because it will make our lives easier if you don't, okay?" She tousled his dark red hair to camouflage her disquiet about withholding the truth, both from Alexandre and her son. All these years, Richie had been convinced his father was dead. She had told him Boyd was no longer alive in order to save Richie from heartache, to keep him from wishing for a father who would never arrive or to yearn for the love of a man who didn't care a thing about him, and probably never would—since ten years of no contact was a good indication of Boyd's paternal interest.

Richie pulled away. "I don't want to lie to Mr. Chaubere. It'll make me feel creepy."

I know you don't like it, but the less he knows of us, the better."

"Aw, Mom!"

"I'm your mother, Richie. And I know best how to manage things."

"But—"

"Come on." She opened the door. "I'm going to be late if we don't hurry."

9

Later that evening Alexandre drove down to Savannah, Georgia to check on his boat. Usually when he went aboard, he felt a rush of freedom and the call to adventure. But this time when he inspected the progress on his schooner, he felt no excitement, no anticipation of his upcoming voyage. Always before he could count on the sea to turn his thoughts from the land and his troubles with women, but he worried that such would not be the case this time. Alexandre returned to his car, telling himself that once he reached the open sea, he'd forget all about Olivia Travanelle. She'd be like all the others. A forgotten face, a fading name in his memory.

Upset, Alexandre got into the Spider and headed back to Charleston. He didn't want to forget Olivia. Her feistiness charmed him and her reserved mannerisms challenged him in a way he'd never experienced before. And he wasn't certain if it would be possible to dash the vision of her face from his thoughts, no matter how far away he sailed from her.

On his return to Charleston, he decided to visit Gilbert at the Le Jardin Hotel and discuss travel plans with his friend before going on to Harry's. Alexandre parked the car and walked through the lobby, found Gilbert's room, and knocked on the door. As he waited for Gilbert to answer, he felt a sharp twisting pain inside, so sharp he doubled over, clutching his abdomen. His guts churned and lurched. Was he rotting from the inside out, like his alchemist friend so long ago? He couldn't imagine a more horrible way to die and prayed the same fate was not happening to him. Alexandre's vision shifted, spun, and then turned into sparkling blobs through which he could not see. Panting, he turned and propped himself against the wall, his knees trembling. He reached to the side and threw his fist against the door, hoping Gilbert would hear the single loud thump.

"For God sake, du Berry," he gasped through clenched teeth. "Open the door."

While he stood against the wall, his eyes shifted back to normal, just in time for him to glimpse two young women coming toward him. Both of them gave him dark scathing looks and a wide berth as they passed.

Then the door opened, and Alexandre turned toward du Berry as his friend stepped into the corridor.

"*Alors*, Alexandre!" Gilbert exclaimed in surprise, reaching for him.

"Get me inside," Alexandre blurted. He draped his arm around du Berry's narrow shoulders and hung on his friend as they stumbled through the doorway.

"What is the matter with you?" du Berry cried, guiding him to the bed.

Without answering, Alexandre collapsed upon the gold comforter, face down, completely exhausted. He couldn't talk. It was all he could do to breathe.

Du Berry skittered backward and pushed the door shut

and then darted back to the bed. He sat down on the mattress beside Alexandre. "Is it the elixir?" he asked.

Alexandre nodded.

"Just relax." Du Berry reached out and stroked Alexandre's hair. Ordinarily Alexandre wouldn't let himself be touched so intimately by Gilbert, for he was well aware of his friend's sexual preference even though du Berry had never made any kind of advances toward him. But the gesture was one of simple support, not seduction, so Alexandre let himself be comforted.

"Can I get you something, Alexandre?" du Berry questioned. "Water? A warm cloth? Anything?"

"Nothing."

"Is it really bad?"

"Yes." Alexandre closed his eyes.

"Where?"

"In my guts." He pulled himself into a fetal position.

"Alexandre!" Gilbert jumped to his feet. "What is happening now?"

"Rest. Just let me rest."

Alexandre felt himself slipping in and out of consciousness, felt the cool quilted pattern of the comforter beneath his cheek, and then all went black.

When Alexandre came to, he found Gilbert standing over him, his face dark with worry. Alexandre rolled onto his back.

"Blessed Virgin, I thank you," Gilbert declared to the heavens. Then he clasped his hands together under his chin. "Alexandre, are you all right?"

"Yes. The pain has gone."

"Thank God!"

Alexandre ran a hand over his forehead. "How long was I out?"

"Two hours."

"What?" Alexandre lurched up to a sitting position. "Two hours? What time is it?"

"Just past midnight, *mon ami*." Gilbert reached for a blue silk shirt draped over the back of a nearby chair. "You slept like a babe."

"I can't believe I was out that long! Two hours? We've got to get out of here."

"What is the rush?"

"I wanted to go to Harry's tonight."

"*Vraiment?* Why? Is it that a good band plays there tonight?"

Alexandre rubbed the back of his neck. "I don't know."

"You don't?" Gilbert stopped buttoning his shirt in amazement. "Then why go when you have just been so ill?"

"I just wanted to, that's all." Alexandre got to his feet. "I felt like getting out, away from the lab, maybe having a nip of cognac."

"I don't believe you should have a nip of anything tonight."

Alexandre shrugged. "I still intend to go."

"Do you feel up to it?"

"I'll be all right. I just need to wash my face. May I?"

"*Certainement.*" Gilbert tilted his head. "So!" he exclaimed in a suspicious tone, as he followed Alexandre to the bathroom and watched him splash water on his face. "This is not about cognac that you go to Harry's, I am thinking. This is about something different, entirely different. But what, exactly? This intrigues me!"

"Gilbert, I simply wanted to get out of the house. No ulterior motive." Alexandre glared at him over the towel as he dried his cheeks. "Now, are you coming with me or not?"

"Oh, I shall come simply for the rare treat of watching you in public, *mon ami*." Gilbert tucked his shirt tails into the waist of his summer-weight cream wool pants and fastened his belt. "The female tourists will flock to you, Alexandre."

"No they won't. It's Tuesday. Harry's will be quiet."

"*Au contraire, mon ami.* Tonight, this is ladies' night!" Du Berry laughed and pulled a suit jacket off a hanger in the closet.

Alexandre had forgotten about ladies night. Frowning, he glanced down at his black jeans and deep purple shirt, never having even thought of changing into something more dressy. But what the hell, they were just going down to a bar. He wasn't the type of man to fuss with his clothes anyway, especially for a woman who seemed immune to his outward appearance.

Over the years he had learned to value those who judged people on qualities other than their looks and clothes. Olivia was such a person. While most females gave him appreciative appraisals and made no secret of their physical attraction to him, Olivia had never revealed such thoughts. He liked that about her. And the best part was, he couldn't tell what she thought of him, which only intrigued him more. She had stared into his face at length on two separate occasions, but both gazes had been full of searching intensity, not sexual interest. Her ice-blue eyes were impersonal and businesslike, her body language aloof and dignified, and her conversation limited to her work and her son. He didn't fault her for her cool façade, even though he wished he could crack it, because he knew she was a married woman and obviously dedicated to her husband. Yet what kind of man would leave a woman like Olivia on her own for years on end? Her husband was a damned fool.

"Are you sure you are up to this, my quiet friend?" du Berry inquired, startling him from his thoughts.

"Yes. I'm fine now."

"Then here we go." Gilbert laughed gaily, snatching up his room key. "Lambs to the slobber."

"*Slaughter*," replied Alexandre, dryly, following his compatriot out the door. "And I don't think I like the sound of it."

They sped to North Market Street in the Spider and parked on a side road. Then, walking in the shadows to avoid the townspeople as was their custom, they slipped in unobtrusively and went upstairs to the jazz and blues club. The place was noisy, crowded, and smoky, which reminded Alexandre of the reason he usually stayed away from bars.

He stopped near the doorway and surveyed the lay of the room until he saw which section the other barmaid was working. Olivia wasn't in sight and he was disappointed momentarily until he caught a glimpse of her coming from the back room behind the bar. She didn't notice him and quickly moved toward the band, where she stooped and delivered four beers to a bunch of overdressed, overly made-up women at a table near the front.

"This way," Alexandre said, weaving a path between the tables to the left hand section. He ignored the upturned faces of the women he passed. Such attention had once been highly gratifying, and he had enjoyed the idea that women found him attractive. Over the years, however, he had come to feel more like a commodity, a prize to be won, a medal to be pinned on the bosom of a woman— until she found out she would never make it into his bedroom. Not just the women suffered, either. His heart had broken numerous times over the centuries, until he learned the cruelest lesson of all: he could never allow himself to fall in love. He had discovered the best way to avoid the pain of the inevitable unhappy ending was to avoid ladies altogether.

Usually he lost himself in work and found that when he was occupied with a puzzling scientific problem, or a complicated invention, his life was bearable and he didn't miss the companionship of women. When it came to Olivia Travanelle, however, he considered the possibility of breaking his own rule of avoidance. His work suddenly didn't fascinate him as much. He found himself pacing the laboratory; his patience for packing short, and his thoughts far away from his trip to South America.

In truth, he didn't want to avoid Olivia Travanelle. She fired something in him—joy, a new way of seeing things, a feeling of well-being and home—all sensations he was certain he had lost long ago. When he thought of talking to her, seeing her, or kissing her—Alexandre swallowed hard at the thought of kissing her determined little mouth—he felt happy and eager to meet the day with a newfound appreciation of life.

Alexandre located a table at the far wall, well away from the band and nearly hidden by the shadows. He sat down, knowing he wouldn't be easily recognized in the darkness. Gilbert pulled out a chair and sat down across from him.

"Could you have found a darker place, Alexandre?" Gilbert complained. "It is as if we are out on the hinges of civilization here."

"My intention exactly."

"How will the ladies see you if you hide in the shadows?"

"Perhaps I don't want them to see me."

"Have you no sense of sport?" Gilbert countered.

"Not when I am the quarry."

"Quarry, pah!" Gilbert heaved a dramatic sigh. "You are no fun anymore, my friend. No fun at all, do you know this?"

They fell silent and idly watched the band. Alexander had heard better groups, but still he enjoyed the music. Absently, he tapped his foot and let the melody take him far away, to one of his trips to New York where he had enjoyed his first taste of jazz in the late 1920s. He'd liked that dark era of gangsters and speakeasies because the danger reminded him of his younger days when he had plundered British ships and lived life much closer to the edge than he did now. The only danger in his current life was his gamble with the Everlasting Lily elixir, and it just wasn't the same.

"Ah," Gilbert crooned. "There is one who stares at you. There, *voilà*."

Alexandre followed Gilbert's gaze to a blonde across the room. She was a lithe and attractive creature with long slender legs, and her bold stare sliced through him with a message no one could misinterpret.

Du Berry poked him in the ribs. "What did I tell you?"

Alexandre looked down at the table. "Not interested."

"Shall we place a wager on how long it will take her to come to you?"

"No, we shall not."

Gilbert made a face and leaned on his palm. "*Eh, bien.*"

At the beginning of the next song, Alexandre felt someone coming up behind him and got ready with an excuse that he wasn't in the mood to chat. But as the woman approached, he could feel the energy in the air change and knew without a doubt that Olivia was coming his way. On more than one occasion when standing next to her, he had experienced a strange vibrancy between their bodies, as if the frequency of her body's electrical system was in sync with his, creating an amplified field between them. He wondered if she felt the same thing, for it seemed too strong not to be obvious. Just as he thought, Olivia appeared at his elbow.

"Mr. Chaubere, Mr. du Berry, it's nice to see you," she greeted. "What can I get for you?"

Olivia had pulled her mass of russet curls back with a clip, but tendrils escaped to frame her ivory face, lending her a soft, feminine delicacy that made Alexandre want to reach up and stroke her cheek. Her skin looked as soft and creamy as a child's, her neck a long slender column that cried out to be kissed. Her expression was pleasant but reserved, her unique light blue eyes friendly but direct, the epitome of a business-like demeanor. How could a woman be so cool and straightforward and still seem so seductive? He realized he wanted to enjoy the music with her, in a slow dance with full body contact, a chance to capture her lithe waist and slender hips in his hands, and an opportunity to lean down to that graceful neck of hers and breathe in her scent. Alexandre shifted uncomfortably in his chair. He had no business even thinking such thoughts about a married woman, let alone acting upon them.

"Mrs. Travanelle, a pleasant surprise!" du Berry exclaimed. "Alexandre did not tell me that you worked here."

"Only for a few more days."

"You must be tired—toiling all day in Alexandre's garden and coming here afterward. Alexandre, you must go easy on this poor creature!"

"It's my choice," Olivia put in briskly before Alexandre could speak. She perched the edge of her empty tray in the small of her waist and raised her eyebrows. "Now, what can I get for you gentlemen?"

"Cognac for me," Alexandre said, wondering at the extra frost in Olivia's voice. Was she still angry at du Berry for his teasing a few days ago?

"A nice red wine, *s'il vous plaît*," du Berry added. "What do you have in an '89 Cabernet Sauvignon?"

"Ste. Michelle or Knudson's."

"I'll have the Ste. Michelle."

"Thank you. I'll be back in a moment." Olivia turned and left the table, and Alexandre watched her move through the room. He frowned. Her mind and talents were wasted in a place like this, and he didn't like watching her wait on people who didn't appreciate her. He saw a man lean back in his chair and ogle her as she headed for the bar. Anger and jealousy flared in Alexandre, and he half-rose in his chair to go over to the guy and tell him to keep his eyes off his waitress.

Gilbert looked up. "Where is it that you are going, Alexandre?" he asked.

Alexandre paused, half-standing and half-sitting, and realized he was as guilty as the ogling man. He was doing the same thing—openly staring at beautiful Olivia Travanelle as she plied drinks for the citizens and visitors of Charleston. Scowling, he sank back to his seat.

"Just stretching."

Gilbert tilted his head and studied him. "Alexandre, you are hardly what I would call good company tonight."

"Pardon?" He turned in his seat.

"I said, you are hardly good company."

"Sorry, du Berry."

"Is it that you are distracted by something or some-one?"

"What are you implying?"

"That your eyes follow Mrs. Travanelle."

"You are mistaken." Alexandre twirled the napkin on the table.

"*Non, mon ami*. I think that I am not. And you know better than I that *une affaire* is not for you."

Alexandre sighed.

"She is married, Alexandre. And you are leaving the country."

"I know." His scowl deepened. Even though his mind recognized the obvious, his heart did not.

"You have told me before of the futility of these things, and that you will never do it again."

"I know. I know!" Alexandre glared at the band gyrating

before him. "But why the devil have an everlasting life if I can't really live it to the fullest?"

"It depends on how you define living." Gilbert looked up and smiled. "Ah, here is Mrs. Travanelle with our refreshments."

"Your wine," Olivia said, setting a goblet before du Berry.

"*Merci*," he said.

"And your cognac." Just as she placed the drink in front of Alexandre, someone jostled her from behind. With her arm extended, she lost her center of gravity, which nearly pitched her into his lap. She caught herself against his shoulder to keep from falling forward.

Alexandre reached around her torso to steady her, and for a brief instant enjoyed the sensation of her breast pressing into his upper arm and the vision of her mouth hovering a few tantalizing inches from his.

"Pardon me!" she said, gasping.

"Madame," he began, slowly freeing her as she stood up. His other hand leisurely slid down her bare ivory arm. He was reluctant to release her. "Are you all right?"

"Yes!" She blinked, obviously confused and flustered. He relished the sight of her firm red lips opened slightly in surprise and the uncertainty hanging in her remarkable eyes. For a moment they stared at each other, his hand around her wrist and her palm upon his shoulder, until du Berry's laugh broke the spell.

"Fortunate for you, Alexandre, the tray was empty," du Berry chuckled. "Or you would be wearing that brandy."

Suddenly Olivia snatched her hand from his arm and backed away, apparently realizing she was touching Alexandre. "I'm so sorry, Mr. Chaubere. The drinks are on the house."

"Don't worry about it," he replied. He would gladly suffer the chance to have her fall in his arms again. "I didn't mind."

She surveyed his face for a moment and something

dark flashed through her eyes. Then she raised her tray and her expression returned to its normal businesslike demeanor. "Well, enjoy your drinks, gentlemen."

As soon as Olivia left, du Berry inclined his head toward Alexandre. "She's a cool one, our Little Miss Green Thumb."

"That she is. But I think the frost is only on the surface, du Berry."

"But you will not be finding this out, *mon ami*, eh?" Du Berry raised his goblet in a toast. "Here's to a life without bothersome entanglements."

Sighing heavily, Alexandre raised his snifter.

Gilbert smiled. "And to the knowledge that beauty is only skin tight."

"Skin *deep*, du Berry."

"Ah yes, and to your next voyage, my friend."

"To South America," Alexandre grumbled, woefully disinterested in his upcoming trip. "To the Southern Cross."

A half hour went by. After another dose of Alexandre's moody silence, du Berry engaged two young men at the next table in conversation. Alexandre sipped his cognac and watched the band, wondering why he had come. Sitting here in Olivia's world was a torment he didn't need to endure. He wanted to watch her move through the crowd, and yet protect her from all the rude stares by men who didn't deserve to be in the same room with her. But he could do neither without drawing attention to himself.

After the last break, the lead singer of the band came out in a different outfit, a slinky number of metallic silver with slits in the sides of her dress. She took the microphone out of its stand and bowed her head. Realizing something new and different was about to occur, the crowd hushed. The stage lights dimmed, all except for a spotlight on the black woman. Then the keyboard player hit a single chord and the singer slowly raised her head.

"Someday he'll come along," she began in a rich raspy voice perfectly modulated for the Ira Gershwin song.

So enthralling was the song, no one moved. An appreciative silence fell over the crowd. Alexandre glanced to the side and located Olivia while the singer continued the slow, heartfelt ballad about the perfect man, the perfect love, and the perfect life in a house of love.

Olivia stood at the end of the bar, hugging her tray to her chest with both arms, her profile turned toward the band, wholly engrossed in the song. She swallowed and raised her chin a fraction as Alexandre watched her. Did the song reach her in some way? Did she miss her husband? Had they shared a perfect life together until something had gone wrong? Had her dream lover turned out to have feet of clay? One thing Alexandre had learned over the years was that most lovers were a disappointment, given enough time to show their true hearts.

Alexandre watched her choke back her emotions as the song continued. He could see it in her throat and in the way she forced her small shoulders back, a sure sign that she was struggling to be strong.

The song drew to a mournful close and the crowd exploded in applause. Alexandre didn't join in, because as the song ended he saw Olivia wipe at her cheek, and he felt a painful twisting sensation inside his chest. Olivia must be in love with her husband—the unappreciative bastard. She must be desperately missing him, waiting for him to return, and working her little heart out to mark time until he came back to her.

Her devotion made him feel like a heel for even considering the possibility of wishing her into his arms.

"Come on, du Berry," he blurted.

"Why? This chanteuse, *elle est magnifique!*"

"We're going!"

Alexandre pushed back his chair, stuffed a twenty under the candle, and turned to leave, his emotions roiling so hard he thought he would burst. Why had he come here? What had he thought to accomplish? For a man who had lived more than three-hundred years, he was an utter idiot.

The place was even more crowded than when they had come in over an hour ago. He stormed through the patrons, trying not to jostle anyone, but anxious to put his disappointing evening behind him and go back to the lab where freaks like him belonged. Just as he reached the doorway, however, his eyes caught a strange glint to his right. He glanced to the side, surprised to see a man in a dark suit holding a black and white photograph to the light. Why Alexandre looked at the photograph, he didn't know. But look he did, and was shocked to see the likeness of Olivia Travanelle staring back at him.

He stopped so suddenly that du Berry ran into his back.

"*Qu'est-ce que c'est?*" du Berry sputtered, pushing away.

"Sorry," Alexandre replied absently as he watched the man in the suit stuff the photo in the chest pocket of his jacket. Why would someone have a photograph of Olivia? Was someone looking for her? He glanced at the man's face, a pale circle with fleshy lips and a receding chin, and took in his rumpled clothing and cheap shoes as well. He didn't like what he saw.

"Alexandre?" du Berry questioned hotly. "What is it that is happening?"

"Hold on," Alexandre replied.

"What? Are we going or are we staying?"

"Staying for the time being."

"You are acting peculiar tonight, *mon ami*," du Berry squeezed around him. "And I must say, it is not amusing."

"I've decided to have one more drink."

"Tiens, Alexandre!"

"Are you game, du Berry?"

"No, I am not game! I am going to find more congenital company than you!"

"Congenial." Alexandre knew he was rarely considered congenial company. He was never chatty enough for du Berry, even on his good days. "Do you want to take the Spider?"

"Non, certainement! You know that I do not drive. *Bonsoir."*

"See you later, Gilbert."

Alexandre found a stool at the bar near the man in the dark suit and sat down. He ordered a beer from the bartender and casually looked over at the stranger.

"The lady's got a great voice, eh?" Alexandre commented, forcing himself to come up with small talk in order to draw out the man in the suit.

"Yeah. A great ass, too."

Just for something to do, Alexandre glanced at the singer, even though he wasn't interested in the woman's figure. "You're not from around here," he said in an off-hand tone, hoping the man would offer more information.

"Nope."

"Well, this is the best jazz club in Charleston."

"Then I guess I got lucky." The man took a swig of his beer and put his bottle down.

"Are you here on business or pleasure?"

"Business." The man raked him up and down with his bleary eyes. "You from around here, buddy?"

"I've lived here for years," Alexandre replied, hoping he was getting somewhere.

The man slipped his hand into his chest pocket and pulled out the tattered photograph. "You ever seen this woman?"

"Let me have a closer look." Alexandre took the photo and pretended to study the face as he weighed his answer. He was fairly certain the man must have noticed Olivia in the bar. If he went along with the man and gave him a bit of information, maybe he could acquire much more information in return. "Yes, I've seen her. She works here."

"I thought that was her. The photograph's kind of old and it's hard to tell."

"What's her name?" Alexandre asked, feigning ignorance.

"Olivia Williston."

Alexandre nodded and handed back the photo. "Your sister? Niece?"

"Nope. No relation to me."

"Then why are you looking for her?" Alexandre cocked his head. "You are not from the FBI or the IRS, are you?"

"Nope. A private investigator. Someone's trying to locate her. It's a family matter."

"Ah, I see." Alexandre pretended to take a drink of his beer. He had already ingested a few sips of cognac and didn't want to overload his hibernating system and possibly suffer another attack like the one at the hotel. He had no intention of repeating last night's painful experience in the garden and didn't know if alcohol would cause a spell or not.

"What time does this joint close?" the man asked.

Alexandre glanced at the clock above the bar. "In about ten minutes."

"Good. I'm beat. Got jet lag."

Alexandre nodded. "How about introducing me to this Olivia person? She's a real knockout."

"Buddy, you don't want to get involved. The lady's in trouble with a guy who can make your life miserable. Know what I mean?"

The information shocked Alexandre, but he forced his expression to remain impassive. Was Olivia running from a man? Her husband? But why would she cry because of an old song? Had she had an affair with someone else and now was running from an enraged spouse? What would her story tell? He wanted to know everything about her— her past, her problems, her hopes and dreams—yet if she disclosed the fact that she was passionately in love with someone, the information would disturb him. Greatly.

Regardless of the consequences, Alexandre took a gulp of beer. Whatever was going on, he was going to get involved with it. He wasn't about to let this crusty private detective harass Olivia.

10

Just a few minutes before the bar was due to close, the private investigator stood up from his stool.

"See ya," he said, nodding toward Alexandre.

"What about Ms. Williston?"

"I'm going to wait for her outside." The detective put a few bills on the bar. "And like I said—stay clear of her, if you know what's good for you."

The detective slipped into the crowd and disappeared. Alexandre located Olivia walking back to the bar with a tray full of empty glasses. He tried to catch her eye, but she was concentrating on getting through the noisy throng that mobbed the blues singer. The lights in the bar flicked on, and more people joined the standing room only crowd as customers got up from their chairs to leave.

Alexandre remained on his stool for several minutes, even when the balding bartender wiped down the bar and told him it was time to hit the road. The crowd slowly filtered by him, until he and an inebriated man were the only customers left in the room.

"Bar's closed," the bouncer said, coming up behind him.

Alexandre rose from his stool and turned to face the huge bouncer, a man he'd seen grow up from a kid who ran the streets to this towering hulk who muscled drunks out of Harry's. "I wish to speak with Olivia."

"Sure you do. You and a hundred other guys." Ed crossed his arms and jerked his head in the direction of the door. "Beat it."

"Just give me a minute, all right? It's important."

"You can talk to her outside."

"Ed?" Olivia called behind him. Alexandre could hear her footsteps approaching.

"This guy wants to talk to you."

Alexandre turned slightly, enough to catch a glimpse of Olivia's face, which was pale and drawn in the greenish light of the bar. No doubt she was exhausted. Who knew how early she had risen this morning.

"Mr. Chaubere?"

He heard Ed suck in a breath. "You Alexandre Chaubere?" he asked.

"Yes." Alexandre glanced back at the bouncer.

"We-ell, I'll be damned!"

Alexandre ignored his surprise and faced Olivia. "Is there a back door to this place?" he asked.

"Yes, why?"

"Let's go then. Hurry."

"Wait a cotton-pickin' minute," Ed protested, throwing a beefy arm between Alexandre and Olivia. "She ain't goin' nowhere with nobody, especially you."

"Hold on, Ed," Olivia put her hand on Ed's forearm. "What's wrong, Mr. Chaubere? What's going on?"

"There's a man downstairs waiting for you."

"Who?"

"I don't know his name, but—" Alexandre broke off and glared at Ed, who listened avidly to their conversation. He was certain Olivia wouldn't want news of a private investigator tracking her to spread through Charleston. "—can't we talk somewhere else? I'll give you a lift home."

"I have my van."

"I think you should leave it. It's still got Washington plates on it, doesn't it?"

"Yes."

"It would be best to leave it in case he follows you."

Olivia's brows drew together. "Was this man asking questions about me?" she inquired.

"Yes."

She frowned and threw a glance around her. "I should help clean up before I go. But what if they find Richie?"

Sherry sauntered up to them, drying her hands with a towel and giving Alexandre a thorough once over.

"What's up, Liv?"

"I need to leave quickly," Olivia turned to her. "My son might be in trouble."

"What's wrong?"

"Something's come up. I can't talk about it now, okay?"

"Yeah, but I'll want a full report tomorrow."

"Sure." Olivia pushed back her hair. Alexandre saw her hand shaking and wished he could take it in his own and assure her that everything was going to be fine. "But I can't leave without—"

"You go on, Liv. I'll take care of the place tonight. Don't worry about it."

"Thanks!" Olivia pulled off her apron. "I owe you one."

"I owe you, for coming in at the last minute and not leaving me in the lurch!" Sherry shot another glance at Alexandre. "But when you have time, I want an introduction to Mr. Chaubere here."

Alexandre gave Sherry a slight smile while Olivia grabbed her purse and slung the strap over her shoulder. He took her elbow. Olivia didn't pull away this time.

"See you," Sherry said. "Hope everything's okay."

"Bye." Olivia said. "Bye Ed."

"Watch yourself," Ed warned, glaring at Alexandre.

He urged her along. "Where to?"

"This way."

Olivia hurried to a door behind the stage and pushed it open. The stairwell was dark, and she fumbled for the light switch.

"No lights," Alexandre warned in a low tone, stepping in front of her. "He might see you."

"We could fall and break our necks!"

"I can see very well in the dark." He reached out. "Here, take my hand."

After a brief pause, he felt the cool soft skin of her fingers slide across his palm, and the touch of her flesh sent tingles streaking across his skin. Her hand was delicate and small, not much bigger than a child's. In fact, she wasn't much taller than a child—barely taller than her ten-year-old son. How could a woman so small defend herself against a brute of a man—for that was how he was coming to think of Mr. Travanelle or Williston, or whoever the hell she was married to. A wave of desire to protect Olivia and see her through her problems swept over him, as intense as any sexual hunger he'd experienced. Why must this woman affect him so deeply? She was troubled. He was scheduled to leave Charleston soon. He couldn't afford to make her problems his own. Telling himself he would not get involved any further than seeing her home, Alexandre gripped her fingers and guided her into the gloom below.

"How can you see where you're going?" she whispered. "It's pitch black in here."

"I have unusually good vision," he replied. The Everlasting Lily heightened all his senses—sight, smell, hearing, taste, and touch—especially touch, which was evident in the way her skin hummed against his. He wondered what it would be like to feel her naked against him. Perhaps such closeness would be too much to bear. He put the thought out of his mind and kept walking.

At the bottom of the stairs was a short hallway and another door. Carefully, Alexandre cracked open the door and looked out. Beyond them was a narrow alley filled with Dumpsters and a single line of parked cars. The Spider was a block away and around the corner, to the north.

"Come on," he whispered.

Still holding her hand, he slipped into the alley. They didn't say a word as they sprinted up the lane, keeping in the shadows of the buildings. Alexandre scanned the territory up ahead and saw no one. With hope, the private investigator hadn't lost patience and was still standing on the sidewalk outside the entrance to Harry's.

As they approached the Spider, he let go of her hand and reached into his jeans for his keys. Quickly, he unlocked the door and pulled it open. She sank into the car and he shut the door, and then loped around the front to get in his side.

"Did you see him?" Olivia asked.

"No. He must still be out front."

Alexandre watched her ease back her head and close her eyes. She looked so weary, so vulnerable. He longed to lean over and kiss her lips when she sat there like that, seemingly unaware of his desire for her. But she was far too worried to have her troubles compounded by his advances, be they welcome or not—and he knew his kiss probably wouldn't be welcome, not after having seen her cry during the song a half hour ago. Besides that, he didn't know how overwhelming it might be to touch her lips. One taste of Olivia Travanelle and he might explode from an overload to his senses. Forcing his thoughts to the matter at hand, Alexandre started the engine and pulled away from the curb. He made a U-turn and headed toward North Market.

"I'm going to drive past the front door," Alexandre commented. "See if you recognize the man."

Even at such a late hour, a long line of traffic eased down the cobblestone street. Alexandre turned into it and flowed past Harry's.

"Do you see him?"

"Not anyone I recognize."

"There he is," Alexandre said, pointing at a man who strode toward the side parking lot. "See the guy in the suit?"

"Yes." Olivia had to twist her body and peer around Alexandre's shoulder to view the detective. The smell of her hair wafted up to him, and he felt another aching surge inside at the nearness of her shoulders and breasts and the vision of the side of her face with the swirling ridges of her neat pink ear. He gripped the steering wheel. Tightly. He was losing control and he knew it.

"Ever see him before?"

"I don't know. Maybe. It's hard to see his face."

She returned to her original position. He relaxed a fraction.

"What did he say about me?" she asked.

"He showed me a photograph of you. One when you were younger."

"He did?"

"Yes. He said your name was Olivia Williston and that someone wanted to find you, someone who could make trouble for you."

"Did he ask about Richie?"

"No. He didn't mention him."

She sighed.

"Well?" Alexandre glanced at her again, anxious to hear an explanation.

"Well what?"

"What's going on?"

"It's personal. I don't want to talk about it." She crossed her arms and set her jaw. He tried to read her expression, but he couldn't see her eyes from this angle, and couldn't tell if she was angry.

"I appreciate your concern," she continued. "But this is something I must handle on my own."

"Why did you change your name?"

"What do you mean?"

"He said your name was Williston."

"It was. Now it's Travanelle. Most women change their names when they marry."

"But I recall you saying the Travanelle name was French, on your grandmother's side."

She shot him a sharp glance.

Ah, he had caught her at her own deceptions, and she knew it.

"So?" she retorted.

"So Travanelle cannot be your married name."

She clenched her jaw and remained silent.

"Travanelle is an assumed name, I take it?" he ventured, still anxious to hear an explanation.

"You can assume anything you like, Mr. Chaubere."

"I only wish to—"

"You can help by staying out of my affairs. I stay out of yours. Kindly return the favor."

"But if you're in some kind of—"

"I'm not. I'm not a criminal, Mr. Chaubere. I won't steal from you, if that's what you're afraid of."

He glared at the street ahead. Little did she know she

had already stolen something from him—his good sense. And she was quickly making off with his heart as well.

"I was concerned for your safety, madame, more than—"

"Well, I can take care of myself."

"I'm sure you can."

"I have for twenty-eight years." She raised her chin. "And I am not in the mood to be verbally attacked like this, like you were storming the Bastille or something!"

"Attacked? I hardly intended—"

"Just let me out here!"

"Why?" Alexandre stared at her. "We're a block away from the house."

"Richie's at Mrs. Foster's." She reached for the handle of the door. "Now would you please let me out?"

"Of course." He frowned in exasperation, knowing he had bungled the attempt to get closer to her. Why was she so prickly, so determined to keep her problems to herself? He eased the car to the side of the road and rolled to a stop.

She jumped out before the car had even come to a complete halt. "Thank you." She closed the door before he could say anything in reply.

Worried for her safety, he watched her sprint up the brick walkway. He had imagined helping her, being her knight in shining armor if she'd let him. Yet something had gone terribly wrong.

Alexandre waited where he had pulled to the side of the road until Richie and Olivia came back out. Olivia ignored him and guided her groggy son down the sidewalk toward his driveway. He kept his eye on them, all the while looking out for suspicious characters on the street, and made sure mother and son were safely in the carriage house before he put the Spider in the garage.

Disappointed that Olivia had refused his help, Alexandre trudged to the main house. He thought of the carriage house apartment behind him, filled with Gilbert's furniture and Olivia's plants, and the warmth shared between Olivia and Richie, two human beings who enjoyed the full spectrum of life. He remembered the night on her piazza when they had talked about the garden plans and Seattle. They could have chatted about anything or nothing at all, and it wouldn't have mattered. Just to be with her, part of her real world, would have been enough for him. And earlier this evening when he had sat down at their table as naturally as if he did it every day, was a moment he knew would make a precious memory, one he would review again and again in his thoughts.

Alexandre pictured his own quarters—the spare rooms, the bare fireplace grates, the cavernous bedchamber with its huge, empty four-poster. He had grown to loathe sleeping and hated the sight of that yawning expanse of linen. He required only an hour or two of rest a night, which was fortunate, for an hour or two was all he could stand in that bed. Alexandre walked slowly up the back stairs, unlocked the door, and closed it behind him. The sound clanged through the hallways and up the stairwell. He paused at the foot of the wide staircase. He could hear his own breathing in this deserted house, amplified by the emptiness of the place and the loneliness of his heart. He cocked his head and listened to the mournful silence of the opaque void of early morning and the reverberation of his eternal solitude. Now that Olivia Travanelle had burst into his life, the echo rang more hollow than ever.

He couldn't face his bedchamber. Not tonight. With slow steps, he retraced his path down the back stairs and turned toward the lab. He should take another blood sample and see if there had been drastic changes in the cell count since his last attack. He'd go over his notes, study his graph, and look for trends—anything to avoid his empty bed.

* * *

At the first light of dawn, Olivia tramped into the garden, hardly having slept at all, and anxious to put her worries aside with hard work. Her goal for the day was to clear the entire quarter of the front garden closest to the drive. She dressed in light cotton pants, tank top, and an old shirt she could discard when the sun climbed higher. Then she stuffed her tell-tale red hair under one of Richie's baseball caps to conceal her identity should the private investigator cruise by. Satisfied that she was unrecognizable, Olivia pushed the wheelbarrow full of tools down the drive and through the oleanders.

She pulled out kudzu, dandelion, and chickweed from around the shrubs and decided to have the stretches of lawn alongside rototilled, treated, and sodded. Her labors did little to ease her mind, however, for the more she worked the harder she thought about Boyd. What would happen once the private investigator found her? Would Boyd show up? Would he try to snatch Richie? And why after ten years would he want her son? It didn't make sense. But what other reason could there be for the search? She'd call the school later on and make it clear they were not to release Richie to anyone but her.

Olivia threw a clump of dandelions in the wheelbarrow and thought of how Alexandre had helped her the previous evening. She should have treated him more kindly, but she had lost her temper when badgered by all his questions. Olivia wished she could share her problem with Alexandre and get his perspective on the matter, but to explain it would reveal the fact she'd lied to him. What was worse, if he learned she wasn't really married, she'd be fair game to any designs he might have on her. She felt certain there was something happening between them, and if she gave the slightest sign of interest in him, she was sure he'd make a move. If he felt free to pursue her openly, she didn't know how long she would be able to resist him, for she had never met a man who intrigued her more than Alexandre.

Yet, she had to resist him. Long ago she had learned her lesson about rich men, their appetites, their selfishness, and the weakness money fostered in the human character—and Alexandre was just another rich man content with his bachelor life.

One time had been all it took to teach her the painful lesson regarding men and their fleeting passions. She thought of the beautiful statue in the corner of the garden, forgotten and fallow, practically invisible to the man who had once considered her a prize. Then she thought of herself and the way Boyd had faded from her life, seemingly overnight. Olivia grimaced at the similarities between the statue and herself and thrust her shovel at another clump of weeds.

Around eight-fifteen, she stopped to see Richie off to school. She asked him the usual questions—did he have his homework, did he have his lunch, did he have his key? Then she reminded him not to talk to strangers. He screwed up his features in protest, reminding her that he wasn't a baby anymore, and backed away, anxious not to miss the bus. Olivia called the school and then hurried back to her work. She promised herself she would take a coffee break around ten. But ten came and went and she continued to work. She could already see the difference in the yard and was determined to meet or exceed her goal for the day. Soon the long-sleeved shirt came off and rivulets of sweat trickled down her torso as the southern humidity closed around her.

Hours flew by. Mockingbirds and wrens sang in the trees behind her. Beetles and spiders scuttled out of the way of her fork and spade, some she had never seen before and couldn't identify. She promised herself to pick up a book at the library on insects and arachnids, for learning the names and characteristics of the flora and fauna around her was part of the joy she derived from her chosen profession. Sometimes she used insects as a form of pest control in the gardens she created. An added benefit to her love of bugs and spiders was that her interest was something she and Richie found as a common bond.

Rich, she corrected herself, with a wry smile. She wondered if her son liked the name. She'd have to ask him.

"Madame?"

She jumped and whirled around. Alexandre stood behind her, a glass in his hand, his dark head framed by the fan of a small palmetto behind him.

"Pardon me," he smiled slowly. "I didn't mean to startle you."

"I didn't hear you coming."

"I have a light step." He held out the glass. "Here, I thought you might like a cold drink."

She stared at the cup, wary of his kindness. She didn't wish to face a barrage of questions. When she didn't immediately reach out, he stepped closer, but not into the direct sunlight.

"Not thirsty?" he asked.

"Actually, I am." She held out her hand for the cool glass. "Thanks."

She took a sip. Refreshing water laced with lemon slid down her parched throat. He couldn't have brought her anything that would have pleased her more.

"This is great," she said. "Thank you." She drank a big draught of the water, thirstier than she had realized.

"You've been out here for hours without stopping. That's not a good idea, especially in this heat."

"I've worked in hotter weather."

"Perhaps, but the southern heat can sneak up on a person. I can't have you collapsing on me."

She wondered if he heard the double meaning in his words and knew full well she would enjoy the diversion of collapsing upon this man. Olivia took another big gulp and surveyed her progress in the garden to get her mind off that particular vision of Alexandre Chaubere.

"About last night," he began, "I think—"

"I want to apologize for being so short with you," she broke in. "But my personal affairs are just that, Mr. Chaubere. Personal." She knew he wanted her to call him by his first name to foster familiarity between them, but she wouldn't allow him even that slight intimacy.

His dark eyes studied her for a moment. "Then I will respect your privacy, madame."

"Great."

"But if you are in danger, do not hesitate to tell me. I would be happy to help you."

She put a hand on her hip, deciding it would be best to get things out in the open. "Why, exactly?"

He blinked, obviously taken aback by the direct question. "Because I want to."

"Listen." She lowered her arm and rested the cup against her thigh. "I don't know what's on your mind, but I need to make something clear."

"And what is that?"

"I'm here to work for you, Mr. Chaubere, nothing more."

"Is there a law against our being friends in the process?"

"Yes. A personal credo of mine. I know men. They say they want friendship. They offer to help, to do for women. But they all want one thing, and I'm not the type of woman to exchange favors for favors."

He crossed his arms. "Some men are different."

"The men I've met haven't been."

"I am unlike any man you have ever known, madame, I assure you." His words were soft but steeled with conviction. "I am a man capable of friendship with a woman."

"Are you?" She glanced at him. "I don't believe such a man exists."

"I offer my help to you free of strings, madame, as a friend."

She studied him as he stood shrouded in the dappled shadows of the oleanders, and took in his direct dark gaze, the grim sincerity of his mouth, and almost believed him.

"But why? Why bother yourself with me?"

"Because you bring light to my shadowy corner of Charleston," he replied softly. "And I hope the light will remain."

His words shot arrows into her heart. No one had ever uttered such a romantic phrase to her. Olivia had suffered hundreds of corny come-ons and scores of suggestive insults, but never words tendered with such poetic honesty. She didn't know how to respond. Honest sentiment from a man was new to her. Confused, she reached for her spade.

"You give no answer," he prodded.

"I have none, Mr. Chaubere. We'll see how it goes, okay?"

"You are always so tough when you are frightened?"

Indignant, she straightened, gripping the wooden handle of the shovel. "I'm not frightened of you!"

"Then perhaps of yourself?"

Again, he left her speechless. At least he had the decency not to smile at her as he usually did when he again pierced her armor.

"Fear can drain the joy from life," he continued gently.

"I'm not afraid of life."

"Then do not deflect it with sarcasm and cold looks, Olivia. I wish to help you, to learn from you, as perhaps you can learn from me. But only with the safety of permission that each of us can give the other."

"Permission can get a person in trouble."

"Choose to permit out of strength, not out of weakness."
He raised his eyebrows, waiting for her to see his point.

Olivia stared at him. She had always considered herself
a strong, hard-working person. But had she chosen a solitary path out of fear and avoidance instead of conviction?
She had never considered such a possibility.

"You are silent again," he put in.

"I'm thinking."

"A good sign, madame."

"I don't trust people, Chaubere, certainly not as readily
as you seem to."

"That's an assumption, madame. And assumptions can
be inaccurate, hmm?"

"*Touché.*"

"Friends then?"

She had to smile. She couldn't help it. "I'll think about
it, Chaubere."

"Alexandre, I insist."

She placed the heel of her shoe on the top of the spade,
aware that in agreeing to call him by his given name, she
was agreeing to the possibility of friendship.

"You're a hard man to say no to, Alexandre Chaubere."

"Then it is a yes?"

She shook her head and smiled, her heart suddenly and
dangerously light at the prospect. "How do you say maybe
in French?"

"Maybe?" He grinned back. "I don't believe there is
such a word *en français*."

"You toy with me, sir," she retorted, using his own
phrase again, and saw the light of appreciation in his eyes.

"I play no games," he murmured in reply. He reached
out for the cup and she noticed his hand shook slightly.
"Let me take that for you."

She gave it to him, even as he slipped the glass from
her grasp and lightly grasped her hand in one smooth

movement. Before she could pull away, he raised her fingers to his mouth. Warmth spilled over her as he kissed the back of her hand, closing his eyes as he did so, and very slowly rising up afterward as if savoring every moment of contact. Olivia stood before him, transfixed by the old-fashioned gesture, as he raised his smoldering eyes to meet hers. Then she realized that the warmth of his hand was unnaturally hot. Did he have a fever? She opened her mouth to remark on his temperature, but he seemed to sense her impending question and drew away.

"Au revoir," he said, his voice husky. Without waiting for her response, he slipped through the azaleas and disappeared from sight.

11

By the time Alexandre got to the rear walk, he was shaking uncontrollably. He staggered to the marble statue and sank to the ground at its base, unable to make it to the lab. As soon as he had kissed Olivia's hand, the trembling had begun and he had broken out in a sweat. He knew an attack would soon be upon him. He hadn't had a chance to tell her how he felt about her, hadn't had a chance to do anything but croak a quick good-bye.

Alexandre drew a shaking hand across his forehead. He was a fool! What gave him the right to tell Olivia anything? He was dying. He couldn't predict when an attack would hit, and the next one might kill him. What kind of man was he to want a woman to care for him when he might have only a few weeks left, perhaps only a few days? It would be selfish of him—cruel even—to chance the possibility that she might fall in love with him at this stage. Alexandre leaned the back of his head on the statue and shut his eyes against the anguish that filled his heart.

He had to forget about her, put her out of his mind, and get on with his packing. Du Berry was right. There was no place in his life for a woman, now more than ever.

After his weak spell abated, he dragged himself down to the lab and once again checked his blood. The immortal platelet count was down, lower than it had ever been. He dated the entry and marked it on the graph. Tired and depressed, he stared at the lines and cursed himself for ever having drunk of the Everlasting Lily. Perhaps the end would come soon and his heart would quit suffering. He'd cling to that notion for strength in the days to come when loneliness would once again be his sole companion.

Later that afternoon Alexandre worked in the shade provided by the carriage house, buffing the newly applied coat of wax on his car and trying to remove any scratches or marks in the paint. He wanted to make sure the Spider was in immaculate condition, for soon it would be sold after he left for South America.

Though he couldn't see Olivia, he knew she worked in his front yard, bringing a sense of orderliness and beauty to his world. He took a deep breath at the thought of her presence on his property and the fact that they were both hard at work in the same proximity, and felt strangely content even though he knew he must have nothing more to do with her.

As he polished the black sheen of his Spider, he heard a scraping noise at the side fence. He paused and looked up. What was the insatiably curious Eugenia Foster doing this time—spying on him to see if he were seducing his attractive landscaper? She'd be happy to learn of his change in plans. He remembered Eugenia as a child, always peeking through the front gate, then as a young woman constantly trying to catch his eye, and as a new mother, shooing her children away from the Chaubere property. During the seventy years she'd been his neighbor, she must have logged decades of surveillance. Alexandre walked toward the back of the carriage house, determined to convince the old woman once and for all to keep out of his affairs. But he stopped short when he caught sight of Rich's backpack as it sailed over the brick wall and landed in a clump of clover. Alexandre paused at the corner of the carriage house, his buffing cloth in hand, and waited for Rich to appear at the top of the wall, wondering why the boy didn't come down the much easier route of the driveway.

He saw the red-brown hair of the boy and his two hands as Rich struggled to pull himself up on the other side. Then he crawled over the top, glanced around to make sure the coast was clear, and dropped to the grass below. Obviously he hadn't seen Alexandre standing in the shadows.

Alexandre watched Rich pick up his pack and slowly straighten as if the movements hurt him. Then the boy turned and started toward him. Alexandre stared in alarm at his face. Rich had been in a fight. His left eye was red and swelling, blood showed at the corner of his mouth, and his shirt hung out of his pants, dirty and torn.

At the sight of the boy, Alexandre forgot he had been concealed from view, spying on the kid. "Rich!" he called, striding forward. "Are you all right?"

The boy's head jerked up and he stopped in his tracks.

"What happened to you?" Alexandre demanded.

"Nuthin'."

"Who did this to you?" Alexandre asked, tipping Rich's head back to have a look at his eye. Rich averted his gaze. He frowned, and his grimace deepened with the line of blood at the corner of his mouth. Alexandre knew that look and knew he wouldn't get immediate answers to his questions, for once long ago he had been a boy himself and could remember the piercing stings of hurt pride.

"You've got to get something cold on that eye to take down the swelling," he said, "Does your mother have some meat in the refrigerator?"

"Yeah, I think so, but I don't want her to see me."

"Is that why you came around the back?"

"Yeah."

"Come on. She's working out front. We can slip in the carriage house and attend to your eye without her seeing, if that's what you wish. Do you have a key?"

"Yeah," he stuck his hand in his jeans and pulled out his key.

Alexandre took it, turned and walked to the door of the apartment, and unlocked it. Then he and Rich tramped up the stairs in silence.

"Go wash up," Alexandre instructed. "I'll get something for your eye."

"Okay." Rich turned in the living room. "But my mom uses a bag of frozen peas, not meat.

Alexandre walked into the kitchen and opened the refrigerator to search for frozen peas, and was surprised by the foreign sensation of looking at so much food. He rarely ate and never kept any food on the premises. In fact, his kitchen in the main house had neither stove nor refrigerator. Since building the house in 1795, he never had a need to prepare meals there. What little food he ate to sustain his hibernating body he ate in outlying restaurants where he was less well-known. He opened the top section of the refrigerator and found the frozen food and a half-used bag of peas. Rich appeared in the doorway, his hair wet around his face and most of the blood on his lip gone.

"Sit down." Alexandre motioned toward a dining room chair.

Rich trudged over to the table, pulled out a chair, and plopped down.

"Tip your head back," Alexandre went on. Rich obeyed and Alexandre carefully laid the flattened bag over his eye.

"How many were there?" Alexandre asked, standing beside him.

"Three."

"Your mother will find out, you know."

"Yeah, but when I get the blood off, it won't look so bad."

"Will she get upset?"

"Yeah. She hates fighting."

Alexandre glanced at Rich's thin frame and innocent face. "Does this happen often?"

"Naw." Rich frowned and shuffled his feet. "Well, yeah. It used to be because of my hair. They'd call me carrot top. But now, I don't know why it happens."

Alexandre adjusted the peas. "How does that feel?" he asked.

"Better."

He studied the boy for a few moments, wondering if Olivia would think he was overstepping his bounds should he talk to Rich about his problem. Fighting was an issue his father should discuss with him, but since his father was not around, he felt someone should step in. Alexandre pulled out a chair and sat down facing the back of it.

"Do you want to hear a theory of mine?" Alexandre asked, propping his forearms on the back of the chair.

"Theory?"

"Yes, about fighting."

Rich squinted at him with his uninjured eye. "I guess so."

"It has to do with animals. Have you ever had a dog, Rich?"

"No. Just a turtle once."

"Well, I've had dogs. Some really great ones. But dogs have an uncanny sense, you know. They can tell when someone's afraid of them."

"They can?"

"Yes. And if a dog knows another animal is afraid or injured, that's when they'll consider being aggressive. But there's an interesting thing I've learned over the years."

"What?"

"No matter how big the dog, no matter how fierce, if you can pretend not to be afraid—call his bluff, so to speak—he won't attack. I've extricated myself a number of times from frightening situations just by knowing how to pretend."

"How can you pretend you're not scared when you really are?"

"By walking firmly, standing very square and tall, calling out to the dog, and staring it right in the eye."

"But what's that have to do with fighting, Mr. Chaubere?"

"Sometimes I think people are a lot like dogs, Rich. They can sense when others are afraid. Just like cowardly dogs, they'll strike when they think the other person can be taken down easily."

"But how can I pretend, Mr. Chaubere? These guys are big. They're sixth graders."

"And they're probably cowards, the lot of them. That's why they have to go around together in a pack and beat up kids younger and smaller than they are."

"I can't pretend I'm not afraid, Mr. Chaubere." He leaned forward, holding the bag to his eye to keep it from falling off. "I know what they can do to me."

"That's why you have to learn one thing, Rich."

"What?"

"You have to learn a defense tactic, something that will surprise them. Usually one confrontation is all it takes.

Then you'll be left alone because they'll think you're not afraid anymore, even if you might be terrified deep down. Bullies will leave you alone when they find out they can't scare you. And the moment you reach that point, your confidence will rise, which will strengthen your defenses even more. Defending yourself is more a state of mind than brute strength, you know, and it's something many people never figure out."

"That's easy for you to say, Mr. Chaubere." Rich shook his head. His shoulders drooped. "You're not a wimp like me."

"Who said you're a wimp?"

"Everybody. And it's the truth. Look at me, Mr. Chaubere. I wouldn't scare a Chihuahua."

Alexandre glanced at the lean frame, long limbs, and soft face of Olivia's son. He didn't know quite what to say to the boy. To buy a few moments, Alexandre leaned forward and gently pulled away the bag of peas. "Ah, much better," he commented, studying Rich's eye. Much of the swelling had subsided. He kept the bag in his hand as he sat back. Rich stared at the table, his arms crossed over his chest.

"You know, Rich," Alexandre began, hoping he could find a way to bolster the kid's confidence. "Some of the finest swordsmen I've ever known were slight like you. That's what gave them an edge. They possessed speed and agility which the larger men could never hope to achieve."

Rich glanced sidelong at him and then back to the table, not entirely convinced. But at least he was listening.

"And I've fought in tournaments against some black belts in karate who were the scrawniest specimens of the human race you could ever imagine."

He saw one corner of Rich's mouth raise in a grudging smile.

"But they knew how to move. Talk about deadly," Alexandre shook his head and whistled softly. "Some of those guys could move so fast you'd swear they were in two places at the same time."

"So what're you saying, Mr. Chaubere?" Rich turned his face toward him and Alexandre was struck by his earnest expression and his direct question, both of which were strikingly similar to his mother's.

"I could teach you a few moves if you'd like," Alexandre rose and walked to the refrigerator. "I've got a black belt in karate and a tolerable sword arm, though I'm a bit out of practice with a blade." He tossed the bag into the freezer section.

"Not many people have swords these days, Mr. Chaubere."

"I know. A pity, too."

Rich gave him a quizzical look and then stood up. "And fancy Kung Fu moves—I don't know."

"Kung Fu moves?"

"Yeah," Rich raised his flattened palms and spread his legs. "You know, like this?"

At that moment, the front door closed loudly and an instant later Olivia appeared in the kitchen doorway. She took one look at her son's stance and one look at Alexandre and her eyes flashed with anger.

"What's going on here?" she exclaimed, striding forward. "Richie, where in the world have you been?" Then she caught a glimpse of Rich's face and her lips parted in shock.

"Richie!" she cried. "What happened to you?"

"Nothing, Mom."

She grabbed her son's shoulders and threw an accusatory glare at Alexandre. Suddenly it dawned on him that she thought he had been the one to assault Rich, and that she had just now interrupted the attack. He couldn't believe she would jump to such a heinous conclusion.

"Wait a minute!" Alexandre held up a hand in protest. "We were just—"

"Get out!" she demanded, not even looking at him. She was too busy surveying the damage to her son.

"But Mom—"

"I said get out, Chaubere!" She whirled to face him. "Or I'll call the police!"

Alexandre stared at her, astounded and appalled, but knew it would be useless to try to reason with the woman until she settled down.

"I'm not kidding, Chaubere!"

"All right. I'll go. But ask Rich if I harmed him in any way."

"I intend to." She clutched her son tightly, her gloved hands crossed over his torso. "Now get out!"

Alexandre exchanged a glance of exasperation with the boy and then strode to the door. He wouldn't have to try very hard to keep away from Olivia. She'd stay away now, for sure.

As soon as Alexandre left the carriage house, Olivia turned Richie around and inspected his face, carefully examining his eye and mouth.

"Was he in here when you got home?" she asked.

"No!" Rich tried to yank his arms out of her grip but she held him fast.

"He came in after you?"

"No!" Rich scowled. "Now will you just let me go?"

Olivia searched his expression, wondering why he so vehemently protected Alexandre. What had the man done—threatened him into complicity with his schemes? Or had he wormed his way into her son's affections with his well-oiled charm, his flashy car, and his damn money, hoping to take advantage of a boy who had little defense against a male who showed the slightest bit of fatherly interest in him? She never should have allowed Richie to meet Alexandre. She never should have allowed him in that car. And she never should have moved onto the Chaubere property.

She felt the twinges of her old battle scars from her war against money and indulged selfish men, and slowly loosened her grip. Richie jerked away.

"You had no right to yell at Mr. Chaubere like that!" he shouted and ran for the hallway.

"Come back here!" she demanded.

"No!" He dashed down the hall to his room and slammed his door.

Tired and exasperated, Olivia pulled off her gloves as a horrible burning feeling still flared in her stomach. She had been frightened when Richie hadn't shown up from school on time, terrified that he had been snatched off the street. She had run to Mrs. Foster's and back, her fears mounting as the minutes ticked by with no Richie in sight. And when she had burst into the carriage house and found him with Alexandre, something inside her had snapped. She was ashamed she had yelled, but Alexandre should have known she would be worried about Richie, especially today.

Olivia sighed. Once again she would have to cajole Richie into opening the door and talking it out with her. Each time he slammed a door on her, she worried she wouldn't know what to say to convince him that their way of life was the best way for them, even though he was weary of their Spartan existence. Her greatest fear was the day Richie would slam the last door and disappear from her life forever.

Olivia slipped off her dirty shoes and padded down the hall in her socks. She stopped at Richie's door and waited, gathering her thoughts. The room on the other side of the door was deadly silent.

"Richie," she began. "I'm sorry I yelled. Let's talk." She tried the latch, but he had locked it.

"Come on, Richie," she continued. "I need to know what happened."

She paused and listened. No noise filtered through the door to her. She waited for what seemed like minutes and then leaned her forehead on the smooth wood. "Please, Richie, if I'm wrong about Mr. Chaubere, you have to tell me, but if he hurt you then we can't live here anymore."

"He didn't!" Richie's muffled response came from just beyond the door. He had to be sitting on the floor, blocking her entrance.

"Come on, open the door, Richie."

"And don't call me that!"

Olivia blanched, taken aback by the fire in his voice. She knew Richie would one day cease being her baby, and had felt confident that she would deal with the loss when the time came. But that threshold had always been far in the future, an event to be faced in his adolescence. Richie was only ten years old—what seemed like eons from adolescence. She hadn't had enough time to get accustomed to the idea that he might be growing up and away from her.

"Don't call me that baby name!" Richie repeated.

"All right, I won't," she swallowed, "Rich. Now open the door."

She heard a rustling and a click. The door eased open a crack.

"Can I come in?" she asked.

"Okay." His face disappeared.

She pushed open the door and followed him across the carpet to his bed. He flung himself down on the threadbare Grand Prix comforter, where faded versions of Ferraris and Lamborghinis followed each other over the side of the mattress. Olivia paced to the window seat and perched on the edge. To add to her disquiet, she could see Alexandre below at the side of the carriage house as he polished his car with hard determined strokes. What if she had accused him of something of which he was totally innocent? It was so easy for her to jump to conclusions and to suspect the worst regarding men. In the long run her suspicions had often been proved true, and she had been grateful for her careful doubting nature. But what if she was wrong about Alexandre? She might have turned him away forever. Is that what she truly wanted?

"So what happened, Rich?" she asked softly, highly aware of the sound of his new name on her tongue.

"Mr. Chaubere was just helping me, Mom."

"Helping you do what?"

"Clean up."

"What did he do?"

"He got some frozen peas for my eye to take down the swelling. And they really worked. See?"

He turned so she could get a good view of his red-rimmed eye. The faint outline of a developing bruise tinged his cheek. Olivia looked away, unable to bear the sight of his battered face.

"How did Mr. Chaubere see you come in when I didn't?"

"I sneaked around the back way, through Mrs. Foster's yard."

"Rich, you shouldn't be running through Mrs. Foster's property."

"I know," he sighed, "but I didn't want you to see me, to see that I had got in a fight."

"So you let a complete stranger come into the house and help you?"

"Mr. Chaubere isn't a stranger. Besides, he understands about fights."

"Oh?" Olivia blinked, as another momentary surprise tugged at her heart. She was well aware that a man could offer things to Richie that she could not, but she still felt an acute disappointment at no longer being everything for her son.

"And what does he say about fights?"

"That I have to look a guy like Eddie in the eye and call his bluff."

"By doing what?"

"Fighting back at first. Then just pretending I'm not afraid after that."

"I don't want you fighting!" Olivia jumped to her feet. "How many times do I have to tell you that violence creates more violence!"

"Mr. Chaubere says that—"

"I don't care what Mr. Chaubere says. He's a man. Men are warlike, violent and aggressive. I don't want you to grow up like that, Rich. I want you to be a thinking person, a sensitive guy, the kind of man that women can trust."

Rich sat up. "But Mr. Chaubere said he'd teach me some moves so I—"

"No! I don't want him teaching you to fight, do you hear? Fighting back is not the answer."

"That's not what he said," Rich countered, swinging his feet to the floor. "He said I needed to learn to defend myself."

"How about reasoning with those boys? Talking it over?"

"Mom!" Rich rolled his eyes. "You don't talk to guys like Eddie. They don't listen to anybody. All they do is hit."

"Which is usually learned at home. They've probably been beaten themselves."

"So I should feel sorry for them?" Rich got to his feet and swiped the end of his nose with the back of his hand. "And let them hit me?"

"No, I didn't say that." She crossed her arms over her chest, suddenly unsure of what she was trying to say. "Can't you just stay out of their way, stay out of trouble?"

"They ride my bus, Mom. They know where I live."

"Then I'll talk to their parents."

"No!" He whirled. "Don't do that. They'll think I have to have my mother stand up for me. My *mother*, of all people!"

She sighed. "Don't you see, Rich, that turning the other cheek is preferable to striking out? Once you start striking, there will be no end to it."

"That's not what Mr. Chaubere says."

"What does he know? How many sons does *he* have?"

"None, but it's obvious he knows about stuff like this."

"Some men are simply older little boys, Rich. They don't have any more answers than we do. They just think they do." She walked to the door.

"But—"

"I forbid you to have anything more to do with Mr. Chaubere, at least in the fighting department."

Rich's face fell.

"I mean it, Rich. Nothing." She put her hand on the door knob. "Do I make myself clear?"

"Yes." He scowled and plopped back onto his bed.

"I'm going down to apologize to Mr. Chaubere right now. But I'm going to tell him the same thing I told you. No fighting."

"Fine!"

He flopped over and presented his back to her.

Olivia studied him for a moment. Rich had never been this stubborn before. Was it because he believed he had an ally this time? She turned and strode down the hall. No matter. She might not be able to reason with her ten-year-old son, for whom she had a desire to be gentle, but she was certain she could tell a grown man to back off. She'd done it plenty of times in regard to herself. Olivia pushed her feet into her shoes, grabbed her gloves, and headed for the front door. Alexandre Chaubere was about to have his meddling ways nipped in the bud.

12

Olivia stormed out of the carriage house and across the driveway to the expanse of lawn where Alexandre was still buffing his car. If she took a moment to stop and watch him and to think about the long-term effects of what she planned to say, she knew she might falter, and she couldn't take that chance. Alexandre was too great a temptation for her, too much the kind of man who appealed to both her senses and her intellect. But his intervention with Richie was much too disturbing, and she wouldn't indulge her own desires at the expense of her son.

Alexandre didn't look up as she approached. He just kept buffing his car. Either he was unaware of her presence or chose to ignore her. Olivia pressed on and positioned herself directly across from him, on the other side of the hood.

"Mr. Chaubere," she began. "I'm here to apologize for what I said a few minutes ago."

He glanced at her briefly and then away, and continued to swirl the cloth over the shining black surface. "I'm listening."

"I'm sorry I accused you of mistreating Richie. Because of that man asking questions about me at Harry's, I worried about Rich all day. And when I saw his face I panicked." She wished he would look at her so she could see his reaction to her words, but Alexandre remained bent over his car. At his cool reception, her temper rose a notch and she continued the speech she had prepared in her head while walking toward him moments before. "However, you had no right to conceal Richie's condition from me or to talk to him about fighting. My son's upbringing is my responsibility, and I insist you leave it to me. I have instructed Rich not to take part in any fighting, and I trust you will not encourage it."

As she turned to leave, her ears burning and her heart pounding, his voice stopped her.

"That's it?" he asked.

Olivia glanced over her shoulder. "What do you mean?"

"You come out here, list your demands and leave, just like that?"

She pivoted at her waist. "I see no problem with it."

"Do you always have such one-way conversations?"

"Only when the other person acts as if they're not going to participate."

"*They* might have participated if you hadn't delivered your message like a manifesto and turned away immediately. Are you so reluctant to hear my views that you refuse me a chance to speak?"

She turned to face him, her hands on her hips. "I'm not afraid of your views, Mr. Chaubere, I'm just not interested!"

She whirled back around and took a few steps toward the front gardens, intending to return to her work, but Alexandre ran up behind her and caught her arm.

"Hold on for a moment!"

"Let go of me, Chaubere," she warned through gritted teeth.

"Not until we talk this over."

"We've talked enough!"

"Not the way I see it. The boy needs to know how to fight back."

"No! Violence begets violence." She yanked her arm out of his grip. "And I don't want you teaching him your violent ways!"

"Madame, I am not violent!"

"Listen to yourself. Your every word just now has been violent."

"You confuse passion with violence."

"No, I don't. And I won't have you teaching my son anything. I don't want him near you!"

"*Alors!*" He tossed back his head of dark hair. "Would you have me as one of your plants to be pruned and trained? A shrinking violet, perhaps?" He took a step closer, his expression clouding as only his could darken, and it took all her willpower not to step backward. "Shall I be a pansy and not pursue what I know is right for Rich?"

"Rich is none of your damned business!" She didn't want to be forced to look up at him and cursed her diminutive size, but more importantly, she wanted him to feel the full force of her blazing eyes, so she tilted her chin upward to glare at him. "He's too young to fight his own battles. With his father being gone so much—"

"*Oui*, and a pox on the man for shirking his paternal duties!"

Olivia blinked, once again highly conscious of how guilty she felt when she lied to Alexandre about her phantom spouse. "I am perfectly capable of standing up for him."

"It is the worst you could do for him, Madame. It is time for Rich to stand up for himself. If he doesn't learn to do this now, he'll go through his life avoiding confrontations. Of all kinds. Do you want that?"

"No, but brawling in the streets isn't my idea of teaching a boy coping skills."

"Brawling isn't what I had in mind either. What Rich needs is some self-esteem building."

"You think you know how to raise my son better than I do?"

"In this instance, yes. In Rich's case, I think lessons in self-defense are in order."

"You're saying he has to learn violence to avoid it?"

"In a way, yes. He must learn to fight in order to choose *not* to fight and come away with his self-respect intact."

"That's a twisted way of thinking, Alexandre."

"Perhaps to you. But not to a male. You see, Olivia, if Rich has no choice but to walk away because he is afraid, he will lose pieces of his self-esteem until he'll no longer be capable of growing into the man you want him to be."

Olivia glared at Alexandre, still unconvinced, but finding it difficult to refute his logic. Alexandre's way of thinking was unfamiliar and shocking, and she would have to take time to digest his words before she arrived at an opinion on the matter. She also found it difficult to maintain an intense level of anger toward him, which was her only sure way of keeping Alexandre at a safe distance. Disturbed by the notion that the foundations of her tenets had just been irrevocably shaken, Olivia tugged at her gloves, even though they securely hugged her hands.

"I've got weeds to pull," she declared, certain that attending to her duties would dash away the disquiet from her mind and blot his disturbing words from her thoughts.

"Pull away then, madame. May the saints strike me dead should I detain you from your task." As she walked past him, he swept the air with a graceful bow.

Olivia stormed away from him. He was enough to drive

a woman completely crazy, what with his theories and his undeniable charm. She fought back her reaction to him, determined to remain detached and unaffected.

"Olivia," Alexandre's voice stopped her again. "Just one more question before you go."

She turned and studied him warily, reminding herself that she had no obligation to respond to any questions better left unanswered. "Yes?"

"Are you going to work at Harry's this evening?"

"No."

"Good. I've been worrying about the man who asked questions about you."

"If they call me in to work later in the week, I plan to say no."

"What about your van?" Alexandre put in. "It's still parked in the alley behind the club."

"I'd completely forgotten about it!"

"I'll walk over there this evening and get it."

"I couldn't ask that of you."

"You needn't. I'm offering."

She stared at him, trying to figure out why he would extend kindness to her after they had just had an argument. What did he want in return? Men always wanted something in return. He had a big surprise coming, however, if he thought he'd be granted any special favors for his acts of chivalry.

"All right," she said. "I'd appreciate it."

"I'll stop in after dinner and get the keys."

"Fine." She turned to go. "See you then."

She hurried to the front garden, hoping to make use of the remaining daylight, shocked at the way her anger had subsided. Her first impression of Alexandre had been one of an unenlightened insufferable man and it would be best for her to cling to that opinion, to keep him at arm's length. Why, then, whenever she talked to him, could he so easily change her opinion? It must be that he could work his charm overtime, arch his brow, and smile his winning grin enough to blind her to his true character. She'd simply have to double her defenses.

Later that night, after Rich had gone to bed, Olivia slipped out of the carriage house. Heat from the afternoon lingered in the apartment, and though she was tired from the long hours she had put in the past few days, she couldn't sleep. She had tried sitting on the piazza for a while, but felt too restless, and chose to take a walk instead.

She strolled across the grass, passed through the break in the oleanders, and stepped onto the walk that meandered to the front garden, confident that the darkness would hide her from the eyes of the private investigator, should he be watching the house. Even in the darkness, she could see the tidiness of the left side of the yard, and a pleasant wave of satisfaction at her progress washed over her. She glanced back at the house. Her initial view of the mansion had been one of disrepair, even ruin. But upon closer inspection, she had found the bricks and mortar to be in good shape, the stone stairs level and solid, and the foundations uncracked. Once the trim was painted and the shutters repaired or replaced, the house would look presentable. And when the gardens were finished and in full bloom, the property would be a showplace. She ambled toward the wilder section of the yard where the Everlasting Lilies grew, and wondered what tidy sum Alexandre could get for his estate. It was such a shame to sell a house that had been in his family for so many years. Why would he abandon the place after living here so long? Could he be short of money?

Olivia frowned. She should never have started the job without signing a contract and getting money from Chaubere for her supplies. What if he talked big but didn't have the funds to back up his plans? Charmers like Alexandre were often impractical dreamers who couldn't be depended upon, and she couldn't afford to hitch her wagon to a ne'er-do-well. Tomorrow for sure she would finish the draft of the contract and have him sign it, just so she'd have legal means to go after him, should he turn out to be neglectful of his financial responsibilities.

She knelt near the Everlasting Lilies and inspected them. Most lilies grew on tall stems and had long slender leaves, but these flowers sprang from a twisted mass of woody vines, and reached only about a foot off the ground. Carefully she tipped one of the leaves to the light of the moon and was surprised to find it hairy and succulent, like the leaf of a poppy, instead of the smooth blade-like foliage of a lily.

"Olivia, is that you?"

Alexandre's voice startled her. She snatched back her hand and jumped to her feet, while a slight tingling sensation remained in the finger which had touched the lily leaf.

"Yes," she replied to the dark shape quickly approaching.

"What are you doing out so late?" he inquired, pulling aside the delicate curtain of willow catkins.

"I couldn't sleep." She rubbed her finger with her thumb, hoping to chafe away the sensation that had set in, but her skin kept tingling.

He noticed the movement. "You didn't touch the lilies, did you?"

"Actually, yes. Just a leaf."

"You mustn't, Olivia. I told you the plant is poisonous."

"Then why keep it on your property, if it's so dangerous?"

"Because I'm not certain of the strength of its poison, and whether or not its benefits outweigh its drawbacks."

"I'd like to send a cutting to a professor I know in Seattle, to see what he says about it."

"Absolutely not," Alexandre replied. He held out his hand. "Come."

Without thinking, she put her hand in his and was led away from the huge willow tree. Once they gained the walkway, she slipped her hand from his.

"Did you get the van?" she asked, setting off toward the side of the house.

"Yes. Here are the keys." He reached into his pocket and pulled out her car keys. "I passed through Harry's and didn't see the private investigator hanging around. Either he wasn't there looking for you, or he already found out enough for his client and left to report it."

Olivia took the keys and dropped them in her pocket. "Thanks."

Alexandre paused on the walk. "Just tell me one thing, Olivia. Are you in danger?"

"Not physically."

"Emotionally?"

"No. It has to do with Rich."

"Is he in danger?"

"I don't want to talk about it, all right?" She increased her pace, hoping he wouldn't follow, but he kept pace with her.

"Why won't you tell me?" he inquired. "I would like to help you, and I am sure there is some way I can."

"Why?" she flung back at him. "So I will be in your debt? So I will owe you something? No thank you."

"I would like to help you. Out of friendship, nothing more."

"Right." She turned and glared at him. "I don't believe that for a second."

"Why?"

"Saying the words is one thing, Alexandre. Proving them is another matter entirely."

"How can I prove myself when you won't permit me to help you?"

"I let you help me. You got the van for me, didn't you?"

She raked him with a scathing glance. "Just don't expect anything in return."

"I don't. I consider it cloud seeding."

"Cloud seeding?"

"Yes. I am willing to do things for you—things that will make your life easier or make you a bit happier—without expecting anything in return. It's part of a theory I developed a long time ago."

"What kind of theory?" she asked.

"Many years ago I came to the conclusion that good things selflessly sent out into the universe bring back positive things eventually."

"That's not a new theory."

"It was when I developed it. Since then, many others have claimed cloud seeding as their own philosophy. Books have been written about it and seminars taught, each author convinced the idea was theirs. I simply smile and shrug."

Olivia shook her head, incredulous. "Most men I've met want immediate results from cloud seeding."

"I didn't say I would help you for nothing."

"Ah, there!" she pointed at him. "You see?"

"Be*cause*," he put in, undaunted. "I derive satisfaction in helping you and Rich. And whether or not you return my favors, I will continue to want to help, simply because it's the way I can make my world the best it can be."

"I find that totally impossible to believe."

"Why?"

"Because my experience has shown that most men just want to jump into bed with women."

"Not an incorrect observation." He chuckled.

"They would do anything to make the jumping occur."

"You think jumping in bed with you is my motivation, do you?"

She blinked and raised her chin, deciding to be brutally frank with a man for once. "Yes."

He took a deep breath, which he let out slowly. "And you think that if I do nice things for you and you are nice to me in return that I will naturally assume I can demand such a privilege?"

"Yes."

"And that you have no control over the matter? You could not say, 'Alex, I wish to be your friend and nothing more?'"

"I suppose I could," she frowned, slightly puzzled by his logic. "But that isn't the point."

"What is your point?"

"I don't want you doing things for me and expecting I'll grant you special privileges. And I don't like the idea of being friends with someone whose goal is to get me in bed." She stared at him, challenging him to answer her, and feeling a bit over her head by talking in such terms to him. She had never had such a frank conversation with a man, not even Boyd. But there was something about Alexandre's personality that drew her out of her usual reserve.

She saw his eyes glinting in the darkness as his gaze traveled across her face and over her lips. She didn't move—didn't want to move, if the truth were told—and waited for his reply.

"Why shouldn't I want you in my bed?" he answered passionately. "*Mon Dieu*, Olivia. You're a beautiful, intelligent woman. Your spirit fascinates me, your strength and drive amaze me. It would be an insult if I didn't desire you. And I would be lying if I told you I didn't." He paused, and his voice rumbled in a much softer tone when he added, "Would you prefer that I lied?"

"No," Olivia whispered, her voice and knees failing her. She didn't know what to do now or what to say, for the thought of lingering in Alexandre's arms was disturbingly enticing. And if he asked her for the truth, what would she tell him in return?

"But I will never act upon my desires," Alexandre continued. "I will not ask you to my bed, on that you can rely."

She gave him a doubtful grimace.

"I am not a beast, madame. You are safe with me. All you must say is a simple yes or no to my friendship. That is all it takes." He reached out and touched her cheek, cupping her jaw in the palm of his hand. The gesture was feather-light, the most tender caress she'd ever received. His hand slipped to the back of her neck, drawing her closer as he bent down. And then his mouth sank upon hers, warm and unbelievably gentle. She had thought he would be the type of man to grab her and plunge his tongue into her mouth. But Alexandre's kiss was far from invasive. In fact, he didn't press her to open to him, yet she did so—willingly, shamelessly, and eagerly—wanting more of him than she cared to admit. Boyd's kisses had never been like this—tender and restrained and full of appreciation. Olivia longed to close her eyes and wrap her arms around him, to sink against his solid body and let the kiss go on forever. Instead she pulled back, too flustered and confused by him to know what she did want. She drew away from him, blushing because she had waited too long to retreat with her honor intact.

"The answer is no, Alexandre."

"No? You are certain?"

"Yes. You know very well I'm unavailable."

He gazed at her with a wry smile playing at the corner of his mouth, obviously not fooled by her poor attempt at righteous outrage.

"And will you tell me of your husband someday?" he asked at last.

"Why?" She rubbed her arms, nervous that he might delve too deeply and learn the truth.

"Because I want to know what kind of man would leave a woman like you alone."

"Perhaps it was my choice," she countered.

"To spend your days and nights away from a man you love?"

"Yes."

"How can this be? I can tell you are a passionate woman, Olivia. Why would you choose to live a life without passion?"

"I choose it for my son, Alexandre, as I choose all things. That's why I asked you to stay away from him."

"To protect him from my friendship?"

"To protect him from disappointment and heartache."

"As you believe you must protect yourself?"

She looked at the house behind him, to avoid meeting his intense gaze. "My needs are not the issue here."

"Ah, but I think they are." His knowing tone snagged her attention. Why couldn't he be more mocking, more flippant, so she could lapse into her usual sarcasm and extricate herself from this uncomfortable intimacy?

Yet Alexandre said nothing more. He fell silent and studied her again. A sudden breeze rustled through the garden, bringing with it cool air off the bay. Olivia pulled together the fronts of her oversized shirt, crossing them over her tank top, too nervous to remain in Alexandre's presence, but unwilling to leave him, even though it was long past time to return to the apartment and her bed. She knew if she stayed, she would give Alexandre the opportunity to dig more deeply into her thoughts, and she realized from the last few minutes, this was a dangerous area for either of them to explore.

"Your husband," Alexandre began, "is he a violent man?"

"He is not your concern," she replied. "Good night, Alexandre."

"Must you go?" He touched her sleeve. "The night is still young."

"Not for me. I've had a long day."

"I shall walk you back, then."

"No." She edged away, wary of her desire to talk to him all night and realizing she must cut off the conversation. "I prefer to go alone."

"It seems you do," he murmured.

"Well, good night." Olivia turned and hurried through the oleanders, aware that he stood in the darkness watching her. She had said things to him that she had never discussed with a man before and touched on levels of sexuality and intimacy that she had always avoided. Alexandre had admitted to his desire for her, had blatantly told her that he wanted her in his bed. Any other man who revealed such sentiments would have received a harsh reply or at least a cold shoulder. Why hadn't she subjected Alexandre to her usual icy retorts? Because his words had been soft and romantic?

"Why shouldn't I want you in my bed? Mon Dieu, Olivia."

She strode down the gravel drive, trying to outdistance the seductive echo of his voice in her head, but heard him all the same.

"It would be an insult if I didn't desire you."

She had ceased to lash out at him because his words had been honest and heartfelt, and somehow she knew his opinion of her wasn't based purely on lust and selfishness. That was the difference between Alexandre and all the other men who had come on to her. That and the fact that she wanted Alexandre Chaubere as she had never wanted another.

Other women had told her they had made love to men just to get them out of their systems. She hadn't understood their need to do such a thing—not until now. Would it be best to fall into Alexandre's arms and get it over with? Should she decide to make love with him in order to douse her burning curiosity? Alexandre's lovemaking might be as flat as Boyd's. Why not find out the sad truth and cease fantasizing about him? Once she discovered he was just an ordinary man, she would no longer be consumed with desire. Then her mind would be free to concentrate on her work and her son, and she could get her life back on track.

Olivia ran up the stairs of the carriage house and down the hall to her room. She slipped out of her clothes, hung them up, and got into bed, sighing as her naked body stretched upon the cool clean sheets. She slid her hands up over her ribs and cupped her breasts, pulling at her nipples as she slowly drew her hands away. A flush of arousal spiked down her body, and she closed her eyes and sighed, imagining Alexandre's wide masculine mouth closing upon her flesh, and remembering how gentle his lips had been upon hers.

The flush of arousal deepened and fanned out in faint warm waves. For over ten long years she had lived without love from a man—ten long years of sleeping alone in a bed that was too wide, too quiet. Ten long years of staving off her needs until Richie was raised. How could she go on like this?

Olivia dragged the spare pillow onto her chest and hugged it fiercely, imagining that it was Alexandre pressed to her breast, that the edge of the cushion was his shoulder wedged beneath her chin, and that the width of the pillow was the powerful span of his back. She bit her lip and pressed away tears of aching loneliness, forcing herself to retreat to her usual calm and unwavering center. She knew better than to indulge in useless emotionalism. Such lapses only left her frustrated and unhappy. She clung to her old thoughts, trying to convince herself that her life was fine just the way it was, that she would be an idiot to consider reaching out for Alexandre. But after a few moments, she knew her usual way of thinking lay in tatters, ripped to shreds by the compelling theories of Alexandre Chaubere. Cloud-seeding, indeed. Yet his cloud-seeding had already worked on her. She could no longer keep him out of her head and heart. Olivia wanted to talk to him, spend time with him, and come to know what it felt like to embrace him.

How she longed to hold him! Olivia squeezed the pillow and then slowly pulled it away and set it aside as she set aside her hunger for him as well. She stared up at the ceiling, knowing she could never allow herself the pleasure of seeking Alexandre's arms. The night closed in upon her, cloying and vast as she lay pinned to the bed, feeling adrift and small. Was the air so much different in the South that she felt oppressed by the weight? Or was it the heaviness of her heart bearing down upon her?

Alexandre returned to his lab, his senses on fire. Every part of his body that had come in contact with Olivia— his fingers, palms, mouth, and tongue—felt hot and tingling, unlike anything he had ever before experienced with a woman. His ears rang with a high-pitched tone, and the smell of her soap and shampoo lingered in his nose. If he closed his eyes, he could instantly conjure up the vision of her pale face tipped toward his, the sweep of her auburn lashes against her cheek, her straight, sharp nose, and her lovely sensual mouth, as deeply rose-colored as the tips of the red bud tree. She had kissed him back. Lord, how she had kissed him—fire for fire, just as he had suspected she would.

Alexandre strode across the floor of the lab to his microscope, more energized than he had felt in months. He knew the cause without running any tests. But he knew he couldn't indulge in this wonderful sensation. He had vowed to keep away from Olivia Travanelle. Where was his willpower?

With steady hands he took a blood sample from his finger, and tried to subdue the giddy, soaring delight in his heart with a heavy dose of reality. If he had any feelings for Olivia, he would stay out of her life altogether. He finished his platelet counts and stepped back in surprise. Just to be sure he hadn't made a mistake, he repeated the screening. The results were the same: inside his unique third platelet group of immortal cells, the count had plunged dramatically. He entered the figure on his graph and drew a line from the dot which recorded the figures of the last test. The line sloped downward at a much steeper angle than ever before. What did it mean? That being around Olivia was healthy for him—or was he closer than ever to death?

13

Olivia massaged the small of her back as she watched a late model sedan slowly drive down Myrtle Street. She glanced at her watch. It wasn't yet nine o'clock in the morning, but she'd been out since dawn, working on the front garden. Richie would soon be getting up and turning on his favorite Saturday morning cartoons. She'd take a break in a half hour and make sure he ate some breakfast and then encourage him to come outside with her.

She sighed and tucked some stray tendrils of her hair under her baseball cap while she glanced back at the dark windows of the mansion behind her. A sad frown pulled at the corners of her mouth. Since their kiss Wednesday night, Alexandre had changed. She had seen him only once since then, on Thursday, when he had finally signed a contract for her services and had given her a three-thousand dollar advance. His manner had been abrupt and reserved, as if he were angry with her. Had she offended him by saying Richie wasn't his business? Had he taken her "no" to mean everything was off between them, including friendly conversation? She tried not to let his silence bother her, for after all, it was what she wanted. The less she saw of him the less she was tempted to want more. Still, his absence was harder to endure than she would have imagined, and his silence had put a damper on the last few days.

When she bent to return to her pruning, she noticed the same blue sedan pass by the house and park at the front gate. Then she heard the muffled sound of a car door closing. Who would visit the Chaubere house this early on a weekend morning? Her trouble antenna went up like a warning flag. Olivia stepped behind the curtain of willow tree branches which concealed the Everlasting Lilies, certain that her tan cotton shorts and beige tee shirt would blend in with her surrounds, and watched a tall blond man push through the gate.

He was attired in a pair of crisp blue dress slacks and a cotton short-sleeved shirt which accentuated his thick shoulders and torso. She would have guessed him to be a young man in his late twenties, except for the fact that his thinning blond hair receded from a round florid face, adding a considerable number of years. With long strides the man approached the house, and when he got closer, Olivia was stunned to see Boyd Williston III. How he had changed! He was the spitting image of his father, and once his midriff thickened a bit more, there would hardly be a difference between the two men, except for gray hair. Olivia stared at her ex-husband, knowing her world had just changed for the worse. Boyd had tracked her down! What would she do now? She didn't want to leave Charleston, but she had to protect Rich.

Olivia watched Boyd trot up the front steps of the mansion and knock on the door. He waited and then knocked again, harshly pounding the brass knocker against its plate. She doubted Alexandre would answer the summons, and was glad for his aversion to visitors. Perhaps Boyd would give up and go away.

After a few minutes with no response, Boyd paced the porch, looking around at the house and yard. Olivia hung back, her heart pounding, hoping he wouldn't catch sight of her behind the willow strands. Then, with an impatient sigh, Boyd ran down the other flight of steps and strode toward the carriage house.

Olivia burst from her hiding place. She had to stop him before he knocked on the door of the carriage house or Rich caught sight of him. She couldn't let Rich meet his father. She didn't want the truth to come out yet, for Rich was too young to understand why she had lied to him about his father being dead. If he discovered her necessary falsehood, her credibility would surely crumble, and all the good things she had built with her son would topple as well.

"Boyd!" she called, running after him.

He turned in front of the oleanders. "Olivia?"

She halted a few feet from him and stared at her ex-husband. His once Nordic face had transformed into jowly roundness, accentuating the blunt circles of his nose and the high curve of his forehead. Olivia couldn't believe the way ten years had added nearly twenty to Boyd's face, and wondered how she could have ever considered him attractive.

He stared at her as well, sweeping a critical and condescending glance across her soiled shorts and faded tee-shirt, and ending with a quick perusal of her face. He probably thought she was nothing more than a day laborer, making minimum wage on a southern plantation. She didn't care if he had the wrong information and wasn't about to set him straight.

"Olivia, it's great to see you." He smiled and held out his hand. "How are you?"

Blind with anger, she ignored his hand. How could he smile and step into her life like this, conveniently over-looking the fact that he'd turned his back on their marriage, left her to deal with her pregnancy alone, and never once inquired about the welfare of his son. How could he act as if the years had been nothing? "What are you doing here?" she demanded.

He gave another quick smile, nonplussed by the caustic edge of her voice, and retracted his hand to slip it into the pocket of his slacks. "I have business in Charleston for a few days. I thought I'd stop by and see you and Richard."

No one had ever called her son Richard. The name sounded foreign, more foreign than Alexandre's French pronunciation of his name a few days ago. If Boyd had cared to find out anything about them, he would have at least known to call their son Richie. "So you've come to visit at nine o'clock on Saturday morning?"

"Too early?" He smiled his country club smile again, his composure smooth and confident. "I wanted to get a jump on the day. Maybe take you and Richard out for brunch. What do you say?"

"No thanks. I'm working."

"Then I'll take Richard."

"I don't think so."

"Come on, Olivia," Boyd urged. "I'd like to get to know the boy."

"Why?"

"Because he's my son, that's why." He glanced at the ball cap hiding her hair and then back to her face. "I know I haven't been the best father all these years, but I'm will-ing to make up for it."

"How? With money?" Olivia crossed her arms. "Sorry, Boyd. Richie is not for sale."

"Hey, I'm reaching out here, Olivia. Meet me halfway at least."

"Like you met me halfway ten years ago?" She took a deep breath, desperately trying to contain her anger. In a moment she would either burst into an uncontrolled rage or break down crying, she wasn't sure which, and she had no desire to succumb to either. She jerked her head toward the gate behind her. "It's best that you leave. Rich knows nothing about you. Let's just keep it that way."

"Look, I'm sorry about the past, Olivia. But we gave you some options, you know."

"Right," she retorted sarcastically. "Sorry, but money and surgery can't fix everything, Boyd."

"I married you, for Chrissake! You were the one who divorced me."

"You call what we had a marriage? You didn't even have enough backbone to tell your folks about the wedding!"

"I was young. I didn't know what to do."

"Like hell you didn't, you spineless bastard!"

He tried to smile his way out of his shocked surprise. "Olivia, just—"

"Leave me alone!"

"Wait." He held up both hands. "I just want to see him. See what he's like."

"I don't believe you. Get out!"

Suddenly Boyd's expression slackened and he glanced over Olivia's shoulder. Wondering what had captured his attention, she turned and saw Alexandre Chaubere striding down the walk at the side of the house, his dark hair flowing behind him. She hoped he hadn't heard any of the argument between her and Boyd, but her worry was eclipsed by her relief at the sight of Alexandre's stormy expression. If anyone could induce Boyd to leave, it would be Alexandre.

"Is this man bothering you, Olivia?" Alexandre questioned without glancing at Olivia.

"Yes!" she replied.

Boyd turned his red face to Alexandre. "And just who the hell are you?"

"I'll ask the questions, *monsieur*," Alexandre snapped. He planted a hand on his hip, in his peculiar gesture of unassailable obstinacy. The early morning breeze rustled the generous sleeve of his white shirt. "You are trespassing on my property. Why?"

"I came to see Olivia here."

"It is obvious she doesn't wish to see you. I suggest you leave."

"Hey, wait a minute—"

"I resent my work being interrupted by a common row."

"Common row?" Boyd retorted. "Listen, buddy—"

"Remove yourself from my property or I shall call the authorities."

Boyd glared at him for a long moment and then glanced at Olivia, abandoning his false charm to red-faced anger. "You haven't seen the last of me," he warned, shaking a finger at her. He turned and stomped toward the front gate.

When she saw Boyd reach his car, Olivia sighed and glanced over her shoulder at Alexandre. "Thanks," she said.

He leveled his dark gaze at her, neither smiling nor frowning. "He is the one in pursuit of you?"

"Yes."

She felt him step up behind her, to better hear her restrained replies. "I couldn't help but overhear some of your discussion. He is Rich's father?"

Olivia's shoulders drooped with the futility of keeping the truth from Alexandre. "Yes."

"And your husband?"

The question hung on the morning air, which suddenly seemed too humid to bear. Olivia stared across the front garden and waited until the blue sedan roared away before she answered.

"My ex-husband."

"And your present husband?"

"I have none." She sighed and raised her chin. "I lied."

"I see."

By the brusque tone in Alexandre's voice she couldn't tell whether he was disappointed in her or not, but she felt a deep sense of self-reproach for having lied to him.

After a long pause, Alexandre continued. "How long were you married?"

"Two months." She stood near the path, her back to Alexandre, unable to make her feet move. Her shirt stuck to her back.

"Only two months?"

"I think Boyd decided a wife and child was too much of a responsibility."

"And raising a son too daunting?"

"He left long before Rich was born," Olivia replied, losing her battle against her emotions. Tears pooled in her eyes and rolled freely down her cheeks. She wiped them away with the back of her gloved hand, uncaring whether she spread garden soil on her cheek. Husky, tear-filled vehemence filled her voice. "The bastard never once came to see his son. Not once!"

"Or you, eh?"

She swallowed, refusing to look back at the months of private anguish spent waiting for Boyd to come back to her, sure that his love for her would return him to her side. But months had grown to years. She had learned to harden her heart against suffering such unhappiness again, and was proud of the fact that she had never cried for Boyd once she had made up her mind to put him out of her thoughts. Yet here they were, the tears she had never released, pouring down her cheeks and around her nose.

After a moment, she felt Alexandre's hands on her shoulders and his squeeze of support, and she lost all hope of suppressing her grief. Great sobs wracked her body, compressing her into a hunched wraith. Olivia didn't want Alexandre to see her face or witness her breakdown. She tried to pull away, to flee to a dark corner of the garden where she could fight her battle in private as she had always done. But Alexandre held her tightly.

"Olivia," he whispered. He stepped even closer, until his warm body hummed against her back and his strong arms encircled her, surrounding her with protection and support. At first she stiffened, but he wouldn't release her. His strange personal energy descended upon her, wrapping her in a blanket of care, and she felt the shattering release of her long-hidden heartache.

"It's all right to cry," he murmured, his words forming a pool of heat at her left temple. "There is no one to hear but the sparrows."

Allowing him to support her with his arms, she leaned her head back against his chest and wept, knowing he couldn't see her face because of the bill of her hat. Sorrow and loneliness flowed out of her in a black stream that seemed to last forever. She gave herself up to his arms, to the healing embrace of him—to the kind of father, brother, and lover she had never had. The males in her life had always taken from her, never giving back what she needed in return, and she had come to believe that all men took without giving. Yet the one who held her now seemed to be offering her the sustenance she required but had never received, believed in, or could even name.

"He broke your heart," Alexandre said softly.

She nodded, still unable to speak.

"But like a brave *chevalier*, you never let it show."

She shook her head in a slight back and forth motion, knowing it certainly showed now.

Alexandre lowered his head until his lips were close to her ear. "It has been far too hard on you to keep this secret."

"I know." She choked.

"To keep such a secret, you had to ignore your heart all these years."

"Yes."

"Even the beautiful songs it might have sung to you."

She swallowed, crying again. "Yes."

In one fluid movement Alexandre turned her and drew her against his tall and powerful body. His arms enclosed her and she let herself succumb to his embrace. A sigh escaped from her soul, a sigh of release and longing that had nothing to do with desire, and everything to do with completion. Tentatively she reached out and slid her hands around his torso and across his back. An incredible sensation of well-being and gratefulness burgeoned inside her at his touch. She rested her cheek and temple against his chest, and felt a rightness in sharing such closeness with him. His left hand moved up and took off her ball cap, releasing her hair. Her curly tresses fell down around her shoulders and Alexandre pushed his fingers into her hair, spreading his long slender hand over the back of her head to keep her gently pinned to his heart.

For a long moment they didn't speak as they stood in each other's arms. Olivia had never known such a healing silence. She sighed and stroked his wide back and the strong column of his neck where his soft sable hair brushed her fingers, and knew she would find it difficult to release this vibrant, giving man.

Finally Alexandre spoke. "What will you do now?"

Olivia shrugged her shoulders. "The only thing I know to do. Move."

"Why?"

"He knows where I live. And I don't want him to approach Rich."

"Is moving the only solution?"

"As far as I know."

Alexandre's hand slid down her neck. "Do you want to move?"

She pulled back and glanced up at him, mostly seeing the underside of his sharp jaw, and wondered whether his question had a double meaning. Did his inquiry pertain to leaving him as well as Charleston? She could be truthful on both counts with her answer. "No, I don't want to move."

"Then don't. You can't run forever, any more than Rich can run from Eddy."

"But Boyd'll come back. I know he will."

"Let him come then." In a tender, solicitous gesture, he brushed the dust off her cheek with two fingers. "I'll be here."

"I can't ask you to protect me."

"You aren't asking. I'm offering." He touched the side of her face, caressing her cheek with his gentle hand. "Olivia, let my home and my gardens be your haven."

She pulled back and studied his face. How she longed to remain in his world, to continue to enjoy the happiness she had known with him. For a long moment they looked deeply into each other's eyes. What they had just shared in his garden had forged an unspoken bond between them that she was now unwilling to break. The bond went beyond friendship, far beyond anything she had ever experienced with another human being.

"Olivia," he whispered again, pleading with her to remain. Then he leaned down while at the same time pulling her into him. A kiss was inevitable—she knew it as surely as her own heart beat. His serious face lowered to hers. She wanted his kiss. She wanted his arms, his lips, and his heart. How she wanted him! Olivia raised up, never breaking from his smoldering gaze, until her mouth met his. She watched his dark eyes closing and she slowly shut her own while she opened in all other ways to him, heart and soul. A vision of a rose unfolding in the strange ballet of time-lapse photography burst in her thoughts as he kissed her, as his arms enfolded her with grace and appreciation. Olivia thought she'd start crying all over again. But this time her tears would be full of joy instead of sorrow.

The heart she had quit listening to so long ago soared up into her throat and into her kiss. With trembling hands, she framed Alexandre's face and sank her fingers into his deep brown hair, bringing him even closer to her. His tongue slipped into her mouth as his hands passionately swept over her back.

I love you. She wanted to whisper the words to him, to tell him what he had just done for her, to explain how his support and understanding had set her on the road to healing. Perhaps soon she would be ready to love Alexandre in a way he deserved to be loved. But she remained silent, afraid of her shaky emotions and not sure if Alexandre was ready to hear such a confession. Instead she told him with her lips what she couldn't say out loud—that she cherished him and wanted him.

His kiss became heated, insistent. He pressed his mouth to her jaw and throat, sighing raggedly as he brought her hips to his. Their bodies caught and fused and Olivia let out a gasp of desire. Her breasts swelled and pressed against his chest, her nipples hardening against the firmness of his body. Her mouth went dry as he bent to her lips again, kissing her with such passion, she thought he'd crush the breath out of her.

And yet as they arched into each other, she could feel no

mark of his arousal. She was on fire for him, ready to sink to the ground and make love to him right then and there, but Alexandre had yet to sexually respond. Did he not find her desirable? Was his kiss a gesture of support, not of passion? She couldn't believe he would hold himself back so thoroughly as to prevent his own arousal. Maybe there was something about her that men found lacking. Was that why Boyd had left her? She couldn't—wouldn't—repeat the experience of a similar rejection again.

"No!" She pushed away, confused and hurt.

"Olivia!" Alexandre exclaimed. His face was flushed, and his breath came in labored heaves. "What's wrong?"

She grabbed her cap off the ground and dashed away, angry at herself for letting his lack of arousal affect her so deeply, but not knowing what else to do but run.

Olivia ran to the north side of the property, as far from Alexandre as she could get, where the brick wall separated the Chaubere lot from the Foster place. Standing by a red bud tree, she wiped her eyes and cheeks with her sleeve and stuffed her hair back under the baseball cap. After a few heavy sighs and a promise to herself not to let any man make her cry ever again, she raised her chin and looked up at the clouds, just in time to spot Mrs. Foster ambling down the sidewalk toward her.

"Yoo-hoo, Olivia!" the older woman called, waving a white paper in her hand.

Olivia steeled herself, hoping her eyes weren't bloodshot from crying. She had no desire to be quizzed about her emotional state. She forced a smile onto her lips. "Mrs. Foster, how are you?"

"Just fine, thank you! Wonderful morning, isn't it?"

"Beautiful," Olivia replied, hoping her neighbor hadn't heard the flatness in her tone.

"I won't keep you but a minute, young lady. I just wanted to give you something."

"Oh?"

Mrs. Foster held out the white paper, which upon closer inspection, proved to be two envelopes. "Invitations," Mrs. Foster explained, urging Olivia to take them.

Olivia looked at the flowery script on the fronts of the envelopes. One was for her and the other for Alexandre. She glanced up at Mrs. Foster.

"They're invitations to the Charleston Horticultural Society's Spring Ball. As secretary for the society, I'm pleased to invite you to our annual do. This year the theme is Waltz of the Flowers. Isn't that clever? Right out of The Nutcracker."

"Very clever." Olivia absently fanned the envelopes, wondering how Alexandre would receive an invitation and then deciding she shouldn't care less what he did or thought. "But I didn't know you were a member of the Horticultural Society."

"Lord yes! For the last thirty years. We hope you'll come and bring that mysterious Mr. Chaubere with you."

"Don't expect miracles, Mrs. Foster."

She giggled and touched Olivia's forearm. "Oh, work on him, girl. Why, you're living at his place, which is more than anyone's done as far back as we can remember. Maybe you can convince him to come."

"I don't know. When is it?"

"Next Saturday night. Nine o'clock. Do come, Olivia. The Horticultural Society wants to show you off as their scholarship winner. There will be tons of people there. It might do wonders for your business, I would think."

"Without a doubt." She smiled. "All right. I'll be there, Mrs. Foster. And I'll do my best with Mr. Chaubere."

"Good!" Mrs. Foster beamed. "I wouldn't miss this for the world!"

14

Alexandre watched Olivia hurry away from him. He had never felt so frustrated in his entire life—all three hundred years of it. What had caused her to pull away, just as she had begun to melt in his arms? She had felt so soft and yielding and on the verge of total surrender. Strange, but he had felt the same urge to surrender to her, enticed by the notion that if he gave his heart to her, she might have the power to bring him totally alive, even the most dormant part of him. He ran a hand through his hair and closed his eyes, caught in the residual humming still vibrating his skin where she had pressed into him. How could such a petite woman fit so well against him? How could such small ivory hands make his heart race and his blood catch fire? She had touched the sides of his face and stroked his hair, hardly aware that she had nearly sent him to his knees with desire. The thought of her firm breasts and cloud of russet hair made him want to cry out in anguish, to regale the jealous God who begrudged him no pity because of his stolen immortality.

His body still sang for her as he returned to the lab. Work was the only way to purge her from his thoughts, if that were possible. He had spent the early morning hours mixing more Everlasting Lily elixir to make up for the portion he had spilled during his last attack. Now, instead of tending the distillation process, he turned to his blood testing, anxious to discover how his cell count would appear after having spent the last half hour intimately connected with Olivia.

He took a sample of blood, screened it, and repeated the test, just to be sure he had not made a mistake. God knew he would be prone to error, for he found it impossible to keep his mind on his work with thoughts of redhaired Olivia Travanelle haunting him at every turn.

Alexandre cleaned the slide and then picked up a pencil to graph the results. Frowning, he tapped the eraser on the counter, deep in thought. The immortal platelet count had again plunged dramatically. In fact, there were few dark red cells to be found anywhere. If he were a man to jump to conclusions, he would theorize that the way Olivia made him feel had much to do with the destruction of the immortal cells. Dare he stop taking the potion? Or did the potion plus Olivia's effect on him work in tandem to produce these results? If he continued to build a relationship with Olivia, would his cell count improve even more? Or were his feelings for her interfering with the whole process by introducing male hormones, which then adversely effected the Everlasting Lily potion? There were far too many variables in this experiment.

He thrust a hand in his hair, and rubbed the top of his head. If Olivia was a good influence, why all of a sudden were his attacks getting worse? Was she hastening his route to mortality? If so, wouldn't his attacks increase in severity until they killed him?

His thoughts racing, Alexandre plotted the results on his graph and drew another downward sloping line. Then he stared at the graph as a horrible realization dawned on him. Ever since Olivia Travanelle had entered his life, his immortal platelet counts had steadily decreased. But at the same time, he had begun to suffer painful physical distress. Was she giving him life or causing his death?

Alexandre slumped against the counter, shocked. Olivia's affection could literally be killing him. He prayed the supposition was flawed and that he was drawing the wrong conclusion. But over the years he had learned to trust his instincts when it came to experimentation and research. So many times his instincts had steered him in the right direction. This time he hoped they proved to be wrong.

Alexandre pushed away from the counter and paced the floor. There was only one way to find out whether Olivia was connected to his physical well-being. He'd have to stay away, at least long enough to see if the immortal platelet count raised again and if the attacks lessened in severity. If he found that Olivia was linked to his mortality, he'd have to make the hardest decision of his life—to stay with the woman he loved for the short time he'd have left, or step out of Olivia Travanelle's life and spare her the heartbreak of witnessing his decline.

In mid-afternoon when the sun was the hottest, Olivia stopped to get a cool drink, heading back to the carriage house for the second time that day. After running from Alexandre earlier in the morning, she had hurried to the apartment to check on Rich. As she'd expected, she found him sitting on the floor with a bowl of cereal in his lap, watching cartoons. She'd hung in the doorway, feeling sick at heart, knowing she would have to tell him the truth about his father before anyone else did. She didn't have the luxury to wait until he grew older. But she couldn't tell him now, not when he was absorbed with the television and she was feeling so emotionally ragged. She'd tell him at the end of the day, the time they usually sat at the supper table and talked.

Before returning to her work, she'd told Rich to come out and help her at ten o'clock. After lunch, as long as he didn't leave the grounds, the day would be his to do whatever he liked.

The entire day in the garden was spent going over and over in her mind what she would say to Rich, how she would explain her past, and her reasons for protecting him with lies. She prayed he would be old enough to appreciate why she had done what she'd done, but worried nonetheless about his reaction. No peach cake or car models would make up for her Big Lie. Only her sound relationship with her son would help him weather the truth. Tired and worried, she walked down the side path of the mansion toward the break in the oleanders. As she passed the house, she heard the distinct metallic clink of swordplay somewhere above her head. Olivia looked up and saw most of the second story windows open on the north side of the house.

"*Touché!*" Alexandre exclaimed. More metallic clinks played a staccato in the air above her head.

Then a high-pitched voice cried, "Gotcha!"

Olivia froze. Rich was in Alexandre's house, and by the sound of things, he was engaged in some form of combat. She glared up at the open windows. Not only had Boyd burst back into her life with his underlying threat of taking Rich away from her, Alexandre had gone against her request to stay away from her son. Seething and distraught, she plowed down the walk to the back of the house. She took the back stairs two at a time and pushed through the rear door. Stale air met her in a pungent wave and momentarily halted her in her tracks. She'd never been in the Chaubere mansion before, and wasn't prepared for the sight before her.

Olivia stood in a spacious vestibule where two massive staircases flanked a central hall leading to the front of the house. She was amazed to see wall sconces containing candles in the hall, and peeling wallpaper panels not much larger than sheets from a big drawing tablet—the kind of panels installed in the 1700s which depicted bucolic landscapes and garden scenes. A huge brass chandelier hung from the second story ceiling forty feet above, a masterpiece dripping with crystal and candles, hundreds and hundreds of candles. She gaped at the light fixture, wondering if Alexandre could possibly still be using candles to illuminate his house. She'd read somewhere that wealthy homeowners long ago had employed a servant exclusively to tend the candles in their houses, and she could see how that might have been necessary in the Chaubere house.

The staircase on the left was shrouded in dust and cobwebs, and it rose to meet a heavy curtain of gold velvet that blocked off the south wing of the second floor. The right staircase showed heavy use and the mahogany balustrade was dusted and polished. She had been in enough museums to know that the furnishings, woodwork, and wallpaper in this house were the real thing, and had gone unchanged since the late eighteenth century. Alexandre Chaubere lived in a virtual showplace—an ancient but still impressive showplace. His house would have been an excellent addition to any historic tour. Yet she couldn't imagine him allowing visitors to tramp through his hallways gawking at his home. She briefly wondered why he had never remodeled the house, if only to add a few modern conveniences, but her thoughts refocused on the noise above.

Intent on catching Alexandre and Rich fighting, she dashed up the stairs to the second story, where a deep red and gold carpet decorated the floor. She ran past a huge mirror and was startled by the flash of her reflection as she hurried by. Olivia reared back and bumped into a side table, nearly knocking a Ming vase to the floor. Luckily, her quick reaction allowed her to catch the vase and right it on the table with shaking hands. What if the vase had fallen to the floor and shattered? She could never have found a replacement, let alone come up with enough money to buy it. Flustered, Olivia glanced around the dark corridor, trying to steady her pounding heart.

The metallic sound rang through a doorway on the right, near the center of the house. She ran in that direction, and burst through the doorway into a huge ballroom, where Alexandre and Rich furiously practiced fencing, their bodies and faces concealed by masks and protective clothing. Rich looked ridiculous in his oversized outfit, which had been rolled up on his arms and legs, and she worried that at any moment he might trip and injure himself.

"Rich!" she shouted over the noise.

He jerked around at the same time Alexandre halted in mid-lunge, the button of his épée raised to shoulder height, and his tall elegant form outlined by the light from the bank of windows behind him. He straightened in a sinuous movement, and despite the bulky white fencing gear, he appeared lean and commanding. She found it hard to believe that a few hours ago she had stood in his arms and contemplated making love to him while at the same time he had remained physically removed from her. A flush of shame spiked through her and she tore her gaze away.

"What's going on here?" Olivia demanded, striding across the parquet floor toward them. She felt flustered and hot, anxious to get away from Alexandre's intent regard, which pierced through the mesh of his mask.

Rich lowered his blade. "We were just practicing fencing, Mom."

Alexandre swept off his headgear and shook out his hair. "Rich is a natural. He reminds me a bit of myself when I was a lad."

Olivia turned to Alexandre, her blood pounding in her ears. "I thought I told you not to encourage Rich to fight."

"I am not. Fencing will improve his reflexes and keep him nimble on his feet."

"And teach him to use a weapon."

"Aw, Mom," Rich unfastened his mask. "It's fun!"

"Fighting is not fun, Rich. It's violent."

"Fencing is a sport these days, madame." Alexandre unsnapped his metallic plastron at the neck and shoulder. "Entirely. I consider it a reasonable alternative to teaching him hand to hand combat."

"Yeah, Mom," Rich put in. "How many times have you seen someone sword fighting in the street?"

Olivia glared at Alexandre, upset once again for being in the wrong according to Rich, and hating the feeling of her own pettiness for wanting to be in the right, regardless of the logic or the obvious parental response.

"Still, I asked you to stay away from my son, Mr. Chaubere."

"Rich has come far in three days, Olivia. It would be a shame to prohibit his progress."

"Three days?" she cried. "You've been teaching him for three days?"

"Yeah," Rich stepped forward. "After school, Mom."

"He's a fine student." Alexandre unsnapped the rest of his plastron. "I couldn't ask for a better pupil."

"Please don't make me quit," Rich pleaded. "This is the most fun I've ever had."

Olivia surveyed his serious face, his mussed hair, his imploring blue eyes. Should she deny him this? Except for the very basics, hadn't she denied him many other things in life, especially the fun things? Was fencing really an innocent sport after all, and nothing to worry about? She shook her head, hating to appear wishy-washy by conceding to his request, but wanting more for Rich than she was able to provide.

"Please?" Rich added, as if he could see her changing her mind and thought to tip the scales.

"Oh, I don't know!" Olivia replied, exasperated. She shook her head. "I suppose it wouldn't hurt anyone if you continued with it. But I have to clear up some things with Mr. Chaubere before this goes any further."

"Thanks, Mom!" Rich leapt forward and threw his arms around her. She couldn't remember the last time he had voluntarily hugged her. She hugged him back and smoothed his hair. "But I don't want your fencing to leave this room, do you understand, Rich?"

"Yeah!"

"And if I hear about you challenging anyone to a duel, that's it. I mean it!"

"I won't!"

"And no more going behind my back or I'll ground you, and you won't be doing anything for weeks."

"I'll be good, Mom, I promise! Thanks!"

Alexandre drew off his gloves. "That's enough for today, Rich. We'll continue tomorrow morning when it isn't so hot, eh?"

"Okay, Mr. Chaubere. What time?"

"Ten, if it's all right with your mother." He glanced at her.

Rich turned to her, his eyes bright and shining as she had seldom seen them lately.

Olivia nodded and crossed her arms, aware she'd just been bulldozed, but suddenly certain she'd made the right decision. Perhaps in a limited way, Alexandre could be a good influence on her son.

"Go change, Rich," Alexandre instructed, "We'll wait for you here."

Rich sprinted off to a salon on the side of the old ball-room and shut the door. As soon as Rich disappeared from sight, Alexandre turned to Olivia.

"From now on, Alexandre, I insist that you discuss your activities with Rich with me first."

"Would you have consented to him learning to fence?"

"Probably not."

"Why do you run from things you do not understand?" She looked up at his face. "To protect Rich and myself."

His dark eyes glittered down at her. "Why do you run from me?"

Olivia stared at him, struggling with an answer that wouldn't alienate him, but would still hide the bald truth.

At her silence, Alexandre tossed his gloves upon a side chair and glanced back at her, his eyes stormy. "Do you know when I first met you, Olivia, I thought you were different from other women, that you were outspoken and frank."

Olivia stuck her hands in her pockets, choosing silence over self-defense.

"I thought you were honest," he continued, pulling off his plastron, "and unafraid to speak your mind."

"I'm not afraid."

"Bullshit." His eyes locked with hers, heated and damning.

She should have slapped him and walked away. She should have grabbed Rich, gotten in her van, and driven out of Charleston. Instead she stood glaring at Alexandre, facing the truth about herself, that she could be a coward and a liar. He stared down his sharp nose at her, challenging her to deny it.

"You lied to me about being married. There is no husband."

"No."

"You have lied to Rich as well, telling him his father is dead, haven't you?"

"Yes!"

"And you push me away, as if you have no feelings for me. But you do, don't you?"

Olivia blushed. No one had ever challenged her integrity before and she didn't know how to defend herself or if she should even try. "Leave my feelings out of this!" she hissed.

"Why should I? Your feelings are the reason for your dishonesty."

"No they're not. I lied to protect Rich. That's the only reason!"

"And is Rich the reason you ran from me this morning? I don't think so." His voice lowered. "Tell me the truth for once, Olivia, for God's sake. *Accouchez!*"

She glanced toward the salon where Rich dressed, desperate for him to finish so she could extricate herself from this uncomfortable conversation with Alexandre. But the door to the salon remained closed, forcing her to remain in the ballroom and speak the truth. So be it. Olivia breathed in and threw back her shoulders. Alexandre wanted the truth? He wanted to know the reason, even if it insulted him? She'd tell him, and maybe he'd learn the value of gentle dishonesty.

"You want the truth?" she responded, glaring up at him again.

"*Oui.*"

"I ran because I don't want to get involved with you."

"Why?"

"Because I have learned the hard way how painful it is to care for a man who holds himself back from me."

"I hold myself back?"

"Yes."

"In what way?"

He seemed unaware of his failure, just as Boyd had seemed unaware of his. She couldn't believe Alexandre would be so insensitive, so imperceptive. And she didn't know what words to choose to tell him the truth without sounding crass. Angry and hurt, she crossed her arms again. "Must I spell it out?" she retorted.

"Please. I will appreciate your honesty, Olivia, however brutal."

"All right." She breathed in again. "I want to be with a man who respects me and wants me—who wants me a lot."

"What makes you think I don't?"

"The way you were in the garden this morning."

"And how is that, precisely?"

"Unaroused." She glanced away, her face heating.

Alexandre stared at her and two blotches of crimson appeared above his cheekbones. He looked as if she had slapped him. Before either of them could say another word, however, Rich bounded across the parquet floor, oblivious to what had just passed between the two adults.

"Mom," he exclaimed. "I just remembered something you've got to see!"

Distracted, Olivia glanced across at him and hoped her knees wouldn't buckle. Her legs trembled and her head spun. "What should I see?"

"Mr. Chaubere's models." Rich smiled at Alexandre. "Would it be all right if I showed them to her?"

Alexandre turned away. "Fine. Go ahead. I'll put the equipment away."

"Great." Rich touched his mother's sleeve. "Wait until you see his ships, Mom. They're unbelievable!"

Olivia shot a glance at Alexandre, wondering if she should leave so abruptly without tempering her words.

How could she accuse him of impotence and then walk away, as blithely as if she'd commented on a poor choice of clothing?

Alexandre met her glance. "Things are not always as they appear, Olivia," he commented.

"But some things can't be faked."

"I am always genuine, Olivia. But all that I am is not for you to know." His black eyes, full of troubled lights, held her suspended and unable to move, even though Rich pulled at her hand. She longed to remain, to ask him what he meant, to plumb the depths of the sudden and unmistakable sadness in his eyes. Had the sadness always been there, hidden in the darkness, concealed by the wry smile and the hooded glances? Her anger slowly cooled toward compassion. Had she been so obsessed with her own needs and fears that she had overlooked the possibility that Alexandre had problems, too? Perhaps she had been the insensitive one, the imperceptive one all along.

"Mom, come on!" Rich urged.

"I'm coming," she answered. She gazed at Alexandre a moment longer, trying to convey her change of view. Slowly he raised one eyebrow, relaying the fact that his humor, though battered, was still intact. Grateful for the gesture, she raised her free hand.

"Bye," she said, simply.

"Good-bye."

"See you later, Mr. Chaubere."

"*Bonjour, Richard.*"

Rich pulled her out of the ballroom, down a corridor, and into a smaller chamber at the back of the house. The room was full of a score of models kept inside glass display cases and surrounded by four walls of books, many of which appeared exceedingly old. Rich showed her the wooden models, meticulously detailed, which Alexandre had built over the years, and gave her a brief history of each craft. Apparently Alexandre had acquainted Rich with the background of the ships, and Rich had effortlessly memorized the information. Her son never ceased to amaze her.

"Look at this one," Rich pointed to a glass-enclosed schooner named the *Bon Aventure*. "Isn't she a beauty?"

Olivia bent down for a closer look. Her eyes saw the ship, but her heart and thoughts were far, far away, with the man whose careful hands had built the tiny craft. How would she ever face Alexandre again? Yet how would she ever be able to live with herself if she turned her back on him now? No matter what, she couldn't leave Charleston. Not just yet.

15

Olivia had every intention of speaking with Rich about his father after dinner, but her plans were changed when Willie Lee, Mrs. Foster's grandson, invited Rich for pizza and an overnighter at his house across town. Willie's house seemed a much safer place for Rich to be for the evening, now that Boyd knew where they lived. She dropped Rich off with strict instructions not to leave with anyone but her, and then went to the grocery store to buy milk and bread. At a visitor's rack near the entrance of the store she saw a brochure about plantation tours and decided to celebrate her day off tomorrow with a short excursion. Perhaps on the way to the plantation with Rich she could bring up the subject of his father. Heartened by her new plan, she bought picnic supplies and splurged on a quarter-pound of chocolates she thought Rich would like.

When she returned to the carriage house, she felt restless and lonely without Rich. She fixed a sandwich and a cup of coffee and took her small meal out to the piazza where she could watch the sun melt behind the rooftops and trees. Olivia sat down and slowly ate her sandwich, trying to appreciate the evening calm, but feeling too unsettled inside to pull her thoughts away from Boyd and Alexandre. She had the strongest urge to seek out Alexandre's company and discover what he'd meant with his last cryptic words, that she couldn't know all that he was. She picked up her cup of coffee and wandered to the end of the balcony to look across the lot toward the mansion. The house was dark. No light from the lab spilled out to the marble statue of Venus in the back garden. Alexandre had probably gone out for the evening. She sighed and returned to the house. A long bath and an early bedtime would do her good.

With an early start the next day, Olivia and Rich traveled a few miles up the Ashley River where several plantations had been preserved in their original condition, and were now open to the public. The Dryer Plantation, a huge brick house built in the 1700s, was situated on a hundred sprawling acres of lawn, cypress swamps, and groves of huge live oaks festooned with Spanish moss. Olivia and Rich took the hour-long tour and then went back to the car to get their picnic supplies. They found a rhododendron-lined path to the river and walked in companionable silence to the river bank. Olivia spread a small blanket over a patch of grass while Rich held the paper bag containing their picnic lunch. Most of the people on the tour had already left the grounds, and because of the midday heat not many had taken the walk to the river. But the shade of the live oaks and the lushness of the tall grass by the water afforded them a surprisingly cool haven. A locust sang in the bank of trees behind them.

"What kind of pop did you bring?" Rich asked.

"Root beer."

"Good." Rich glanced around at the slow moving river and took a deep breath. "I like it out here."

"It's peaceful, isn't it?"

"Yeah." He set the bag on the blanket. "A person could camp out here and no one would ever find them."

"Probably not."

"You could get water from the river and catch fish, kind of hide out while the tourists were around, and then have the place to yourself the rest of the time."

"I think that person would miss taking a bath," she countered, teasing.

"Naw, I'd just jump in the river every so often."

"With the alligators?"

Rich stared at the water. "You think there's gators in there?"

Olivia suppressed a smile as she opened the picnic bag. "You never know."

She sat down and took out their simple lunch: peanut butter and raisin sandwiches, apple slices, and a small bag of chips. Her smile slowly faded as she opened her can of pop.

"Rich," she began, not really knowing how she'd explain herself, but plunging in anyway. "There's something we have to talk about."

He swallowed a lump of sandwich and squinted his eyes. "Not about the birds and bees, Mom, okay? I know all that stuff."

"You do?"

"We learned about it at school."

"I see." She took a sip of root beer, not sure what she had known of sex when she was ten years old, but certain her knowledge had contained plenty of ridiculous notions she'd accepted as fact. "Well, sex education isn't what I want to talk about, but it has something to do with what I have to say in a way."

He looked down and fiddled with his aluminum can. She knew Rich well enough to recognize that when he acted obviously disinterested, he was listening to her intently and hiding his reactions by averting his eyes and keeping his hands busy. "What do you mean?"

"Well, you know how I've always told you to tell people that I'm married, even though I'm not?"

"Yes."

"Do you know why?"

"So guys wouldn't bug you."

"Yes. I've always felt that men would take my time and attention away from you, and they might even treat you badly, since you weren't their kid."

"Not Mr. Chaubere. He's nice to me."

"I'm sure there are other good men in the world, too, Rich. But I didn't want to take the chance or the time to look for one. I wanted to raise you in a safe environment and give you all the attention I could."

Rich nodded and glanced up. She noticed the bruise around his eye was fading to a yellowish color. Rich returned his attention to the pop can. He had stopped eating, just as she had, and she sympathized with the tenseness he might be feeling at a potentially touchy conversation. Olivia reached out and put her hand on his shoulder.

"I know it's been tough for you sometimes, Rich, not having a dad. But I always thought no father would be better than a cruel stepfather. And I never wanted to subject you to a string of boyfriends. So I chose not to have any men in our lives at all."

He pushed the still-connected pull tab around and around with his index finger.

"That's why I told people I was married. I thought it

would be easier for us if I fibbed a little." She released his shoulder.

Rich pursed his lips and peered up at her. "Does this have anything to do with Mr. Chaubere, Mom?"

"No."

His shoulders slumped.

He seemed intent on fostering a relationship between her and Chaubere, and it dismayed her to see his spirits sag. Yet she wouldn't give him false hope, only to have him experience greater disappointment when Alexandre left Charleston. She straightened and took a sip of pop. "Above all things, Rich, I want your happiness. I don't want you to hurt or suffer. I've tried to do my best. But I'm human, you know? I don't have all the answers. I'm learning as we go along, just as you are."

He shook his head and picked up his plastic bag full of fruit.

"So to protect you, Rich, I told another lie, an even bigger one."

Rich shot a glance at her. "What do you mean?"

How could she tell him the truth? What would he think of her? What would happen afterward? Still, she pressed on, knowing she had to finish what she had begun. "You know how I've told you that your father was dead? It's not true."

For a moment he stared at her, the bag hanging in his hand. "You mean . . . he's . . . alive?"

"Yes."

Shocked beyond words, he gaped at her, forgetting to close his mouth.

Her heart went out to him, seeing that incredulous and innocent expression on his face. "I told you he was dead to protect you, so you wouldn't cling to the notion that someday your father would come for you, that someday your father would realize what he was missing and come back into your life. I knew better, Rich. He was just a boy himself. He wasn't ready to be a father. He disappeared before you were born and I never saw him after that. He never once asked about you or supported us in any way. For all intents and purposes he might as well have been dead."

"But he isn't? How do you know?"

"He came to Mr. Chaubere's house yesterday."

"He did? My father came to the house?"

"Yes."

"Why?"

"To see you. But, why, I'm not sure."

"He came to see me?" Rich jumped to his feet. "And you didn't let him?"

Olivia remained seated, even though she wanted to grab Rich and hug him to her breast, afraid that this new information would create an unbreachable rift between them. But she was afraid if she reached for him, he'd bolt. Torn and apprehensive, she watched him pace the edge of the blanket. "I couldn't let him see you until we had this talk, Rich. Do you understand that?"

"No!"

"Rich, we have to be careful in dealing with your father. Maybe he's changed, but maybe he hasn't. I need to find out why he's looking for you after all this time before I'll trust him."

"Maybe he just wants to know what I'm like!" Rich retorted. "He's my dad after all!"

"Yes, he is. But don't pin all your hopes on him, Rich, that's what I'm trying to tell you. There's a lot of difference between a dad and a biological father."

"I can make up my own mind!"

"I'm sure you can. But you don't know him like I do."

"If he was so bad, why did you marry him then?"

"He wasn't bad. Just irresponsible and not the type of man for me. I was young. I thought I loved him."

"And you didn't?"

"I thought I did. But I didn't know what love was then, Rich. Neither of us did."

Rich stood at the edge of the blanket for a long moment and then threw his half-eaten apple slice in the river. "What's his name anyway?"

"Boyd Williston III. He comes from a wealthy family in Seattle."

"You mean my real name is Rich Williston?"

"No. Your real name is Richard Travanelle." She returned her uneaten sandwich to the bag. "By the time you were born, your father was away at college and I had divorced him. The Willistons were quite against you being born in the first place, so I had no intention of giving you their name. I gave you one that's been in my family for hundreds of years, and changed mine at the same time."

"Do I look like him?"

"No. You favor my side of the family."

"Do you think he'll come back again?"

Olivia recalled Boyd's angry parting words, that she hadn't seen the last of him. "Yes, I think he will. But I'm not going to let you see him until I know what he's up to."

"But I want to see him!"

"Rich, trust me, it might not be a good idea."

"He's my father!" Rich cried.

"Rich!"

He glared at her and then dashed off. Olivia ran after him and spent the better part of an hour searching for him. She finally found him in a tree along the riverbank and convinced him to return to Charleston with her. She dropped the remnants of their lunch into the bag and stuffed the blanket under her arm. Rich stomped across the lawn ahead of her, climbed in the van, and refused to talk with her the rest of the afternoon.

*   *   *

When Olivia turned onto Myrtle Street and drove toward the Chaubere House, she spied the same blue sedan from the previous morning parked out front. No one sat in the car. Was Boyd looking for Alexandre or hanging around the carriage house? Her heart sank as she drove to the gate, stopped and opened it, and then climbed back in the van.

"Who's that?" Rich asked, nodding toward a man sitting in front of the carriage house door in the dying light of late afternoon.

Olivia surveyed the tall form and blond hair of the man as the sunlight streamed over him. He raised a hand to shield his eyes and slowly stood up as he watched them approach.

"Your father," she replied at last, rolling to a stop in front of the garage. She wasn't at all pleased to see him, for she wasn't prepared to face Boyd so soon after their discussion. But more importantly, she wasn't ready for Rich to see him. She turned to her son.

"Looks like it's out of my hands," she said. "If you want to meet your father, go ahead."

Rich scanned the figure of his father, his face drawn and serious but his eyes bright with curiosity. "Okay."

"Please remember what I told you." She reached over to touch his arm, but Rich was already opening his door to get out.

Olivia tried not to frown so she wouldn't unduly influence Rich's first meeting with his father, but found it difficult to pretend that she wasn't upset. She grabbed her purse and the picnic bag and slipped out of the van.

"You must be Richard," Boyd said in a voice that was overly loud and full of forced friendliness. Olivia watched Boyd extend his hand. Hesitantly Rich reached out and shook it. But afterward he stepped back to keep his distance and studied his father without the slightest hint of emotion on his face.

"Do you know who I am, Richard?" Boyd went on, chuckling nervously.

"You're my father." Rich answered. "And the name's Rich."

"Sorry!" Boyd laughed again. "I wasn't quite sure what your mother called you." Boyd glanced at Olivia and then back at Rich, his face flushed. Obviously Rich's reserved behavior surprised Boyd, who had probably thought his son would run to him with open arms.

Secretly applauding Rich's cool reception of his father, Olivia stood by, letting the conversation unfold without any intervention on her part. She had no desire to make the meeting easier for Boyd. It was his own fault if he couldn't connect with Rich, since he had never bothered to foster a relationship with his son until now.

After a moment of strained silence, Boyd slipped a hand in his pocket. "Say, where've you two been? I've been waiting here for over an hour."

"We were gone," Rich replied, his voice flat.

"Well, the wait was worth it, seeing you, Rich. You're a good-looking kid. But what happened to your eye?"

"Some kids at the bus stop beat me up."

"Really?" Boyd made a concerned face and put his hand on Rich's shoulder. He shot an accusing glance at Olivia. "I hope something was done about it, Olivia."

"We're handling it," Rich replied calmly and shrugged off his father's hand. Olivia wondered what he meant by that statement, but now wasn't the time to ask.

"Well, I bet you're one heck of a soccer player anyway."

"I don't play soccer."

"You don't?" Boyd chuckled nervously and Olivia could see worry flicker in his eyes. "I thought every ten year old boy played soccer."

"Not me. Mom can never get me to the practice games. She always has to work."

Boyd glanced at Olivia again. "Well, maybe we can do something about that, Rich. In fact," he said, reaching behind an azalea bush and lifting up a large shopping bag that Olivia hadn't noticed sitting there, "I've got something here that might set you on the right track." Boyd pulled out a black and white ball and tossed it to Rich. He caught it, but his expression didn't change, and he tucked the ball under his arm without a second glance.

"Thanks," he said.

Olivia watched him, well aware that Rich could have used a larger baseball mitt instead of a soccer ball.

"I've got some other stuff here, too." Boyd reached inside the bag. "SuperMario Land!" he exclaimed, holding up the small box. Rich accepted the software and smiled shallowly at the irony of the situation. His father assumed he owned a Game Boy, like most kids his age, when in fact he had rarely held one in his hands. The gift of a software disk wasn't much use without a machine to run it.

"And!" Boyd announced, too insensitive to comprehend Rich's tight smile. "How about this? A radio controlled helicopter!" He struggled to pull out a large carton and held it up for Rich's approval. "Pretty cool, huh?"

"Yeah." Rich nodded. Olivia's heart went out to him. Rich would have been delighted with the much smaller gift of a radio controlled car. He had asked for one repeatedly for Christmas, but she could never afford to get him a good one, and she knew Rich wouldn't be satisfied with a cheap version. If only Boyd had known, he might have won Rich over on the spot.

But Rich was not to be won over with gifts. She saw it in his expression and was proud Rich could see through Boyd's attempts to buy his acceptance.

"If you want, I could help assemble this copter," Boyd ventured.

"That'd be great," Rich replied. "But I've got some homework to do—"

Olivia stared at him in surprise, but quickly recovered, recognizing an excuse when she heard one. She stepped toward the door. "I hate to break up this chat, Boyd, but Rich and I have things to do."

"How about I take you and Rich out to dinner tonight? I could use the company."

"No thanks." Olivia unlocked the door to the carriage house.

"Come on, Olivia!"

"Perhaps some other time."

"How about you, Rich?"

Rich looked to his mother for a response.

Boyd threw up his hands. "I just want to get to know him, Olivia. That's all."

Olivia opened the door and looked back at Boyd. She'd hate herself if she thought she had ever denied Rich the opportunity to truly get to know his father. The choice was up to her son to accept or reject his father, and she knew how damaging it would be to project her past hurts and prejudices onto Rich's life.

"All right, Boyd. Tomorrow, though. Pick us up at six."

"I'll be here."

"We'll see you then."

"Just one more thing." Boyd reached into the bag and pulled out an expensive camera. "Would you take a picture of us, Olivia?"

Rich turned to Olivia with a grimace. She shrugged. "I don't see what harm it would do."

"Great!" Boyd snapped off the case while she put down her purse and grocery bag. Then Boyd gave the camera to her and stepped back, sliding his arm around Rich's shoulder. The boy held himself stiff, hands at his sides. "How's this?" Boyd asked.

"Okay." Olivia focused. "Say cheese."

"Cheese!" Boyd exclaimed and laughed as he squeezed Rich's shoulders. Rich pulled away as soon as the shutter closed and dashed for the door.

"Hey, Rich, don't forget your loot!" Boyd called after him while Olivia returned the camera.

"Oh, yeah." Rich pivoted and scooped up his gifts.

Boyd held the camera in front of him. "See you, Rich. Hope you like the presents."

"Yeah, thanks."

"I'll be back at six tomorrow." Boyd waved and walked off.

Olivia watched him go and glanced at Rich. "What do you think?" she asked. "Do you want to have dinner with him?"

He smiled bitterly and held up the SuperMario Land box. "Think if I go, he'd buy me a Game Boy?"

Alexandre stood at the door to the carriage house and breathed in the simple but heavenly scent of frying potatoes and onions. His stomach growled loudly and he glanced down at himself in shock. He hadn't heard his body make such a sound for as long as he could remember. With a painful twinge, his salivary glands surged into action, flooding his mouth. He opened the door to the bottom level, hoping his stomach noises would quiet down and not embarrass him in Olivia's presence. His body had already made life difficult enough for him in that regard.

The fragrant aroma grew more intoxicating as he ascended the stairs, and Olivia's musical laughter drifted through the evening air as he gained the landing. He didn't want to disturb Olivia and Rich, yet he longed to be part of their activities. Even though Alexandre knew he risked an inconvenient interruption of their supper, he knocked on the door.

Rich answered the door and grinned when he caught sight of him. Alexandre's heart lifted, for he valued the affection of Olivia's son, independent of his feelings for her.

"Hi, Mr. Chaubere!" Rich exclaimed.

"Good evening." He smiled and glanced across the living room toward the kitchen. A second later Olivia appeared in the doorway, a spoon in her hand, wearing a light blue blouse and denim shorts. She gave him a hesitant smile.

"Come in," she motioned with the spoon. "But I've got to get back to the potatoes."

"I just came by to see if everything was all right with you two."

"What do you mean?" Rich asked, shutting the door.

"I saw Mr. Williston lingering at the doorstep earlier. Is everything all right?"

"We're going to have dinner with him tomorrow," Rich replied. "But hang on. I've got to show you what he gave me. I'll be right back."

Alexandre paused in the living room while Olivia hung in the doorway of the kitchen. He could see that she was uneasy.

"I didn't mean to intrude on your supper," he explained. "I was worried."

"Boyd seems innocuous," she answered. "So far."

He stepped closer and lowered his voice so that Rich couldn't hear. "Olivia, if he threatens you in any way, you will tell me, won't you?"

"Thank you. I will." She glanced at the stove and then back to him. "Alexandre, I've been meaning to give you something."

"Oh?"

She hurried to the table by the door and retrieved an envelope, which she held out to him. "Mrs. Foster gave me this to give to you."

"Mrs. Foster?" He tilted his head, suspicious.

"Now before you get your hackles up, just look at it, would you?" She thrust the envelope into his hands. He opened it and slipped out the card.

"It's an invitation," he murmured, scanning the flowery script.

"I got one, too. It's for the Horticultural Society's Ball. Won't you go with me?"

"To a ball?" Alexandre's lip curled in disdain. "Certainly not."

"You don't have to dance. Just go as my escort. They're dying to meet you, you know. If you go, you could dispel a lot of rumors and I could make a lot of client contacts."

His eyes narrowed. "Dispel a lot of rumors? What rumors?"

She glanced at him, and he could tell she wished she had been more careful in choosing her words. Then she turned toward the kitchen. "You'll have to excuse me— the potatoes are about to burn."

Alexandre followed her into the kitchen. "What rumors, exactly, Olivia?"

"That you are some sort of weirdo."

"Perhaps I am."

She shot a glance over her shoulder and grimaced in disagreement. "You're no more a weirdo than I am," she retorted. "But if you can't bear the thought of appearing in public, don't bother. I'll go by myself."

She stirred the potatoes with agitated strokes. Alexandre watched her, contemplating his decision. She'd probably attended most functions in her life alone. Why would one more make a difference to her? And yet the ball would give him the opportunity to pamper her, perhaps take her to dinner, and share a few hours of pleasure with her before he left Charleston altogether.

"I'll think about it, Olivia."

His stomach growled again. She glanced at him and he excused himself.

"Hungry, Mr. Chaubere?"

"Actually, I believe I am."

"Why don't you stay and have dinner with us?" She stirred the contents of a large skillet. "As you can see I misjudged the quantity. I've made enough food for an army!"

He gazed at the pan, fighting the urge to step up behind her and take her in his arms again, as he had done in the garden yesterday. She looked delightfully feminine in her shorts and sandals with her hair pulled back in a simple knot. He longed to push his nose into her fragrant curls and feel her soft body melting into him. He wanted to hold her, he wanted to eat the food she prepared with her own hands, wanted to hear her laugh with Rich, and see her gaze grow heavy with desire for him as it had the last time he had embraced her. Alexandre stuffed his hands in his pockets.

"I don't wish to impose," he replied, hoping to be overruled.

"It wouldn't be any trouble. But it's just going to be eggs and potatoes—nothing fancy."

"It smells wonderful!"

"Then stay." She smiled at him over her shoulder.

He felt his heart swell at her open friendly expression. "All right. Thank you."

A moment later, Rich returned from his room with his arms full of toys.

"Here's what my father just gave me," he declared. "Wait until you see this stuff!"

Alexandre tore his gaze and attention away from Olivia and allowed himself to be dragged into the living room. He sank to the cushions of the couch and watched Rich open a box. Dare he eat Olivia's eggs and potatoes? Yet, how could he not? He hadn't been this hungry for hundreds of years, in fact not since he could remember. Alexandre decided to quit worrying about the state of his health and focused on what Rich was saying instead.

16

A wave of pain passed through Alexandre's mid-section and he shifted on the couch in the carriage house. After a wonderfully relaxed dinner, he and Rich had read through the directions of the radio-controlled helicopter and set it up for take-off the next day. Alexandre suggested that he wait for his father for the maiden flight, but Rich brushed him off, saying it wouldn't matter if Boyd was there or not.

Olivia ventured out of the kitchen, wiping her hands on a towel. He remembered the way she had laughed and smiled at him during dinner. Something had changed in her. He could sense it in her more open manner and could see it in her eyes, as if a barrier had fallen and she was allowing him a view of her more natural self. He was anxious to speak to her alone, to ask her what had changed, and to try to explain his odd behavior in the garden. Yet he had no idea what explanation he would make for his lack of arousal. He simply couldn't tell her the truth—that he was a man who could live forever but was forever denied the normal male response to a handsome woman.

Alexandre felt himself flush. How could he be critical of Olivia's falsehoods when he himself had hitherto withheld important information? In addition, he hoped he hadn't been a complete bore at dinner when he'd recounted some of the Chaubere "family" stories, which of course were highlights from his own life during the last two hundred years he'd spent in America. He'd told them about his privateering days, when he'd been captured and thrown into Charleston's Provost Dungeon for a few weeks. He described his audience with Napoleon and showed them the watch he'd been given as a gift, explaining the engraved name inside as belonging to his namesake great-great-whatever grandfather.

Three hours later, Alexandre found himself sitting on the carriage house couch, fiddling with batteries in a child's toy, stuffed with Olivia's delicious meal, and gazing up at her. She stood bathed in the soft light of evening which diffused through the gauze of her wild red hair. Regardless of the unanswered questions between them and the increasing pain in his abdomen, he felt extraordinarily contented.

"Would you like a cup of coffee or tea, Alexandre?" she asked, breaking him from his musings.

"Thank you, no." Another wave of pain, like heartburn, tore through him. Damn! What had possessed him to eat, and to eat as much as he had? He should have known better than to overeat after having consumed nothing more than mouthfuls of food over the last few months. Judging by the way he felt, he might pay a stiff price for the precious time he'd spent at Olivia's table.

Alexandre's vision blurred. He tried to stand, but his legs gave out under his weight, because his bones felt as if they'd melted.

"Alexandre!" Olivia lunged forward. Her red hair and blue blouse merged into swirling blobs of color.

"*Tiens*!" Alexandre gasped, trying to stand up again. He had to get away before Olivia and Rich witnessed the severity of his malaise.

"Mr. Chaubere!" Rich jumped to his feet. "What's the matter?"

The boy's hands caught his right arm and kept him from pitching forward. Rich's grip was surprisingly strong, and Alexandre made a mental note to tell the boy later that his strength was growing in many ways.

"What's happening?" Olivia cried, catching him around his torso as he staggered to his feet. "Is it your heart again?"

"No," he replied, barely above a whisper. Her light scent overwhelmed him, billowing in his head like a silken scarf in the breeze. She mustn't see him like this. And Rich—he couldn't display such weakness in front of the boy, not without scaring him.

"I must—" He hit the door and fumbled for the knob. "—I must get back."

"You'll never make it down the stairs!" she exclaimed, still holding him up.

"I have to," he replied, panting through the pain and the buzzing noise in his head. He was aware of Rich hovering behind him.

"Rich!" Olivia instructed over her shoulder. "Get the keys and the flashlight."

"Right!" He dashed off.

"Alex," she tightened her grip around him. "I can't get you down the stairs. You're far too big for me."

He gritted his teeth. "I'll make it," he replied. "Come."

Half-blind and staggering, he pushed through the door. Valiantly she sustained a good part of his weight as they struggled down the steps with Rich at their heels. As soon as they descended to the foyer, Alexandre realized he was going to be sick. He practically shoved Olivia away and lurched for the door and the outside air. Using the last of his strength, he reeled toward the bank of azaleas, leaned over them, and retched.

Olivia hung back, until she saw Alexandre's wide shoulders straighten slightly. What was wrong with him? It couldn't be the food, for neither she nor Rich were experiencing any stomach trouble. In fact, until just a few minutes ago, she had felt perfectly wonderful. With Alexandre at their table relaying his family history and Rich laughing and asking questions, all had seemed right in her world. She'd even forgotten about Boyd's looming presence. Why was it the good times with Alexandre seemed so fleeting and puzzling? And what was wrong with him that caused him such fits of pain? He probably hadn't seen a doctor since his last attack.

She and Rich guided Alexandre through the oleanders and around to the back of the mansion.

"Do you want to go to the lab?" she asked.

Alexandre shook his head.

Olivia hoped she could get him up the stairs. The huge mahogany staircase rose up to the second floor, daunting in its length. Rich valiantly supported Alexandre on the left while Olivia set her shoulder under his right arm and against his torso. They practically dragged Alexandre up the steps, huffing and gasping for air by the time they reached the top.

"Do you know where his bedroom is?" she panted.

Rich nodded toward a gloomy hallway on the left. "Down that way, I think,"

"*Oui,*" Alexandre added weakly.

"Shine the light in that direction, Rich," Olivia

instructed, taking stock of the hall before them. "Okay, run ahead now and open the door."

She swayed under Alexandre's weight, surprised at the load Rich had obviously supported during the trip to the house and up the staircase.

"Can you make it?" Alexandre questioned.

"Yes."

He shuddered and clamped his teeth together to keep them from chattering. She could feel the heat from his body flooding out of his skin and the damp folds of his shirt clinging against the planes of his body. He had to be suffering from a fever, but she'd never seen one come on this suddenly. The sooner she could get him in bed and under some blankets, the better.

They stumbled down the short hallway and passed through a door into a large chamber, furnished with a pencil post bed, an armoire, a wing-back chair near the fireplace and a plain side chair against the wall, but nothing else to soften the starkness of the huge room.

"Pull down the sheets," Olivia said. Rich obeyed immediately and watched with eyes huge with worry as Olivia guided Alexandre to the bed. He collapsed upon the mattress with a burst of air, too weak to pull his feet onto the bed or take off his shoes.

Olivia bent to the task, slipping off his finely-made loafers and easing his legs toward the center of the bed. Alexandre shivered violently. She was alarmed to see how pale he'd grown. In the dim light of the room, the white rectangle of his face glowed against the linen pillowcase. Olivia placed her palm on his forehead.

"You're burning up," she remarked tersely.

His eyes remained closed while his lips parted slightly and his breath rasped through his teeth.

"Have you gone to a physician? Is there any medication you need to take?"

Alexandre shook his head slightly.

"What's the matter with him?" Rich asked, hovering at her elbow while she carefully draped the sheet and comforter over Alexandre's prone shape. "Does he have the flu or something?"

"I'm not sure. But I'm not leaving until I know he's okay."

"Me neither," Rich put in solemnly.

"I'm going to see if I can find something to bring down his fever," Olivia said, brushing the hair out of her eyes. "The kitchen has to be downstairs somewhere."

She held her hand out for the flashlight. Then she scanned the room, searching for a light switch, but found none. She couldn't believe it. But then irrefutable proof met her eyes as the flashlight beam glinted off a brass candleholder on a nightstand near the head of the bed. Beside the candle was a box of matches.

"Light that candle, Rich," she said, "And I'll take the flashlight with me."

Rich jumped to the task, always eager to use matches with his mother's blessing. He was also anxious to participate in any important task, and few were as important as helping Mr. Chaubere. The flame caught and held, throwing a flickering, eerie glow across the bed, a much more vibrant illumination than the steady beam she held in her hand.

"I'll be right back, Rich," Olivia said. "Call out if he gets any worse."

Olivia hurried out of the master bedroom and retraced her steps through the dark corridor, down the wide staircase, and turned to the central hallway that led to the front of the house. Shrouded by the black organdy veil of twilight, the house seemed far older to Olivia than she had previously thought. What had appeared gracefully aging in the daylight took on a haunted, sinister aspect at night. She took careful steps down the hall, directing the beam of light into the nooks and crannies around her, chiding herself for being frightened in Alexandre's house, but inspecting her shadowed surroundings all the same.

One by one she poked her head into chambers off the hall, only to find them unused and festooned with dust and cobwebs. Most of the salons were furnished with splendid pieces of furniture upholstered in brocade and velvet, the walls hung with huge paintings in gilt frames, the windows draped with yards and yards of now fragile silk. One touch and the draperies would probably disintegrate. She could almost picture Marie Antoinette floating across the floor, flitting her fan and trilling French witticisms. Yet Marie Antoinette and her court were long since dead, as dead and silent as the air in these closed-off rooms. It oppressed her, like the air of a tomb.

Olivia quickly closed each door and hurried away, all of her senses on edge. The floor creaked beneath her feet and something moved on her left. With a gasp, Olivia lunged backward, throwing the light to the left, half-expecting to see a ghost or a household servant Alexandre had failed to mention. She was surprised and a bit chagrined to find her ghost was nothing more than a grandfather clock whose door had swung open. Rattled and grinning foolishly in relief, Olivia stepped forward and closed the door on the old clock.

She shook her head at her own temerity. How could an inanimate object such as this house unnerve her so thoroughly? She should concentrate on Alexandre, suffering upstairs in his bed, and find the kitchen instead of allowing her imagination to run wild.

With new resolve and firmer steps, Olivia explored the north portion of the first floor. She found a large coat closet, a dining room with nothing but a huge dusty table in the center, and after another few steps down the hall, she found a pantry. The shelves were empty except for a carton of candles and a tin box decorated with faded rose decals popular before the turn of the century. Curious, she opened the box and found more matches. She returned the lid to the box and looked around, hoping to find some aspirin, but not expecting any success. Alexandre obviously kept no extra supplies of food on hand, for he didn't like visitors and probably never entertained. She wondered if he ate most of his meals in restaurants.

Olivia closed the door on the pantry and opened the next one, sure that the kitchen had to be on the other side. Her assumption proved correct, but the kitchen was no ordinary one. The room was one of the dustiest in the house, with cupboards closed upon stacks of china and filmy glassware. She could see where someone had walked through the dust on the plank floor to a cupboard. Olivia followed the faint tracks and pulled open the door, surprised to find a partially filled bottle of mineral water and the shriveled wedge of a cut lemon—the remains of the drink Alexandre had offered her in the garden days ago. Why hadn't he put the items in the refrigerator? She shined the light around the hoary room and found no refrigerator or stove—no modern appliances whatsoever. A sink of sorts sat below a window, but instead of a faucet a huge black pump handle rose up on the right, like a giant chess piece.

Olivia leaned back against the edge of the counter, unmindful of the dusty line she'd get on her clothes. How could a person live in a house and never use the kitchen? Not even for breakfast? Or for making coffee? Didn't Alexandre ever want a midnight snack? Amazed, she gaped at the abandoned room. Like a rumor that couldn't be squelched, Mrs. Foster's words came back around, filling her head and filling the room.

"Do you believe in vampires, Olivia? I'm not saying he is, I'm not saying he isn't. I'm just saying I can't explain what goes on over there."

Olivia shook her head, trying to dislodge such preposterous thoughts. Just because the man never used his kitchen didn't make him a vampire. He had odd habits, that was all, and she couldn't condemn him for that. What she couldn't explain, though, was why had he became ill after eating dinner with them, why he suffered such terrible attacks, and why she rarely saw him during the daylight hours.

Suddenly the thought of Rich alone with him upstairs hit her full force. She blanched, struck by the thought that Rich might be in danger, and that she had left him alone up there. Yet, how could she think such heinous things about Alexandre? So far he'd done nothing to cause her to distrust him. But what if it were all a ruse to earn her confidence, to lure Rich and her into his clutches, and then swoop in for the kill?

Olivia rubbed the back of her neck, unwilling to jeopardize the safety of her son or herself, but equally unwilling to believe Alexandre capable of deceit or malevolence. Alexandre had done a lot for her and Rich, and she intended to allow him to explain himself before she made any kind of decision. Even more, she was falling in love with him, monster or not, and couldn't turn her back, especially when he was suffering. Whatever he was, a vampire or just an eccentric scientist, she'd at least stay by his side until he recovered. She cared about him too much to walk away.

With shaking hands, Olivia opened cupboard after cupboard until she found a basin for water and a clean cloth. Then she struggled with the pump, pressing it down time after time until the muscles burned in her arms, wondering all the while if the pump were still connected to a

source of water. Finally the pump coughed up a thin red-
dish stream. She kept pumping until the stream turned
clear and strong. Then she filled the basin, dropped the
towel in the water, and carried it to the second floor.

When she arrived, Alexandre's hair was damp with
sweat. Rich stood near him and glanced up af his mother
in concern, his features starkly outlined in the candlelight.
"He's been saying all sorts of stuff," Rich reported. "But
mostly in French. He's been calling your name a lot,
though, Mom, and asking you not to leave him."

Olivia was thankful that the darkness hid her flush of
pleasure at hearing such a sentiment. What else had
Alexandre said about her? "He must be delirious," she
replied, sitting down on the mattress, "and talking nonsense."

Alexandre muttered a string of unfamiliar words and
tossed his head back and forth. Beads of sweat popped
out on his forehead and upper lip. Olivia squeezed out the
cloth and gently wiped his face. He grew quiet for a few
moments, as if the cool water gave him some relief. Then
he thrashed even harder, forcing Olivia to stand so he
wouldn't dump the water.

"Hold this for a minute," she said, handing the basin to
Rich. "I'm going to get the chair."

She tried to lift the wing-back chair so as not to scratch
the oak floor when she moved it, but the chair was too
heavy. Instead, she lifted the weight off the two front legs
and carefully slid it close to the bed. Rich gave her the
basin, which she settled in her lap. Then she took
Alexandre's right hand and bathed it, pushing up his sleeve
and sliding the cloth up and around his forearm. She
couldn't help but notice the sinews of his arm, the cords of
veins from elbow to wrist, and the fine bones of his slender
fingers. His were the hands of a gentleman with his
tapered fingers and clean nails—the hands of a sensitive,

thoughtful man. But the lines of his forearms and biceps spoke of the strength of an athlete, and the set of his jaw defied all notions of a sensitive nature. Such a mixture of characteristics were more than a little intriguing.

She put the basin on the night table beside the candle and stood up. "Rich, help me take off his shirt, would you?"

"Okay."

"I'll lift him up while you pull it off his arms."

"All right."

Swiftly Olivia unbuttoned his loose white shirt and pulled the tails out of his trousers. Then, straddling his lean hips, she pushed her arms around him and hoisted him forward. He babbled incoherently and dropped his face into the small of her shoulder. Before she could stop him, he began kissing her neck and fumbling for her breasts. Olivia blushed, hoping Rich couldn't tell what was happening.

"Pull his shirt off," she gasped, fighting a quick surge of arousal that bloomed in her as Alexandre's hot lips pressed into her neck and his damp hair tickled her throat. Though his loins remained unresponsive to the nearness of her, there was no mistaking the arrangement of their intimate position. A faint throbbing pulsed between her legs, but she managed to ignore it because of Rich's presence in the room and her worry for Alexandre.

"Why is he kissing you?" Rich questioned, staring at her.

"He's out of his mind," Olivia stammered. "He probably doesn't even know who I am."

"Olivia!" Alexandre moaned, making a liar of her as soon as the words were out of her mouth.

"Just get his shirt off!"

Rich tugged at the cotton fabric and crawled onto the bed to complete the task, which proved difficult because Alexandre kept wrapping his arms around Olivia. He was heavy in her arms, and she wasn't certain how long she could hold him upright. Finally Rich yanked the shirt free and scrambled off the bed, holding it up like a prize.

"Got it!" he exclaimed.

Olivia smiled at him and gratefully lowered Alexandre to the bed. She glanced at Alexandre's supple torso, smooth and gleaming in the candlelight, his shoulders intoxicatingly wide, his abdomen seductively lean and muscled. Olivia let her gaze travel over his beautiful figure. Upon closer inspection, she noticed scores of little scars on his skin, and a long vertical one where she was certain Jimmy Dan Petersen's knife had ripped his flesh a few weeks before. How could he have healed so quickly from a wound that had produced such a large scar? And what kind of life had he led to sustain so many injuries?

"Mom?"

She heard Rich's voice, but for a moment she remained numb to everything in the room but the mystery of Alexandre Chaubere and the way her body longed to lay upon his. His feverish skin would be hot—a furnace of heat—and smooth, like marble left all day in the sun.

"Mom?"

Olivia snapped out of her daze. "Yes?"

"What should I do with his shirt?"

She glanced around the room and spotted the straight-backed chair near the armoire. "Just put it on that chair over there."

She knew she should get out of the bed and away from Alexandre's body, but she lingered a moment longer while Rich carried the shirt across the room. Olivia closed her eyes for an instant, imagining what it might be like to make love to this man, and knowing she would probably never find out. Still, she couldn't deny that she wanted him, and it took every ounce of her willpower not to sink down upon Alexandre and kiss his beloved body, his scarred and feverish skin.

Hours later, Olivia jerked awake after a terrible dream in which Rich stole Alexandre's Spider and crashed it into Boyd's blue rental sedan. She sat up, rubbing the side of her neck which ached from her uncomfortable sleeping position in the wing-back chair, and glanced at Alexandre sleeping peacefully in his bed. The room was bathed in shadow, and the house made no sound whatsoever, poised on the cold quiet line between darkness and dawn. She glanced at the sputtering candle, halfway spent, and then at her watch. Four-thirty.

Olivia rose, twisting the cramp out of her back. After Alexandre's fever had broken around one o'clock in the morning, she had collapsed in the chair. Three hours of sleep had passed like three seconds, and she was weary and sore. Rich was bunked in the ballroom down the hall, having gone back to the carriage house for his alarm clock and sleeping bag earlier in the evening. She hadn't wanted him to be alone in the apartment, especially with Boyd in the neighborhood, but had sent him from Alexandre's lighted bedroom so he could get some sleep.

She padded down the hall to make sure Rich was safe and sleeping soundly and then returned to the master bedroom. Sighing, Olivia sank to the edge of the mattress to check on Alexandre. She touched the back of her hand to his forehead to confirm his fever was gone, but her hand was cold and she couldn't be sure of an accurate reading. Instead, she leaned over him and lightly lay her cheek against his skin, just above his brow.

Satisfied that his temperature remained normal, Olivia slowly sat up. Knowing she was alone and he was asleep, she let her gaze languidly travel up his bare chest, along the strong cords of his neck, over his sharp jaw line, his obstinate mouth, and determined nose, drinking in the sight of him. She loved to study him and had spent hours during the night just watching him sleep. But her slow perusal changed to shock when she looked up to find his black eyes open and gazing right back at her.

"Alexandre!" she gasped, embarrassed to have been caught staring at him. She pulled back, intending to jump to her feet, but found she could go nowhere.

His hands had wrapped around her wrists like iron bands.

17

"*Olivia,*" *he rasped.* "Don't go!"

She quit pulling at her bonds for a moment, until she could determine the state of his health. "Are you all right?"

"Much better," he replied, "But thirsty as hell."

She glanced at the bottle of mineral water she had retrieved from Alexandre's kitchen and he followed her line of sight. As if he read her mind, his hand loosened on her left wrist. She slipped from his grip to reach for the bottle. Alexandre pulled himself to a sitting position and accepted the bottle to lift it to his lips. Closing his eyes, he drank greedily, but never once loosened his hold on her right arm.

"Not too much," she warned. "It might make you sick again."

He lowered the bottle and sighed. "Thanks," he said, his voice much stronger this time. He stretched to replace the bottle on the nightstand. The covers fell away from him and she couldn't help watching the play of muscles over his ribs as he extended his arm and then sat back again.

Alexandre leveled his eyes upon hers. "You're cold as ice, Olivia."

"It got chilly last night." She refused to look down at his chest again. "But I was afraid to leave you."

"You woke me up with those icicles you call fingers."

"I'm sorry."

"I'm not. Come here."

Before she could move away, he grabbed her left hand again, and in a surprisingly subtle movement pulled her down to the bed while he scooted sideways. She rolled onto her back in the warm spot he had just vacated, and an instant later found herself half covered by his chest and thigh.

"Alexandre!" she gasped in alarm. Yet even as the protest slipped out, she realized she appreciated the cloud of heat from his bed and body. He fluffed the coverlet around them both, disregarding the fact that she still wore her sandals, and brought the covers up to her chin. "Ah!" she added, her voice trailing off. She had to smile as the chill melted out of her. His left arm remained draped across her and she felt her breast tingle in anticipation of his touch. She couldn't believe she lay in his bed as though it were the most natural place to be.

He looked down at her, his eyes dancing. "Better?" he asked.

"I'm getting warmer," she replied

"Good." His eyes grew more serious. "And I thank you, Olivia, for coming to my aid last night."

"I worry about you when this happens. What's wrong with you?"

"Whatever it is has passed." He pulled his arm down and eased his hand slowly across her chest. She closed her eyes and held her breath, while his strong fingers combed her nipple and then pushed the fullness of her breast upward and into his palm. Every cell on the surface of her skin cried out to be caressed by him, to be stroked, to be kissed. But she couldn't allow herself to get aroused this time, not until she knew why he refused to surrender to his feelings for her.

"Alex," she mumbled, reaching up to push him away. "We've got to talk—"

"Not now, *ma petite*," he whispered, "not now."

"But, Alex—"

"Let's enjoy these few minutes together without thinking of anything else."

"How can we?"

"By concentrating on the here and now. Only you. Only me."

In another smooth movement he reached under the coverlet, peeled off her sandals, and dropped them to the floor. Then he slipped his arms around her and brought her to him, enfolding her in the blazing curve of his chest and shoulders. She snuggled against him, giving up her fight to resist him just long enough to partake of his glorious heat. She pressed her cold cheek upon the planes of his chest and curved her arms around his torso. His skin was as hot and smooth as she had imagined and unusually taut. Alexandre was all muscle and sinew, as sleek and strong as a big cat. She closed her eyes, reveling in the strength of him and the comforting way he had wrapped her in his arms.

"Alex," she began, "I—"

"No protests, Olivia." His warm breath in her ear spread tingles up and down her spine. "No have-tos, *ma petite*, no shoulds, just want-tos, eh? What do you want me to do?"

She turned her head just enough until their mouths

were inches apart. She gazed up at him, certain her eyes burned as intensely as his.

"Tell me, Olivia," he whispered, his eyes never wavering. "What do you want?"

"I want you to kiss me."

"Granted, and with much pleasure." His expression softened and his head lowered to hers with unbearable, aching deliberation. She tipped her chin to hasten the meeting of their lips, and her mouth came up against his. His lips pressed into hers with lingering sweetness and then she felt his mouth opening, slanting across hers, and his strong warm tongue pushing into her. Olivia moaned, swamped by the sudden desire to consume Alexandre in every way possible, and took him in, drawing her hands up on each side of his jaw. He crushed her to him, and his kiss hardened. She had never known such ardent kisses, such passion in a man. He kissed her eyelids, cheeks, the tip of her nose and chin, and then along her jaw line and down her neck until she abandoned her vow to remain unaroused. All too soon, however, he rose up, his cheeks flushed.

"Enough?" he asked, his eyes glinting.

"Hardly!" She stared at him. "Is that it?"

"It is but the beginning." He smiled, and the left corner of his mouth pulled up in a rakish grin. "But you must ask me now what *I* want."

Olivia felt a thrill zip through her. "What *do* you want, Alexandre?"

As if considering his answer, Alexandre let his gaze travel across her forehead, down her nose and over her mouth. The tension between them stretched to the breaking point. Then he slowly raised his regard and looked her in the eyes. "I want to taste your breasts, Olivia—your creamy silken breasts."

He paused after each word in the last phrase, watching the blush she felt spreading across her cheeks. "How do you know they're creamy?" she countered to hide her nervousness.

"I have imagined them so. Am I wrong?" He raised an eyebrow and smiled at her. "Well?"

"You may find out for yourself." She sank back upon the pillow.

He gazed down at her. "Only if you will take pleasure in the discovery."

"I'm certain I will." She couldn't help but smile back, even though her senses screamed at her to slow down. She hadn't been naked in the sight of a man for ten long years, and thought she would die from sheer anxiety.

With maddening precision, Alexandre unbuttoned the front of her blouse. Olivia watched his fingers work the fasteners and couldn't help noticing the rise and fall of her own chest. Her breath came hard and fast, and her breasts seemed to swell in anticipation. Boyd had never been like this, so deft and unhurried, and she had to admit that as the moments lengthened, her desire for Alexandre heightened in response. This man knew what to do with a woman, how to play her, tease her, and set her on fire. She swallowed, no longer thinking of her nakedness, and hardly able to endure the time it would take until his mouth lowered to her aching breasts.

Alexandre folded back the front edges of her unbuttoned blouse, from her waist up. For a moment he surveyed her lacy bra. Then he kissed the buds of her nipples through the thin fabric, pushing his wet tongue against the lace. Gasping in delight, Olivia arched upward. Alexandre took the opportunity to slip his hands behind her back and unhook her bra. Gently he urged her even higher off the mattress, and with a smooth movement, he slipped off her bra strap and the shoulder of her blouse, first the left side and then the right. Olivia felt cool air pass over her bared flesh and attempted to lie back, but soon lost all thought as his hands spread over her shoulder blades to hold her in the air like a plate of ripe fruit before him. She let her head fall back upon the pillow. He could do whatever he liked to her, for whatever he did, she knew it would be exquisite.

"I was right," he murmured. "You're like ivory, all warm and smooth."

She closed her eyes in ecstasy. Nothing she had ever experienced had prepared her for this moment. He kissed her, licked her, and then sucked at her nipple like a child while shafts of longing coursed from her breast to her womb, bursting deep inside her in nearly unbearable waves. Olivia squirmed and moaned, and plunged her fingers into his soft brown hair, pinning his head to her and caressing the back of his neck. She wanted to give him everything, anything—anything he wished.

Alexandre bit her, lightly at first and then harder until she gasped with shock and wonder. She went rigid, unable to take a breath, and her hands grabbed fistfuls of the sheet as his lips and teeth took her far beyond her wildest imaginings. Her universe shrank to the single world of his mouth and her breasts.

Breathing heavily, Alexandre moved on top of her, covering her with his hard heavy frame, and pressed her lips in a most savage, uncivilized way. She thought the bed would burst into flames with the heat of their hunger. Olivia felt his hips surge against her thigh, pressing into her soft flesh, as he sank his face into the small of her shoulder with his chin locked against her collarbone. She knew what he wanted, and she wanted it right back. Olivia was wet with desire, and ran her hands over the tight mounds of his rear. She reached around and could feel the effects of arousal in him, though not as much as she had expected. He tensed.

"*Mon Dieu!*" Alexandre gasped.

"It's my turn again," she panted, still barely able to breathe because of his weight but hoping he would pin her down forever. She was ready with her second request—that he make love to her, passionate, lingering love that would last for hours. Olivia ran her hands up his back and felt his spine stiffen.

He raised his head, and she saw regret smothering the fire that had raged in his eyes moments before. What was the matter?

"Olivia, no. I never meant to take it this far before I—"

"Before you did what?" she asked, incredulous but aware that his demeanor signaled another retreat. She was mortified. He had brought her to the brink of surrender again only to reject her once more. What was wrong with him? With her?

Olivia couldn't look at him, afraid he'd see how much he had hurt her. She had to pretend it didn't matter, that she had harbored no expectations, that she could choke back her hunger for him in a matter of seconds just as he could deny his own.

"Olivia, there is something you must—"

Suddenly a harsh metallic clanging ripped through the early morning air. Alexandre reared up and rolled to a sitting position while the noise stopped as abruptly as it had begun. "What the devil was that?" he demanded.

"Rich's alarm clock. He's in the ballroom." Olivia scrambled away from him, partly out of alarm, for Rich would appear in the master bedroom any moment, and she didn't want to be found half-dressed. But mostly she fled from Alexandre's crushing rebuff. She didn't want to hear his explanations, his excuses, or look into his eyes. She felt like a fool and stung from the way he'd toyed with her emotions to see how far she'd go. She'd go all right. She'd clear out of his room so fast it would make his head swim.

Olivia snatched her bra from the floor and stuffed it into the pocket of her shorts. Then she yanked on her blouse and stabbed her arms through the sleeves, hurriedly buttoning the front with angry jerks. Not once did she glance at Alexandre. She didn't want to see the bastard ever again.

"Olivia, it's not what you think—"

"I need to get Rich off to school," she said.

"Olivia—"

She ignored him and pushed her feet into her sandals. Then she swept up the flashlight and strode away.

After Olivia left the house, Alexandre dragged himself out of bed. He'd made a mess of things. Why had he kissed her in the first place? Yet, what man could have resisted the temptation to pull her into his arms? He was human after all, perhaps not an ordinary human, but a man never the less. Alexandre padded to his armoire and threw open the left door, revealing a mirror on it's interior side. He pulled off his jeans and glared at his body, staring at his damnable cock. Miraculously it had stirred to life while pressed against Olivia, but just barely—certainly not enough to do justice to his feelings for her.

She'd run out of his room, her face flushed, and her shoulders stiff with anger. What woman wouldn't be upset by his lack of response? Alexandre rubbed the back of his neck, upset and frustrated. In the old days he could last all night and had brought much pleasure to his women. They'd whispered in his ear that he was the best lover they'd had, that he was the most wonderful man they'd ever taken to their beds. Yet, now, when he longed to give his love to the most important woman in his life, he couldn't manage more than a half-hearted erection. How could he explain his body's failure to act? He couldn't tell her the truth, and anything else would sound equally preposterous. Besides, he didn't want to lie to Olivia.

Swearing and scowling, Alexandre dressed. Now more than ever he must stay away from her. He couldn't take the chance of hurting her any more than he'd done a few minutes ago.

Though Alexandre was in a mood more foul than an offshore squall, he forced himself to go down to the lab. Dejected and out of sorts with himself and the world, he took a blood sample and sat down to screen it. Just as he suspected, he could not find a single immortal platelet. Making love with Olivia, or as close as he could come to the act, had dropped the cell count of the sample to zero.

Alexandre charted the results and sat back down on his stool. He dropped his head into his hands with his fingertips over his ears and stared at the black counter top until his vision blurred. Just as he'd theorized, his physical well-being was linked to Olivia. It was doubly imperative that he stay away from her. The task shouldn't be difficult. He'd seen the hurt surprise in her face and then the hard look of recrimination. Olivia would probably never speak to him again.

That evening, six o'clock came too swiftly for Olivia. She barely had time to run in from the garden, shower, and change before Boyd showed up at the door with flowers for her and a carton of baseball cards for Rich. During the entire drive to the restaurant, Rich sorted through his cards while Boyd tried to make small talk. Olivia sat in the back, thankful she wasn't required to participate. She was tired from her scant three hours of sleep and miserable from her morning with Alexandre. Try as she might, she couldn't keep him from creeping into her thoughts. She played the bedroom scene over and over again in her mind, trying to figure out why Alexandre had pulled back. Yet try as she might, she couldn't explain the sudden shift from his ardent kisses and warm embraces, to the tense, reluctant person he'd been right before the alarm clock went off. Dejection pressed down upon her like a black cloud. She worried she'd burst into tears at any moment, and kept her lips tightly pressed together and her gaze on the old houses along the street. But she saw nothing of the scenery except Alexandre's haunting face.

"Where are we going?" Rich finally asked.

"A place that comes highly recommended. Edward's."

"Do they have burgers at Edward's?"

"No." Boyd chuckled. "No burgers tonight, Rich. We're celebrating. It's champagne for your mom and me and lobster all around."

"I've never had lobster," Rich replied.

"You'll love it!" Boyd slapped his son's leg.

Olivia stared out the window, disgusted with Boyd's display of forced gaiety.

"What are we celebrating?" Rich asked.

"Being together, Rich. Just being together, the three of us."

Olivia frowned. There would never be such a thing as "the three of us". She'd straighten Boyd out on that point as soon as got a chance to talk to him alone.

All through dinner, Olivia worried that she'd fall asleep and drop her head in her food. She was conscious of Boyd's low tones as he told Rich all about growing up in Seattle, and all the things they could do together if Rich lived in the Northwest.

"Wait a minute," Olivia countered. "We're not about to go back to Seattle. I'm going to attend college in the fall in Charleston, and Rich has made friends here."

"He can make new friends in Seattle."

Olivia glared at him and was thankful that Boyd dropped the subject.

By the time the meal ended, Boyd had fallen silent, having depleted all the subjects he commanded for a one-way discussion with his son. He tried to interest Olivia in a chat but she answered him in monosyllables and then asked to be taken home. She was too tired to last any longer, even though it was only nine o'clock.

Silent, Boyd drove them back to the carriage house, taking the narrow twisting streets far too fast, throwing Olivia against the door a few times and bringing back memories of his reckless driving. He hadn't changed. Boyd dropped them off at the end of the drive.

As Olivia stepped up to the gate to open it, she heard Boyd roll down his window. "I have to return to Seattle for a few days," he called out. "But I'll be back by the weekend. We can talk then."

Olivia paused and turned slightly. "About what?"

"About Rich. About you."

Olivia put her arm around Rich's shoulders. "There's nothing to talk about."

"Oh, but there is. I can offer a lot to Rich, more than you'll ever be able to give him. You know that as well as I do."

Olivia flushed with anger, wishing Boyd would have been sensitive enough to make such a remark in private, not within earshot of Rich. She felt her son tense up beneath her hand. Damn Boyd and his thoughtless comments. How secure would Rich feel after hearing such a remark?

"Come on, Rich," she said.

"Don't think you can keep him all to yourself, Olivia!" Boyd called out behind her, making the situation even more unsettling for Rich. "I've got legal rights as his father, and you know it!"

"What's he talking about, Mom?" Rich asked, pulling away and gazing up at her with worried eyes. His look confirmed her fears that Rich doubted the security of his place with her.

She turned to him. "Custody. But don't you worry, Rich."

"Olivia!" Boyd shouted, obviously peeved that she was walking away without responding to him.

She pushed open the gate and walked through, refusing to give Boyd an answer, and closed it without glancing back at his car.

Rich walked alongside her, not saying a word. But she noticed he inspected the Chaubere house as they crunched up the gravel drive. Just before they reached the carriage house, he stopped.

"Do you think Mr. Chaubere is home?" he asked. "There's a light on in his lab."

"Maybe. But it's late, Rich."

"We never flew the copter this afternoon. You think he forgot?"

She glanced at the mansion, her heart heavy with guilt, knowing full well her trouble with Alexandre was the reason for his absence. "Maybe something came up, Rich."

His shoulders sagged. "I thought he'd at least tell me. I waited for him for an hour."

"Rich," Olivia slipped her arm around his shoulders again. "I know you like Mr. Chaubere, but he's got his own life to lead. Remember that. Don't get too attached to him, or you'll only end up disappointed."

She stepped into the foyer with him, knowing she was speaking less to Rich than to herself.

The rest of the week dragged by. Minutes seemed like days, days like months. She worked like a fiend to try to outdistance her aching heart. Fired by anger and resentment and with no interruptions by Alexandre or Boyd, she made incredible progress. She cleared the weeds from the reflecting pool, removed the silt and distributed it along the side garden, and checked for leaks. Finding none, she refilled the pool, and was gratified by the sparkling change the clean water lent to the front garden.

A few times in the evening on her way back to the carriage house, she caught a glimpse of Alexandre standing in a window, or walking from his lab to the garage, but she quickly averted her gaze. A pall of silence surrounded the house, as if a force field had risen between them, and she didn't intend to breach it. But in her weak moments she wondered who suffered more from their refusal to talk—her or Alexandre.

On Friday, she arranged for a crew of men to move the statue from the rear garden to the front, near the reflecting pool. The task took most of the afternoon. Olivia held her breath as the wrapped marble was hoisted off the ground. If anything happened to the Venus, she would never forgive herself. The statue, like the Ming vase, was irreplaceable. She orchestrated each move, every turn, and watched in concern as the forklift slowly rolled down the drive, through the break in the shrubbery, and across the tilled soil to the pond. There they placed the marble statue in the spot she had prepared, just in front of a stone wall deliberately constructed to appear old. The movers offered to unwrap the Venus, but Olivia replied that she wanted to do it herself.

By the time the crew left, the sun was melting behind the house. Olivia returned to the reflecting pond. The sight of the water soothed her and she felt her troubles fading as she approached the statue.

"New digs, old girl," she commented to the statue, stepping up to pull off the masking tape and burlap. "And I think you'll like the view."

"Undoubtedly," a male voice replied behind her.

At the sound, Olivia whirled around, her heart pounding wildly. There in the shadows of a rhododendron stood Alexandre.

18

"*You startled me!*" Olivia said, gasping.

"*Pardon,*" Alexandre replied, bowing slightly. "I did not mean to."

Olivia pulled at the masking tape, determined not to let his presence fluster her, and did her best to ignore him. She heard him step up behind her.

"Olivia, please don't turn away from me."

"Why not?" she answered sharply, without looking at him. "You turn away from me with amazing ease."

"Why do you assume it is easy for me to step away?"

"Because you've done it every time that we've, that we've—" She broke off, struggling for the right words. "—well, you know what I mean!"

She continued to unwrap the Venus, concentrating on keeping her hands busy and her emotions suppressed. All the while she was acutely aware of Alexandre's presence just beyond her right shoulder.

"I hope you understand," he said at length, "that my turning away during those instances was anything but easy."

He waited for her response, but she kept her mouth shut and continued to yank at the tape.

"Olivia, why won't you talk to me?"

"Why should I?" Her words rang with disappointment and pain she could no longer hide. "What do we have to say to each other?"

"Plenty. You know that as well as I."

Olivia yanked at the burlap, too blinded by the tears welling up in her eyes to see what she was doing. At his last few words, a thousand questions sprang to mind, but she bit them back, refusing to encourage him and court more heartache.

"You were the one who pulled me into your bed," she declared. "It's not like I jumped in."

"I got carried away. You have that effect upon me, you know."

"Do I?" She shot a hot glare at him and then threw a wad of burlap toward the pile of the packing material on the ground, but missed, which made her even angrier.

Alexandre reached down and tossed the rag onto the mound of coarse brown fabric. Then he straightened. "People like us don't have to base their friendships on activities in the bedchamber."

"That's fine and dandy if friendship is all you want." Olivia turned slightly. "But you could have fooled me! And I'm not the type of person who likes to play games, Alexandre."

"Nor am I."

"Then quit playing with me!" She whirled back to the statue and grabbed the tape with both hands. Most of the burlap covering had been removed, revealing the serene face of the Venus. Olivia couldn't look at the statue's mocking, unperturbed features without feeling like an idiot for allowing her emotions to boil over and get the better of her.

"It's not a matter of playing, Olivia. I told you once I was not like any man you'd ever met. And it's true."

"What are you saying?"

"I'm saying that friendship is the best we can expect to have together."

She balled up a length of masking tape. She wanted to know just what type of medical problem he had, but wasn't certain if Alexandre felt comfortable discussing his physical limitations. So she let the question die and continued to squeeze the ball of tape between her hands.

"Olivia?"

She looked up.

"Is the prospect of friendship with me that disappointing?"

Olivia studied his pale worried face. Mere friendship with Alexandre would devastate her; she knew that as surely as she knew the sun would come up in the morning. How could she tell Alexandre that she wanted everything with him, that she didn't want to hold back her desire for him to the level of friendship, that she might not be capable of repressing her love for him. Yet what positive outcome would there be in speaking the harsh truth? He only wanted to go so far with her. She would either have to take it or leave it. As he had told her before, the decision was hers.

"Why should I be disappointed?" she said at last, as the hard grip of logical resignation locked around her heart. "You're leaving soon anyway, aren't you?"

"In a few weeks."

She nodded, confident she could maintain a pretense of friendship for a few weeks.

"However, if you still plan to attend the Horticultural

Society Ball tomorrow night," he continued, "I would be honored to accompany you."

His offer genuinely surprised her. "Really?"

"Yes. Perhaps dinner beforehand?"

She paused, wondering what it would be like to spend time in public with Alexandre. The townspeople would be shocked to see him. What with stares and whispers all around them, she and Alexandre might not have a moment's peace—although solitude with Alexandre Chaubere was a danger she knew best to avoid. "All right," she answered. She could allow herself to look forward to an evening with him in the limited setting of a social affair. "That would be nice."

"Excellent. I shall call for you at five."

The next day Olivia worked until noon. Then she took a quick shower and dragged Rich downtown to help her find a dress. She had nothing appropriate in the way of evening wear, and her usual simple black dress wasn't good enough for a society "do." Rich protested that he hated shopping, but Olivia didn't feel safe leaving him alone because of Boyd's unsettling visit earlier in the week. She offered to make the trip short and buy him a late lunch. With the promise of food, Rich's attitude improved. They rushed through a few shops, and finally settled on a sale item—a midnight blue silk dress with a sash on a dropped waist. Even Rich looked twice when she modeled the outfit. Olivia quickly ran through a mental list of her personal belongings and decided her navy pumps and zircon earrings and bracelet would do to accessorize the outfit. She purchased a fancy pair of navy silk stockings and then they hurried off for lunch at Harry's.

Late in the afternoon she dropped Rich off at Willie Lee's house across town with a couple of videos and a bag of junk food for late-night snacks, and then sped back to the carriage house. Frazzled and keyed up about the night to come, Olivia slipped into the bathtub at four o'clock and tried to relax. She shut her eyes and eased back, but visions of Alexandre leaning over her and kissing her filled her thoughts. He would always fill her thoughts.

Alexandre stepped out of the shower in his lab where the only running water in the mansion was located. He rubbed himself dry, shook back his mane of wet hair, and wrapped the towel around his hips, just as he heard the lab door open. He glanced up in surprise, doubtful that Olivia would burst in unannounced, and aware that Rich wasn't home. To his relief he saw Gilbert close the door behind him.

"*Bonjour*, Gilbert!" Alexandre called, picking up his clothes and smiling broadly.

"*Tiens*, but we are happy," du Berry replied, "as happy as a shark, *non*?" He wore navy slacks, a light blue shirt, and an expensive gold bracelet on his left wrist. "What happened to the tortured Alexandre Chaubere I have come to know and love?"

"He's changing. Let me show you something." Alexandre clutched his towel at the waist and strode toward his microscope. He threw his clothes on the counter and picked up the graph where he had recorded his blood cell counts for the past few months. "Take a look at this."

Du Berry leaned over the paper and pursed his lips. After a moment he turned to Alexandre. "I am hopeless with such scribbling, *mon ami*. You must explain to me what it means."

"I've been keeping track of the number of immortal platelets in my blood. See here?" Alexandre pointed to the portion of the line that represented the previous autumn when he had first drunk the elixir. "Last fall my blood was full of immortal platelets. That's why the line is way up here on the graph."

"Ah," du Berry answered, nodding.

"See how the line gradually goes along without much change until February 10th, when it begins to dip downward?"

"What happened on February 10th?"

"Madame Travanelle interviewed for the gardening job."

Gilbert's glance darted up to Alexandre's and then back to the graph. He followed the line with a manicured nail. "And here, on February 18, what happened then?"

Alexandre peered at the graph where it plunged dramatically downward. He thought back to February 18, which had been a Friday, the day Rich had been beaten by his classmates. He passed the rest of the events of the day through his mind—his discussion with Rich, the argument with Olivia near his car, and the words they'd shared late that evening in the garden. Friday had been the first time he'd kissed her.

"I spent most of the day with Olivia and her son, in one fashion or another," he explained.

"And look at February 19," du Berry continued. "Another turning point."

Alexandre reviewed Saturday in his mind. Boyd had arrived that day. After Williston had left, he had taken Olivia in his arms and tried to comfort her with another heartfelt kiss.

"Since Olivia's arrival in Charleston, my cell counts have continued to improve. Look there, Gilbert, at yesterday's platelet counts and today's."

"None?" du Berry raised his eyebrows and scanned the graph again. "Can this be true?"

"Yes!"

"But," du Berry let the paper fall to the counter top. "What does it mean?"

"That I've found the antidote in the lily elixir, just as I had theorized. However, there is one drawback."

"And that is?"

"The success of the antidote is linked with Olivia Travanelle."

"How?"

"I'm not sure. Some chemical reaction within my body takes place when I'm around her. That reaction, plus the daily intake of the Everlasting Lily, has practically rid my system of the immortal platelets."

"Are you becoming a mortal, then?"

"I'm not sure. But I've experienced hunger, du Berry."

"Did you eat?"

"Yes. Unfortunately, I didn't keep the meal down. But I've continued to eat small portions of food all this week and haven't become ill."

"So!" du Berry studied Alexandre, as if to detect a physical manifestation of the changes taking place inside him. "Is that all?"

"I had a partial erection a few days ago."

"What?" du Berry's mouth fell open. "*Incroyable!*"

"*Sans char.*"

For a moment they grinned at each other.

"How are you feeling otherwise?"

"That's the puzzling part. Sometimes I feel great. And sometimes, du Berry, I'm sure I'm going die." He grabbed his clothing and headed for the staircase at the back of the lab, which led up to the pantry on the first floor. Du Berry trailed after him.

"You think the way you are feeling is tied to your beautiful gardener?" du Berry asked.

"Undoubtedly. I believe her presence is hastening the

effects of the lily, perhaps far too much. I've had some serious attacks, Gilbert. You haven't seen the worst of them."

"And these attacks didn't occur until she came into your life?"

"Not with such severity. "

"So the lady is killing you?"

"It is a possibility."

"Is this not what you wanted—to die?"

Alexandre paused on the stairs and studied his friend. "Yes. It *is* what I wanted, at least last fall. But now that I have met Olivia, I long for a life with her, at least a few years. But the way my health is declining, I doubt I'll last a fortnight."

He turned and hurried up the stairs, trying to outdistance a feeling of self-pity and despair that he normally wouldn't countenance in himself.

Du Berry accompanied Alexandre to his bedchamber. "What will you do about this, Alexandre?"

"Continue with my initial plan and go to South America."

"And if you find you cannot live without her?"

"Physically?" Alexandre opened the door to his bedroom. "Then I shall die and be done with it."

"And emotionally?" du Berry inquired. "What does your heart have to say about this?"

"I can't indulge my heart in this matter."

"Hmmm." Du Berry's voice faded as he sank down upon the wing-back chair, while Alexandre searched through his armoire for something to wear.

"Where is it that you are going?" du Berry asked, crossing his right leg over his left and making sure the crease of his slacks wasn't destroyed in the process.

"A local club's annual ball."

"*Vraiment?* Why was I not invited?"

"You must not be a member of the Charleston Horticultural Society."

"And you are?"

"No," Alexandre said, pulling on an ecru-colored shirt. "but I support a valuable member of their league."

"As in our little shepherdess?"

"Her name is Olivia." Alexandre buttoned his shirt. "You offend her when you make light of her, you know."

"Women these days!" Du Berry clucked his tongue and shook his head. "They are so sensitive to every little thing, every little jest."

"Perhaps they're through pretending our jokes amuse them."

"It was never my intent to be cruel, merely to tease."

Alexandre frowned, more at himself than du Berry. "I've discovered some women tire of trying to find a difference between cruelty and jest." He reached into a small drawer for his favorite pair of cuff links—sapphires set in gold—a prize he had taken at gun point from a vicious British admiral during the American's Revolutionary War.

"Enough of women, Alexandre. What are you wearing?" Du Berry rose from his chair.

"This silk dinner jacket," Alexandre replied, slipping the cream-colored garment from the rack and holding it up to view.

"Acceptable. What trousers? Tie?"

Alexandre showed him the articles of clothing and watched a grimace pull down the corners of du Berry's mouth.

"Not that tie, *certainement*. It's ancient. And those trousers, Alexandre, they are the wrong color." He stepped forward and Alexandre backed away, knowing du Berry couldn't resist the challenge of selecting the proper dress for him. Saints knew he could use the help. He pulled on a pair of socks while du Berry sifted through his wardrobe, shaking his head and heaving hopeless sighs.

A half hour later, Alexandre slipped his wallet inside the pocket of his jacket, picked up his car keys, and walked down the stairs, confident that he looked as good as possible, his limited wardrobe notwithstanding. He had never been a clothes horse, even in the old days when he maintained a busy social life and multiple residences throughout Europe. Du Berry had claimed it was nearly impossible to make do with Alexandre's sparsely stocked closet, and then later had remarked with an enviable sigh that some men could look attractive, no matter what they wore.

Descending to the lab where his phone was located, Alexandre dialed the number for the carriage house and waited for Olivia to answer.

"Hello?" Her husky voice floated seductively over the phone line.

Alexandre closed his eyes and let the sound seep into him before he answered. "Olivia, this is Alexandre."

"Oh, hello." Her tone changed, became lighter.

"Are you ready to go?" he asked, wondering what she looked like in something other than casual summer clothes.

"Yes." She paused. "Is something wrong?"

"Not at all. My friend Gilbert just stopped by. You remember him, do you not?" He heard her take in a long breath and smiled, imagining the scowl that must be crossing her pretty face.

"Of course."

"We thought we'd have a nip of brandy on the piazza. Would you care to join us?"

"If I wouldn't be intruding."

"Not at all. Come to the lab. I'll meet you outside."

"All right. Bye."

"Good-bye."

He knew he shouldn't indulge in his feelings for Olivia,

but he couldn't help anticipating the coming hours with her. Just the thought of her sent a delicious wave of desire through him, which had a slight but undeniable effect on his loins. He'd have to concentrate on other things if he was to survive the evening without embarrassing the both of them. Alexandre smiled, feeling like a schoolboy again, and not minding it at all. Just for tonight he'd pretend there was no end in sight to their relationship. He wouldn't think twice about leaving Charleston, or dying, or never seeing Olivia again. Tonight he would put all that aside and enjoy the time he had left with her.

Alexandre locked the outside door of the lab and slowly ascended the steps. Beyond the stone arcade lay the rear garden, bereft of the Venus. The garden seemed bare to him, but soon he wouldn't be around to notice. And before long, Olivia would finish the transformation of the entire yard, increasing the value of his home to prospective buyers, not that it truly made much of a difference to him. A movement near the oleanders caught his attention and he turned to see Olivia gliding toward him. Alexandre paused, appreciating the graceful way she walked in her high-heeled shoes, and the way the heels accentuated the feminine lines of her ankles and calves. She wore a dark dress that hugged her slight curves to perfection, and a bracelet that defined the delicacy of her wrist. In the dying afternoon light, her dark red hair, loose and luxuriant, flamed gold and carnelian. He breathed in, unaware that his feet still touched the ground, and held out his hand.

"Olivia," he said, slowly raising her hand to his mouth. "You look *magnifique!*"

"Thank you," she replied. Her glance took him in and then centered on his mouth. Her lips opened almost imperceptibly, showing the barest ridge of her teeth, as she waited for him to kiss her fingers. He did so, fighting the urge to pull her into his arms as a strong rush of desire

swept over him. Tonight would be special; he was certain
of it—if he could just keep his head.

"Come. I'll show you to the piazza." Lightly he cupped
her bare elbow and guided her up the back stairs, his
palm buzzing where it made contact with her skin. He
hoped Gilbert had finished cleaning the long-abandoned
piazza, enough to at least make it presentable.

He and Olivia didn't speak as they climbed the stairs.
He opened the door for her and she passed into the main
hall, her dignified beauty strangely suited to his home.
For the first time in his long life in Charleston, Alexandre
imagined a woman in connection to his house, and knew
that Olivia Travanelle was meant to be the mistress of
these rooms. His heart swelled, but he immediately
stepped forward to put aside the unbidden emotional
response. There would be no mistress of the Chaubere
House. There never had been one and there never would
be one. He knew better than to entertain such nonsense.

"This way." He led her up the second flight of stairs,
down the hall to the front of the house, and through the
doorway of the piazza. At their appearance, du Berry
turned and his face lit up with a surprised smile.

"Ah!" he exclaimed. "Madame Travanelle. *Enchanté!*"

"*Monsieur,*" she replied.

"A lovely dress," he remarked, clasping his hands
together under his chin. "Simply *exquisite.*"

"Thank you."

Alexandre strolled to the small table where du Berry
had set out a bottle of cognac and three snifters. He
poured them each a portion of the thick amber liquid, and
then offered one to Olivia.

"Thanks," she said, glancing at Alexandre with eyes full
of warmth. He returned the smile and motioned toward a
white wrought iron chair which du Berry had managed to
wipe clean. The disrepair of his piazza was lost in the

dying light. Unkempt details were granted grace by the forgiving haze of dusk, and for that he was grateful. He took great care of the possessions that meant something to him, such as his car and his scientific equipment. But until this moment, the house had meant nothing more to him than a place to sleep. Now he saw it as a place to shelter Olivia, a place to gather with friends and enjoy the evening—a place to fill with light instead of shadow. He gave a drink to du Berry and then lifted his own.

"A toast," du Berry declared, raising his glass. "To the wonderful garden. *Voilà!*"

Alexandre shifted his gaze to the grounds two stories below, to the gleaming rectangle of the reflecting pond, to the luminous statue glowing at the far end where it could be seen from the house and glimpsed from the street, to the peace and beauty Olivia cultivated in his yard as well as in his soul.

"To the garden," he added.

"To Charleston," Olivia put in with a smile. "Such a lovely city."

They clinked their glasses together. Alexandre knew that Charleston was a lovely city, but only through Olivia's eyes had he rediscovered the charm of his longtime home. Because of her friendship, he was becoming what he hoped to be—more in tune with the world around him and the people that inhabited his sphere. She might very well be bringing death much closer, but she had certainly brought life and light to his dark world. He longed to tell her what she had done for him. Painfully aware of the heartache involved should he put thought to word, Alexandre tore his gaze away from her beautiful ivory face and glanced at du Berry instead. Obviously he had not been able to conceal his feelings from Gilbert, for his friend caught his eye and slowly, sadly shook his head, warning Alexandre to guard his secrets well.

19

Olivia sat back and watched Alexandre sign the credit slip for dinner, appreciating the slender lines of his hand and the deft way he wrote his name. Comparing her dinner with Boyd to this repast with Alexandre was like comparing poplin to velvet. Boyd had been stiff and proper, struggling for topics of conversation and abrupt with the waiters, while Alexandre was relaxed and elegant, his excellent manners impeccably invisible, and completely at home in the crystal and linen surroundings of the French restaurant where they had spent the past two and a half hours. He ordered their food in French and charmed the stuffy waiter until the man was smiling and friendly by the time he returned with their appetizers. Over the course of the evening, they chatted their way through slivers of duck, butter lettuce, miniature vegetables, lamb and rice, and a wonderful bottle of pinot gris, most of which Olivia was sure she had imbibed, judging by the glowing feeling inside her.

Her misgivings about appearing in public with Alexandre were dispelled by the discreet employees of the restaurant. The wine steward and waiter treated them with special care, as if they could sense the attraction buzzing between Alexandre and Olivia and wished to foster their budding relationship. Though Alexandre hadn't eaten very much and hadn't said a single word regarding his feelings during dinner, his eyes continued to hold a conversation with her on another level, letting her know that he found her compelling and fascinating, and was so absorbed by their conversation that he was oblivious to the rest of the people in the room. Olivia had never felt so pampered, so happy, or so alive.

Never once had Boyd made her feel as special as Alexandre was this evening. Alexandre didn't even have to speak. He simply had to look at her, his eyes smoldering. Yet, they spoke of everything over dinner—of Charleston, of Rich, of her hopes and dreams. She bubbled over with conversation as years of silence and the lack of a confidante fell away. Alexandre listened and chuckled, told his own stories, and nodded his head often. He seemed just as eager to talk to her, and she listened intently to everything he said. As she sat there with him, she realized this was the way it should be between a man and a woman, intimate and supportive, a glorious give and take of views and philosophies between the sexes.

Perhaps she'd been wrong to hinge everything on his lack of arousal. There should be more between a man and a woman than making love, and tonight Alexandre was showing her just how amazing a male/female connection could be. She might have been too hasty to run from him, too quick to label his behavior as rejection. Perhaps his problems were medical and out of his control. In her own hurt, she had been cruel to him.

After dinner, Alexandre walked her to the car. He

offered his arm and she curved her hand around his biceps. Alexandre gently pulled her closer as they strolled in intimate silence down the walk to the parking lot. Olivia felt warm with the wine they'd enjoyed, warm with the attention and care this man showered upon her, and bathed in the balmy breeze that fluttered in the palmetto trees.

"Thank you for the marvelous dinner, Alexandre," she said as they approached the Spider.

"It was my pleasure," he replied. "Entirely."

Suddenly he paused near a rhododendron bush and slipped his free hand into the curls of her hair. Before she could reach for him he leaned down and pressed an impassioned kiss upon her lips. Then he straightened.

"Off to the ball then?" he asked, his voice husky.

She lay her palm on the side of his face and his long dark hair rippled over her fingertips. For a long moment he gazed at her, his nearly black eyes glinting in the darkness. Could he be longing for complete privacy with her as much as she yearned for it with him? Friendship be damned. All she wanted was to end the evening with Alexandre, naked in his arms, no matter what else happened or didn't happen between them later. "Must we?" she asked softly.

"We can't disappoint Mrs. Foster."

"All right," she murmured. Then she raised an eyebrow, mimicking his usual expression. "But the night is young."

"Indeed," he replied. Smiling, he opened the car door and helped her inside. She sank onto the leather seat, lolling her head back against the headrest, awash in the magic.

The ball was held in the assembly room of the Exchange Building a few blocks away. Alexandre parked on the street and guided Olivia up the stairs toward the hum of voices and the throb of music. Everywhere they looked people stopped to watch them pass by. Some stared openly at Alexandre, but most of them smiled as she and Alexandre walked by arm in arm. Was it obvious she loved him? Could they tell? It seemed likely, judging by the pleasant expressions on the faces of the people who turned to look at them. Most of the crowd passed by in a big blur, however, for she was preoccupied with Alexandre's wry comments in her ear, and the sensation of his strong shoulder close to her cheek. She felt proud to be on his arm, for he was by far the finest looking man in the room and more than likely the kindest.

"Olivia!" a familiar voice called out, bursting her delicious bubble.

She turned and spotted Mrs. Foster mincing toward them.

"Olivia," Mrs. Foster repeated, beaming in delight. "And Mr. Chaubere! Why, I am so gratified you could attend our little get together."

Alexandre bestowed a slight bow upon her.

"The decorations are lovely," Olivia commented, glancing around at the festoons of netting sprinkled with real flower blossoms.

"Do you like it?"

"I've never seen anything so beautiful!"

She looked at Mrs. Foster to find her inspecting Alexandre. The older woman tilted her head.

"Would you care to dance, Mr. Chaubere?" Mrs. Foster asked.

Alexandre began to protest, but Olivia slipped her hand away from the crook of his arm, sure that one dance with the mysterious Alexandre Chaubere would make up for a lifetime of curiosity for Eugenia Foster. "Go ahead, Alexandre," she urged. "I need to freshen up."

She left without waiting for a response and glanced back just long enough to see the eager glow of anticipation on

Mrs. Foster's face. Olivia slipped through the milling crowd to the hallway beyond. She hoped it would lead to the ladies' room, but the hallway intersected with another corridor. She bore to the right and found herself in a meeting room with a long table and countless chairs. She was just about to turn around, when she caught the reflection of the hallway light on someone standing near the adjacent wall. Startled, Olivia pulled back sharply, surprised to discover a man lurking in the shadows. Something was odd about him, and she quickly deduced the man couldn't be standing on the ground, for his head was at too great a height for a normal man.

While her heart pounded in her throat, Olivia swept the wall beside her, frantically trying to locate the light switch. She felt the familiar cool switch and she flicked on the lights, ready to dash backward if necessary. Much to her chagrin, she saw she'd been looking at a painting, a life-size portrait of a sailing man from another century, judging by his clothing and the ship in the background. Shaking her head at her high-strung reaction, she stepped closer to see more of the man who had nearly frightened her to death. She was thankful she hadn't cried out in alarm, for if she would have screamed, half the town of Charleston would have come to her rescue, only to learn what an idiot she was. Olivia chuckled to herself and glanced up at the man's face. The laugh died in her throat.

She was looking at a painting of Alexandre Chaubere.

"Wait a minute," she mumbled to herself. She edged closer. The man in the painting wore high black boots, doe-skin breeches, and a russet-colored frock coat trimmed with huge cuffs and gold buttons. A cascade of lace fell over the neckline of a velvet waistcoat, and a black tricorne was tucked under his left arm. He wore a rapier slung at his lean hips, a pistol stuck in a sash tied around his waist, and a silver watch hanging from a fob in his waistcoat. Olivia squinted at the time piece to see it in detail, and discovered it was exactly like the watch Alexandre had showed her and Rich a few nights ago. She glanced up at the man's face, a striking likeness to Alexandre Chaubere, except that this man's hair was drawn back and tied with a black ribbon. The black intelligent eyes, square jawline, and obstinate mouth and chin were exactly like his. The only thing different was a dark spot, most likely a mole, on the side of his neck, just above the white neck cloth. She didn't recall seeing a mole on Alexandre. Yet he always wore his hair loose around his shoulders, which concealed most of his neck.

In the background, Olivia could see a schooner in full sail, which the artist had labeled by painting a banner to one side. The *Bon Aventure*, the banner read. Wasn't the *Bon Aventure* the name of one of the model ships Alexandre had built? She glanced down at the bottom portion of the heavy gilt frame, to see if an identifying plaque had been affixed to it. Sure enough, she spotted a small brass tag. Olivia leaned over and read the words.

Capt. Alexandre Chaubere, 1795, Charleston, S.C.

Olivia straightened, hoping to find a reasonable explanation. Was this Alexandre Chaubere in the painting another one of her employer's namesakes? How many were there? Was every male member of the Chaubere family named Alexandre? Unease flared in her stomach as she studied the painting. There were so many things about Alexandre that were hard to explain—his eating habits, his peculiar malaise, his bare kitchen, his preference for the hours of night, his formal manners and old-fashioned speech patterns, and his strangely unchanged house, not to mention his sexual dysfunction. And precisely what relation did he bear to the man in the painting?

Mrs. Foster's words came back to her, in a haunting, disquieting refrain. *"Do you believe there are such things as vampires, Olivia? I'm not saying he is and I'm not saying he isn't. I'm just saying I can't explain what goes on over there."*

Olivia walked from the room and shut off the lights, her romantic mood tempered once again by Alexandre's mysterious character. She had allowed his charm and her desire for him to dull her perceptions, to blunt her wariness, when she should have been practicing extreme caution in dealing with him.

She found the ladies' room, touched up her lipstick, and returned to the dance floor, vowing to keep her head. She danced a few songs with a dapper elderly gentleman, chatted with some ladies about the cultivation of roses versus dahlias, and answered question after question about Alexandre Chaubere. Before she knew it, two hours had flown by. Every once in awhile she'd catch a glimpse of Alexandre standing on the sidelines. Sometimes she saw him talking with members of the horticultural society, and sometimes she looked up to see him regarding her, his eyes dark and serious. She knew she shouldn't avoid him all evening, and finally made her way slowly around the room to where she found her handsome escort standing near the punch bowl. Alexandre noticed the change in her immediately.

"Is something wrong, Olivia?" he asked, cupping her elbow in his hand.

To break from his light hold, she pulled away from him with the pretense of reaching for a drink. "We need to talk," she replied, picking up a dainty glass cup.

"About what?"

"You."

"Me?"

"Yes. I have some questions. I'm sure you'll have a reasonable explanation, but I need—"

"Yoo-hoo, Olivia!" Mrs. Foster called, pushing through the crowd. "It's time for the special event."

"Special event?" Olivia asked, her mind still on Alexandre, and not pleased to be forced to switch gears. She felt Mrs. Foster touch her arm.

"Your introduction!" Mrs. Foster replied. "And the formal award of your scholarship for autumn quarter."

Surprised, Olivia glanced at Alexandre. He nodded toward the dais at the end of the room where the band played.

"We'll talk soon," he said.

"Don't go anywhere," she replied, forcing a lightness she didn't feel into her voice.

"Don't worry. I won't."

"Oh, Mr. Chaubere, we want you to join us, too. I believe our president would like to introduce you as well, and have you say a few words."

"Words?" Alexandre's eyes hardened. "What about?"

"Your garden. Everyone's talking about it. I believe the city wants to offer you an official place on the Charleston tour of historic homes."

"Thank you, no." Alexandre bowed slightly. "It is not something I prefer."

"But it's an honor!" Mrs. Foster continued, flustered by his quick refusal. "And think of the publicity it will give Olivia when everyone sees her work."

Olivia glanced away, not about to ask any favors of Alexandre. She placed her cup on the table, highly aware that his gaze followed the movement of her hand.

"It would be a wonderful business opportunity for her," Mrs. Foster put in. "Don't you think?"

"Well," he replied, "for Olivia's sake, I will take it under consideration."

"Wonderful!" Mrs. Foster crowed. "Do follow me, then, you two. They're waiting for us."

While the president of the Charleston Horticultural Society droned on with his speech, Olivia stood on the dais beside Alexandre. She wondered how many people had seen the painting in the other room and if anyone made the connection between that Chaubere and the one standing before them. Yet the sea of faces below showed interest and goodwill, not suspicion, and lively applause followed each of their introductions.

Both Olivia and Alexandre were mobbed after the award presentation. She couldn't tell if Alexandre was amused by the attention or only put up with it. Side by side they stood, answering all kinds of questions and receiving countless invitations to dine with the best families in Charleston. The entire group seemed fascinated by Monsieur Chaubere, and everyone assumed that Alexandre and Olivia came as a matched pair, to be invited together, and treated as a couple. If Olivia had been feeling more confident about Alexandre, she would have welcomed the link between them, but she couldn't accept him as openly and easily as the townspeople, since her relationship with him went well beyond the occasional dinner party.

After an hour of constant talking, she felt Alexandre clamp her hand. Shocked by the unexpected heat of his fingers, she looked up to see the color had drained from his face. He glanced down at her, his eyes glassy and his lips white around the edges.

"Are you ill?" she asked, keeping her voice down so no one else could hear.

"I must leave," he said. "Now."

She saw a bead of sweat trickle down from his temple. The assembly room was hot, but not that hot. Had Alexandre's mysterious and sudden fever returned? Would he collapse on the dance floor? She had to get him out of the Exchange Building immediately, for she knew he'd be embarrassed to have all these people witness his illness.

Olivia snatched her award and purse from a nearby table and then curved her arm around his back. "Come on," she urged. "I'll help you to your car."

Mrs. Foster broke from the ring of onlookers. "Is something wrong?" she asked, her eyes wide circles of gray-blue.

"I'm afraid Mr. Chaubere's had a touch of flu lately," Olivia replied, guiding Alexandre toward the door. "He's not feeling well."

"Oh, dear!"

"Thank you for the wonderful evening. And please give our regrets to your president and his wife, would you? But I really have to take Mr. Chaubere home."

"Of course, Olivia." Mrs. Foster followed them to the door. "Oh, dear, Mr. Chaubere, I hope you're feeling better soon!"

"Thank you," he managed to reply. He grabbed the stair rail and Olivia noticed his knuckles were white.

"Good night!" she said, and guided Alexandre down the stairs. He swayed against her at the bottom, and she nearly toppled under his weight.

"Is he okay?" a white-haired gentleman inquired as he descended behind them. "Do you need some help?"

"We're doing fine," she said. "I just lost my balance momentarily."

"Let me get the door for you," the man said, reaching for the latch. "Too much champagne punch, eh, Mr. Chaubere?" He winked at them as Olivia helped Alexandre cross the threshold.

"Something like that," Alexandre replied, his words slurred as if he were indeed drunk.

Olivia struggled with him down the sidewalk to the car. With every step he became heavier, his breathing more labored, his face more pale.

"Alexandre!" she cried as he collapsed against the side of the Spider.

"You drive," he wheezed. His damp hair stuck to his cheeks and forehead. He pushed his hand into his pocket, started to cough, and then his legs gave out. With a muffled cry, he sank to the ground and rolled onto his back, unconscious.

"Alex!" She grabbed his arm and tried to pull him to his feet, but his dead weight was far too much for her to lift. She would never be able to get him in the car or back to the house.

By that time, a small crowd had gathered on the sidewalk behind them. She glanced over her shoulder, desperate and frightened. "Somebody call 911!" she shouted. "I think he's having a heart attack!"

Olivia sat on the edge of a chair in the emergency room of the hospital, staring at Alexandre and silently willing him to wake up. His pale stillness terrified her. He had awakened from his fever before, but this time he might pass out of her life forever, never to speak to her or look into her eyes again. She couldn't bear the thought. No matter what secrets Alexandre kept from her, she knew she loved him. There had been no doubt in her mind when she had watched him being lifted into the aid car, or now, when she watched him lying so still in the hospital bed. He had regained consciousness, enough to waylay fears of a concussion, but had once again slipped into unconsciousness. Olivia reached out and slowly caressed his forehead, smoothing back his damp hair and praying that he would survive this bout.

The physician on duty had ruled out a heart attack and then had disappeared when the victims of a multiple injury car accident had taken precedence over Alexandre's inexplicable collapse. The doctor had promised to return as soon as possible, but he'd been gone for nearly an hour.

Every once in a while a nurse would check on Alexandre, write on his chart, and hurry away, leaving Olivia to sit and worry, her hand wrapped around his.

Shortly after midnight, Alexandre stirred, startling Olivia out of her stupor. She jerked to attention and saw him open his eyes.

"Olivia?" he croaked.

"Thank God!" she exclaimed. "Oh, Alexandre!"

He looked around, squinting. "Where am I?"

"In the emergency ward at the hospital."

"Hospital? *Jamais!*" He threw off the sheet and blanket, and lurched to a sitting position.

"Alex, no!" Olivia jumped to her feet in alarm. Alexandre shouldn't try to move, much less leave his hospital bed.

"Why the deuce am I here?"

"You collapsed. We called 911. I had no choice. I couldn't move you!"

He glanced around the room. He looked terrible, with his wild hair and white skin. "Have any physicians examined me?"

"Not thoroughly. It's been too busy around here."

"Good. Where are my clothes?"

Olivia stared at him. "You can't leave!"

"I must!"

"You're sick! You need medical attention!"

"Nonsense." He pushed off from the mattress and slid to his feet. For a moment he stood there, squinting and clutching his forehead, too dizzy to take a step.

"Alexandre, please don't leave! You don't know what it's like seeing you collapse! It scares me! Something is dreadfully wrong with you!"

"That's my concern."

"Well, it's mine, too!" she retorted, her voice rising.

His bleary eyes met hers.

"I care about you," she continued, too ragged with worry and fatigue to keep from shouting. "Don't you know that? I care what happens to you. And I want you to find out what's wrong before it kills you!"

"Maybe there's no alternative but death."

"I don't accept that!"

"Once begun, some journeys are irreversible."

"What journeys!" she stepped toward him, her eyes blazing. "Why must you always speak in riddles? You say you're my friend. But you must not be—not if you don't trust me!"

"It isn't a matter of trust." He looked aside. "Now where are my clothes?"

She snatched them off the hook behind her chair and shook them in the air. "Here they are. And you're not going to get them back until you level with me!"

"Olivia!"

"Tell me, Alexandre." She backed toward the door until she felt the knob bump her in the back. "Tell me what the problem is with you, or so help me, I'll take these clothes and run!"

20

Alexandre sighed and crossed his arms over the blue and white hospital gown. "So, you threaten me, eh?" he asked. "Is that the way you treat a friend?"

"You aren't my friend! Friends trust each other."

"I trust you, Olivia."

"Bullshit!" She felt the familiar heat of anger spike up her neck. What was it about this man that made her lose control? "I know next to nothing about you!"

"Are you sure?"

"I don't know anything about your past, what you do for a living, who your friends are—nothing!"

"But are those things truly important, Olivia?" He took a step toward her, obviously recovering quickly. "What about kindness, understanding, and compassion? Have I not shown such qualities to you?"

"Yes, but—"

"Why must you know my past to trust the present?"

"Because there are things about you that are, that are—strange!"

"Strange?" He raised a brow. "Such as?"

Olivia frowned and glared at the ceiling, hardly knowing where to begin without sounding preposterous. She decided to state the most ridiculous claim and go from there.

"Well, for one thing, do you know what Mrs. Foster thinks you are?"

"I live for the woman's opinion of me," he drawled.

Olivia ignored his sarcasm. "She thinks you're a vampire."

"A *what*?"

"A vampire."

Alexandre stared at her, his eyebrows raised. Then they slowly lowered as he considered the words. Olivia had expected him to blurt out an immediate denial. Instead he confounded her by giving a thoughtful, "Hmmm. Why does she think that?"

"Because of your habits. You aren't seen much at all during the day. You don't produce garbage. You don't have a normal appetite for a man. And your kitchen, Alexandre—it's absolutely bare!"

"That makes me a vampire?"

"How do you explain it, then?"

"I have a limited diet. Whatever meals I choose to eat, I prefer to take away from the house."

"Every one of them?"

"My life is simplified by such a routine."

Olivia studied him, unconvinced by his calm answer. "What about your aversion to daylight?"

"Who said I disliked the sun?"

"You rarely are seen except at night."

"I simply prefer the evening hours. I am a private man, Olivia. You know that."

She narrowed her eyes. "I've seen your body, Alexandre. You're covered with scars. Everywhere. How did you get them? Explain that!"

"I've lived an eventful life." He ran a hand over his tousled hair, as if his explanation was enough to answer her question.

"All right." She gripped his clothes to her chest. "Then explain to me how you survived that knife wound?"

"You mean when Jimmy Dan Petersen tried to run me through?"

"Not *tried*, Alexandre, *did*. I saw that knife cut into you!"

"Are you certain?"

"Yes. You tried to convince me otherwise, but I know what I saw. And you healed just like that." She snapped her fingers. "That's not normal."

He nodded, apparently unwilling to deny her observation. His unruffled manner frustrated her.

"So?"

"I don't disagree," he replied.

"Then how do you explain the way you can heal?"

"I have an unusual physical makeup. That's why I don't want a doctor to examine me." He sighed when she continued to glare at him, waiting for answers. "First of all, a doctor wouldn't recognize what he's looking at, and second of all, I don't want to be the object of some scientific study—for that's what they'll do, Olivia, once they start probing and prodding. They'll hound me until I have no privacy left whatsoever. They'll make a medical sideshow curiosity of me."

"But why do you have an unusual physical makeup? What sort of man are you?"

"I'm a man. Let it end at that."

"No!"

"Why dig deeper, Olivia? You may learn something you wish you never had."

A wave of apprehension passed through her, but she quickly doused it. "I've never been afraid of the truth."

"But you've been known to twist it to suit your own use upon occasion."

"Not anymore, Alexandre," she replied, her voice softening to a tone just above a whisper. "No longer with Rich, and not with you." Her eyes locked with his, challenging him to confide in her and gambling on his need of her friendship to tell her the truth.

He gazed at her and his regard poured over her face until she was certain he was going to finally break down. He opened his mouth, licked his lips, and then sank to the mattress. "I have never lied to you," he said.

"But you haven't told me everything."

"I don't intend to, Olivia." He glanced up, hard and unyielding. "Perhaps some day. But not now. I'd like to, but I can't."

"Why not?"

"Because I don't know everything yet. I don't know the outcome, the possibilities, or the dangers."

"Of what, dammit?"

"Of my physical condition."

She closed her eyes and shook her head, no nearer to understanding him than she'd been at the outset of their discussion. Scowling, she opened her eyes and looked at him from the side.

"Alexandre, level with me. Do you have some kind of disease?"

"No."

"Maybe some kind of new virus no one knows about?"

"No."

"Then what are these attacks all about?"

"I'm not entirely sure."

"Don't you want to find out?"

"I'm working on it."

"But you're not a doctor."

He got back to his feet. "Why do you assume a doctor would know more about this than I do?"

Exasperated, she shrugged, tired of her questions being answered by yet more questions. She was ready to tell Alexandre that she'd had enough of their so-called friendship, yet she couldn't bring herself to say the words.

"Olivia," his voice grew softer behind her. "Something went wrong at the Horticulture Society Ball. Your attitude changed toward me. What happened?"

At first she considered not giving him an answer, but then she foresaw no positive results in withholding herself from him just because he wouldn't share himself. It wasn't like her to play such childish games. "I saw a painting," she replied at last.

"A painting?"

"Of you."

"Me?"

"Or someone who looked exactly like you with a mole on his neck, someone who had your name, your watch, and a ship just like the model in your house."

"I know of that painting. Why would it upset you?"

"Because of the questions I have about you!" She whirled, her anger flaring. "Because sometimes I wonder if you're a normal human being!"

"Olivia, that painting is two hundred years old."

"I know! I saw the date. 1795!"

"Surely, you realize that the subject of the painting was—"

"What? Another damned relative? Your great-great grandfather perhaps?"

"Olivia!" He stepped toward her as if to induce her to lower her voice.

She sidestepped, reaching for the doorknob behind her. "If you have so many damned relatives, why don't you tell me about them! What's the big secret?"

He glowered at her, his mouth set in a firm tight line.

"Maybe you *are* a vampire! Maybe you *are* two-hundred years old. Hell, maybe you're older than Moses! That would explain all your scars and your so-called *eventful* life!"

"Olivia!"

"Here's your damned clothes!" She threw his shirt at him. He let the shirt fall to the floor and took another step toward her. "Go ahead," she cried. "Leave the hospital! Why should I care what happens to you anyway!"

Tears of frustration pooled in her eyes. He didn't trust her enough to confide in her. He wasn't perceptive enough to realize how important it was for her to know him honestly and completely. Couldn't he see that his treatment of her made her feel untrustworthy and immature, like a child?

"Go back to your precious laboratory!" She swiped at her tears with the back of her hand. "Your computers and test tubes won't ask you any personal questions! You can handle them!"

She threw his pants as hard as she could, hitting him in the abdomen. Alexandre flung them aside and strode toward her, barreling down upon her like a locomotive, his face flushed. Olivia staggered backward, bumping into the wall beside the door, furious and alarmed by the fierce expression on his face.

He pinned her against the wall without laying a hand upon her, using the force of his personality to keep her captive.

"You want the truth?" he rasped through gritted teeth. "Do you, Olivia? Think you can handle it?"

Mutely, she nodded.

With his eyes locked on hers, he raised his hand and pushed his hair back from his neck. A mole, the size of a pencil eraser marked his skin between his ear and shoulder.

Olivia gaped at the spot, never having seen it before, not even when they had been in bed together.

"You saw the painting. Now you see the man."

She blinked, not believing her own eyes for a moment. What did it mean? What was he saying? What was he?

"Satisfied?" His eyes flashed at her, as black and hard as shards of coal.

Her first reaction was to bolt, to run away from him as fast as she could. But her heart made her think twice, kept her feet firmly planted on the floor, and her love for him made her body relax, and the expression in her eyes soften.

"Yes," she whispered. "I am."

He stared at her mouth and then deep into her eyes, his expression still hard. Then quite suddenly he turned to grab his garments, which he threw on the end of the bed. He ripped off the hospital gown and turned to face her.

"I'm not a man, Olivia. You're right. I'm a freak. Still like me?" He yanked on his trousers. "I'm three-hundred and fifty-four years old. I've fought in more wars than you've blown out birthday candles. I don't age. I can't be killed. The Exchange Building where we were tonight holds the Old Provost's Dungeon in its basement. I was jailed in it. Not some made-up long-lost relative. Me!" He thrust his arms through the sleeves of his shirt. "Most of my body is in a state of prolonged stasis, like hibernation—including my cock, which you've had the decency to point out to me on more than one occasion. And it's all due to that excellent member of the lily family, the *Lis Perpetual*. So you see, you'd best heed my warning about the plant, or you may end up immortal like myself, which, by in large, I do not recommend!"

He grabbed his shoes, snatched his car keys off the table by the bed, and stormed out of the room. Olivia stared at the open doorway, too flabbergasted to move.

Olivia took a cab home from the hospital, paid the driver, and slowly walked through the front garden of the Chaubere House, feeling shattered and alone. It was too late to pick up Rich at Willie Lee's house, and he wouldn't have wanted to miss an overnight stay anyway. She'd have to wait until a decent hour of the morning.

Even though dawn glowed on the horizon, the air still held the warmth of the previous evening, heralding a hot, humid day to come. Olivia paused at the statue and tiredly leaned her hip against the base. Beyond the gleaming length of the reflecting pond rose the mansion, dark and silent as ever. She wondered if Alexandre had returned home, or if she would ever see him again. She brushed back the tangle of her hair and noticed her hands were shaking. She'd been trembling since his confession at the hospital, for his words had shaken her to her very core.

How could she believe him? There was no such thing as an immortal, not any more than there were ghosts or angels or the Easter Bunny. Did he expect her to believe a man could actually live for three-hundred and fifty-four years? She had seen such preposterous claims in tabloids at the supermarket checkouts, but nothing compared with the outrageous words Alexandre had flung at her. What nonsense. He couldn't be killed. He couldn't age. Impossible!

With a jerk of indignation, she straightened and walked along the pool toward the side of the house, careful not to turn her ankles on the shrouded path. With every step she took, however, she thought of the strange aspects of Alexandre's life she'd uncovered in the past few weeks, all of which defied rational explanation. Though she couldn't accept his confession outright, she knew in a place deep within herself that no ordinary reasoning could apply to such an extraordinary man.

Olivia wished Alexandre hadn't stormed out of the hospital room without waiting for her response. He might have been surprised to learn that no matter who or what he was, she loved him. She'd love him for the rest of her days. Some men came once in a woman's life, and Alexandre was such a man for her.

Olivia poked her head around the corner of the mansion, peered through the shadows of the arcade, and looked for the light that might signal Alexandre's presence in the laboratory. The stairwell and windows were black. She sighed, wishing she could confront him before more time elapsed. Each day spent in silence would further drive a wedge between them.

After putting away her clothes and taking a shower, Olivia climbed into bed and lay atop the sheets, staring at the ceiling, wide awake. She'd hoped to spend the end of this night in Alexandre's arms. Instead, she was alone, more alone than ever before.

Alexandre didn't return to the house on Sunday. The garage remained empty, as did Olivia's heart. She worked, too distraught to interact much with Rich and incapable of relaxing. That night she fell into bed, exhausted but unable to sleep, listening for the quiet hum of Alexandre's Spider, but he never returned.

Rain fell lightly on Monday morning. After the showers let up, the day was filled with intense work, spent with a crew from a pruning service that she'd hired to trim the bigger trees. The job took all day. Olivia was grateful for the diversion, thankful to be surrounded by the easygoing, good-natured group of young men in their late-twenties. She returned their banter all day, went to lunch with them, and was sad to see them drive off just before dinner time.

After the crew left, Olivia returned to the front garden and sat on the side of the pool to rest for a moment before she returned to the carriage house to prepare dinner. Slipping off her work boots and socks, she dangled her feet in the cool water. The water soothed her. She closed her eyes and tried not to think about Saturday night. If she hadn't goaded Alexandre to the breaking point, he might still be talking to her. Yet, if she had kept her questions to herself, she would always have wondered about Alexandre and the doubt would have poisoned her feelings for him. In the long run, the truth was best, even if the truth still left many questions. She wasn't sure what she believed in regard to him. But she was glad he had begun to reveal himself and wished the circumstances had been less confronting so he would have answered more of her questions. If she had been more gentle with him, he might not have stormed out.

She missed him acutely. And she worried about his state of mind. Where was he? Was he thinking about her in the same way she thought about him, wishing things had gone differently between them? Olivia hugged her legs and perched her chin on her knees, wishing she had a crystal ball in which she could conjure an image of Alexandre, just to let her know he was all right. What if he had another attack and no one was around to help?

With a shudder, she pulled her feet from the water and scrambled to a standing position, unwilling to let her mind flash on the vision of Alexandre being sick and alone. She couldn't allow herself to think the worst or she'd drive herself crazy. It would be best to keep her hands busy and her thoughts on something other than Alexandre. She'd see what Rich was doing at the carriage house, make dinner, and turn in early. Olivia reached for her boots and socks, and out of the corner of her eye caught a glimpse of a man at the front fence.

She straightened, her heart pounding furiously, until the man stepped past the iron gate and she saw that his hair was blond, not dark brown. Olivia waited, the boots hanging off her hooked fingers, as she watched the man approach. A few moments later she realized the visitor was Boyd. Her spirits plummeted. She dropped her boots and yanked on her socks, wishing she could ignore him and in doing so, make him disappear.

"Olivia," he greeted in a brisk tone.

"What are you doing here?" she asked.

"I told you I'd be back. I want to speak with you."

"About what?"

"Rich." He glanced around. "Can we go somewhere to talk?"

"No. And I don't have all night, so make it brief."

Boyd swept a cool glance down her slight frame. "You're awful tough these days, Olivia."

"I've had to be to survive." She glowered at him, willing him to turn around and leave.

Trying to deflect her glare, he crossed his arms and planted his feet wide apart. "You know, I came here to Charleston last week and tried to be nice to you, and what did I get for my trouble? A cold shoulder."

"Oh, for God's sake, Boyd. What did you expect?"

"Cooperation. Decent cooperation."

"Why?"

"I thought you'd want to make up for the years I've been gone, at least for Rich. Don't you know how different his life could be once he takes his rightful place in the Williston family?"

"Such a life might not be an improvement, Boyd, considering what comes with the Williston name."

"What do you mean by that?"

"I mean that money doesn't make anyone happy, not if the right values aren't nurtured."

"Like what?"

"I don't care to go into it, Boyd. Not at this point. It makes no difference now."

"The hell it doesn't. I want to be a father to Rich. I intend to gain custody of him."

Olivia's breath caught in her throat. "Custody? You're not serious!"

"I'm dead serious. I'm almost thirty years old. I want to know what it's like to have a kid. I don't want to miss out on soccer games, playing catch, going camping—you know, all that fun father and son stuff."

Olivia stared at him, amazed at his view of fatherhood and the notion that parenting was nothing but fun and games. She stuffed her foot into her left boot. "If you want to know what it's like, have a child of your own."

"I can't. I got sick after college and ended up sterile."

"What?" she retorted in disbelief.

"I can't have any more children. Rich is the only son I'll ever have."

Olivia studied his face, sure he must be lying.

"It's true, Olivia. When my wife and I had trouble conceiving a child, I had myself checked and found out that I don't produce sperm."

"You're married?" She pulled on her other boot.

"Yes. And she likes kids. She's all for adopting Rich."

Olivia stood up, shocked. "Adopting?"

"Yeah." He looked around again, his gaze darting across the bushes and pool. "It'll be easier on you, too. I've heard you're planning to finish college in the fall. Your life will be a whole lot easier, Olivia, if I take Rich off your hands."

"You're not going to take Rich off my hands!" she blurted, her voice constricted to a whisper. How could he make such a heart-wrenching proposal and use such heartless words? "That's the last thing I want! He's my son!"

"He's just as much my son as yours."

"No, he isn't. You gave him up long ago, Boyd. You have no right to appear on a whim like this and demand him."

"I have every legal right, Olivia. Make no mistake. And if you want to make this difficult for everybody, I've plenty of grounds for proving your incompetence."

"My *what*?"

"Your incompetence. Dragging our son around from school to school, apartment to apartment, leaving him with sitters all the time, providing only the minimum in food and shelter, hitting him—"

"Hitting him?" Olivia felt the blood draining out of her cheeks.

"I've got proof of abuse—that shiner he was sporting the other day."

Olivia thought back to the photograph she had inno-cently taken of Boyd and Rich, never dreaming he would use the photo against her. "But he got that black eye from some kids on his bus!"

"Says who?"

"Me. And Rich will back me up. Plus Alexandre Chaubere."

Boyd laughed in derision. "I've heard about your boss. No one will believe him. In fact, a judge might think you and Alexandre were in on the abuse together, because Rich got in the way of your plans."

"How could you do this?" she cried. "How could you!"

"I want a son, Olivia. You can either cooperate, or I can arrange things so you'll never see him again. It's your choice."

"You have no right to do this!" Her hands balled into hard fists at her sides. "You've no right!"

"I'm taking him back to Seattle with me, just in case you decide to run off again and disappear, which—by the way—would be against the law. You'll be getting a subpoena for the court date."

"You wouldn't dare, Boyd! I'll call the police!"

"Go ahead. I'll show them the photograph." He patted his shirt pocket. "If I were you, Olivia, I'd get a lawyer."

Enraged, she lunged for him, forgetting that she was just a tiny woman and he was a tall, once athletic man. He caught her and pushed her away with enough force to send her toppling to the ground. She landed on her fanny with a painful thump, in a clump of irises.

He stood above her, his face flushed and his blue eyes full of gloating triumph. "Don't try to stop me, Olivia. It will be best for Rich and you know it."

"Like hell, you bastard!" she declared through clenched teeth.

Boyd took off for the carriage house, trotting across the grass and weeds. Olivia scrambled to her feet and took out after him, her tailbone smarting and tears of frustration pulling out of the corners of her eyes. No matter what he threatened, she would never give Rich up to him. Never. Once she relinquished him, she'd have to fight the Willistons and their money to get him back, and Rich would be lost to her forever.

"Stop, you bastard!" Olivia yelled as Boyd reached for the door of the carriage house.

He turned. "You'd better get a hold of yourself, Olivia," he warned. "You want to make this hard on Rich?"

"You're the one making it hard!"

"That's how you see it now, but in the long run—"

"There isn't going to be a long run!"

Boyd's face flushed crimson. She recognized the outward sign of his quick anger, and noticed the way the false smile slid from his mouth. "Listen, Olivia," he declared. "I'm doing this, no matter how much you scream and kick. You get that? A judge will decide in my favor."

"What judge? A friend of the Williston family?"

"Maybe. Connections never hurt. That's something you should keep in mind." He twisted the knob. "I can give connections to Rich. You can't." He pushed into the foyer.

Olivia followed. "You're not just going to barge in here and take my boy. I won't let you!"

"He's coming with me, one way or another. And if you'd cooperate, Olivia, it would be a whole lot easier. For all of us."

"He just got settled here. He needs me!"

"Then come back to Seattle. No one's stopping you ."

"I can't! I have a job here, a scholarship for the fall, a real future."

Boyd shrugged and climbed the stairs.

"Boyd!" She grabbed at his shirt sleeve. "Don't do this!"

He wrenched his arm out of her grip. "Keep your voice down, Olivia, or this will get ugly, I'm warning you."

"It already is ugly."

He shook a finger in front of her face. "You either encourage Rich to come with me or I'll call the police and have abuse charges brought against you. Today. Do you understand?"

She understood, all right. She was being manipulated by the Williston clan again. Rage and helplessness boiled inside her. Nothing she could do or say would change Boyd's mind, or change the fact that Rich was in danger of being taken away from her. She had to keep her head. If she let loose of the anger inside her and Boyd summoned the authorities, she'd appear to be the violent abuser Boyd claimed she was. She'd come off as the distraught unstable woman and Boyd would come off as the calm collected man who had searched for years for his son, only to find him living near poverty level in some apartment near a run-down mansion.

She gritted her teeth, biting back her anger.

"I see the light is dawning," he commented with a smug smile. "Tell Rich he's taking a trip to meet his grandparents, and that he'll be able to see all his old friends."

"You tell him," Olivia replied in a flat tone. "I'm not going to lie to him."

"Looks like it won't be necessary," Boyd said, glancing past her. "Hi, Rich."

Olivia whirled around and saw Rich standing in the foyer at the bottom of the stairs. How much had he heard of their argument? Distraught, Olivia ran down the stairs to him and flung her arms around him.

"Rich!" she cried. "How long have you been standing there?"

"I heard everything," he replied, his voice strangely toneless.

"Everything?"

"I came out to see when you'd be done working, and heard everything you guys said."

"Oh, Rich!"

Boyd stood at the top of the stairs, still red-faced with anger, and no longer attempting to put on a show for the boy. "Then you know you're coming back to Seattle with me. Tonight."

Rich glared at Boyd, his face full of bitterness and belligerence. Then he turned back to Olivia. "I don't want to go, Mom." His eyes pleaded with her to do something, to make the situation better by applying the magical touch only mothers possessed. Olivia longed to make it better, but this was one problem against which she was nearly powerless. Fury and dread sapped the strength from her limbs, but she stood up straight, refusing to acknowledge her trembling knees.

"You don't have to, Rich." She pushed him toward the door, gambling on the fact that she might be able to bluff

Boyd out of his scheme, at least for enough time to get legal advice and protection from the police. "Run to Mr. Chaubere's lab. There's a phone there. Call 911 and tell them there's an intruder."

"Olivia," Boyd warned. "You're making a big mistake!"

"Go, Rich. Run!"

"Who do you think the police are going to believe?" he thundered, running down the stairs as Rich darted across the driveway. Olivia backed against the door.

"Get out of my way!" Boyd shouted, reaching for the doorknob.

Olivia pressed against it and wedged her palms onto the door jamb. He'd have to pry her away from the door to get past her.

"Olivia, so help me, step aside!" His face had turned crimson with rage.

"No!" she retorted. "You're not getting Rich!"

He reached for the front of her blouse, grabbing the fabric and yanking her toward him. She screamed and pummeled him with her fists, her fury adding strength to her already fit arms, which were toned to perfection from years of hard work. She hit him square on the nose and heard it crunch.

"Why you little bitch!" Boyd cried, clutching his left hand over his face. Blood streamed down to his upper lip.

"Get out!" she exclaimed, not allowing herself time to think about the violent act she'd just committed in self-defense.

"Oh, I'll get out all right." He glared at her over his hand. "But I'll be back at nine o'clock tomorrow morning with the police. Better have Rich's bags packed. And don't try running. I've got a detective watching the house."

She stood aside finally, sure that he would make a retreat, now that she had wounded him. Boyd brushed past her with a dark look on his face, and stomped down the driveway to his waiting car.

Olivia ran to the Chaubere House, anxious to make sure Rich was safe. She met him on his return from the lab. The door to the cellar entrance was locked tight and he hadn't been able to make the call. She told him not to worry, and reassured him that everything would be all right. But as they returned to the carriage house, Olivia glanced toward the street, wondering what on earth she was going do to keep her son out of the clutches of the Willistons.

$\overline{21}$

For most of the night, Olivia paced the floor of the carriage house living room, trying to come up with a scheme to spirit Rich away from the Chaubere Estate. She had checked the grounds earlier. And sure enough, she spotted a man sitting in a car at the side of the road, watching the house and smoking a cigarette. There was no hope of driving the van past him, or even sneaking down the walk to the street, unless the man fell asleep at his post.

She returned to the carriage house, decided to take her chances and call the police, but discovered the phone was dead. Someone must have cut the line.

Only one recourse remained. Hoping the stake-out man would drowse during the early morning hours, Olivia awakened Rich at 3 A.M., grabbed the suitcases she had packed a few hours ago, and slipped quietly down the stairs. She instructed Rich to steer the van while she pushed it silently down the gently sloping driveway. If the detective were dozing, he wouldn't hear the crunch of gravel as they rolled onto Myrtle street. If she could just get past him, jump in the van, and speed away, they might have a chance at escape.

Straining with all her might, she pushed the van toward the gate, while Rich did an admirable job of guiding the vehicle in a straight line. Olivia thanked her lucky stars that Alexandre had allowed Rich to drive the Spider, and in doing so, had given the boy a now valuable skill. With the van still rolling slightly, Olivia sprinted ahead to open the gate. She pulled at the heavy wooden door and tried to ignore her racing heart. She caught sight of the same car parked outside the gate and was dismayed when the hired man stepped into view, blocking their passage.

"Going somewhere?" he asked, around the stub of his cigarette.

Olivia wilted in disappointment. Rich hit the brakes and the van pulled to a stop while Olivia put her hands on her hips.

"Just going out for the morning paper," she replied with frustration, her words hardening into her old sarcasm.

"I'll bet you were." The man threw his cigarette butt on the sidewalk. "Does the kid always drive? Kind of irresponsible of you, wouldn't you say, Ms. Travanelle?"

Olivia ignored him and pulled open the door on the driver's side. Rich scooted out of the way. Without another word to the man, she started up the van, backed it up, and returned to the carriage house.

"Now what?" Rich asked, his hair still mussed from sleep.

"I don't know." Olivia grabbed her purse. "We've got to get away, though."

Rich jumped out of the van and followed her out of the garage. "I know a way we could go."

She looked down at him in surprise. "Where?"

"Over the back wall. There's a path through Mrs. Foster's garden. The wall's kind of high, but it's pretty easy to climb up the old bricks."

"It's worth a try." Olivia glanced back through the open bay of the garage and saw a door at the opposite corner. "I bet that door opens to the back yard," she commented, nodding toward it. "Come on."

She shut the large door of the garage bay behind them and walked across the cement floor, acutely aware of the empty stall where Alexandre usually parked his Spider. Rich opened the back door.

"You're right!" he exclaimed. "Let's make a run for it."

"We'll just have to leave everything here." Olivia followed him through the door to the gray light of the back yard and stepped across the dew-laden grass to the brick wall separating Chaubere property from Foster land.

They had just begun to scale the wall when Olivia heard the unmistakable sound of a gun being cocked. She glanced over her shoulder to see a different man from the one at the end of the drive. This one was tall and thin, with an ugly face and dull eyes.

"Back to the house," he ordered, waving the pistol. "And no funny stuff."

"Geez!" Rich swore under his breath as he dropped to the ground with a thud.

"And don't try anything else," the man added. "I'll be right outside the door."

Olivia draped her arm around Rich's shoulder and guided him back to the carriage house. The second guard escorted them to the door and made certain they entered the foyer. Tired and angry, Olivia trudged up the stairs. A second guard! Had Boyd hired an entire army to imprison them? She had no choice but to remain on the estate. They were trapped. Boyd would arrive in a few hours to claim Rich, and there was nothing she could do about it.

Back in the apartment, she fixed Rich a cup of warm milk and sat with him in silence while he slowly drank it. No matter how much she longed to speak words of encouragement, she wasn't about to give him false hope when she knew her options for keeping him from Boyd were spent. When Rich was finished, he looked at her dejectedly and headed back to bed, since it was still well before dawn. Olivia sank onto the couch, exhausted from her long sleepless night, and sat back to wait for Boyd. Soon, however, her eyelids grew heavy and she drifted into nothingness until a loud thumping noise startled her awake.

At first the noise had been part of her dream, a nightmare about the last time her father had come home drunk, banging on the front door in the middle of the night and yelling obscenities while her mother stood in the living room, white-faced and terrified, refusing to give in to his demands any longer. Olivia hung in the hallway, pressed against the wall, worried that her father would find a way to break down the door and come after her mother. Sweat trickled down her face as he banged and banged, hurling threats through the door at the top of his lungs. Olivia ran to call the police and strained to reach a dream telephone in the kitchen, but it melted into the wall and flattened into the recent photograph of Rich and Boyd standing outside the carriage house.

"Rich!" she screamed, jerking awake to a sitting position on the couch, as the fear of losing her son hit her full force.

The thumping continued even when she opened her eyes. Staggering from the couch, Olivia pulled at her wrinkled T-shirt as someone rapped on the apartment door.

"Olivia!" a familiar accent-laced voice called. "Are you in there?"

Relief swept over her. She pulled open the door and flung herself into the arms of Alexandre Chaubere.

"What's going on?" he asked, trying to hold her back so he could look at her face.

She held him tightly, however, and pressed her cheek against his chest. "Boyd's coming for Rich in a few minutes. He's hired hoodlums to keep us trapped here all night!"

"I dispatched one of them down below."

"Did you hurt him?"

"No, I disarmed him and tied him up in the garage where he won't bother you."

"Oh, Alex, what am I going to do?"

"Get Rich and come with me. We're going to take this to the police."

For a long moment, Olivia gazed at him, wondering if justice would serve her or punish her. Yet what other choice did she have? She wasn't going to become Boyd's victim, forced to go on the run to retain custody of her son.

"Okay," she replied at last and drew away. She walked down the hallway and opened the door to Rich's bedroom. She peered into the darkness. The bed was empty. Alarmed, Olivia flipped on the lights and glanced wildly around but saw no sign of the boy. She dashed into the room and pulled open the closet door. No Rich.

She ran back to the hallway and noticed her bedroom door stood open and the curtain covering the French doors leading to the piazza had been pulled back. Had Rich climbed from the second story to the ground?

"Olivia?" Alexandre called, striding down the hall. "What's wrong?"

"It's Rich!" she cried. "He's gone!"

°   °   °

A few minutes later, Boyd pounded on the door. Olivia answered it. Alexandre watched, certain that Boyd had somehow managed to snatch Rich and was now coming to gloat over his victory. From his vantage point at the couch, Alexandre could see the patrol car of the police Boyd had brought as a back-up.

"Where is he?" Olivia demanded, without giving Boyd a chance to say anything.

He looked from Olivia to Alexandre and back again. His nose was bandaged and taped, and Alexandre wondered what had happened to him. "What do you mean?" Boyd asked.

"You've taken Rich! Where?"

"What are you talking about?" Boyd retorted. "I didn't take Rich. He's here and you know it!"

"No, he isn't!"

"Don't play games with me, you frigid little witch!"

Boyd tried to push his way into the apartment and past Alexandre, but Alexandre didn't budge. Hearing Boyd speak to Olivia in such a rude fashion made him want to break the man's neck. Instead, he shoved Boyd against the doorway and clamped a hand to his throat, nearly cutting off his air supply. Boyd's eyes bugged out in surprise, perhaps at the speed with which he had just been throttled, or at the exception Alexandre took to his treatment of Olivia.

"Speak civilly to Olivia," Alexandre ordered. "Apologize."

Boyd shot a glance at Olivia and then back at Alexandre. His nostrils flared. "Hey, she's the uncivil one. She broke my nose!"

"Apologize!"

Boyd blinked, startled by Alexandre's vehement demand. "Sorry," he wheezed. "Now come on, Chaubere, let up. You're choking me."

"Not until you've learned some manners."

"Okay, okay!"

Alexandre glared at Boyd, staring him straight in the eye until he saw the last flames of challenge die there. Then with a snort of disgust, he released Boyd.

"Where is Rich?" Alexandre growled.

"I told you—I don't have him." Boyd coughed and massaged his throat.

Alexandre gave Boyd a scathing glance. He couldn't imagine Olivia married to such a sniveling bully of a man. The idea revolted him.

"He must have run away!" Olivia hugged her arms. "Oh, God! Where could he be?"

Alexandre reached for Olivia and gave her arm a squeeze of support. "Why don't you call Mrs. Foster and Willie Lee's mother. See if Rich has shown up there."

Olivia nodded. He could see tears swimming in her eyes and longed to hold her close and say he would throw all his energy into making things right, and that they'd find Rich before she knew it. But the best thing for her now was to be kept busy doing positive things. She hurried to the phone which sat on the end table near the couch. Then she remembered the line was dead. "I can't." She glared at Boyd. "The phone line's been cut."

"Then we'll use the cellular phone in the lab."

She nodded and reached for the address book near the telephone.

"If Rich isn't at his friend's house, we're going to have to search for him," Alexandre said, turning to Boyd. They'd have to work together, for Rich's sake. "We'll talk to the police on the way to the lab. You check downtown Charleston. Olivia and I will search the surrounding areas." Alexandre pulled out a pen and piece of paper from his jacket pocket, scribbled his phone number, and gave it to Boyd. "If you find him, call this number. I'll have my portable phone with us in the car."

"Okay." Boyd stuffed the paper in the pocket of his slacks.

"If you don't find him, meet us back here at noon. That's three hours from now."

"Okay." Boyd slowly shook his head. "But I don't understand it. Why would the kid pull a stupid stunt like running away?" His eyes raised to meet Alexandre's. "Doesn't he know what's good for him?"

Alexandre shrugged and glanced over his shoulder to see what Olivia was doing. He had no answer for Boyd Williston. A man like Boyd didn't view the world in the same way as a young boy and didn't possess the selfless imagination to see into the head or heart of anybody, let alone a ten year old.

Olivia rushed toward him, grabbing her purse from a side table as she came. "Come on! We've got to find him!"

Alexandre closed the door behind her, touched that she gave no thought to her tousled hair or wrinkled clothes. Olivia's attention was focused solely on her missing son. From somewhere deep within her, she had found a reserve of strength that fired her eyes and movements with purpose and resolve. Though her hair needed brushing and her faded gardening clothes hung on her in wrinkled folds, he saw nothing but her magnificent love for her son. At that moment he knew he loved not just Olivia's spirit, but her heart and her courage as well. He loved her as he had loved no other woman, and the feeling swelled in his chest until he thought he'd explode.

"Come," he said gruffly, taking her elbow, when what he really wanted to do was enclose her in his arms and tell her how much she meant to him. "Let's talk to the police and then make those calls."

o   o   o

Hours later, night had fallen over the city and the muffled street lights emerged like glowing mushrooms from the fog that rolled in off the bay. Olivia trudged along The Battery for the second time, calling for Rich. She and Alexandre had gone everywhere she had thought Rich might run to—all the places she had taken him in the city. But they had found nothing. Not one clue. The police hadn't come up with a single lead to his whereabouts either.

"Rich! Rich, where are you?" she called.

Olivia crossed over the walkway of heaving concrete slabs to the cement railing of the breakwall, and leaned upon her forearms while the water lapped ten feet below her. She could hear the waves but couldn't see them in the fog. Nothing existed in this strange gray world but a few feet of concrete, a single light above, and the mournful song of a foghorn far from shore.

"Where could he be?"

Alexandre came up behind her, and she felt his strong arms surround her. She welcomed the comforting press of his cheek against the top of her head. "Wherever he is, Olivia, he's all right. I feel it."

She wished she could share his optimism. "I hate to think of him out in this fog, all alone. Frightened."

He gave her a squeeze. "Knowing Rich, he just might like the fog."

Olivia couldn't muster a smile, but his words warmed her all the same. He was right. Rich's favorite holiday was Halloween. He loved mysteries, the scarier the better. The Swamp Thing was practically a hero to him. And he had always loved lightning storms and mist. How could Alexandre have come to know her son so well after a mere few weeks?

She relaxed somewhat in Alexandre's embrace, drawing strength and support from him, and let her weight sag into him. "I'm so glad you came back, Alex," she murmured. "I don't know what I would have done without you today."

She felt his chest expand behind her as he took a deep breath.

"I wish I had returned last night," he answered tersely. "Perhaps none of this would have happened if I'd been there."

"Don't blame yourself." She turned slightly, enough to look up into his face, but the mist and darkness hid his expression from her. All she could see was the glint of his eyes and the sheen of his right cheekbone. She touched the sheen with her fingertips and cradled the side of his face in her hand.

He smoothed back the hair at her temple, touching her as gently as she touched him. "We'll find him, Olivia," he said. "*Ne t'inquiet pas, ma petite.* Don't worry. We'll find him."

For the second night Olivia paced the floor of the carriage house until Alexandre insisted she go to bed. She'd be no good to anyone, including Rich, if she didn't get a few hours of sleep. Gilbert, having joined the search earlier in the day, lay sleeping on Rich's bed.

Alexandre accompanied her down the hallway and lingered in the doorway of her bedroom, leaning against the jamb with his arms crossed over his chest.

"Did you love Boyd at one time?" he asked.

"I thought I did. But I was too young then to know what love really is," she replied.

"And now?"

"Now?" Olivia glanced at him and then away, suddenly afraid to confess her feelings for him, in case the truth might scare him off before they had a chance to really talk. She gave him a quick smile, hoping to keep the conversation light, and sat down on a chair near the bathroom door to take off her shoes. "I think I'd recognize love if I saw it."

"I always thought love was to be felt, not seen."

"Have you ever felt it?" she asked, pausing to look up at him. Surely in three-hundred years, he must have been in love numerous times. "Have there been any special women in your life?"

"A few," he replied. "But one very special lady."

She felt a surge of jealousy at the thought of any woman capturing Alexandre's heart. "Your wife?" she asked.

"No. I've never married."

Olivia thought she saw the old sadness pass through his eyes. He pulled away from the woodwork, and she realized her question had disturbed him.

"I'm sorry," she began, "I didn't mean to bring up painful memories."

"How do you know it is a memory?"

"I assumed we were talking about old loves."

"Not necessarily." He reached to the side for the doorknob. "Sweet dreams, Olivia," he said, changing the subject before she could ask him anything more. "I'll be in the parlor should you need me."

"Thanks," she said. "Goodnight."

Alexandre closed the door and her shoulders drooped. Why couldn't she have told him she needed him now, that she wanted him in her bed, that she longed to lay there with his arms around her. He made her feel safe and cherished, and she sorely needed comfort tonight. Olivia slipped out of her clothes and fell into bed.

Early the next morning Olivia awoke from another dream about Rich in which she replayed the time she told him about his real father. In the dream, they sat on the blanket eating lunch, just as they had done at the Dryer

Plantation, except this time she told him that Alexandre Chaubere was his father. Rich jumped for joy and Olivia jumped with him, bouncing higher and higher in the grass until she was jumping far above the live oaks along the river. At first the buoyancy was marvelous, like a carnival ride, and she laughed like a school girl. When she looked over to see how far Rich was leaping, however, she discovered that he had bounced to the side and was headed for a swirling mass of alligators in the Ashley River. The moment he hit the water, he would be ripped to shreds.

"Rich!" she'd screamed, jerking awake. Instantly she came to her senses and realized she'd been dreaming. She shook her head, grateful the alligators had been figments of her imagination, and hoped her cry hadn't been as loud as it seemed in her dream, for she didn't want to awaken anyone. Much to her chagrin, however, she heard running footsteps coming down the hall and a moment later her bedroom door flew open. Alexandre, still dressed and wide awake, burst into the room. Olivia grabbed the sheets to cover her nakedness and gawked at him, too surprised to utter a syllable.

"Olivia, is everything all right?"

"I just had a bad dream," she sputtered. But as soon as the words were out of her mouth, a thought struck her like a bolt of lightning. "Alexandre," she exclaimed. "I think I know where Rich is!"

$\overline{22}$

"Where?" Alexandre asked.

"The Dryer Plantation." She scooted to the edge of the mattress. "I should have thought of it before."

"Why would Rich go there?"

"It's fairly remote. And he made a comment when we were there that a person could camp out along the river and not be found by the tour staff."

Alexandre frowned as he considered the idea. "The plantation is seven miles out of town, Olivia. Do you think he would have walked that far?"

"If he were determined to get there," Olivia replied, "Rich would walk as far as he had to."

"Get dressed then. I'll meet you outside."

"All right."

Alexandre turned and headed for the front door, passing through the living room. He backed Olivia's van out of the garage and sat in the car, waiting for her and trying to imagine what she would say to her son to convince him that they had to stay within legal parameters, which meant they might have to return to Seattle. *Only temporarily*, Alexandre vowed to himself, tightly gripping the steering wheel. He intended to do whatever was required to ensure that Rich continued to live with his mother.

Alexandre knew he would have a fight on his hands in persuading Olivia to avail herself of his resources and wealth, but hoped that she would accept his offer for Rich's sake. He had seen enough of the world and the power of money, to know a battle against the Willistons without the proper financial backing was a battle she would lose, no matter who was ethically or morally right. He wouldn't let her lose. He couldn't imagine Olivia without Rich, or the boy without his mother. Worse, he couldn't imagine a slick, insensitive man like Boyd Williston guiding Rich into adulthood. What kind of man would Rich become if he were counseled by someone who was little more than a boy himself?

The door to the carriage house opened and Alexandre looked up to see Olivia and Gilbert coming toward him. Alexandre got out of the car and opened the door for her, surprised to see his old friend up so early, even to rescue a lost boy.

They drove in silence down the drive and were surprised to find Boyd waiting in his blue sedan, just beyond the gate. The moment he spied them, he fired up the engine of his car.

"Oh, great!" Olivia exclaimed. Her scowl told Alexandre that her worry regarding Boyd paralleled his own thoughts.

"I hope we get to Rich first," Alexandre said, turning toward the Ashley River.

"Me, too," Olivia replied. She leaned her head back against the seat. "He'll listen to you, Alexandre. Of all of us, I know he'll listen to what you have to say."

Alexandre felt a swell of pride at her statement, but also a twinge of despair. He and Rich shared a special bond, deeper than a mentor/student relationship. Potentially he could have an enduring and positive influence upon the boy, and yet he was soon to abandon the child and never see him again. The thought disturbed him, almost as much as the wrenching feeling that twisted inside him when he thought he'd soon be saying good-bye to Olivia as well.

Boyd followed them closely the entire seven miles on the freeway. Then, as soon as he saw the sign for the Dryer Plantation and realized it was their destination, he zoomed ahead, cutting dangerously close in front of them.

"He's going to kill someone someday," Alexandre commented, slowing a bit.

"All so he can be first." Olivia sighed. "Competition is everything to Boyd. It always has been."

"He sees Rich as a prize to be won, too, does he not?"

"Unfortunately, yes. And he will win at any cost, no matter what it does to Rich."

The road split and Alexandre veered to the right toward the Dryer Plantation. He'd been to the plantation many times when it had been a showplace—an island of culture and luxury amidst endless acres of indigo and rice, shacks full of slaves, and the rotting sink of cypress swamps. Now it was just a shell of a house, bereft of furniture, but even more bereft of the people who had established a fiefdom in the wilds of South Carolina. Without the Dryers and the play of life and death, of joy and tragedy, the house was just an empty box sitting in a trimmed wasteland of lawn and oaks.

A metal barricade spanned the lane leading to the main house, and Boyd's blue rental sedan was parked to the side of the gate. He must have set out on foot, but Alexandre couldn't see him up ahead in the darkness of early morning. Perhaps he had already arrived at the house, for Boyd would have made much better time getting to the plantation, judging by the speed with which he'd careened past them. If Boyd found Rich first, there was no predicting what the boy would do. Run again? Hide? Alexandre frowned at the thought, switched off the lights of the van, and pulled out the key.

He and Olivia slipped out of the car. Gilbert, uncharacteristically silent, climbed out of the slider door and locked it. Alexandre glanced around. Dark cypress sentinels draped in Spanish moss rose up from the swamps on either side of the single gravel lane, and the sweetly pungent smell of the earth lingered like an aftertaste upon the crisp breath of the coming dawn, like wine on the lips of a beautiful woman. Alexandre reached for Olivia's elbow, a gesture of almost second nature between them now, and welcomed the tingle of contact. With Gilbert at her other elbow, they hurried toward a house they couldn't see, neither of them speaking a word, and too consumed by worry to voice their fears. Once or twice Alexandre caught himself gripping Olivia's arm with too much force as his thoughts dwelled on Boyd and how he had treated Olivia over the years, but she neither winced nor made a comment. She was so obviously concerned for Rich that she didn't register the press of his fingers.

To Olivia, the plantation house she had visited a week ago had looked nothing like the monstrous hulk she now saw rising from the mist beyond the dew-swept lawn. Even the two-hundred year old oaks had lost their grace and looked more like giant claws thrusting out of the earth than living trees. She searched the gray expanse, looking for the slightest movement, the barest out-of-place shape that would signal the presence of a ten-year-old boy, and found nothing but drooping branches and silent buildings.

"He mentioned camping on the river bank," Olivia commented as they hurried up the drive toward the back of the mansion and the remnants of the cookhouse foundation.

"We'll check the house first. He might have sought shelter there for the night."

Alexandre slid his hand down her forearm and held onto her cold fingers. "Let's try the cellar and work our way up."

"I will check the front," Gilbert volunteered.

"Good. We'll catch up with you," Alexandre replied. "Call out if you find something."

Like Alexandre's house, the foundations of the Dryer home sat half in the soil and half out, providing windows all around the cellar and an arcade-style entryway in the back. They passed through the white arches of the arcade and picked their way across the shadowed flagstone floor. One by one they poked their heads into the empty workrooms and pantries where slaves had once toiled between the low masonry ceilings and uneven stone floors.

Suddenly Alexandre halted and Olivia bumped into his side, not expecting him to pause.

"Did you hear that?" he whispered.

"No, what?" she replied. Most likely his hearing was as acute as his sight. She looked up at his face.

"I heard voices." He cocked his head and then pointed up to the right. "There."

"Maybe it's Rich. Let's go!" She clutched his upper arm, ready to retrace their steps to the rear entry, but Alexandre turned in the opposite direction.

"I know of an interior stairway," he said. "Unless it's been closed off."

"You've been here before?" she asked. "I mean, long ago?"

"Many times. Come."

He led her to the south wall of the house where a narrow servants' stairwell climbed from a pantry and wine cellar upward to the main floor. The passage was dusty and full of cobwebs, which Alexandre waved away with his hand. They didn't speak a word, not sure who or what they would accost once they gained the next level. Carefully, Alexandre turned the latch and pushed the door open inch by inch, until he was certain the room before them was unoccupied.

The strained discussion came louder now and Olivia recognized the pitch of Rich's voice. She squeezed Alexandre's hand and urged him forward. They crept toward the doorway that opened upon the formal parlor at the eastern corner of the house. Gilbert appeared in the hallway to the left and followed close behind. The sun had begun to rise, sending enough light filtering into the empty rooms to reveal two figures in the parlor. Boyd stood in front of Rich, his legs spread and his hands on his hips in an aggressive stance. Rich faced Boyd, his back to the fireplace, his slight frame stiff with rebellion.

Olivia sank against the doorway, weak with relief that they had found Rich, but anxious to hear what Boyd and Rich were saying. She wanted to learn what Rich thought and what had prompted him to run away, so she hung back to listen. Alexandre sensed her decision and waited behind her, his hand on her shoulder, giving her support that she sensed subconsciously more than felt physically. Gilbert glanced in their direction, but Olivia put a finger to her lips in hopes he wouldn't betray their presence.

"Rich, you don't have a choice," Boyd shouted. "Now quit dragging your feet and let's go."

"No!"

"You can't stay here."

"I'm not leaving Charleston. I like it here!"

"You'll like Seattle."

"I hate Seattle!"

"Not if you live with me."

"I don't want to live with you. I want to live at Mr. Chaubere's house! I like it there!"

Olivia felt Alexandre's grip tighten.

"Rich," Boyd took a step toward the boy. "You're my son. I want to take care of you."

"No you don't, or else you would've looked for me a long time ago!"

"I couldn't. Your mother made it difficult to find you."

Olivia bristled at the lie and straightened in indignation. She hadn't run from Seattle and Boyd. Her scholarship had taken her away from the Northwest, and just happened to coincide with Boyd's first attempts to locate them. She was about to break into the argument, when Rich shouted, "Liar!" and dashed away from his father, heading toward the side of the room where another door opened to the main hall. He turned at the threshold.

"I heard what you told my mom. You can't have any more kids. I'm the only one you've got."

"That's only part of it—"

"So now that you can't have any more kids, you'll settle for me—the one you never wanted in the first place."

"I never said that." Boyd ran a hand over his hair, as if perplexed by a confrontation with a child whose perception went far beyond his young age.

"You don't have to. Think I'm stupid? And who said I wanted you for a father, anyway!"

"Rich, how can you say that? You don't know me. All the things your mother has told you about me are probably lies! She's a manipulative female. I know her kind."

"No! She's the greatest. She loves me!" Rich wiped his cheek with the back of his hand and Olivia wondered if he were crying.

She wanted to run to him, hold him in her arms, and

promise she'd protect and love him forever. Olivia broke from the doorway, but Alexandre's gentle hands urged her to remain where she was and let the drama unfold without them. The instant she felt the pressure of his hands, she knew Rich would be far better off if he finished the confrontation with his father without interruption.

Boyd advanced toward Rich while the boy backed farther through the doorway.

"You don't care about me!" Rich shouted. "You just want a kid to show off to people, like some kind of trophy. I've seen dads like you. They want their boys to win at soccer and softball and get good grades, but they don't really spend any time with them. They're too busy. And they don't listen. They never listen. They treat their boys like things, not human beings."

"Come off it, Rich, you don't mean that!"

"I do, too!" Rich turned and pointed to Alexandre. "Mr. Chaubere's been more like a father to me than anyone!"

Boyd whirled around in surprise, aware for the first time of his silent audience.

"Mr. Chaubere's the man I'd choose for a dad!" Rich declared. "Not you!"

Boyd gaped at Alexandre, his angry expression a mixture of surprise and chagrin. Then, apparently deciding force was the only way to handle Rich, Boyd grabbed the boy's arm and yanked him forward. Rich, his eyes blazing, wriggled free and fell back against the door.

"I'm not going anywhere with you!" he shouted. "I'm not!" Then he jerked to his feet and bolted away.

"Come back here, you little bastard!" Boyd lunged after him while Alexandre and Olivia joined the pursuit, with Gilbert trailing behind them.

Rich pounded up the stairs to the third story, where the ballroom and master bedroom were located. He struggled to open the door to the bedchamber, which allowed Boyd just enough time to catch up with him. Rich threw open the door as Boyd reached out to grab him, and both of them tumbled into the bedroom. Olivia dashed through the doorway, with Alexandre right behind her, skidding to a stop in surprise.

There in the bedchamber stood Jimmy Dan Petersen, the drunk who had attacked her on the street weeks ago, and another man who was short and squat in comparison to Jimmy Dan's string-bean height. At their feet was a nylon bag, the kind used to carry sports equipment. Its zipper yawned open to expose a pile of door knobs and light fixtures they had pilfered from the house. Olivia glanced at the bag in alarm. During the tour of the Dryer Plantation, she had heard the museum docent complain about thieves who stripped old plantations of priceless hardware and sold the loot to ruthless antique dealers. The robbers gave no thought to the irreplaceable heritage they dropped in their satchels, or the history they defaced. They cared only for the few dollars they could get from a fancy brass door latch or a crystal chandelier pendant. Her gaze traveled from the bag to the thieves. The short man still held an implicating screwdriver in his hand. Jimmy Dan, however, held a gun. As if amused by her outrage, he snickered and his unshaven face broke into an unfriendly sneer.

"Well, well, well," he drawled rocking back on his heels. "We meet again, Sugar Pie."

Too angry with Boyd and the thieves to be properly concerned about the weapon, Olivia leveled her accusing glare upon Jimmy Dan. She didn't bother to answer him. Surprised at the greeting, Boyd craned his neck to look up at Olivia as he clambered to his feet. Rich slowly rose, too, his eyes wide with alarm.

Jimmy Dan snickered again. "Thought you'd never get done with all that hollerin' and yellin' downstairs. Kind of got us off 'n our schedule, trapped up here and waitin' for you to clear out."

"Have a full day of sales ahead of you, do you?" Alexandre inquired, slipping from behind Olivia and stepping to the side as if ready to defend the others.

"Not so fast," Jimmy Dan warned, aiming his gun at Alexandre's chest. Then his expression changed. "Hey, I thought I ripped you up pretty good a while back."

"I'll hold no grudge, as long as you let us go."

"Oh, right! Don't you learn nothin'?" Jimmy Dan snapped. "You go messin' with me, and I'll finish you this time, y'hear?"

"Just let the others go, Petersen."

"They seen my face. Sweetie Pie here even knows my name. Think I want to visit the state pen again? You're crazy."

"Then let the boy and his father go. They don't know who you are."

Jimmy Dan narrowed his eyes, his glittering perusal traveling over Rich and Boyd. Olivia held her breath, praying the man would release them.

"He could still ID me to the cops." Jimmy Dan pointed his gun at Boyd. "Nope. They stay."

At the pronouncement, Boyd grabbed Rich and pulled him against the front of his body. His face had paled and his hands shook as he dragged Rich backward toward the doorway. Olivia couldn't believe Boyd would use Rich as a shield. Boyd's astounding immaturity came to the fore as he jeopardized the life of his son in order to save his own.

"Rich!" Olivia screamed.

"Freeze!" Jimmy Dan sputtered, lunging forward.

Then, as if in slow motion, Olivia watched the action play out before her disbelieving eyes. Rich, in a quick twist of his hips, kicked up and sideways, knocking the gun from Jimmy Dan's grip, just as Alexandre leapt through the air, taking the man to the floor. The force of Rich's kick sent Boyd and Rich plunging backward onto the planks of the ballroom, knocking Gilbert off his feet like a bowling pin, while the gun spun like a top through the open door of the bedchamber.

Alexandre and Jimmy Dan rolled in the doorway, clutching at one another's throats. Olivia watched Rich struggle to his feet and dart away from Boyd, who rose, panting for breath, and took off for the staircase behind him. Then Olivia remembered the gun and realized that someone should take command of the weapon before Jimmy Dan could reach for it. She turned in stunned confusion, just in time to see Jimmy Dan's cohort bend down and lift the gun in a graceful, deadly ballet.

The short man ran forward and took aim, his face contorted with fear, and Olivia followed his line of sight. Not Alexandre, not Gilbert, but Boyd was his target, who paused in silhouette against the distant bank of windows behind him, frozen like a deer in a blaze of headlights at the top of the stairs. She heard the click of the hammer, heard the crack of the gun, saw Boyd's expression of incredulity an instant before he jerked, spun, and fell, tumbling down the stairs and out of sight.

Shocked from her galvanized state, Olivia whirled and thrust her hand into the bag of plunder behind her. She snatched up a set of doorknobs, fastened together by a rod to form a miniature set of dumbbells. She grabbed one end of the heavy brass fixture, lunged toward the squat man, and before he could turn to shoot Alexandre, she hit him over the head. Grunting in surprise, he sank to his knees. She bashed him again, and watched in horror as he pitched forward over the legs of the now unconscious Jimmy Dan. For the second time in two days, she had struck a human being. First Boyd and now this man.

While she stood transfixed by the sight of the thief on the floor, Alexandre retrieved the gun and jumped to his feet. He glanced back at Olivia with eyes dark with worry, but before Alexandre could make a remark, Gilbert du Berry appeared in the doorway. He surveyed the sprawling bodies of the thieves on the floor and then stared at Olivia with an expression of amazement on his face.

"As they say in that barbaric land of England," he quipped, "Good show, Olivia."

She grinned shakily, her knees trembling as she stepped over Jimmy Dan and his friend, too intent on Rich's safety and too shocked at her own concession to violence to make a reply.

"Rich!" she called, running into the ballroom. He was standing at the top of the stairs, but when she called to him, he dashed across the floor and flung himself into her arms.

"Rich! Rich, are you all right?"

"Mom!" he cried, hugging her with all his strength. "I'm sorry! I just didn't want to go with him!"

"I know, Rich, I know." She held him close, one hand clasped around his bony shoulders and her other pressed to his russet hair. In that moment she knew they would forever be close, that they loved each other boundlessly, no matter how they might become separated by miles or time. No matter what the Willistons tried to take from them, she and Rich would always have their love for each other to bind them together and their past to link them to the future. "Oh, Rich! Thank God you're safe!"

"I'm okay, Mom. Really." He pulled back and looked over his shoulder. "But you've got to come over to the stairs. I think my fath—I think Mr. Williston is dead."

23

Olivia hurried down the stairs with Rich at her side. Blood formed a crimson pool around Boyd's head where he'd been shot. He lay so still with his arms bent at such an unnatural angle, she was certain he was dead.

"Stay back, Rich," Olivia advised, stopping midway down the stairs when she realized the sight was too gruesome for her son. "I'll check on him. You stay here."

"I can take it, Mom."

"You'll prove nothing by seeing your father in this condition. And you might regret it later."

"No I won't. It's not like he means that much to me or anything."

Olivia turned and clutched both of Rich's arms. "No matter what, Rich, that man was your father. You'll think about him someday, I guarantee it. And I don't want you to fill your memory with this vision of him. Do you understand?"

Alexandre came down the steps behind them, taking in

the sight below. "Listen to your mother, Rich," he said. "She's right."

"Okay, Mr. Chaubere."

Alexandre placed a hand on the boy's shoulder. "And by the way, Rich, that was some fancy footwork you did back there, kicking the gun away."

"I did it just like you taught me, Mr. Chaubere!"

"You certainly did. You probably saved our lives with that move, son."

Rich nodded seriously and Alexandre tousled his hair. He continued down the stairs and paused next to Olivia.

"He's dead," Olivia stated.

"I thought as much."

"I never dreamed it would end like this." She stared at Boyd's body. "Not like this."

"Are you all right?" he asked, his voice full of gentle concern. She raised her gaze to Alexandre.

"Yes. And you?"

"Just bruised a bit. I'm going back to the car to call the police. Don't move him," he nodded toward Boyd and then looked back at her. "Gilbert's holding Petersen and his friend at gunpoint until I return."

Olivia nodded and searched his face, suddenly unbearably tired and achingly relieved, now that the danger had passed. "Alexandre?"

"Yes?"

"Thanks for your help." She reached up, longing to sink into his arms but instead brought his head down for a quick kiss. She would have been satisfied with a simple press of lips, but Alexandre's mouth opened upon hers and she felt his arms wrapping around her. With a sigh of homecoming, she reached around his torso and embraced him tightly, as tightly as Rich had hugged her moments before. Their kiss sang with relief and joy, and a powerful appreciation of one another. For a long moment she held him, unwilling to break away, giving to him what he seemed to need from her and taking a good deal of comfort in return. Then Alexandre slowly drew back and opened his eyes. He ran his thumb across her lower lip.

"I'll be back," he murmured. "And soon we can all go home."

"Hurry," she replied. Their hands lingered together as he backed down the stairs, and then finally broke apart when he reached the bottom.

Alexandre loped across the floor to the hallway, turned, and disappeared from sight. Olivia sighed and looked up at her son, who stood behind her at the top of the stairs. Rich was grinning from ear to ear at what he'd just seen pass between her and Alexandre.

"I'm going to help Mr. du Berry," he blurted as a blush swept across his face. He raced off, leaving Olivia standing on the stairs above the broken remains of Boyd Williston III.

Though Alexandre had promised they'd return home soon, they were still at the plantation at ten o'clock that morning. The police arrived, the coroner came, and then the officers questioned everyone for hours, separately at first going over the events with each person to make sure the stories were straight and no cover-up had occurred. Then in a group session. Olivia had to explain over and over again why Boyd planned to take Rich from her and how he had threatened her, until her emotions were so strung out she thought she'd scream. Alexandre's quiet presence kept her strong, kept her from lashing out at the officers when they seemed not to believe her at first, and kept her from breaking into tears of frustration when she had to explain why she didn't want her son raised by the Willistons.

Surprisingly, it was Gilbert who finally came to her rescue. He listened to the last few minutes of questioning with his arms crossed, tapping his foot impatiently.

"*Alors, monsieurs!*" he declared. "Have you no compassion? Cannot you see this poor woman is at the end of her thread?"

The policemen glanced at each other.

Gilbert took their pause as more evidence of their determination to make the investigation last all day. "She has been out searching for her boy for the last twenty-four hours. Cannot you see she's dead on her foot?"

Olivia looked down, trying to hide her small smile. Gilbert passed behind her and laid his long hands on either side of her neck. "She is tired. She is hungry and upset. She meant no harm to Monsieur Williston—the bastard. Cannot you accept her innocence in his death? He brought it all upon himself. The shooting did not occur until he used the boy as his shield."

"Conveniently for her," the heavier officer replied.

"It appears to be convenience but it is synchronicity, gentlemen, of the highest and most satisfying order, *non*? Nothing more."

"Maybe. Maybe not. We don't know yet whose prints are going to be found on the gun."

The second officer tipped back his hat and scratched his forehead.

"Any jury in the State of South Carolina would find this wonderful lady innocent of all wrong doing," Gilbert added.

The second officer shook his head. "All right, bub," he said, rising to his feet. "We'll recommend to our sergeant that no charges be filed. You're free to go, all of you. Just don't go leaving town, in case we need to ask more questions."

Olivia draped her fingers over Gilbert's and gave his hands a squeeze of silent gratitude. Then Alexandre put his arm around her shoulder and led her from the Dryer house, with Rich carrying his suitcase, and Gilbert bringing up the rear. They passed by the patrol car where Jimmy Dan and his companion were sitting handcuffed in the back seat. Then they trudged up the lane to the main gate where the cars were parked. A yellow police barrier spanned the road, closing the plantation to tourists and staff officials alike. Alexander raised the plastic tape and held it up for the others to pass beneath.

Then Alexandre unlocked the van and climbed in the driver's seat. Olivia was grateful that he chose to drive. She was so tired she could barely move.

"Can I sit up front with Mr. Chaubere?" Rich asked, gazing back at his mother.

It was obvious to Olivia that he was torn between his loyalty to her and his eagerness to ride with Alexandre. She no longer needed for Rich to decide between her and Alexandre to prove a point. There was no undertone of rivalry anymore, and certainly no jealousy. She was glad Rich admired Alexandre, and was happy such a fine man—regardless whether he really *was* a man or not— was willing to give of himself to her son.

"Sure," she said. "I'll ride in back with Mr. du Berry."

"A delightful prospect," Gilbert remarked, winking.

Alexandre raised an eyebrow. "When are you going to learn to drive, Gilbert, and let *me* sit with the ladies?"

"*Jamais, mon ami,*" Gilbert said with a laugh. "Never!"

Olivia turned to Gilbert as Alexandre started the van. "You don't know how to drive? That's unusual in this day and age."

"I'm an unusual man," he replied with a dramatic shrug.

"That's exactly what Alexandre has said about himself."

"Ah. Alexandre and I—we are much alike in some ways."

Olivia studied him closely, wondering just what he meant. But she didn't ask. She'd had enough excitement for one day. She'd ask questions later, after she got some rest.

While Rich and Olivia slept through the afternoon, Alexandre sought out Gilbert and found him on the piazza nursing a brandy. Gilbert looked up when he heard Alexandre's step in the doorway.

"Ah, you have caught me stealing your liquor."

Alexandre waved him off. "You know I begrudge you nothing, Gilbert. But I thought you'd be headed for your hotel by now."

"I didn't feel like going, *mon ami*. I hope you do not mind. I wanted to sit here and look out at the garden for a while. It is so peaceful here now, with that view."

"It is, isn't it?" Alexandre strolled toward him and poured himself two fingers of cognac. He carried his glass to the banister and leaned upon it, gazing out at the statue and the reflecting pond. "When Olivia finishes the garden, it will be *magnifique*," he commented. "I regret the fact that I won't see the finished product."

Gilbert nodded. "I see why you are in love with her. One does not come across such a woman very often."

"She is one of a kind." Alexandre sipped his brandy and savored the fire of the liquor as it slid down his throat. "For me, she is the end of a long search."

"But I thought you were leaving."

"I am. But I will leave with the knowledge that there is such a thing as true love, my friend. I have found it in her."

"Have you told her?"

"No. It would only complicate matters when I leave."

"*Quel dommage*," Gilbert sighed. "Such a waste!"

Alexandre took another drink in an effort to melt the hard lump in his throat. He swallowed and straightened. "I've drawn up new papers, Gilbert. They're with my lawyer, but I wish for you to know."

"Of what are you talking, Alexandre?"

"I'm giving the house to Olivia. She belongs to it as much as it should belong to her. In addition, I'm putting half of my assets in a trust for her. You'll get the other half."

"Never mind about me, Alexandre. I have plenty, you know that."

"It's my decision."

"Very well." Gilbert shrugged one shoulder. "But what if you don't die? What will you do then?"

"I'll start over."

"With nothing?"

Alexandre smiled sadly. "It will not be so difficult. And you know I'm a man who likes a good challenge."

Agitated, Gilbert rose and strode to the edge of the piazza. He turned. "I worry about this. You'll be in South America. I will be here. I will not know in what condition you are in, if you are suffering, if you are dying—"

"It has to be this way, Gilbert."

"But you and I, Alexandre. We are old friends." He jabbed his chest with the side of his hand. "*Old* friends. I cannot imagine my life without you!"

He stared at Alexandre, his eyes more serious than Alexandre had ever seen them. For the first time he realized the huge impact his actions would have on his closest companion. Yet there was no turning back.

"Gilbert," he began, setting his glass down on the table. "You must forget about me. I will either die as a result of this extended experiment, or I will live out my days as a mortal and die a natural death. Either way, our paths will part, as paths between friends must part in this world."

"But Alexandre! How will I go on?"

"Like you always do. You have a million friends, Gilbert. You'll make a million more."

"But none like you, *mon ami*." Gilbert turned suddenly, presenting his back to him. Alexandre stared at the older man, sure that he was crying, and not knowing what in the world to do. A weeping Gilbert was a Gilbert he had never seen before, and the sight positively unnerved him. He didn't feel comfortable with the idea of offering a shoulder for Gilbert to cry on, but he stepped forward anyway, and put a reassuring hand on his back.

"Why is it that you cannot stay until we know for sure what is happening with you?" Gilbert asked, still facing away from him.

"Because as long as I stay near Olivia, and my body is affected by her, I will continue to decline. It wouldn't be fair to her."

"You are thinking always of her." Gilbert pivoted, his eyes piercing their target. "She is not the only one who loves you!"

Alexandre stared at him, unwilling to ask Gilbert to clarify his remark, but knowing full well what he meant.

"Let me go with you to South America," Gilbert continued, stepping forward, his body infused with eagerness. "I can nurse you if you become ill, or help you to get settled. You know you have a horrible sense of decor, Alexandre. How can you expect to set up housekeeping when you seem totally color blind?"

Alexandre shook his head, struck by Gilbert's touching display of loyalty. "Your company would be welcome, you know that. But my need for you to stay here and attend to my affairs is greater."

"But what about afterward? What if you need me then?"

"Gilbert, truly," Alexandre said, grasping the man's shoulders. "The elixir attacks are happening with greater frequency and much greater physical distress. I will surely be dead in a fortnight. I don't want you to witness my decline. I want you to remember me the way I am now—always."

Gilbert's eyes shone with unshed tears. "All right, my friend. *Eh bien*. I cannot fight this crazy notion of yours, this determination to die. But it will be a prison sentence for me, to live life without you!"

He pulled away from Alexandre's grip and rushed toward the doorway of the piazza, his head held high, never looking back. Alexandre watched him go, his heart breaking at the despair he had caused his old friend, surprised at the depth of feeling between them, and worried that saying the same things to Olivia would bring yet more pain.

His hands shook as he poured himself another glass of brandy. He would need the fortification, for tonight he would say good-bye to Rich and Olivia. There was no reason for him to stay, now that Boyd Williston was out of the picture, and every reason to believe that time was his enemy, now more than ever. The more time he spent with Rich and Olivia, the more attached he would become to the both of them, and the harder it would be to leave. He'd say farewell tonight and leave for Savannah where his ship was moored. The *Bon Aventure* would be seaworthy in a matter of days. He'd simply sleep on board until she was ready, and then set sail for South America.

"To adventure," he toasted aloud to his gardens, raising his glass. He tried to picture Rio, the excitement of a new city, new people, and a new language. Portuguese had a romantic sound to it, he'd been told. It had been years since he'd taught himself a new tongue. But the call to adventure didn't stir his blood the way it once had fired him. All he could see was Olivia's face and her blue eyes gazing at him in that serious probing way she looked at him. He closed his eyes and felt the velvet softness of her lips, felt her small hands on his face, and remembered the way her body pressed against his as if tailor made.

"No!" he wailed, squeezing the snifter so hard it shattered in his hand. Bright red blood appeared where one of the shards had sliced his palm. Alexandre blearily stared at his skin, and for one heart-stopping moment, he thought he could see the scarlet line filling with blood, about to overflow and run down his hand. Seconds later, however, the blood faded and the wound healed into a neat scar, just like all the others.

"No!" Alexandre wailed again, sagging against the banister, distraught. He still couldn't bleed. He was still an immortal—a freak. And there could be no place in Olivia's life for a freak.

Olivia and Rich had just sat down to a light meal of soup and sandwiches when someone knocked on the door. Olivia looked at Rich, not sure any more if they should answer the door or sit quietly until the next intruder passed into the night. Boyd's ghost would take a long time to fade from their thoughts.

"I'll get it," Rich offered, scooting back his chair.

She placed a restraining hand on his wrist. "No, you stay here. I'll get it."

Olivia rose and put her napkin beside her plate. Then, full of misgivings she walked through the living room to the door. She peered through the peephole and was relieved to see Alexandre. Immediately she opened the door.

"Hello," she greeted. "Come in."

Alexandre moved past her and then stopped. "You are eating. Once again I interrupt your meal."

"That's all right." She gazed at him, never getting her fill of his dark handsome features, or his lean, broad-

shouldered figure. He was dressed in his black jeans and
dark green shirt, which brought out the golden tones of
his skin.

"No, I will come back later."

Rich turned in his chair. "Want some soup, Mr.
Chaubere? It's cream of broccoli. My mom makes the
best soup, even if it is just made out of vegetables."

Olivia shook her head and smiled at Rich's undying
effort to make her look good in Alexandre's eyes. He
smiled at Olivia, but Alexandre's smile didn't hide the
sadness she had often seen there before, a sight which
made her heart thump painfully. Had he come with bad
news? The smell of brandy drifted from his clothes. Had
he been drinking? Why?

She touched his elbow. "Come. Please join us."

"Only if you sit down and finish your supper without
fussing about me."

"I promise."

"Want me to get you some soup, Mr. Chaubere?" Rich
asked, half-rising from his chair.

"No thanks, Rich. It looks wonderful, but I've already
eaten."

Rich sank back down in his seat and attacked the rest of
his meal while Olivia pulled out her chair. "Can I get you
anything, Alexandre? Coffee?"

"Not a thing, Olivia. I'll just sit here if you don't mind."

They chatted about inconsequential matters, about the
garden and what might happen with the Willistons. All
were relieved to note how the Williston topic had lost its
threat of consequence. Alexandre helped them tidy up
the kitchen, just as he had done the first time he'd come
to their table, an event that seemed to have occurred
years ago. Olivia brewed coffee while Rich showed
Alexandre the car posters in his room. When the coffee
was ready, she filled up two cups, put a drop of milk in

Alexandre's—as he had taken his coffee at the restaurant—and carried the mugs to the back of the apartment. She found Rich and Alexandre sitting on his bed, side by side, talking. Rich had his back to the door and was staring intently at the older man, his attention completely focused on Alexandre's face. Olivia paused with the hot cups in her hand, sensing that she shouldn't interrupt them, and waited in the doorway as Alexandre spoke.

"I want you to know, Rich," Alexandre said, "that it made me very proud today when you said you'd choose me for a father."

"I wasn't lying either."

"I know you weren't. And it meant a lot to me." He put an arm around Rich's shoulders and hugged him briefly, jostling him in a rough masculine embrace. "No one's ever said that about me before."

"How come? You're a neat guy."

"I haven't known many children. But I can honestly say that if I had a son, Rich, I'd want him to be just like you. I was very impressed by you today."

Rich hung his head, flustered at the praise.

Alexandre patted his leg and stood up. He glanced at Olivia and then back down at the boy. "Your mother's told you that I'm leaving Charleston, hasn't she?"

"Yes, but I don't see why you have to go exactly."

"I planned for this trip long before I met you and your mother, Rich, and I must take it. But I want you to do something for me."

"What?"

"I want you to take care of my models."

"Sure, but Mr. Chaubere—"

"I want you to have them, Rich. You, more than anyone else, will value them, and I'm sure you'll take care of them."

"But won't you want them back someday, Mr. Chaubere?"

"Perhaps, but it's unlikely. I'd prefer they live with you rather than in a box, waiting for an absentee owner."

Rich stared at him and then ran a hand through his hair. "What about my mom, though? Could you fix it so we could live here in the carriage house when the new people come?"

Alexandre briefly glanced at Olivia again. "What new people, Rich?"

"The people that will be buying your house."

Alexandre relaxed and crossed his arms. "There won't be any new people. I've decided to give my house to you and your mother."

"What?" Olivia gasped, nearly spilling the coffee.

He turned to her. "You and the estate belong together, Olivia. I'd like for you to have it."

"But, Alexandre!"

"I would like to think my old house was being lived in by someone who cared about it. In your hands, Olivia, the Chaubere House will be the pride of Charleston once again. And I'll know you and Rich will have a place to live for the rest of your lives. I'd like that."

"It's far too generous of you! I don't know what to say!"

"Don't say anything. We've been good friends, Olivia, have we not?"

"Yes, we have." Her hands shook as the heartfelt words slipped from her lips.

"That in itself is thanks enough. Good friends are rare in life. Very rare." Alexandre turned back to Rich. "So, don't you worry about your mother, Rich. Both of you can rest easy now, all right?"

"All right!" Rich exclaimed, but almost immediately his enthusiasm waned. "Except it won't be the same without you, Mr. Chaubere."

Olivia gazed at Alexandre, knowing her heart cried the same thing, only silently and over wounds which would be much more difficult to heal.

"It will be fine, you'll see."

"But—"

"I'm leaving tonight. I just wanted to say good-bye and tell you both how fortunate I've been at having the chance to know you."

Olivia pinched her lips together, pressing back tears, while Rich stared at Alexandre, his eyes also glistening and wet.

"Tonight?" he cried, shocked. "No, Mr. Chaubere! What about my fencing lessons? What about my French and karate?"

"Rich!" Alexandre bent down and pulled the boy against him. Olivia watched Rich fling his thin arms around Alexandre's neck and bury his face into the older man's green shirt. The sight of Rich standing there in a grown man's embrace brought a flood of tears to her eyes. He had never known a father, never known such closeness to an adult male, and the little taste he'd had was quickly coming to an end. Why did it have to be this way? Why was life so unfair for some children? Scalding tears spilled from her eyes and ran down her cheeks as she saw Rich's fists grasp the fabric of Alexandre's shirt, trying to keep the man in the control of his grip.

"I must go, Rich," Alexandre explained gently. "Promise you'll take good care of your mother."

"I will." Rich's voice was muffled and hoarse. "But how can you leave us? I thought you liked her. I saw you kiss her like you really meant it!"

"I did. And I do like your mother very much," he replied, smoothing Rich's hair. "But the time has come for me to go. And I must." Alexandre sighed heavily. "Are you all right now, Rich?"

The boy nodded and backed away, keeping his head down in an effort to hide his tears, but Olivia could see his red-rimmed eyes and wet cheeks. Alexandre stood before him, his hands on Rich's shoulders.

"Can you say good-bye in French, as I taught you?"

Rich wiped his eyes and gained control of his trembling lower lip. He looked up, and squared his shoulders. "À *bientôt*."

"That means see you later, not good-bye."

"I know." Rich stared defiantly at Alexandre.

"Rich," Alexandre said with a sigh of sadness and exasperation.

"That's all I'm going to say, Mr. Chaubere. *À bientôt*." He held out his hand while he mustered a brave smile that broke Olivia's heart. Alexandre shook his hand in the French way—one good shake—and then stepped away.

"*Adieu, Richard*," he said, giving the boy a quiet smile. Then he turned and strode from the room, passing Olivia without a single glance her way. She looked back at Rich.

"Are you all right?" she asked softly.

He nodded. "Yeah. Can you shut my door?"

"Sure." She transferred the second cup to her left hand and quietly closed his door with her right. Then she followed Alexandre down the hall, surprised and dismayed to see him heading for the front door. Had he no parting words for her? No embrace? She slid the untouched coffee onto the kitchen counter and hurried toward him.

"Alexandre!" she called.

24

"*Are you going to walk* out of my life," she asked, "just like that?"

Alexandre stopped, his hand on the doorknob. He didn't turn to face her. "Olivia, I can't talk now."

Olivia could tell by the tight sound of his voice that he was deeply upset. She stood in the center of the living room, uncertain what to do and touched by the difficulty he had obviously experienced in saying good-bye to Rich.

"Please," she said. "Don't leave without saying good-bye to me."

"I won't." He opened the door, still not glancing in her direction. "Meet me at the lilies at eleven, all right?"

"All right."

Alexandre disappeared into the shadows of the carriage house stairwell. Olivia drifted toward the window and watched him walk across the yard and through the oleanders, his head tilted at a downward angle, quite unlike him. Then he was gone and she felt abysmally alone.

This was how it would be for the rest of her life. Once Alexandre Chaubere left Charleston, she would suffer a loneliness far deeper than the solitude she had known before. Since she had never really loved a man until now, she'd been able to endure her single life. But after having enjoyed one small taste of life Alexandre, she could never again be satisfied with her empty plate.

Olivia checked on Rich and much to her surprise found him asleep. The events of the last few days and the late nights he'd spent must have worn him out. She kissed his exposed cheek, and gazed at him, overwhelmingly grateful to have him back in his own bed, safe and sound, and without a worry of Boyd to cloud their future. Yet he would never have a real father, just as she had never known a healthy, stable father, and that would affect him for the rest of his life.

Carefully she tucked the sheet and blanket around his shoulders, turned off his lamp, and quietly left the room. Then to pass the time, she took a long bath, washing away the past two days and trying very hard not to break into tears. She would only make Alexandre's departure more difficult than necessary by succumbing to emotional outbursts. He made it seem imperative that he leave, and he had never given her a reason to think he'd change his mind. She would honor his choice by remaining in control of her private feelings and not betray her nearly desperate sorrow.

Olivia dried her hair, stroked lotion over her white skin, and slipped into a cotton dress of light lavender with swirls of darker purples. She grimaced at herself in the mirror. Pinched with sadness, her face looked more pale than usual, and her eyes stared back at her, dark with the prospect of losing Alexandre. She dabbed blush onto the hollows of her cheeks, but soon realized that no cosmetic could camouflage the pallor of despair written like a headline across her face.

By the time she tidied the bathroom and slipped into a pair of sandals, it was nearly eleven o'clock. She wrote a short note explaining she'd be back soon from talking with Alexandre in the garden, just in case Rich should awaken and wonder where she was. Then she walked to the front door. Before she opened the latch, she threw back her shoulders and promised herself to be strong and self-contained. There was no other way to handle the situation.

Outside, the night air curled around her bare shoulders, only a few degrees cooler than inside the carriage house. Still, she shuddered in anticipation as she passed through the oleanders and headed for the narrow walk near the house. With every step, she composed her farewell speech to Alexandre: how she had enjoyed working with him, how generous he was to give his house to her, and how grateful she was for the care he had taken with Rich. She wouldn't say a single word about how he had changed her opinion of men, how she had lost her bitterness to the gentleness he had shown her, how she would miss him, and how she longed to wrap her arms around him and keep him close forever, no matter who or what he really was. She didn't dare say such words, for she would surely burst into tears if she so much as hinted at the effect he'd had upon her.

When she reached the willow tree, she parted the lush branches and passed into the protected darkness beneath the giant limbs. To her left sprawled the woody vines of the Everlasting Lily and beneath her feet spread a soft expanse of moss that reached to the trunk of the willow. Alexandre had not yet arrived. Olivia ambled to the base of the tree and turned, leaning upon the rough ridges of the trunk and gazing into the night. Through the veil of willow catkins she could see the glint of the reflecting pond and the calm profile of the Venus. Far beyond the statue and azaleas rose the tall iron fence and the street. A couple stood on the sidewalk, hand in hand, gazing at the transformation of the Chaubere property as people had begun to do the past few days. Certain they couldn't see her, she watched them, thinking how wonderful it had been to stroll arm and arm with Alexandre. Then she saw them kiss briefly, and her heart surged with despair. The couple walked on, leaving her feeling even more forlorn.

Her gaze drifted back to the statue. Once she had pitied the marble woman for her connection to exasperating Alexandre Chaubere. Now, however, Olivia knew she would have jumped at the chance to have spent all those years in Alexandre's world. At least she would have been able to see him and share parts of his life. How like the statue she'd been before she met Alexandre—cold, unapproachable, and rigid—and then he'd brought her heart to life, warmed the ice inside her, and helped her see the world with new eyes. And how quickly she'd revert to the statue's stoic personality after Alexandre's departure.

Then Olivia heard a soft clinking sound behind her, like glass upon glass, and she looked over her shoulder to see Alexandre duck through the willow branches, a folded blanket under one arm and a decanter and two glasses in his other hand. He paused when he saw her straighten and step away from the tree. She stared at him, all words of greeting clogged in a painful lump in her throat, for there were no words to convey her feelings as she watched him walk toward her for the last time.

Alexandre seemed overcome by the same muteness. For a moment he simply stood there, gazing back at her. Then he jerked into motion and held out the blanket.

"If you spread this upon the ground, Olivia," he said, "I'll pour the cognac."

"Fair enough." She shook out the blanket and let it settle upon the softest portion of moss, straightening the edges while Alexandre poured two glasses of brandy and set the decanter against a clump of columbines.

He turned and handed a glass to her. Then, raising his snifter, he looked deeply into her eyes. "To you, Olivia Travanelle."

She gazed back, trying to keep the corners of her mouth from trembling and betraying the tears that pooled just below the surface of her eyes. She swallowed and moved her glass toward him until the rim softly pinged against his. "And to you, Alexandre Chaubere," she whispered.

Slowly, he raised the cognac to his lips and took a sip. She felt the warm regard of his eyes pour over her as the heat of the brandy coursed down her throat.

"That's so smooth," she commented.

"My private reserve, saved for special occasions."

She nodded and took another sip.

"Sit," he said, sweeping the air with a graceful movement of his arm. He wore his white shirt with the generous cut and dropped shoulders, his black breeches and boots—the same outfit he'd worn the first time she'd set eyes upon him. She smiled, and sat down quickly to hide her expression.

"Why the smile?" he asked, sinking down beside her.

"Oh, you just look like a pirate in that outfit."

"And what if I *were* a pirate? Would that frighten you?"

"No."

"And the other matter of which I spoke when we were at the hospital—the fact that my body does not age—does that not alarm you?"

"At first it did. But not now."

"Why?"

"Because." She took another sip of brandy, uncertain how to proceed with the conversation. She longed to tell him that she didn't fear him because she loved him. But this was not a night for confessions of love. She sighed and glanced up. "You've given me no reason to fear you."

"And do you believe it possible that I am what I claim to be—an immortal?"

"You have given me no reason to doubt your word." Olivia drank in the sight of his dark eyes and wonderfully masculine mouth, with its wide strong lower lip.

"You have become uncharacteristically accepting as of late," he commented with a slow smile.

"I have learned the benefit of opening to possibilities, of thinking in new ways—something you've shown me the value of, Alexandre."

He looked down and swirled the amber cognac in his snifter.

"In many ways I've become a better person for having known you," she continued. "I want to thank you for that."

"No thanks are needed between us, Olivia," he murmured, glancing sideways at her face. "We have brought much goodness to each other's lives. The benefits have been mutual, believe me."

"I can't see what I've done for you, Alexandre, except intrude upon your peaceful routine."

"That's just it." He replied. "You've given me the greatest gift, Olivia. You and Rich have given me a taste of life the way it was meant be."

"Have you never lived a normal life?"

"I've never had a family. I've never known the joy of having a son, of seeing that look of admiration and affection I've seen in Rich's eyes. What a heady draught." He sighed. "And you—you accepted me with an open mind and showed me a caring heart, unconnected to anything but sincere friendship. I value that highly, Olivia. Very highly indeed."

"Surely you've known women who have loved you."

"Rarely. And sometimes not for the man I am, but for what I possess. I have, until late, lived in a style which attracted those who counted material possessions far above the appreciation of the man I aspire to be."

"Have you ever led a normal life—a mortal life?"

"Once. But the time I spent as a mortal was so long ago, it is like a dream I can barely recall."

She stared at him, marvelling that she was talking to a person who had been born shortly after the Pilgrims landed on the shores of America. "How did you come into your immortality?"

"I was an alchemist living in Paris. Many of my brotherhood were conducting experiments in the transformation of matter and in the pursuit of immortality. I developed a potion made from the Everlasting Lily which, when administered to rats, extended their lives considerably. Next I tried it on hares and swine. And when I decided to try a human subject, for ethical reasons, I could only choose myself."

Olivia examined his face as he spoke, struck by the seriousness that had stolen across his features. She longed to reach out and stroke his cheek, smooth back his hair, and kiss away his troubles, but this was not a night for caresses. This was a night for drawing back with dignity and hearts intact.

"What happened when you took the potion?" she asked, realizing he had lapsed into a dark silence.

"I found I could not bleed. Physical injury had no effect upon me. Soon my appetite ceased. My beard quit growing and my male organs ceased to function normally."

His male organs ceased to function? He had mentioned the hibernating state of his body during their argument at the hospital. She had come to believe that a lack on her part had been the reason he'd so frequently pulled away from her, seemingly unaffected by desire, but had never had the opportunity to discuss it with him. So it was a medical problem.

Olivia dragged her thoughts away from lovemaking, because the barest mention of making love with Alexandre filled her with a painful ache. "How long before you knew your experiment had succeeded?"

"A few months passed and my bodily functions slowed down to what seemed a standstill. After a time, I saw my friends going gray, getting fat and wrinkled. Eventually most of them died of one thing or another. I, however, remained fit and healthy. At first it seemed a gift from heaven. But after a while, I knew I had created my own hell."

"Why do you say that?" Olivia asked. "I would think that knowing you'd never die would be a wonderful release. Everyone worries about dying. You don't have to."

Alexandre took a sip of brandy and stared at the reflecting pond beyond the willow branches. He shook his head sadly and took another drink. His manner made it evident he was having difficulty trying to explain. Olivia wondered if she had misunderstood something. What important concept had she failed to grasp that would help her see the negative aspect of immortality? She held back her questions, however, and waited until he decided to continue. After a few moments he turned to her.

"For centuries, I've had to watch my closest friends die, one after the other. I've been forced to move from place to place so people wouldn't realize I don't age naturally. I lost the luxury of old friends, kin to go home to, or a spouse to share my life. Then my laboratory burned. A horrible fire. All my animals—" He shook his head at the devastating memory. "I had nothing left. And the formula to the immortal elixir was lost forever. So I left Paris for the sea, and settled here years later." His glance turned hard. "That's the life I've known, Olivia. Sure, I've had adventures. I've made and lost vast fortunes. I've read acres of books and traveled the globe so many times I've lost count. But all these things have not nurtured my heart. The years I spent on the earth ate away at my heart, you see, until it no longer had the will to continue alone."

"So what did you do?"

"I decided that death was better than a loveless life."

"But you cannot die—"

"I think that I can." He set aside his glass and ran a hand through his hair. "And I think that I *am*. The episodes I've suffered and you've witnessed are proof of my impending mortality."

"You're dying?" she cried. "But how can you? You're immortal!"

"Not anymore. For the past fifty years I've been working with the molecular structure of the Everlasting Lily, and have found a way to affect the strands of its DNA, enough to reverse the effects it has upon my physical body."

"So that it will kill you?" she questioned, distraught, "instead of sustaining you?"

"I am not certain what long-term effect the antidote will have upon me. I only know that I am slowly changing and that my bodily processes are beginning to work again, but only with the accompaniment of extraordinary pain. That is why I am determined to leave Charleston. I will not suffer anyone to share the consequences of my latest and final venture into the dark world of alchemy—not Gilbert, not Rich, and most of all, not you. I've seen what the lily can do to others when something goes wrong. I'll not have any of you witnessing that."

"But Alexandre, you haven't asked any of us what our opinion is on the matter."

"No, I haven't. I regret this is not a choice to be offered." He rose. "I must walk this path alone."

"No!" Olivia set aside her glass and scrambled to her feet. "It's not fair!"

"It isn't a matter of justice."

"What if we want to be with you, regardless of your condition?"

"Not acceptable." He glared down at her, his mouth grim. "What if I become incapacitated, Olivia? Out of duty you'd stay beside me, doomed to spend your lifetime nursing a man who will never be anything but a mindless mass of flesh. Do you realize how unbearable it's been for me to cope with the inability to make love to you? How do you think it would be to lose the ability to talk to you, to think, to dream? I won't damn you to that kind of life."

She stared at him, searching her mind for the words to convince him that she was willing to take the chance, that come what may, she'd stand by him. Yet she knew that Alexandre could be as obstinate as she when it came to making an important decision and then sticking to it. She knew no matter what she said to him, he'd still walk out of her life.

"And so it is good-bye?" she said. "That's it? Will you at least write to us?"

He shook his head. "I say it is better to cut this off now and not drag it out."

"Why!" she cried.

"Olivia." He reached out and enclosed the tops of her arms in his warm hands. "You must forget me. It will be easier in the long run."

"I'll never forget you!" she declared, gazing at him as her vision blurred with tears. "I don't want to forget you, Alexandre. I love you!"

He regarded her face in sorrowful silence, his hands squeezing her arms as if her confession might travel up through his fingers and reach his heart. "Olivia," he murmured with a sigh, and gently pressed her back, setting her aside.

"No!" she cried. "You can't do this! You can't leave me like this, Alexandre! How will I go on without you? Who will I talk to?"

"Please don't make this harder than it is already." He released her arms, but she flung them around his neck and hugged him fiercely.

"Don't leave me!" She pressed her cheek against his jaw and forgot her vow to remain in control. "I know you love me, Alexandre. I know you do!"

His hands moved up to frame her rib cage with his thumbs just below her breasts and his fingertips clamped around her torso. She felt the rasp of his warm breath upon the small of her shoulder.

"So help me, Olivia, I do," he whispered. "I love you, more than anything in the world."

Olivia closed her eyes, letting his words sink into her as he gathered her fully into his arms. He pressed kisses upon her shoulder and neck and then raised to her lips. Their mouths came together, desperate with hunger and love, and she plunged her right hand into his hair and caressed the back of his head. Tears slipped out of the corners of her eyes. Tears of joy at the realization her love was equally returned mingled with tears of sorrow at his determination to walk away.

"And that," he said, hugging her tightly, "is why I must go."

"Make love to me then," she murmured against his lips. "Share that with me, Alexandre."

"I don't think it would be wise. It will make your life and what future I have left that much more difficult to endure."

"We'll deal with that when the time comes." She stared at him, challenging him to deny the inevitable, to veer from the course they were destined to take the moment they laid eyes on each other. His dark eyes regarded her seriously, probing her face and searching for a shred of doubt in her expression. He would find none, for she had no qualms whatsoever about making love with him now.

"I'm not sure what will happen," he ventured at last.

"It's all right," she replied, reaching for the buttons of his shirt. "I am willing to try it with you, Alex. I love you."

He reached down and raised her chin with the crook of his finger. "Then let's do this right," he said. "And go to my bed."

"No," she countered. "Let's stay here in the garden. Just you and me in this beautiful place where no one can see us but the moon."

His eyes shone as he peered up at the slice of silver glowing high above. A small smile raised the corners of his mouth. *"Très bien,"* he said, leaning down for a kiss. She surrounded him with her arms and pressed into him, and soon she was lost to his strong and heartfelt embrace.

25

From that moment on, they didn't speak a word. Everything they told each other was communicated through their lips and hands, and in their sighs and caresses—a powerful language that required no voice. As they stood together upon the blanket, he slowly unbuttoned her dress and slipped it off. She returned the gesture by divesting him of his shirt, warm and fragrant with his scent. She let the garment drop to the ground while he unhooked her bra and slipped the straps down her arms. Her panties and sandals came next. Then Alexandre straightened and reached for her hands, raising them up and outward as if to lead her into a dance. But he took no step back or forward. He simply gazed at her for a long intense moment until she thought she would burst with desire for his touch. She felt no shame in her nakedness in the garden either, for her entire universe was comprised of the man before her.

She looked up into his face and saw his eyes smoldering as he regarded her slight frame. Waves of the unusual vibration between them buzzed in her ears and danced over her skin. She wanted to tell him it would be all right if he couldn't carry through, that she would be happy to lie in his arms, and that she'd love anything they could do together. But she remained silent, and pulling from his light grip, reached for his waist instead, just above the line of his breeches. Her hands looked delicate and pale next to the golden muscles of his abdomen, and she drew her fingers upward to fan across his ribs and over his chest. He breathed in and dipped down to bring her close to him, and their bare skin met like steel to flint, igniting them both.

Olivia's body burst to life in the crush of Alexandre's embrace. His hands swept over her back and into her hair, bringing her mouth to his for a shattering lingering kiss. The tips of their noses touched and she felt a rush of desire at the odd contact with his sharp, determined nose. Then he kissed her jawline, her ear lobes, and eyelids, and pressed bunches of her curls to his face, breathing in the scent of her hair as though it were the most intoxicating fragrance on earth. She couldn't believe he'd gone without love for centuries, for his movements were restrained, appreciative, and damnably deliberate. Her years without physical love were only fleeting moments compared to the time he'd spent alone, and yet she could barely contain herself. She wanted to sink back down to the blanket, desperate for Alexandre to cover her with the glorious press of his weight. She longed to be his if only for this one precious night.

Olivia kissed his chin, his neck, his chest and abdomen, framing his torso in her hands. Slowly, as slowly as she could force herself to go, she moved down his body, kissing him until she sank to her knees before him. She glanced at the fabric of his breeches, but the darkness of the black cloth concealed his body from her eyes. With hands far more steady than her heart, she reached for the buttons that secured the flap of his breeches. Before she could unfasten the first one, however, her wrists were surrounded by Alexandre's long hands and he gently urged her away. Flustered, she sat back on her heels and looked up. Why had he stopped her? Wasn't he ready? Did he think her too brazen?

He stared down at her, his head backlit by the pale light of the moon filtering through the branches of the willow tree. She knew she'd never forget the sight of him like that, with his dark hair brushing the straight sweep of his bare shoulders, and the rise and fall of his powerful naked chest. Moonlight beamed over his scars, turning them to threads of silver. Then he reached down and pulled off one boot and then the other. Still regarding her with a steady gaze, he unbuttoned his breeches and let them drop.

Olivia felt her entire body flush at the sight of him. There was nothing lacking in Alexandre Chaubere now, nothing to worry about, nothing to sacrifice in loving him. Awestruck at the sight of him, she felt her lips part, her nipples harden, and her breasts swell in response. Something deep inside her surged to life with such driving intensity that she almost closed her eyes against the flood of sensation. But she kept her eyes open. She wouldn't allow herself to even blink, for she didn't want to miss a single instant of this vision before her. Alexandre was so beautiful, all of him, and she couldn't wait to feel the curved jutting length of him inside her.

She reclined on the blanket and invited Alexandre to do the same. He slowly lowered to his knees. She lay back and reached up for him, pressing her palms to his shoulder blades to urge him toward her.

"Come into me," she whispered. "Come into me, Alexandre."

"It is too soon for you," he replied, his voice husky.

"No. It is long past time, for both of us."

He gazed deeply into her eyes and she gazed back, each of them studying the other, looking far beyond their bodies to something more primal and communal than their present-day earthly forms. He lowered himself to her inch by inch until their lips met and his tongue slipped into her mouth. She arched up, meeting his tongue with hers, pushing her aching breasts into his chest, and lifting her hips to his. She felt his warm firm length against her and gasped in his mouth. The sound seemed to set him on fire. In one quick movement he shifted his lower body until he was between her legs and pressing against her most intimate flesh. She moved upward, tilting her hips a fraction and he nudged into her.

Alexandre sucked in a sharp breath and planted his hands on either side of her head as he stared down at her, intent with the feelings their hearts and bodies shared. Olivia was swept away by his gaze, losing herself to the glorious onset of their joining. She ran her hands down his back to clutch his firm rump, and urged him to continue.

"Alex!" she moaned, opening to him with a hunger she had never known. As her legs moved to accommodate him, he pushed inside her. Alexandre groaned as she received him. The sound of his voice coursed through her, raising the hair on the back of her neck and lighting a wildfire inside her. He pulled back and then thrust farther, deeper, and harder until their breathing came fast and ragged, a chorus to a dance as old as time.

Olivia held him in her arms, her cheek angled against his, her body straining to his rhythm, as her heart and soul broke free to rise up and meet a man's for the first time in her life. She had never known such completion, such a belonging to another human being or to her intended place in the universe. As the seeds she had often planted found their way through black soil to the sunlight above, so she had found the true love of her heart after years upon years spent in darkness. Alexandre was her sunlight, her source of nourishment, the place her lonely soul had drifted to earth and taken root. And now, with him in this still and sacred place beneath the willow tree, she burst into bloom, blossoming in a glorious riot of color—reds, yellows, and golds—color that exploded from the splendid fire of their union, rippling and surging through her body, through her feet and legs, her hips and chest, her breasts and arms, and up, up, up her throat, until the colors sang through her clenched teeth in a cry of unbelievable release.

"Look in my eyes," Alexandre gasped. "Olivia, look at me!"

His voice pulled her from deep within herself where she was linked with Alexandre in a pounding chanting place. She opened her eyes to find him staring down at her, his irises like knife points boring straight into her soul.

"Look at me," he demanded hoarsely. She looked at him. And through her eyes the love she bore for him poured out in a torrent of heat as he poured himself into her—each of them renewing the other in a cycle that had no beginning and no end, like one season rolling into the next, full of life and death and life yet again.

Olivia turned and sighed contentedly, reaching for the warmth of Alexandre's body and expecting to find him lying beside her. He had lain with her for hours beneath the willow tree, making love to her time after time, until they both trembled and clung to each other in speechless incredulity. Yet this time her hand found nothing but a stretch of cool percale and the soft pad of a pillow.

A pillow? She jerked up, suddenly and fully awake, to find herself in her bed in the carriage house—alone.

"Alex?" she called softly. The sky was still dark beyond the piazza, but the moon had set. She switched on the lamp and sat up, the sheet and blanket falling from her naked breasts as she searched in vain for an indication of his presence. She jumped out of bed and ran across the floor to the bathroom, praying she would find him there. But the bath was empty and still, except for the fronds of her Boston fern gently rustling in the breeze caused by opening the door so quickly.

She pivoted and faced the bed once more. "Alex?" she cried. How could he have left her like this, to wake up without him? How could he have gone through with his original plans to leave after their amazing night together? How could he not trust her love enough to believe it would take them through whatever he had to face? She felt wretchedly, impossibly betrayed.

"Alexandre!" she cried again, softer this time, her shoulders drooping. She knew in her heart that he was already gone, either to his ship moored in Savannah or already out to sea.

Then her eyes caught sight of a flower on her night-stand at the vacant side of the bed. She padded closer and looked down to find a sprig of the Everlasting Lily wrapped in paper and lying across a note. She picked up the flower, careful not to touch the woody stem or crimson blossom. Its sweet, sharp fragrance, like cloves mixed with ginger, wafted upward as she reached for the note.

"Yours forevermore," Alexandre had written. At the bottom he had signed the initial of his first name, in a flourish of three pen strokes.

Olivia gazed at his note of farewell until the vision swam with her tears. For a long while she stood near the bed, reliving the past few hours with Alexandre until her heart was breaking. Then the lily seemed to sharpen into focus, capturing her attention. She looked down at the flower and suddenly found a new perspective.

She wasn't going to take this. Like the Everlasting Lily which bloomed forever, so would her love for Alexandre last for all time, no matter if he were a normal man or not. Her place was beside him, through summer or winter, life or death. If he hadn't yet set out on his journey, she'd make him see that the world without each other was worse than any hell imaginable, and that she wanted to share her life with him one way or another.

Olivia threw on some clothes and dashed across the hall to Rich's room.

"Rich, wake up!" she called, knocking on his door. "Wake up! We're going to Savannah!"

After a two-hour drive, Olivia and Rich pulled into Savannah just as the faintest glow of dawn tinged the sky pink above the bay.

"Red sky at morning, sailors take warning," Rich said, and then took a bite of the breakfast sandwich she'd bought for him a few minutes before.

Olivia tried to ignore his comment. She had enough to worry about in regard to Alexandre. Tragedy at sea hadn't entered her mind and she wouldn't let it. "Help me look for Mr. Chaubere's ship," she said, hoping he hadn't already sailed. She angled the van down a street and headed for the waterfront. "Keep a lookout for masts, or anything that looks like a tall ship."

"Okay," he answered, staring out the window.

After nearly an hour of driving around and asking anyone they could find on the street that early in the morning about wooden ships, they located the dock where the *Bon Aventure* was moored.

"There's the Spider!" Rich exclaimed, pointing to a side alley.

"And there's Gilbert," Olivia observed, catching sight of the slight man as he walked toward a coffee shop on the corner. She rolled down the van window and waved her arm.

"Mr. du Berry!" she called, making a U-turn in the nearly deserted street. Hearing his name, Gilbert glanced back, and seeing the van, stopped near the curb. Olivia drove up to him and lurched to a stop. He came around to her side.

"Where is he?" she inquired.

"Alexandre?" Gilbert replied. His eyes looked as red and bleary as hers felt.

"Yes! Where is he?"

"He has set sail." Gilbert looked over his shoulder and nodded toward the bay. "You might be able to catch sight of him if you hurry."

Olivia grabbed the keys. "Come on, Rich," she exclaimed. She hopped out of the van and locked it, while her son trotted around to join them. Gilbert led them across the road and down a ramp between two buildings. There, a walkway led out to a pier.

"*Voilà*," Gilbert said, pointing toward a dark speck on the horizon. "Our friend, Alexandre Chaubere, sails out of our lives."

Her heart sinking, Olivia watched the speck grow smaller and smaller as it approached the glowing ball of the rising sun. She was too late. Her chance to convince Alexandre to stay was lost. She crossed her arms and heaved a sigh.

"Did not he tell you he was leaving?" Gilbert asked kindly.

"He told me. I just wanted one last chance to talk him out of it."

"Sometimes there is no talking Alexandre out of anything."

Cold and upset, Olivia chafed the backs of her arms. "Isn't there some way to contact him? A radio? The Coast Guard? Couldn't we hire a launch to catch up with him?"

"Alexandre does not want to be caught, Olivia," Gilbert said, touching her shoulder. "We must accept that."

"I tried to convince him not to leave, that we wouldn't care what condition he might end up in, but he wouldn't listen."

"He is a proud man, Olivia. To show any weakness, especially in front of you, would be very difficult for him."

"And leaving wasn't more difficult?"

"It was the lesser of two weevils," Gilbert added solemnly. Rich glanced at him sideways, his features contorted with confusion and a half-smile.

Olivia thought back to the times she had heard Gilbert speak with Alexandre and make such comical blunders. The thought brought Alexandre's loss into clear, unrelenting focus. She hung her head and tried not to start crying again. Rich edged closer to her.

"It's okay, Mom," he said, putting his arm around her. "He'll be back. I just know he'll come back."

Olivia raised her glance to the speck on the horizon, wishing she shared Rich's innocent faith. But she had seen too much of the world and knew too much of life to harbor any hope of Alexandre's return. He might be sailing off to a horrible death, solitary and doomed, like a fallen warrior on a Viking funeral ship.

They stayed on the pier in the early morning chill, watching Alexandre's ship until it sailed out of sight. Then Gilbert offered to buy Olivia a cup of coffee and Rich some hot chocolate.

"I have to find someone to drive Alexandre's car back to the carriage house," he explained. "I'm sure someone will be happy to oblige."

"I would," Rich put in, "if I were a little bit older. I've driven the Spider, you know."

Gilbert glanced at him and smiled. "Have you?"

Rich nodded proudly. "Out to the street and back. Mr. Chaubere told me I was a natural." He trailed beside Gilbert as they walked from the pier. "When I grow up, I'm going to have a car just like his."

"Of course you are," Gilbert replied. "The exact model."

"You bet. A '73."

"The same car, as a matter of fact."

Olivia stopped in her tracks at the edge of the street as his words sunk in. "What are you saying, du Berry?"

"Alexandre wants Rich to have the Spider."

"What?" Rich gasped, his eyes as round as half-dollars.

"He thought you'd do well to have the car on your sixteenth birthday."

"He did?" Rich whipped around to his mother. "Can I, Mom?"

"Well, I don't know. This is quite a surprise, Rich, and there are lots of considerations—like the title, driver's training, and—"

"All the paperwork will be taken care of, madame," Gilbert said with a wink. "It is my specialty."

Rich hooted with joy and jumped up and down, barely able to contain himself. Olivia watched him, her heavy heart still bearing down upon her, dampening the happy moment. Both of them had benefited from knowing Alexandre. Rich had got his car and she had got his house and half of his assets in the form of a trust, whatever they might be. Though both gifts were unexpectedly generous offerings, they were not enough to make her happy. All Olivia had wanted of Alexandre Chaubere was his love.

"Come," Gilbert said, taking her elbow. "You look like a woman who could use a cup of coffee."

She allowed herself to be led across the street to the waterfront cafe, even though she hadn't the slightest thirst or hunger. It would be a long time before she'd work through this numbness to feel anything again.

Later that week Olivia hired a company to prepare the dirt for the front lawns and sod the large areas between the oleanders and the walk. The transformation was astounding, and more and more people stopped to admire the progress taking place in the yard beyond the ancient iron fence. Many of them chatted with Olivia when she worked within earshot, and Mrs. Foster often strolled by with fresh flowers or cookies and a long chat. As the weeks passed Olivia began to feel more and more a part of the community, an allegiance she had never experienced before and found she enjoyed.

She hadn't begun work on the mansion, however, and the idea that she owned the house still hadn't sunk in. In fact, she hadn't set foot in the place since Alexandre's departure. The rooms were still too potent with his memory, and she wasn't ready to face them yet. Perhaps his memory would always be too painful to bear and she would never be able to make the mansion her residence. Besides, the carriage house was ample space for her and Rich.

Though she no longer had to worry about money, thanks to Alexandre, she continued to work, keeping to a schedule that would have the yard finished before her fall college classes started. She had already registered and planned to hire a housekeeper to cook and watch over Rich once school began.

Olivia worked until sundown, until she spotted Gilbert strolling past the statue toward her, dropping in for a visit as he so often did these days. He'd fallen into the habit of joining them for dinner, often cooking a gourmet meal for them, but eating very little himself. She suspected that Gilbert and Alexandre had shared a secret past, and that Gilbert was most likely an immortal himself. But she never asked him, and he never volunteered the information.

"*Bonsoir, madame,*" he called, waving to her.

"Gilbert," she replied, brushing back a tangle of her red hair. "*Comment allez-vous?*" She asked him how he fared, practicing her French which she had picked up during Rich's daily instruction from Gilbert.

"*Ça va,*" he replied. "I have brought you this delightful shrimp. Shall I cook them up for you?"

"Would you?" She was as grateful for his cooking as he was for their company, now that Alexandre was gone. "That would be wonderful."

"*Très bien!*" he replied, walking alongside her as they headed toward the carriage house. "And I have been thinking, Olivia, about a party."

"A party?"

"When you are finished with the grounds." He swept the air in one of his flamboyant gestures. "We could invite the whole town. It seems everyone knows of your work here. When will you be finished?"

"I don't know. It will probably be mid-summer before the rear gardens are done."

"July then!" he beamed.

"But Gilbert, a party takes a lot of planning. I don't have the time–"

"Not to worry. *Moi*, I am an expert in these matters. Leave it to me, eh?"

Before she could respond, Rich burst through the row of oleanders with Willie Lee at his heels.

"Hi, Mr. du Berry!" Rich called.

Gilbert smiled and nodded at the boys. Olivia noticed an unfamiliar ball cap turned backwards on Rich's head, and then realized when he tore past her and she saw the emblem, that it was the Charlotte Hornets cap which had been snatched away by the school bus bullies several weeks ago.

"Wait a minute!" she demanded.

Rich ground to a halt and turned.

"Where'd you get that cap?" she asked, walking toward him.

"This?" Rich touched the hat.

"Yes. That."

"It's mine. I got it back."

"From Eddie?"

Rich nodded and grinned.

"Without fighting?"

Rich and Willie exchanged glances. Olivia watched them carefully, wondering what mischief was going on between them. Rich looked back at her.

"Yep. No fighting, Mom."

Willie Lee bobbed his head solemnly. "I thought he was going to get creamed, Mrs. T, but he just walked up to Eddie and told him to give it back, just like that."

"You did?" Olivia glanced at Rich in surprise.

"Yeah. I kept thinking about what Mr. Chaubere had taught me, about pretending not to be afraid. And I just did it."

"Good for you, Rich," Gilbert exclaimed. "Another Chaubere in training. *C'est bon!*"

For a moment Olivia stared at her son, proud of his newfound courage and amazed at the influence Alexandre still had on their lives. "Well, you boys come up to the house in an hour. Mr. du Berry's making dinner."

"Cool!" said Willie Lee.

Olivia watched them dash off. Though her life had grown richer and fuller since she'd settled in Charleston, a yawning emptiness still hung in her heart. Someday she might get over the loss of Alexandre, but he would always remain part of her. The secret was not to lose his memory, but to overcome the sadness. She would do it. Olivia took a deep breath and threw back her shoulders. Another day, another night. She would endure.

Epilogue

July, at the Chaubere House

"A wonderful party, Olivia! Simply wonderful!" Mrs. Foster remarked, taking a sip of punch as she stood near the statue of Venus. "It's the kind of party my daddy used to throw years ago. Why, just look at all those folks enjoyin' themselves!"

Olivia thanked her for coming and moved on through the crowd. She was amazed by the number of people who'd gathered to celebrate the completion of the Chaubere Gardens. More than a hundred friends and neighbors had assembled on the lawn at six, and now at dusk, nearly all of them were still there, obviously having too good a time to leave.

"Did you see the roses in the back?" she heard the president of the horticultural society remark. "The Don Juans? Real beauties!"

"And the bay blossom tree," his wife replied, "I've never seen a lovelier specimen!"

Olivia walked on, flushing with pride, while other snippets of conversation drifted toward her like pieces of a dream. She nodded, smiled to acquaintances, and stopped to answer questions, all the while feeling strangely distanced from the festivities.

She continued her slow progress toward the house. Tables laden with hors d'oeuvres, desserts, and wine lined the walk. People chatted and ate and laughed, while music from the band on the front porch filled the evening air. Sherry had helped her book Lenny Hanfield and the Ambassadors, the group from Atlanta that they'd heard at Harry's and liked so much. Sherry and Ed, the bouncer at Harry's, stood near the reflecting pond drinking wine with Rich's first Charleston baby-sitter, Mrs. Denning, and talking with everyone who passed by on their stroll to the rear gardens. Rich and a group of his friends darted in and out among the adults, grabbing food and having a great time, careful of course, not to trample any of the plants. Gilbert held a plate up, pointing this way and that at the food, most likely explaining the intricacies of a recipe to a captivated audience of women. Olivia smiled. She felt blessed with so many friends and such a warm bunch of neighbors.

At a table near the porch, Olivia stopped to pour herself a small glass of cabernet sauvignon and heard two men talking behind her.

"I'm telling you, Dale, I've never seen anything like it," a man commented. "It's like a work of art! It has to be two hundred years old, at least!"

"You say it's at Griffith's wharf?"

"It was there earlier this evening." The man paused. "You've got to see it before it leaves port. Man, it was like watching a movie, seeing that beauty sail in. Just like a movie! I kind of expected Errol Flynn to come down the gangplank, you know?"

Olivia set down the decanter of wine as she wondered exactly what the men were talking about. But by the time she turned to question them, they had drifted into the crowd. She would feel foolish pursuing them and quizzing them about a ship that could belong to just about anyone. She picked up her goblet and faced the band, hoping the music would restore her spirits.

But the mere mention of a wooden ship destroyed what little festive mood Olivia possessed. She felt her smile slipping, her brave façade cracking. Suddenly she could no longer bear the crush of the crowd or hear another ripple of laughter. Her heart hadn't mended enough to stand the strain of other people's gaiety. She hurried around the side of the house, hoping to escape the crowd, but everywhere she went there were people talking, giggling, and dancing. Olivia fled to the back of the mansion and up the stairs, knowing the only place of refuge would be inside Alexandre's house, which was off limits to partygoers.

She ran up the back stairs and slipped inside, and then continued to the second floor, where Alexandre had spent most of his time. She passed by his vacant bedchamber and dashed into the hollow ballroom. The house stood in the same condition as five months before. Strains of jazz floated upward, filling the old room with soft muted sounds. Out of breath and close to tears, Olivia skidded to a stop in the center of the room, trying to calm herself, trying to talk herself out of the sorrow she knew she could beat if she just developed the right perspective. She hadn't yet figured out how to soften the sharp edge of Alexandre's memory.

"Alex," she whispered, dashing a tear from her cheek and looking up at the medallion design molded into the plaster ceiling. "Alex, I miss you!" She closed her eyes and turned in a slow circle, letting her lonely heart drift away with the music, hoping that her spirit could find him wherever he was in the world. She continued to dance alone in the ballroom, floating with the memory of her lost love, until the music drew to a close.

While the band prepared for another song, she meandered across the ballroom floor and out to the piazza, which overlooked the front yard. From this distance she could withstand the party, and watch over her world without having to interact with those below. She strolled to the banister, and caught sight of a small object lying on the rail. When she got closer, she saw that it was a sprig of the Everlasting Lily wrapped in a linen napkin. Olivia gasped in surprise and whirled around, searching the shadows of the piazza for the shape of a man—the only man who would leave such a sign. But no one was there.

Leaning upon the rail, she peered down at the yard, straining to make out the faces in the twilight below, but couldn't see the familiar broad shoulders and brown hair of Alexandre Chaubere. Olivia's heart raced with anticipation as she ran the length of the piazza to search the northern side of the house. He had to be here! Alexandre *had* come back! That must have been the *Bon Aventure* that had sailed in Charleston Harbor earlier in the day.

Then she heard the music start and she paused at the end of the piazza, propping her palms upon the rail as the lead singer broke into a familiar haunting verse.

"Someday, he'll come along, the man I love—"

Olivia closed her eyes as the words crashed down around her, more poignant than ever. She should have known better than to have false hope. Alexandre hadn't returned to Charleston. He would have contacted her if he'd come back. Surely, she would have been the first to know. The sprig of lily was just someone's idea of a cruel jest, and probably taken from her bedroom. But how could anyone have known its significance to her? To them?

The song continued, reminding her that the big, strong man she'd loved was gone forever. She'd never have a man in her life, not the one she wanted. She was destined to travel life's path alone, learning self-reliance as a skill above all else.

But dammit, she *had* been self-reliant. She'd forged a trail for ten years without help, without a companion, without anything but her own two hands. What more did she have to endure? She deserved to be loved because she knew how to love—purely, completely, and forever. And she knew she had desperately wanted to dedicate her heart and soul to one man.

She hadn't cared if Alexandre was an immortal or that he might have grown more ill as the days passed. She had wanted to share those days with him, here in this house. The singer's words about a house built for two drifted up to her.

No. She'd never roam from this house. It was all she had of Alexandre. She'd never leave Charleston either, not for any length of time. Her heart belonged here as it did to no other place, just as her heart belonged to Alexandre Chaubere, wherever he was, whether alive or dead.

She, of all people, had come to know the value of love—the only thing worth having in the world.

She had waited years for the right man to come along and was sure that once she found him, everything would fall into place. Well, now she knew the truth. Life didn't always work out. In fact, it rarely worked out the way she'd planned or hoped. All she had were her memories, and a fantasy man to live in her imagination.

"I'm dreaming of the man I love—"

"That song gets to you, doesn't it?" a familiar voice commented behind her.

Olivia's eyes flew open at the sound and she turned, barely trusting her sight or hearing. There stood Alexandre

Chaubere, as fit and trim as ever. She stared at him, frozen in place at the banister, afraid he was just a dream, and unwilling to burst the bubble. He stood in the doorway, a tall dark statue framed against the evening sky at the end of the piazza. Was he really there, or had her imagination conjured him from her misery?

"I asked the band to play it for you."

"Alex?"

The statue came to life and slowly raised his hands toward her, offering the haven of his arms. She broke from the rail and flew into his embrace.

"Alex!" she cried, burrowing into his chest. "You've come back!"

He held her tightly. "The first time I saw you listening to that song, I thought you were going to burst into tears." He caressed her. "I thought you were dreaming about your long lost love, aching for him."

"I knew nothing of love then," she replied in a near whisper, holding him close, soaking up the warmth of his body.

"But you wanted a man."

"A man to love."

"I was incredibly jealous of the man I thought you were in love with."

She gazed up at him, still thinking he might be a dream and praying he was real. "I had nothing then but a phantom love—a man of my imagination."

Alexandre paused and looked down, his eyes drinking in the sight of her. "And do you still crave a man to love?" he asked, raising a brow. "A real man?"

She pulled back, hoping she was hearing what she thought he was really saying. "You're a man?" she asked. "A mortal?"

"Yes!" He grinned.

"How do you know?"

"I can eat. My beard grows. I get tired. I can bleed!" He held her, his hands locked together around her waist. "All traces of immortality are gone, even in my blood!"

With a trembling hand, she reached up and stroked his cheek, slightly raspy with a day's growth of beard. "But how? How did it happen?"

"It had a whole lot to do with you," he replied. "The moment you came into my life, you started a chemical reaction in my body that worked in conjunction with the Everlasting Lily potion."

"How did I do that?" she asked, tilting her head.

"It has to do with our body chemistries being just right for one another, as well as our feelings for each other."

"What do you mean?"

"Take plants for example. You know how people say you have a green thumb, because you can make plants flourish?"

"Yes. But it's not hard to see why. I take care of them."

"You do more than that. I have seen you touch plants. I've seen you talk to them. You cherish them, Olivia, and their systems respond."

She had read the results of studies where plants subjected to harsh noises and unhealthy atmospheres, such as cigarette smoke, failed to flourish. She fully believed a person could affect plants simply by thinking about them in a certain way. But she hadn't transferred the theory to the human body.

"Haven't you felt that strange vibration between us?" he asked.

"Yes. But I thought it was just me."

"I feel it, too. My skin literally buzzes when I touch you," he kissed her. "I've never experienced anything like it before—not in three hundred years."

"So you think we have an unusual effect on each other?"

"Assuredly. It took someone like you, a nurturer, a lover of plants, and a person with a pure heart to augment the Everlasting Lily potion."

"So if I hadn't come along, you'd still be an immortal?"

"Exactly. Or dead." He smiled. "Falling in love produces certain chemicals in the brain, Olivia. Did you know that? A drug is released that makes lovers feel wonderful, full of joy, and capable of anything. People think it's love that makes them feel lighter than air, but it's actually a simple chemical reaction."

"I don't know if I like the sound of this," she remarked, touching his face again and smiling at the eager expression she saw there. "You're taking all the mystery out of our romance."

He chuckled. "I think it's an incredible mystery, the way two people can have such strong effects upon each other." He slipped his hands down over her rump and pulled her close. "And you have a big effect upon me, you know."

Her body thrilled to his blatant sexuality and suggestive words. She would never forget what it was like to make love with this man.

"I knew you were having some effect on me," he continued. "but I jumped to the wrong conclusion. I thought you were killing me."

"What?" she gasped.

"I thought your presence was changing me back to a mortal but also destroying me in the process. Some of those episodes were so painful, I thought I'd never survive them."

"So the closer we became, the closer you thought you were to death?"

"Yes. Ever since I drank the first dose of the lily potion last October, I have been taking blood samples, checking cell components in my blood which my immortality created.

Those cell counts dropped dramatically once you came into my life. But my spells got worse, much worse. And then I had that bad spell after the horticultural society ball. I knew I had to leave Charleston because I was certain I was going to die in a matter of weeks, if not days."

"Why didn't you tell me?"

"I couldn't. I didn't want your pity. I couldn't bear it."

She squeezed him and shook her head. "So what happened when you left?"

"I soon realized what I thought was my impending death was merely my body functions beginning to recover from centuries of hibernation."

"But you've been gone for nearly five months. Why did it take so long?"

"I had to be sure." He pulled her even closer, pressing her head against his heart and stroking her hair. His voice rumbled in his chest and into her ear, giving her comfort on the deepest level. "I had to be certain that all was right with me before I asked you to love me."

"You could have asked me back in February, Alexandre." She caressed his wide back. "You know that, don't you?"

"Yes, but it would not have been right." He bent down and kissed her, and for a long moment she heard little of the party below them and thought of nothing but the exquisite taste of him, the firmness of his body in her arms, and the rush of his breath on her cheek.

"Olivia, I want a second chance with you," he said near her ear. "I want to spend the rest of my life—the *rest* of my life—with you. I want to have a family with you, with lots of children and dogs and cats, and noise and bedlam—all of it! I want to make a home with you, right here in this house, starting today, if you'll have me."

"Do you think I'd ever want anyone else?"

"Then you'll marry me?"

She gazed into his eyes, knowing how deeply she could fall into them. "Yes," she answered. "The sooner the better."

He kissed her again, even longer this time, joyfully rocking her in his arms. She laughed and struggled free, nearly choked by his exuberance, just as the piazza door opened behind them. She looked up to see Gilbert gaping at them.

"Alexandre!" he cried. "It is you!"

"I'm back, my friend."

"Blessed Virgin!" Gilbert stood transfixed, his face beaming with happiness, his hands clasped together in front of him. Then he ran forward and flung his arms around Alexandre. "Alexandre! *Mon Dieu!*"

Alexandre patted him on the back and pulled away, laughing.

Gilbert raked him up and down. "You look a picture of health. Are you well?"

"Never better. I'll tell you all about it later." Alexandre slipped his arm around Olivia's waist and turned back to Gilbert. "I'm here because I heard a nasty rumor, du Berry."

Gilbert glanced from Alexandre to Olivia and back again, obviously flustered. "Nasty rumor?"

"Yes, that some rapscallion was throwing a party on my property. I thought I made my position clear regarding parties."

"But Alexandre!" Gilbert sputtered, rushing forward. "I thought you were dead, that is we assumed–"

"Well, you can just forget what I said," Alexandre added in a firm voice. He squeezed Olivia to let her in on the friendly jest.

"Eh?" Gilbert stared at him, a mixture of confusion and affront in his expression. Then Alexandre threw his arm around Gilbert, hugging him tightly to his side.

"From now on you can throw all the parties you want, my friend," he said, grinning. "As long as Olivia approves."

"Alexandre!" Gilbert backed away and stared at both of them anew. "You and Olivia, you are going to tie the pot?"

"*Knot*," Alexandre corrected, shaking his head and smiling.

"Not?" Gilbert stepped backward, even more confused.

Olivia laughed. She couldn't help herself. She burst into ripples of laughter—in joy that Alexandre was back in her life, in relief that he was no longer suffering, and in amusement at Gilbert's endearing slips of the tongue. She hadn't laughed in years, not like this, not since she had been a young child. Alexandre and Gilbert joined in, and Olivia laughed with them, her heart swimming with love for the both of them and knowing there was a lifetime of joy to come.

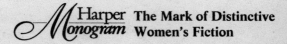

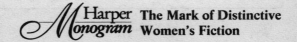